VERA'S WILL

Shelley Ettinger

H\S

HAMILTON STONE EDITIONS

2015

All rights reserved. Published in the United States by
Hamilton Stone Editions, PO Box 43, Maplewood, NJ.

www.hamiltonstone.org

Library of Congress Cataloging-in-Publication Data

Ettinger, Shelley, 1954-
Vera's will / by Shelley Ettinger.
pages cm
ISBN 978-0-9836668-7-5 (alk. paper)
1. Lesbians – Fiction. 2. United States – Social life and customs –
20th century – Fiction. 3. Domestic fiction. I. Title.
PS3605.T49V47 2014
813'.6—dc23

2014020758

Portions of earlier drafts of this novel have been previously published
in the following literary journals:
*Blithe House Quarterly, Epiphany, Hamilton Stone Review,
Lodestar Quarterly, muse apprentice guild.*

ACKNOWLEDGMENTS

For their amazing gifts of material, moral and temporal support, I am grateful to the Money for Women/Barbara Deming Memorial Fund; Norcroft Writing Retreat for Women; the Anderson Center for Interdisciplinary Studies and the Jerome Foundation; and the Lambda Literary Foundation.

Thank you: Dorothy Allison, Lewis Aron, Brent Calderwood, Muriel Dimen, David Ebershoff, Carol Emshwiller, Matthew Fields, Charles Flowers, Katherine V. Forrest, Liz Goren, Martha Hughes, Doug Jones, Edith Konecky, Joan Lebovitz, Suzanne McConnell, Michael Montlack, Michael Nava, Sarah Ocasio, Carol Rosenfeld, Trudy Rudnick, Melanie Suchet, Justin Torres, Barbara Villarreal, Rebecca Villela, Gary Wilson. Thank you also to the archivists, librarians and staff at the Botto House Labor History Museum, Lesbian Herstory Archives, NYU Bobst Library, and YIVO Archives. I wish I could thank Pat Chin.

Special thanks to Rosemary Hiller, Tracy Wittmer, Rebeca Toledo, LeiLani Dowell.

Extra special thanks to Gimbiya Kettering and Carole Rosenthal.

Super special thanks to the extraordinary artist Lallan Schoenstein for making this book beautiful.

I don't know how to thank Meredith Sue Willis, writer, teacher, friend. Beyond grateful, MSW.

Finally, for her generous spirit, sweet support, astute read, sharp critique and political clarity, I thank the love of my life, my comrade and wife Teresa Gutierrez. For letting me, trusting me, pushing me, and waiting for me—thank you, Comandante.

To Teresa

Sugar's

I don't want to go into a whole maudlin song and dance about how sad it was to see Tanteh Vera in her last days. My dad's mother, the grandmother I called aunt. Stuck in a nursing home, where she had vowed she'd never end up. Struggling to inhale some air through the crud in her one remaining lung. It seemed ironic, unfair, that cancer was killing Tanteh Vera. Steel-willed, she had stopped smoking the week the surgeon general's report came out in 1964. All those cylinders she'd sucked through the Roaring Twenties, Great Depression, war, McCarthyism. To be done in by them now, after ten nonsmoking years. A bum deal.

On an occasional Saturday as my third year in college drew to a close, I drove from Ann Arbor to Detroit to see her. I wasn't always sure she knew I was there. Half in and half out of lucidity, she was shut down and silent most of the time. She stopped eating, became incontinent. Well I said I didn't want to go into it, so that's enough of that. But it was shocking, okay? Shocking to see someone like that become someone like this. I remembered how she had awed me when I was a kid in the fifties, on those rare Saturdays Dad took Elliot and me to see her. She was so chic, so stylish—nothing like Grandma Gussie, or for that matter anyone else's grandmother I'd ever met. If you'd ever seen her in springtime in her brown leather trench coat with the wide shoulders, you'd know what I mean. Tall and trim in her tapered tan slacks stepping out of her Chevy Bel-Air, cigarette dangling between darkly manicured fingernails. She reminded me of Joan

Crawford in one of those old movies Mom would let me stay up and watch with her sometimes. And those piercing dark eyes. They seemed, when I was small, to hold the whole world in them.

How could this wheezing geezer be the same Tanteh Vera? She'd stopped bothering to put her teeth in, so her face was sunken at the cheeks. Watching her slip in and out of sleep, I was staring at a death mask.

When she was awake she kept getting weepy. I'd never seen her cry before. I didn't know what to do. At least I didn't let myself bolt out of the room like I wanted to. I just kind of sat there patting her hand.

One afternoon she seemed to be asleep so I sat next to her bed watching TV with the sound off. Then I became aware of her hand on mine. She was awake. I asked if she wanted some water. She shook her head. She gripped my hand tightly, urgently, showing more strength than I'd thought she had left in her. And she looked at me.

Her eyes were clear, her gaze suffused with longing. I flinched. I felt as though I'd been pierced by an arrow dipped in ineffable sorrow. But I held her eyes and gave her a little smile.

She smiled back at me, a truer, deeper smile than I'd ever seen. It transformed her visage. She looked almost young, as if the Vera of long ago was peering at me from behind the wrinkled scrim of her seventy-six-year-old skin.

Her dark eyes shimmered. For an instant I got the old feeling from my childhood, that if I looked deep enough into them I'd see the whole world of woe and wonder. Still gripping my hand, she lifted it toward her face.

Softly, "Oh Mary," she said. She kissed my hand, then held it against her cheek. "Mary." She closed her eyes again. I thought she'd fallen back asleep so I started to extricate my hand. Her eyes flashed open and she pulled me back—with such force that my whole body leaned in toward her. "Hold me, Mary," she said. "Please."

I hesitated for an instant—no one had called me Mary in years, and I had never been affectionate with my grandmother—but then I moved to hug her. As I did, I felt her other hand on my face. We stayed like that for a minute, me suspended just above her, she resting a hand on my cheek and holding my hand to her face as she peered at me.

"Don't be afraid, Mary," she murmured. "It's safe here, darling. No one can see us. No one will know."

Goosebumps prickled up and down my arms. As she kept smiling and whispering, "Mary, my Mary," she drew me closer toward her. I sat down on the bed, bent over and pulled her up so she could rest her head against my chest. Holding my grandmother in my arms, I started slowly rocking her weightless old body.

I don't know how long we stayed like that. It took no effort to hold her and rock her. Tanteh Vera had always seemed so rigid, almost as though she were encased in armor. Now she felt pliant, soft as down. All the tension gone. I peeked at her face. She had a look of—bliss? peace?—somehow, homecoming was the word that floated into my mind.

Her eyes were closed now. For a moment I closed mine too. Then I felt the slightest vibration against my breastbone. Tanteh Vera was humming. So faint. I strained to hear, and I recognized a corny old tune that I was surprised I even knew.

You made me love you. I didn't want to do it, didn't want to do it.

I added my voice, quietly joining words to melody. *Give me, give me, give me what I sigh for. You know you've got the kind of love a gal could die for.*

My grandmother and I sang and rocked.

At the cemetery, as the rabbi muttered prayers in a foreign sing-song not a soul there understood, I closed my eyes and imagined Tanteh Vera standing among the mourners. She'd have on a tailored suit, sharp cut emphasizing her trim figure, skirt ending just at the knee to showcase her shapely legs. Short gray hair swept back in an understated wave. Smoking—that's how I would always picture her—or tapping her silver cigarette case impatient to light up. She'd be standing off slightly to the side, surveying the scene. Alone as always. An onlooker.

I opened my eyes and realized the rabbi had finished. People were coming up, hugging, shaking hands. I figured we would split pretty quick. Mom and Dad had decided against sitting shiva. The plan was to get some take-out Chinese food and eat at the house, then I would drive back to Ann Arbor with my older brother Elliot the medical student. Dad was clearly ready to leave. His jaw was grinding bigtime. Elliot loosened his tie and started walking toward the limousine. I moved to follow him.

Mom grabbed my elbow. She'd spent most of my life keeping her husband's mother at arm's length from me. Now she could relax; I'd thought she'd be relieved. Instead, her eyes were red. She sniffled. She held onto me. I asked if she was okay but she didn't speak.

Aunt Rose approached. She gave Dad an awkward squeeze, then wrapped Mom in a big hug. "Bud would have been so sad," she said. "You know, Ruby?"

Mom nodded, tearing up anew at the mention of her other sister, Rose's twin, my shy, sweet aunt who'd died in a car crash years before. "Yes," she whispered. "I guess she would. They were such friends."

Friends? This was news to me. Before I could ask anything, "oh my gods" were spurting from Mom and Aunt Rose and they were swept up in hugs and kisses from several middle-aged women. I gathered from snatches of conversation that they were old friends of Mom's twin sisters. Why they'd shown up at Tanteh Vera's funeral was beyond me.

A figure broke away from the pack and turned toward me. She was all in black. Tight leather pants clung to big drooping butt. Low-cut polyester blouse struggled to hold full fleshy bosom in check. Shiny plastic purse slung over her shoulder. Platinum blonde hair, the fakest hue imaginable. Crimson-painted lips. Eyelashes dripping with mascara. In the May sunshine, trickles of sweat cut runnels down her cheeks, cracking the thick patina of foundation that pancaked her skin. She took a couple steps. Her jewelry pinged and jingled—dangly earrings, at least a dozen gold-plate bracelets climbing her arms, cheesy glue-and-glass rings on every finger.

Something tingled in the back of my brain. She stopped in front of me, nearly toppling me with potent perfume and brassy voice, loud and incongruous amid the hush of whispered conversation surrounding us.

"Hiya, kiddo," she said.

"Hello," I answered.

"I was awful sorry to hear about your grandmother."

"Thank you," I said, hesitating.

"Vera was one classy gal. Don't let anyone tell you otherwise." She peered at me. "You don't know who the hell I am, do you?"

"I—I think—I'm sorry—"

"Don't be embarrassed, sweetie. You were a little tyke last time I saw you." She leaned into my ear and whispered, "We were all nuts about you, but Ruby—I mean, your mom—she wasn't too crazy about your Aunt Buddy's gang." She pulled back. "Naturally you don't remember your old pal Sugar. I don't take it personal."

"Sugar?"

"Sure, hon, Sugar. As in—" She leaned again, and smacked a big loud kiss onto my cheek. She quickly slipped a compact out of her purse, opened it and held the mirror in front of me. I saw her lips' bright red imprint. I remembered.

I know it's hard to picture me trawling for crawdaddies, slogging through ankle-deep, muddy ditches, flicking mosquitoes off my neck, swishing a pickle jar into the wet in hopes of capturing some slithering creature. Try. Squint into the sun if you have to.

Remember, I was a little kid then, a whole other version, three decades shy of the edgy, bespectacled Brooklyn bookworm I'd eventually become. Northdale was new, too, not yet the bland, shabby starting point of suburban Detroit. A town just a-borning, full of raggedy patches still. Plenty of empty lots, teeming with wildlife. Or so we neighborhood kids believed.

Across Greenbelt Road's four lanes, a few blocks behind our houses, the land hadn't been developed yet. Within a couple of years the world's biggest shopping center would rise there and I'd never again have to squeeze into patent-leather pumps and help Mommy wriggle my fingers into white gloves for the trip to J.L. Hudson's downtown—a good thing since I'd soon refuse to be seen in that stuff. But in the summer of 1958 it was still pretty wild outside just yards from our back lawns. We considered it honest-to-goodness swampland. It sounds ridiculous, I know. After all, this was Northdale, not New Orleans. Our wetlands experience was pretty much limited to riding the Bob-Lo boat or splashing in the water at Belle Isle. What did we know about bayous? Let alone crawfish, which by the way some of the kids would have been forbidden to eat even if we had found any, their households adhering to the kosher laws grandparents had been kind enough to shlep across the ocean along with strange gurgly accents, kooky habits such as drinking tea from a glass, and mysterious behavior like kissing little metal doohickeys hung on doorjambs. So I'll grant you, we were a tad out of our element when we went wading into those roadside marshes as though they were the Everglades. Nevertheless, we were convinced crocodiles lurked in the oozy furrows. Garter snakes, anyway. Which although I really had no desire to touch I felt I should be in on the discovery of.

I didn't want to miss anything. Ever. Even if it scared me I had to see it through. So there I was, T-shirt and pedal pushers, hair all sweaty under, oh god, I admit it, my Davey Crockett coonskin cap because I didn't know the TV was lying when it told me he was a hero. Hot mud gunked onto my legs and squished between my toes inside my gymshoes. I was the only girl on this expedition, trailing along behind the big boys of my block, all except Elliot who was probably home in the basement perfecting some science project to wow his third-grade teacher for extra credit next month when the new school year started. Which worked out well since I had only just turned five and I was definitely not allowed to cross Greenbelt with all its traffic but without Elliot to tell on me, I did.

I didn't find any crawling creatures, about which I was secretly relieved. I managed to pull up some cattails, not an easy task because they were tall and thick and the spikes were prickly, tricky to grab onto. As I tugged I discovered they were rooted deep in the muck. I was determined, however. Something about the lofty brown reeds appealed to me. They were tough and hearty and stood proud, not caring that they weren't all bright and blossomy. I thought if I brought a bouquet of them home it might make Mommy happy.

I headed home feeling pretty pleased with myself. I was hungry. I was thinking I'd swagger in all suave with the cattails, kiss Mommy, hand them to her and ask what's for lunch. I was a daydreamy girl. Scuffing along, gulps of mud squooshing out of my gymshoes, I enjoyed the image I'd cooked up, Mommy tickled pink as I presented her bouquet. It didn't matter that the other kids, older, longer-legged, had left me behind on our trek back from the wilderness. I was on my own block. I knew it like the back of my hand. I skipped in anticipation as I rounded the corner to our house.

But wait! Auntie Bud was here! She was sitting on the hood of her beat-up old white Dodge sedan. Waiting for me, I was sure of it. Man oh man I felt lucky, the way I always did when she'd swoop by our house and carry me away to exotic environs. I wondered where we'd go today. What could top an alligator hunt?

Mommy was standing by the car talking to Bud. She shaded her eyes watching me move down the sidewalk. She turned and whispered something to her sister, and then they both started blowing kisses in my direction. I tried to return the favor but I almost dropped the cattails so I just smiled as I approached. I couldn't wait to hear where Auntie Bud was taking me but I was also torn: should I go ahead and give Mommy the cattails as I'd planned, or should I pretend like they were for Buddy all along?

The point turned out to be moot. As I drew up to the two of them, I saw Mommy's expression change as her eyes slid up and down my filthy legs. Oh no. Why hadn't I thought to grab some leaves, wipe off the sludge, take off my shoes and scrape my feet on somebody's grass before I turned the corner? She'd know where I'd been. Even Perry Mason couldn't defend me against so much evidence. Mommy's big round face started shrinking, tightening down. She turned red. Bracing myself, I stuffed balled-up fists into pockets and clenched my whole body. I even closed my eyes, scrunching them tight so I couldn't see Mommy's anger. I waited.

Whoa nelly! It was Auntie Bud to the rescue! I stood there all hunkered down waiting for Mommy to start yelling for what seemed like hours, but there wasn't a sound. Finally I heard hissing noises like tiny animals skittering. I opened my eyes. Mommy and Buddy were draped over each other, backs shuddering against the Dodge's dirty windshield as they laughed and laughed. I got mad for a minute—I never could stand being laughed at—until I realized I'd been delivered from an awful fate, Mommy's rage on a summer's day. Auntie Bud caught my eye over Mommy's shoulder and winked at me.

I started laughing too. Mommy looked me over again, shook her head, then broke out in a fresh wave of guffaws and reached her arm out for me to join them. As I did, I remembered the cattails. Lying on the ground where I hadn't noticed dropping them, they looked ratty. More like long-tailed, fur-matted rodents than the noble proffering I'd imagined presenting to Mommy. They were also further proof of my misdeed. Better left forgotten.

Twenty minutes later I was cleaned up and strolling across the lawn toward Bud, now waiting behind the wheel. My tiny tomboy self, hands anchored in the pockets of blue jeans, grinning at her. Feeling fine. Me and my Auntie Bud were off for the afternoon.

Where we went was our little secret. Not an actual cross-my-heart-hope-to-die secret. It was more complicated than that. We went to Sugar's, and Mommy knew that. Bud told Mommy that she was taking me out for lunch, "just us single gals, Ruby, just me and my niece," at the little place near Palmer Park her friend Sugar owned. What Mommy didn't know was that Sugar's wasn't really a restaurant. They did serve hamburgers, sandwiches and stuff. But Sugar's was a bar. People didn't go there to eat. They went for the company. What could be wrong with that? Still, when Auntie Bud told me that Mommy wouldn't understand what a nice place Sugar's was if she knew it was a bar, I promised to keep that part of our single-girls-afternoon-out a secret. The real kind, the cross-my-heart-hope-to-die kind.

This was before they built the John Lodge Expressway, so as I watched the world go by from the back seat of Bud's car I marked our progress by familiar landmarks on the roads. Northdale High, where Daddy taught. Boesky's. I'd had brisket there the first time I ever ate at a restaurant, Mommy and Tanteh Vera interrupting each other to show me which forks to use and how to hold my hands like a lady and chew with my mouth closed and not smack. The University of Detroit archway zipped by. We were getting close. Palmer Park Golf Course. When we passed Dutch Girl Donuts I knew we were on Woodward from the Saturday mornings Mommy took me with her on her rounds picking up goodies for the weekend. Soon Auntie Bud swung left, singing out, "McNichols—we're almost there!" and in another couple of blocks we had arrived.

Early afternoon, pale light meandering over mostly empty tables. I liked the way the place smelled. Stale cigarette smoke, hairspray, cologne. Grownup smells. People, maybe a dozen or so, sat in twos and threes toward the back. One lady with short, wavy gray hair and a long neck sat on a high stool at the end of the bar. I could only see her back but something struck me about her. The way she held herself. Erect yet graceful, ankles crossed on the stool's bottom rung, dress dropping just over her knees. Something in how she moved her hand when she picked up her glass, how her other hand drummed lightly on the bar, cigarette secured between two slender fingers. Sugar herself was down there too, behind the bar, leaning on it, deep in conversation with the gray-haired lady. She was so engrossed in talking that she didn't see us come in.

Auntie Bud looked down the bar at the two of them, then grabbed my hand and led me to a booth on the far side of the door. The wooden table was full of carved letters, hearts, doodles. Boy, I wished I could read. Bud waved over to Sugar. "OK, bub. She sees us. Grilled cheese sandwiches coming up." Perfect.

Bud headed to the jukebox, further down the row of booths. I studied the table, running my hands over it, feeling the ridges where someone's knife had etched out a message, humming along when the songs began to play. Before I knew it Bud was back, and then Sugar arrived, piling sandwiches and potato chips and root beers on the table and bowling me over with her blowsy blonde bluster. "Hello there, gorgeous," she bellowed, and planted a loud, smacking smooch that I knew left a cherry lipstick imprint on my cheek. "What's cookin', good lookin'?" The only witty response I could think of was "after a while, crocodile," but that was part of a different joke so I said, "Nothing," but in a hearty voice so Sugar would know I was real glad to see her. She gave a little shove to my aunt, saying, "Go on, sit down and eat, Buddy," and slid into the booth beside her, facing me.

"How's the grilled cheese, sweetie?"

"It's very good, thank you very much."

She beamed at me. "That's real polite. You're very welcome." I didn't know what to say to that except "thank you" again and I knew that would sound dumb so I just kept eating. Sugar took out a pack of cigarettes and started to light up, but Auntie Bud grabbed her hand and said, "Jeez, Sugar, the kid is eating, have a little class, would you?" Sugar lifted her eyebrows and mugged at me, an exaggerated "whoops" kind of face, mumbled "sorry" to Bud, put her cigarettes away. I laughed. Scooting forward to clutch my straw, I slurped root beer and gazed at Sugar as she and Auntie Bud talked. She wasn't pretty, I had to admit, she had kind of a big nose and not much of a chin, but she dazzled me with her bright-white blonde hair teased tall, her long, red-pop fingernails, and the way her eyes seemed to rove around inside a carefully drawn boundary of thick black makeup. She wore a lot of jewelry, big pieces, black and gold, that clanged all over the place whenever she moved her hands or head.

Her clothes were tight. When she'd approached the table I'd been fascinated by how her black stretch pants clung to her. Sitting across from me, her elbows on the table, leaning her chin into her hands, the top part of her nearly spilled out of her low-cut leopard-print leotard. Her chest looked so big and strong yet so soft, cushiony, that I wanted to touch it, reach over with my fingers and press, see if it felt more like a marshmallow or mashed potatoes. Springy or mushy. Well of course you can't go around pressing on people's chests, I knew that, so I made myself look away. Sitting next to Sugar, my aunt looked a little washed out. Her pudgy potato face was pale, floating between her slicked-back red hair and the red-and-tan checked men's dress shirt she was wearing. When she'd picked me up I'd thought she looked really keen. Now, compared to her friend, Bud seemed suddenly bland. Then she caught me looking at her and she gave me a lop-sided Popeye wink and she looked real sharp again.

"Hey—where's the music?" Bud asked. We'd finished our sandwiches and the songs had stopped. I made an "I don't know" gesture, lifting my hands up, and looked over at the jukebox against the far wall. Turning back to my aunt, I held my hand out to her. "Oh, it's like that, is it?" She said to Sugar, "See how they wrap me around their little fingers?" but she laughed and pulled some quarters out of her pocket. Putting them in my palm, she told me to go ahead and pick out some songs.

I ambled over to the jukebox. I waved at a couple of Auntie Bud's friends as I passed their table. I took my time making my record selections. Since I didn't know how to read I didn't have much to go on, but in case anyone was watching I wanted to give the impression that I was really studying my choices. Finally I put in both quarters and started pressing buttons at random, relishing the give against my fingertip. Then the buttons went all rigid, which I knew meant I'd used up my selections. I stood still for a minute, watching the forty-fives inside the jukebox shuffle themselves around until the record player needle set itself down on one.

The first notes filled the bar. Frank Sinatra sang about the way somebody has to love you. At a nearby table Cookie, one of Bud's friends I'd met before, looked over at me and nodded. Well done, pal, I felt like she was saying. I gave a bow. She elbowed her friend and they both laughed. Then I saw that several people had gotten up. They were moving toward the little dance floor in front of me. Neat. I was going to get to watch some dancing. I slid into the last booth, next to the jukebox.

Cookie was up now. She was taller than her friend but the way she leaned you could see she wanted her partner to be in charge. Other people were out there too. I wondered when I'd learn to dance like that. So smooth.

One of the dancers had her back to me. I recognized the elegant lady with the gray hair who had been at the bar when we came in. She was moving differently than the others, as if she were listening to some other song. She held herself erect. Yet I sensed some hint, some urge within her, to give way. She wants to have fun, I thought. She just doesn't know how. She looked like a tree bracing itself against a breeze. I had a crazy urge to blow on her, tickle her, get her to laugh. She held one hand down at her side, cigarette between her fingers. The other hand rested lightly on her partner's shoulder. I wondered what her eyes looked like. I thought if I headed toward the jukebox I might get a look. I stood up.

"Okay, babe, that's about it for us, time to get going." Suddenly I couldn't see the lady anymore. Auntie Bud was standing in front of me blocking my view, gripping my wrist and pulling me so I had no choice but to fall in behind her. I scrambled to keep up with her long, brisk steps away from the dance floor, toward the door.

"Hey! Slow down! Hey! Auntie Bud!"

She stopped. "Do you want to go to the bathroom before we leave?"

We were already even with the cash register, opposite the doorway. Sugar was back at her station behind the bar. She looked at Bud and shook her head.

"Buddy, take it easy." Bud loosened her grip on my wrist. I rubbed it, scowling at her.

"That's her g—"

"—I know, Buddy, but relax." What's her what? What was Auntie Bud mad about?

"If Ruby—"

"—She won't, all right? Just drop it."

"All right." Auntie Bud took a deep breath. She handed me my jacket, offered an apologetic smile and took my hand again, in a nicer way. We turned toward the door.

"Hey, kiddo, you think you can get out of here without giving old Sugar a kiss?" I spun around, hopped onto a bar stool, leaned over the bar and kissed Sugar goodbye. "Come back soon, okay?"

"Okay, Sugar, I will."

"Promise?"

"Promise!"

Mood thoroughly restored by Sugar's attentions, I jumped down off the bar stool and into Auntie Bud's arms. She threw me into the air once, twice, laughing along with me as we walked out the door.

From that day to this, I had never thought about Sugar's again. Now, sixteen years later, I stood graveside, inhaling the wormy smell of fresh-turned dirt and picturing the gray-haired lady barely swaying on Sugar's dance floor.

My grandmother. Vera. And Bud, too. Both of them were like me. I never knew.

Soon after that afternoon at Sugar's bar I had entered kindergarten. I learned to read, I grew, I was weird, a misfit, I went to college, I came out of the closet, I started to not feel as miserable anymore.

And still I never knew.

I do not cry in public, not even at funerals, but as Sugar's thumb lifted my chin, a wavery wet curtain obscured my view of her. She laid her hand onto my face, the fake-diamond rings sliding against my slick skin, and wiped the tears.

"Aw hon," Sugar said. "You remember."

I nodded. "Sugar?"

"Yeah, sweetie?"

"Did my grandmother have … "

"Did she have what?"

"Did she … was there … someone named Mary?"

Sugar stood quietly for a moment. She glanced nervously toward Mom, then she turned back and looked me over. I watched her take me in. My black dress pants, pressed white shirt. Short hair, bitten fingernails. Flat lace-up shoes. No make-up. No purse. The survey done, she took in a deep sigh. So did I. I was seen. So was she.

"Mary?" she said. "Maybe so, hon. A long time ago. Before my time. Yeah, she might have mentioned a Mary once or twice."

"Was there—"

"—Anyone?"

I nodded. "Ever? After Mary?"

"I really don't know, Randy. As long as I knew her, she was always alone."

As long as I knew her. If only I'd known.

Pale Night

It's getting dark. Vitka is falling asleep. Yet the five-year-old is the first to hear a noise.

She struggles to open droopy eyes. Fuzzily she figures she's dreaming when outside she seems to see snow falling. Big, white, fluffy, wafting past her window. How could these silent flakes have awakened her? Yet this is all she can see: a blizzard of fat white snow—strange snow because it is well past winter's end.

No one else seems to notice anything unusual outside. Vitka's little brother Mendel sleeps beside her on the feather mattress. She loves it when she and Mendel have the bed to themselves, before the bigger children crowd in. With all the whispering and jostling, teasing and pinching, they usually wake her. Then she groans grouchily, which only makes them laugh and tease her more so that she falls back asleep with a frown on her face. Mendel generally sleeps through it all, because he is only a baby, not even two years old. Anyway, it's still early. Everyone else is in the other room.

Vitka smells Papa's cigar. She hears paper crinkling as he reads the Bund newspaper from Odessa, which reached him yesterday after being passed among several of his co-workers at the jute mill. She hears him say, "Bring me a glass of tea," and knows he's talking to seventeen-year-old Freyde, the eldest child, and that Freyde, dutiful and quiet as always, moves quickly toward the kettle. Piano keys tinkle softly. That must be Mama. In all, the two-room apartment is pretty quiet. Unusually quiet for this bunch of shryers.

Then she hears Hersh, unmistakable in his stilted earnestness: "Papa, the strategy is all wrong. I repeat, on the national question your beloved Bund has the wrong approach entirely. You are putting not only the class struggle but the Jews ourselves at risk." Vitka is used to political debates between her big brother, next oldest after Freyde, and her father. Yet there is something new in Hersh's tone tonight. Beneath the stridency, is that fear?

Vitka's skin prickles. She comes fully awake. Without moving enough to lose her view of the snow she shifts a little so she can peek past the sheet that hangs dividing the rooms. She doesn't like to miss anything if she can help it. Sure enough, there's Chaya, who is ten and in Vitka's opinion a complete nudnik though Chaya considers herself a wit of the highest order. She's standing behind Hersh, silently mimicking him with exaggerated expressions and gestures. Little ripples of air wisp through Papa's bushy black beard—this is how the children know Papa is amused, the closest thing to laughter they ever get out of him—and the chuckling beard infuriates Hersh into further speechifying.

"How can you laugh when we're talking about the future of the Jews? And on a day like this, especially. A day, let me add, that we should have started by being down there at New Marketplace with our brothers defending our people, appealing to the goys as fellow workers, organizing against the pogromists, not staying by ourselves, not trusting to some fekokteh god. This is where your Bund fails, Papa, precisely here. The czar fills the goys' ears with slanders against us, and we should be countering it, organizing them to join together with us, but what does the Bund counsel instead? That we should huddle amongst ourselves! Discuss, analyze! and meanwhile the mob is coming with clubs and knives and—"

"—Be quiet!" Mama spits. "You'll wake the babies. I want them to sleep through this night. And leave Papa alone. It's a miracle he's laughing at all after a day like this."

Vitka comes completely awake. Why are they talking about this day, this night? A thin sliver of fear glides through her breastbone. It lodges inside her like a tapeworm. Still she peers past the hanging sheet at her bickering family.

"But Mama, what are we doing?" Hersh's tone is querulous. "Just sitting here. All day it's like we're waiting for them to come get us."

"We are not waiting. We are doing what we do. You are pestering Papa. Chaya is driving you meshugeneh. Zalman is rehearsing," Mama says.

What had been a dull drone from over by the eating table now lifts to a sonorous speech, drowning out any answer Hersh was preparing. It is Zalman reciting Hamlet's "to be or not to be" soliloquy. He's rehearsing for the lead role in his school play, in which he will declaim the Bard in Yiddish. Mama's expression softens. The Shakespeare was her idea, eagerly adopted by Zalman's progressive-minded teacher at the otherwise not exactly progressive school for the children of Jewish workers in the eastern outskirts. Mama volunteered to be drama coach, which has turned into something she loves—no, anyone can see it's more than that, something through which she finds herself transported into a dreamy realm far removed from this loud, gritty, drafty place that is itself far from her home—but it has also become yet another household dispute. Papa says Zalman, at twelve, should be studying for his bar mitzvah with Mr. Sislvicz, the shammes at the run-down shul on Skulianskii Turnpike who for a discount fee tutors workers' boys to chant their bar mitzvah Haftorah passage. For two months now Papa has been trying to pin Mama down on setting a date for Zalman's bar mitzvah so he can make a deal with Sislvicz and the rabbi. Mama keeps putting him off one way or another. Little by little it has dawned on Papa that Mama prefers Zalman to read Shakespeare than Torah. She would be happy to skip the bar mitzvah altogether.

Oy oy oy, Vitka hears her father mutter between Hersh's sniping, which has resumed, and Zalman's trilling. "Oy oy oy, this is what I get for marrying a modern woman. She'd rather turn her boy into a Shakespeare reader, an actor, a faygeleh most likely, this she'd rather than a Haftorah reader who becomes a man when he's thirteen like every Jew has for the last five thousand years—"

"—Not every Jew, Leib," Mama says. "Not the women."

"Fine, now you're going to start in on me about women's equality, Lena? Please, enough already. Please may I have a little peace and quiet before I go back to kill myself in the mill tomorrow?"

"I am not the one who threatens your peace and quiet. So please stop with the oy oy oys. I've had enough of them today and to tell you the truth for the rest of my life."

Vitka yawns, relaxing again. This she's used to. For here in the Resnikoff household on Muncheshtskii Road in the mud-poor Jewish section of the Skulanska Rogatka neighborhood on the eastern outskirts of Kishinev, the capital city of Bessarabia, southwestern province in the czarist empire, here live people who would rather express to the highest possible degree of accuracy their various thoughts, observations and opinions than let the chance to do so pass.

Vitka glances out the window again. The snowfall seems to be thickening. She yawns. So maybe her family drives each other crazy a little. It doesn't bother her—especially on a night like this, when, despite tendrils of brisk April breeze that squeeze through gaps in the plank walls, it feels wonderful to be home, inside, snug and warm under a blanket. Vitka is comfortable, contented, before the chill comes. Before she gets out of bed and shuffles into the main room and announces, "It's snowing."

Before Hersh looks at the big window and says, "That's not snow." Before the window suddenly shatters. Before Freyde falls,

Vitka's brooding big sister is on the floor, an inert, crumpled heap at Papa's feet. Her silence is deeper than usual. Papa is bleeding from the temple. Rocks fly through the window. Everyone is paralyzed for a moment before everything speeds up.

All Vitka's senses are under attack. First she feels the cold. Her fingers are icy with April wind whooshing in full force through the broken front window. She tries breathing on them to warm them up.

She looks outside. The air is thick with white particles falling from second-, third- and fourth-floor windows. She sees now that they aren't snowflakes at all, as Hersh saw right away. They're feathers—goose feathers, duck feathers, the downy insides of hundreds of pillows and mattresses. The bedding of every family on Muncheshtskii Road. Tiny wisps of down tickle her nose. She sneezes. There's a full moon and it's a clear night and why is it snowing feathers? Vitka looks across the narrow yard at the wood-frame apartment house where ten families live. Young roughs are flinging bedding out the upper-storey windows—she doesn't know them, they don't live there, she wonders who they are and why they're tearing up her friend Gilda Markowitz's mattress—and then "oh Mama" she whispers as she sees that one of the men has Gilda herself, he's holding her out the window, upside down by her feet, he's laughing and now he drops her too, just lets go and she flutters down amid the down.

But Gilda doesn't drop quietly like the snowy feather storm. She screams, one long shriek as she falls, and now Vitka hears a thousand sounds at once. Screams everywhere—Gilda, and Gilda's mother, who stands at the window howling as her daughter falls, and in the next window Mrs. Damnovner chanting, "Oy Gott Oy Gott Oy Gott" over and over. Now a series of rhythmic dull thuds, each accompanied by a cry, from the window above the Damnovner apartment, a girl Freyde's age it sounds like, maybe it's Freyde's best friend Ruchl Melshoff, she's crying in pain as though something is pounding into her over and over then suddenly her cries stop and now Vitka realizes the loudest noise of all is here, beside her, below her, where Mama lies on top of Freyde, keening, kissing her, holding her, sobbing. Chaya is also crying, and Zalman. Mendel toddles into the room, whimpering. Papa whimpers also. Little wisps of air disturb his beard like when he laughs. He bends over Mama and Freyde and lets out a deep moan. He starts rocking, swaying, murmuring the plaintive opening notes of the Kaddish prayer for the dead. There are shards of glass stuck in his hair. Blood seeps down from his forehead through his beard, and drips onto Freyde's body.

More sounds—windows breaking, things tearing, something cracking, soft surfaces being pounded. Bellowing laughter. Feral howls. They sound like battle cries but Vitka doesn't understand the words. It's Moldavian, the language of the goys.

They are approaching. Close, too close, they're outside, in the front yard, they're next door. Soon they'll be here. Vitka tastes iron and realizes she has bitten her lip open. A whirlpool swirls around her. She is the still, silent center. Maybe if she doesn't move the next thing won't happen.

But it does. "Come on," Hersh yells. "Papa, we've got to get out of here. We've waited too long already." He grabs Papa's shirt, actually lifts him up, shakes him. "Take Chaya and Zalman," he says. "Run out to the back, see if you can find somewhere to hide them. Maybe in Grillspoon's carpenter shed up the alley."

Papa looks down at Mama and says, "Lena, we've got to go. They'll be here any minute."

"Go!" she screams. "I stay with my Freydeleh!"

"But the other children—"

"—Dead! All dead!"

"Lena!"

Hersh intervenes again. "Papa, just take Chaya and Zalman, go." Then, harshly, "Now!"

So Papa does. Now four live Resnikoffs are left in the tiny flat along with the dead one. The noise outside grows louder, nearer. Snapping. Cracking. Dishes? Windows? Bones?

"Mama, we are going right now," Hersh says. "Get up and take your Mendeleh."

He thrusts the crying, confused toddler at Mama. Vitka holds her breath. Does Mama really think they're all dead? Will she take Mendel? Will she leave with them before the monsters come?

"All right, Hersh," Mama finally says, her voice like ice. She straightens up. "Give me Mendel." Vitka breathes fast and shallow. She can't swallow. Fear chokes her. Fear siphons her dry. Holding Mendel, Mama turns to Vitka. "Come."

Vitka starts toward the sleeping room. Hersh grabs her shoulder from behind. "What are you doing?"

His rough handling shakes Vitka. She's on the verge of tears. "Getting dressed," she says. Like Mama always tells her to, neatly, nicely, because a Jew must always make a good impression when she goes out.

"There's no time, Vitka." He turns her around so she's next to Mama, facing the back window. "Now, Mama, take her! Go!"

Vitka takes Mama's hand, which is limp.

"Hurry!" Hersh nudges them forward. "Run, Mama!"

"Where, Mama?" Vitka asks. "Where are we running?"

Mama looks blank. Hersh stands in front of his mother, takes her chin into his hand, lifts so he can see into her eyes. They're dull. He slaps Mama's cheek. Her head jolts back. A curdled roar spurts out of her. For an instant silence splits the room, then an answering, much louder roar of many deep voices comes from just outside the front door. Mama looks wildly at her son.

"Take them," Hersh commands. "Now."

Mama nods. She moves toward the back window with Mendel and Vitka. "And you?" she asks the teenager.

"I'll see you later. I'm going to go into town and find the comrades."

Another slight nod dips Mama's head. Hersh hugs her, taking in the two little ones and blocking their view of Freyde's body. He helps them out the window, hisses again, "Run!"

Where are they running? Vitka must know. She turns back, grabs Hersh's arm through the window and asks. He answers, "Into the woods. Help Mama and Mendel get there. Run fast, Vitkaleh."

Vitka tries to push down the terror and breathe. Into the woods they're going? Into the place where she is never, ever allowed, not even at the very edge, not even to play? The place with wild animals and crazy goys who are like animals if you have the misfortune to run into one of them? We're going to the forbidden, dangerous place? Without even getting dressed properly? How can this be?

But how can any of this be? How can that silent dead thing left behind on the floor be her big sister Freyde? How can Mama's eyes too be so silent? Mama's hand so limp?

No time to make sense of it. The screaming, the crashing, all the sounds rise up again around her. Vitka hears something from inside her own house, where she was asleep just moments ago. Is Hersh inside still? Or has he already slipped away? More glass breaking, now yes it's definitely from inside Vitka's house. Maybe it's Mama's special Passover glasses, and now oy oy oy there's no mistaking the sound, horrible music as the keys fly off the piano, someone is smashing it, pound, crash, wood cracks, wires pop. Oy Gott they're destroying Mama's piano, the only fine thing we own Mama often says. How can they do this to her beautiful mother? Vitka feels Mama wobble, looks at her mother's stunned, immobile face, and realizes it's up to her to get the three of them to safety. Where are Papa and the others? Vitka hopes they're waiting in the woods. Suddenly tonight, the trees don't loom so scary. It seems that all the vicious animals are here. In Kishinev. In her house. Now the Jews belong in the woods.

Vitka runs. Pulling Mama forward, she keeps a tight hold on her hand, checking that Mama in turn is keeping hold of Mendel. Mama does manage to hold him—but not to keep him quiet. His whimpers erupt into wails. Mama has no free hand to cover his mouth. As they run, Vitka and her mother and her baby brother, they are anything but inconspicuous.

They never make it to the woods, not even to the edge where, Vitka has been hoping, they might blend in with the other forest creatures and be safe until Papa arrives to take them home. In fact, they never make it out of their own rear yard with its familiar jumble of wooden buildings. As they hurry past the ramshackle carpenter's shed, its door opens and Papa shoots out. He grabs Vitka, breaking her hold on Mama's hand, and shoves her into the shed. Then he pulls Mendel from Mama, takes his wife's hand, and closes the door behind them as they enter the shed.

It's very dark in here: even so Vitka can feel the presence of many people. No one makes a peep, however. Except Mendel, who's still howling. Papa rocks him. Whispers, "Sha, sha." Finally puts his hand over the toddler's mouth.

Too late. Mendel's wails have been heard. The shed's door is ripped open, hands reach in, grabbing people, dragging them out. Now the screaming starts again. Sobs, cries, appeals to God. In that other language some thug yells something and laughs, and the others shout merrily. Papa and some other men rush forward, out of the shed. They fight the Moldavians, trying to pull the children and women back from them. Mendel's bawls are now only one note amid a discordant chorus, Yiddish laments mixed with calls of "Kill the Jews," the meaning clear despite the language barrier. So many voices, in the shed, outside. Twenty-five people have been hiding in Grillspoon's shed. Mostly children and their mothers. The mob that has at them numbers fifty or sixty. Men and teenaged boys. Some familiar faces. The baker, a postal clerk. One of Papa's co-workers at the jute mill. They carry pipes and clubs. Knives, hacksaws.

It goes fast. Papa, Mr. Grillspoon and the other men try to fight off the mob. Outnumbered, without weapons and unused to fighting, they go down one by one. Mr. Grillspoon and three others are clubbed to death. Bella Grillspoon—kind Mrs.

Grillspoon who always chucks Vitka under the cheek and gives her a hard candy—doesn't have it so easy. Just outside the shed's open door she is set upon—by four, five, six brutes, how is it possible? Vitka doesn't know the word for what she sees but she sees it with her own eyes. Cowering in the front corner of the shed with Mendel she watches, the moon shining a spotlight on Mrs. Grillspoon. Some time after the third or fourth assailant, the old woman ceases to resist or even flinch. Still she lives: Vitka hears her rasping breaths. Then, after the last one finishes, he kicks Mrs. Grillspoon over and over. When he moves away Vitka hears no more breaths.

Vitka turns the other way. There is Papa, lying on the ground. Blood all over his face. One leg bent at a strange angle.

Vitka wants to scream and scream but it's too dangerous. She must stay still. Make herself small. Invisible. Keep Mendel quiet. Which is no longer hard. He's gone silent, stiff. Finally Vitka understands all Mama's fears, all her warnings. These goys are like animals, it's true after all. Or worse. Vitka has never seen animals act like this.

Near the corner where Vitka crouches with Mendel, Zalman and Chaya have been hiding too—under the carpenter's big work table along with Feya Wouller, a girl Zalman's age, and Feya's eight-year-old sister Dvora. After finishing outside, a pack of men howling like wolves sweeps into the shed, kicking children, grabbing women. They topple the table and see Zalman, Chaya, Feya and Dvora underneath. Two of the men make a beeline for thirteen-year-old Feya Wouller. A third rights the table. They lift her onto it, tear at her dress, start at her. Zalman leaps forward, screaming, kicks at the men. One grabs him, punches him in the gut, keeps hold of him while Zalman hunches forward. As Zalman catches his breath, he thrashes, trying to break loose. Meanwhile the ruin of Feya Wouller progresses. One after another, they tear into her. After the fifth she is unconscious.

Zalman calls out to Chaya and Dvora: "Run!" As the girls hesitate, the thug punches him again, this time hard in the face. The boy crumples.

Two sets of grimy hands grip Chaya and Dvora. The men push the girls back down onto the floor. As Chaya's assailant reaches up to loosen his belt, the shed is filled with a guttural cry in no known language. Mama lunges at the beast atop her daughter. She is not completely human herself. A creature of instinct, an enraged, wounded animal, a she-devil rising up to defend her child. This is Mama, carpenter's awl in hand, no language left but fury, and she brings the awl down hard onto the rapist's back, gaping a tear into him that staggers him backward, off Chaya.

While Chaya is spared the gang rape of Feya Wouller proceeds on the table. Vitka smells something foul as the men destroy her. A dozen of them. The thirteen-year-old is already dead as the last two take their pleasure.

Then the thug Vitka's mother bloodied shouts something. Many men—the same dozen who just finished off Feya? fresh troops surging in?—swoop toward the center of the shed. They swipe the body off the table, its skin catching wood splinters as it slides down. Several drag the corpse outside. Vitka hears the hacking sounds of an ax breaking it apart. The table cleared, a hundred hands lift Mama onto it. One by one they rape her. This time Vitka does not see or hear. Chaya has joined Mendel and her in their corner. With shaking hands she pulls Vitka's face against her chest and covers her ears. Mendel has long since rolled himself into a fetal ball. The three children hide and wait for it to end.

For what seems like hours Vitka, Chaya and Mendel wait in the carpenter's shed. They stay silent, hidden, almost molded into the rough, slivered wall until long after the mob peters out. Russian police come. They carry Mama out, and Zalman and the others. They don't see the still, silent shadows in the corner.

At last, when the children hear no more movement, no more voices, Chaya gets up. She struggles to lift Mendel, takes Vitka's hand, and leads them out of the shed into the yard.

Vitka tries to keep her eyes closed, thinking this will maintain her invisibility, but she keeps stumbling on debris—torn clothes, pieces of wooden plank, a metal rod—so she opens her eyes. She slips, nearly losing her footing on some slick red gunk on the ground. She's holding Chaya's hand so tight her sister says "ouch" and tells her to let go, but Vitka cannot let go, no she will not, she must hold on. Look what happened when she lost hold of Mama's hand.

They make their way across the yard and back to their home. They climb in through the same window they'd left by.

Chaya and Vitka gasp at the wreckage. Nothing is the same. Pieces of dishes, glasses, windowpanes on the floor. Cutlery tossed all around. Clothes strewn, furniture overturned. And the piano is no longer a fine thing.

The old upright's legs have been hacked off so it lies on its back. Most of the keys have been pried off; they're scattered around the floor with the other trash. Stiff metal musical strings point out from the innards. Others, bent or cut or stripped, droop onto the floor. The dark wood is torn up. And it smells like someone has peed on Mama's piano.

A wild wire of worry twists inside Vitka. How will she tell Mama what they've done to her piano? The piano Mama calls her saving grace. The stool, also broken now, is Mama's special place, her protected zone, where she goes sometimes to play, sometimes just to sit and stare facing the friendly keys when she's weary or sad or at her wit's end. The household knows to leave Mama alone when she sits at the piano. Mama's retreat, reminder of home, of her own mama and papa, the grandparents Vitka has never met. One sweet spring evening Mama had explained her feelings for the piano to Vitka. She said it was a precious remnant of her life in Odessa, the thrilling, cultured port city Mama left to come to this back-country provincial capital in the Pale of Settlement, the area to which Jews are restricted by the czar's decree, where Papa could find factory work. Mama had shown Vitka a faded photograph of herself at age eighteen, seated at the piano in the front room—Mama called it the parlor—of her parents' flat above their tailor shop. She told Vitka people used to teasingly call her an "Odessa levone"—an Odessa moon, meaning she was stylish, even glamorous—and that the picture was taken on a special night, just before her parents took her to see a touring production of Hamlet in which the great Sarah Bernhardt shocked the world by playing the lead role in men's knickers.

Now where will Mama go when the shrying gevalt drives her mad? Vitka is always able to wait quietly while Mama plays or just sits at the piano, because she knows that when Mama is ready she will reach out for her pet, draw her onto her lap, take Vitka's hands into hers, place them on the keyboard, and then Vitka, magically, is playing music. She knows it's really Mama playing. Vitka herself wouldn't know what to do with her fingers without Mama guiding them, but still it swells her up with pride and love as she hears the notes thump out and feels the vibration rise from the stool up through Mama's lap into her tushy, which she clenches as she squirms with pleasure.

With all that has happened this night, everything she has seen, the piano somehow seems the worst. She frets over how to tell her mother. It doesn't occur to her that anyone else would tell, or that Mama might already know—or that she has more to grieve over than a musical instrument. No, Vitka vows, Mama must never see this sight. She'll get Chaya to help her finish dismantling the piano and drag its carcass out of the flat.

If only she hadn't waited so long to tell them it was snowing. Guilt rises up through Vitka's throat. The piano would be okay. If only she'd told them earlier about the strange snow. The dishes would remain stacked in the cupboard, milcheche on the right, flaisheche in the middle, Passover on the left. Her parent's mattress would be fluffy and full, not torn up with feathers lying all around, and at the foot of the mattress inside the trunk the family's clothes would still be neatly folded and piled instead of torn up and flung all about, like that big, ungainly pile under the front window—

Freyde. Oh God. She lies where they left her. Vitka wishes Hersh were here. He would know what comes next. Where is he? When was the last time she saw him? Her stomach rises to her throat. She swallows over and over. Suddenly she feels very sleepy. She's shutting down. She turns toward the sheet that, incongruously, still hangs between the two rooms, and stumbles onto what's left of the children's bed. Lying down, shivering, she sneezes as the loose downy fluff rises around her. The night wind lets itself in through the broken front window, tickles Freyde's body, then washes over Vitka. She yawns. She couldn't open her eyes if she tried. She feels Chaya place Mendel at her back and ease herself down behind him. Chaya has found the big blanket, in one piece somehow, and tucks the rough wool around the three of them. Under the blanket Chaya lays her arm over Vitka and Mendel. Vitka stops shivering. Exhaustion trumps emotion and the three youngest Resnikoffs sleep through what's left of the night.

I

Modern Girl

"We'll tell her it's a concert, how about that?" Vera proposes.

"Very good," Mary responds. "Your mother is always happy to hear if you're doing something involving music."

"Yes—and happier yet if she comes too. Here, my dear, we have before us the basic problem." Vera wags her finger in a playful imitation of their geography teacher. Mary grabs her finger but Vera pulls it back. "If we tell Mama we're going to an art show she'll want to come. But if we tell her we're going to a concert to throw her off the trail, that won't work at all because she'll want to come to that even more! And what's wrong with us anyway? Why shouldn't we take her along? Doesn't my poor old mother deserve a little pleasure once in a while? Isn't she the one who taught me to appreciate art and music? Didn't she train my golden fingers to skip across the keys—"

"Stop it, you're getting carried away about your darling mother. As you have a tendency to do, dearie." Mary pokes Vera in the belly and keeps poking until both of them double over laughing.

"Well, I worry about her," Vera says when she catches her breath. "All of a sudden she's getting old. Her life hasn't been easy, Mary. If I can bring her some joy once in a while—okay, I see your face, I'm way off the subject, I admit it."

"What was the subject again?"

"Something about art, wasn't it?"

"Oh face it, girlchik. This isn't only about art. This is about going to Manhattan by ourselves. This is about dressing up in the latest Fifth Avenue fashions—"

"You mean the five-and-dime home-sewn version of them—"

"Yes, all right, the latest fashions from Fifth Avenue by way of F.W. Woolworth and smelly old Passaic, but dressing up nonetheless—"

"And hobnobbing with the hoity-toity!" Vera tries to keep a straight face, but Mary is crossing her eyes to get a laugh. It works. The girls burst out in a new round of giggles.

These two have been thick as thieves since soon after Mary moved in with the Resnicks two years ago, crossing the river to New Jersey from New York after her mother's death left the thirteen-year-old alone in their Lower East Side tenement rooms. Mary's mother, a distant cousin of Papa's, had been a widow and Mary her only child. She perished along with 145 other workers when fire swept through the ninth floor of the shirtwaist factory off Washington Square where she worked. Doors locked from the outside, the only escape from flames and smoke was to jump out the window to her death. At first when Papa brought Mary home she was thickly garbed in grief. Vera felt uneasy with the bereaved girl. But under Mama and Papa's care, and amid the constant clamor of conversation, Mary emerged from mourning, soon revealing a boisterous wit that fit right in.

Now, at fifteen, Mary and Vera attend the same classes at Passaic High School. Both love books. They relish the hours spent lying side by side on their shared bed reading—especially now, during their final term in school, before they finish ninth grade and graduate into the grueling jobs that await them in some needle shop.

When they're not reading or talking they're playing piano and singing. Mama has given Mary some rudimentary lessons. Vera herself plays beautifully after years of practice. The pals delight in pounding out duets whenever Celia or Mickey brings home sheet music for the latest hit songs.

They also practice elocution, competing at embellishing their vocabularies, showing off for Mama and Papa. Vera's parents have never lost their thick immigrant accents. They struggle with English, sticking to Yiddish most of the time. For the girls, this is the model of how not to be. They want to be poised. Articulate. Confident. They want to be—they are—modern girls.

Mary manages the trick best. Her smile, movements, gestures, the way she carries herself. Clearly Mary is unburdened by the self-consciousness that constricts Vera. Sometimes, watching her friend laughing, chatting—effervescing, for heaven's sake—seeing people respond to her on the street, in a shop, at school, Vera thinks Mary is like a strawberry phosphate. A fizzy, sparkly, delicious concoction, impossible to resist.

As for herself, Vera told Mary earlier today as they took turns reciting Byron, "I may live among the oy oy oys, the fehs, the puh puh puhs. But that doesn't mean I have to be one of them. I don't have to dress like them. And I certainly don't have to speak like them." She felt a twinge of shame, as though she were breaking faith with her family, but pushed the feeling aside.

All these old-country tics. These sure signs of strangeness. From the day she arrived in 1905, Vera had set about ridding herself of them. Precisely as a surgeon, she has excised these markers of the foreign like bulbous, unsightly growths. She will not be other. She will not stand out.

Nor will she be laughed at if she can help it. This she decided the very first day. That first long day that turned into three long days and nights on Ellis Island. Where they waited while a customs official haggled with Cousin Asher over the size of the bribe necessary to release them. Where a clerk's pen turned them from Resnikoffs to Resnicks. Vitka to Vera. Chaya to Celia. Zalman to Solomon. Mendel to Michael, which quickly became Mickey. And where the guards—immigrants or sons of immigrants themselves, Vera knows now, Irishmen who arrived not so long ago themselves—made fun of her parents. They parroted Mama and Papa's earnest efforts at English. They mocked Papa's Kishinev limp, one of them even tripping him at one point. There was nearly a brawl on the second day when a middle-aged, paunch-bellied, beer-breathed cop reached up to pull on Papa's peyess. Sol jumped in, grabbing the cop's hand and raising his own to punch him before Papa pulled him away.

The greatest shock, for Vera, came later that day when the matrons started in on Mama. They poked, feeling the material of her skirt, pulling at her babushka, prying open her valise and snooping at her underthings. Laughing, they fired a series of questions at her as she struggled to maintain her dignity. They acted as though she were some sort of dumb, comical peasant. Her cosmopolitan mother, who speaks three languages. A classical pianist. As these official representatives of her new country taunted Mama, seven-year-old Vera wanted to shout at them to stop, be quiet. "You are ignorant," she wanted to say. "Stop your bullying." But she was afraid they would turn on her. Better they shouldn't notice her. She stood behind Mama and, like her, stayed silent. And on her second afternoon in the United States of America, Vera watched her mother, a proud, educated woman who loomed in her daughter's life as high and bright as a full moon over Odessa, begin to diminish.

That day, as every day since, Vera had felt torn. She wants to protect her mother, defend her from all that is harsh and unlovely in this land. She is also driven to distance herself. It is unfair that Mama is treated badly. Yet she is, after all, different.

Now me, on the other hand, she repeats to herself as the girls' giggles die down, I'm no greenhorn. Mama and Papa are proud, it's no betrayal of them to speak correctly, they love to hear me speak English, they love that I'm a modern girl, they've told me so a hundred times.

So here she sits with her best chum Mary Freundlich conspiring about how to get Mama to let them go to New York alone to see the scandalous show of modern art at the Armory. It's a delicate proposition—and not because Mama is some philistine who would be horrified to have her daughter view the new surrealist works.

Papa is a different matter. The other night he was reading a piece in the Daily Forward about the show; when he got to the title of Marcel Duchamps' centerpiece work, "Nude Descending a Staircase," he emitted a torrent of Yiddish harumphs and hoo-hahs about what kind of people would go see a picture of a naked woman that anyway doesn't even look like a naked woman except as imagined by a meshugeneh. The plan is to try to keep Papa out of this entirely.

But Mama—ah, with Mama there are, as always, shadings. For all this country has done to wear her down, it has been unable to dull her interest in the arts. And so she is well aware of what's going on over in Manhattan. She's read the outraged editorials, seen the scurrilous cartoons. The other day while she was listening to Vera practice piano, she described to her what she believes these new artists are trying to do.

"Dada," she said. "Can you believe it, Veraleh? A school of art that takes its name from the baby's first word. And who coined this term Dada? Max Ernst. And who is he? No, keep playing, sweetie, don't stop, I'll answer the question myself. Who is this Max Ernst? Why, he is a Jew, of course. Who but a Jew would come up with a punchline like that?"

Vera already knows quite a bit about the Armory show. Her art teacher has been telling the students about it. He's got them dying to see this exhibition that the government tried to shut down for offending public morals.

"But I don't want to take Mama!" Vera tells Mary again. "Is that so awful of me?" It is, she knows. I ought to be ashamed, she tells herself. But, she argues back silently, I'll be in the center of culture and sophistication, New York City, at the most marvelous art exhibition of all time—a show that's drawn all the best people, the patrons of the arts, the writers and thinkers—so why should I have to shlep along my old greenhorn mother? Vera cringes at her own thought. I'm a terrible person, she thinks. How can I be so shallow?

Back and forth, her argument with herself continues, right up until the great day itself finally arrives.

By the time she enters the Sixty-Ninth Regiment Armory at Lexington and Twenty-Fifth Street two weeks later in the smelly, noisy city, stepping quickly through the grand fortress's thick oak-and-leaded-glass doors, holding onto Mary, palm sweating into her friend's as she braces against the jostling hundreds behind them pushing to get in, Vera is so stiff from standing, so bored and hot on this sunny March day, that she has nearly forgotten why they're here. Yet getting here took so much effort.

First the conniving with Mary about how to convince Mama to let them come, and not come herself. Finally the compromise—with Papa, as it turns out, for he set the condition that they can go to the Armory show only if Mickey comes along. What an insult. It's not only that Mickey is two years younger, a mere child at thirteen. Worse, he's a ruffian, a street creature. All he does is run around Passaic with his pack of wild hooligan friends. What does he know of High Art? Here they are, about to partake of the most exquisite, the most sophisticated, the most thoroughly radical art show ever mounted—the International Exhibition of Modern Art, announces a 20-foot-long banner hung above the arched oaken entryway, and Vera's breath catches at first sight of it—here they are at last, and they should be saddled with this lout? It is not fair. But Mickey is a boy and therefore, Papa decrees, he goes to the Armory show with Vera and Mary or Vera and Mary do not go. Papa would accompany them himself, but the mill has been running on overtime and after shul he needs his Saturday afternoons to snooze.

Her brother is no more pleased about his assignment than they are. On the streetcar headed toward the ferry landing, he groused about having to get up so early, and ducked low for fear his pals would see him with his sister. At least on the ferry they hadn't been saddled with him—he'd hung over the railing smoking, watching the buildings approach, all the way to Manhattan. From that moment until this, though, on the crosstown streetcar, on the elevated train riding uptown, then through the two hours standing in line, his constant griping and wisecracks have made the day crawl.

Still, Vera does detect something else underneath his smart-aleck demeanor. She suspects Mickey is as excited about this day as she is. True, he would not choose to look at Art if he had his way. But she knows Mickey loves coming to New York. He especially loves the sounds. Standing in line as they inch toward the entrance she watches his body jerk to the rapid percussive rhythm echoing from the Second Avenue El two blocks away. It's like Mickey's own crazy version of davening, the swaying, bowing motions with which Papa, still frum, chants his morning prayers. Mickey can't help but be aroused by all he sees and especially all he hears here. So if he's more jittery, if he talks faster and louder today, Vera tells herself, this is good. Maybe he'll even enjoy the show.

As for us, she thinks, Mary Freundlich and Vera Resnick, we are serious students of the finer things in life. We are here to contemplate Art. We've spent the day traveling and waiting until we are so bored that even the idea of being back home in our hellhole of a hovel of an overcrowded apartment in Passaic sounds good—but now we are finally about to enter the Hallowed Halls of Creativity so please let Mickey not ruin it. Let's hope he feels free to leave us alone with the Art if he wants to go contemplate the noise outside in his beloved streets.

Vera feels Mary pull at her hand. Her friend, bold as always, is leading the way. At first, as they take several more steps into the interior, they're disoriented under the flickering electric lights. After hours waiting in bright sunlight, staring at the stolid red-brick walls of the Armory fortress, their eyes have to adjust. Their other senses too. Outside it's been all automobile horns bantering with whinnying horses, hagglers hawking newspapers and roasted chestnuts and penny candies, hundreds of voices bickering, talking, laughing, occasional shouts of recognition as a famous vaudevillian or politician arrives. The girls have held their noses as carriages drawn by smelly old nags pass, and coughed as the horseless ones discharge sooty exhaust that fills their nostrils and leaves a gray grit on their tongues. They've been sweating, too, their scalps itchy, because of course the heavy black hats Mama insisted they wear attract the edge-of-spring sunshine straight to their heads.

Now, indoors, Vera, Mary and Mickey step to the side of the entryway for a moment. Vera unpins her hat and takes it off. Cool air tickles the moist skin on the back of her neck. She turns her head to both sides and looks around.

This is astonishing. This is another world.

Something fierce, thick, loud hits Vera. An explosion of sensation. For an instant she feels faint. Then her body restores itself, tapping a muted memory of another room a long time ago where her senses were similarly assaulted. She survived that. Surely she can survive this. Vera pinches her own cheek, yelps, and comes fully to herself with a little laugh of embarrassment. Mary and Mickey are ignoring her anyway. In fact, they've moved off. Good, Vera thinks. Let me collect my thoughts.

But she doesn't think. She drinks it in.

People fill the vast hall. This cannot be the same chattering crew from the streets. Here they speak in bare whispers, sending a susurrous undertone slithering through the air. Snatches of soft conversation sneak past Vera, the words elusive, wafting by with a whiff of pomade from this debonair dandy's hair, brushing her with a tickle of ostrich feathers, an audacious mass of them that blooms from that genteel lady's splendid purple hat. Oh! Vera takes in a quick breath. The lady's plumage is très au courant, the absolute latest thing. Vera looks for Mary, to point out to her in person a fashion that they had previously seen only in drawings in the *Saturday Evening Post*.

Stop getting distracted, Vera tells herself. She steers a path through the milling crowd toward the center of the room. Here, atop a three-foot-high wooden platform, stands—sits? lies?—a sculpture of sorts. It is a human form, she figures, but it is not the human form. It's broken up. The arms are detached. They lie in front of the head, which is propped upon them. It would have to be, Vera supposes, because it has no neck. No mouth either, for that matter. And these stylized slits, they hint of eyes, but how could they ever see? The whole thing is stark in white stone. Vera touches it. It's cool. Hard. A cool, hard, stark person who is broken into pieces. What are you telling me, Mr.—Vera looks at the card propped next to the piece—Mr. Brancusi?

She'll have to come back to this one when she finds Mary. She wants to see what her friend makes of it. For now, Vera steps a half-pace away. She turns slowly around, trying to decide what to look at next.

She's standing in the middle of a big rectangular room. She can't see its full proportions because of all the people, but it seems to be unadorned architecturally aside from a smooth, plain, apparently purely functional pillar in the center. Otherwise it's just four walls, a floor and ceiling. Funny that such a nondescript spot should be the arena for a great battle, the war between the cultural philistines and the free-thinking vanguard. Vera tries to picture the room as it's ordinarily used. National Guard troops lined up, marching, training, doing calisthenics. The walls, she imagines, are probably faded, dirty, no color at all. She doesn't know for sure, though, because they're covered with tacked-on sheets of dun burlap, like a thin layer of topsoil from which extreme new species can bloom.

And that's how it feels—as though the extraordinary is springing out at her from every side. Paintings line the walls. Sculptures clog the floor. A colorful canvas across the room clamors for her attention. Vera strides toward it. This painting is like nothing she has ever seen. What it is a picture of, or if it is a picture of anything at all, Vera doesn't know. Her spine tingles as she examines the vivid riot of hues. Reds, yellows, greens, blues ram into and bleed through each other. Blacks and whites, too, that try in spots to intrude on the tumultuous colors.

Eventually Vera looks at the card posted next to the painting. Improvisation No. 27, it says. Wassily Kandinsky. Vera touches the name card, then brushes the back of her hand along the burlap-covered wall above it. A rough thrill pricks her knuckles.

"Improvisation." Mickey is standing beside her. He's never so still. He never speaks so softly. "He improvised this. Can you believe that? From what he heard inside his own head."

"Vera! Mickey!" It's Mary, rushing up to them. "Come on! It's over there! I've been staring at it for ten minutes!" She grabs each by the elbow and propels them forward. "Vera, come on!"

"What? What already?"

"The Marcel Duchamp!"

Mickey screws up his face. "The what?"

"Tell your brother, Vera. Tell him about the masterpiece he is about to see."

"You mean the one that made the governor try to shut down the show?" Vera laughs. "Nude Descending a—"

"—Oh no," Mickey moans. "You're not going to try to look at naked pictures now, are you? You want I should lie to Papa?"

"Don't worry, Mickeleh." Vera affects an exaggerated soothing tone. "Nobody has to lie. No more than you already will— I mean, look around you, bubbeleh, what do you think all these sculptures are?"

Mickey grimaces, then breaks out into a grin. "I was trying not to look."

"Sure you were, you little angel."

"Well, anyway, Papa didn't say anything about statues. But he did say no naked paintings."

"Too bad, Mickey. Like it or not, we are now going to look at a nude descending a staircase." Vera arches her eyebrow at Mary, who is trying, unsuccessfully, to keep a straight face.

"Oy oy oy!" Mickey grabs his head in both hands. "No! No, Vera. Papa said no nudes. Please, why do you have to get us in trouble after he was so nice to let you come? Okay, what's so funny? What are you two laughing about?"

Mary takes Mickey's left hand and Vera takes his right. "Come along," his sister says. "Let's see for ourselves."

Each one dying to be the first into the apartment to dazzle Mama with tales of the Armory show, they race up the three flights of stairs.

Mickey manages the trick, beating Vera and Mary to the door—unfairly, elbowing Vera as he pushes past her.

He is adept at this sort of thing. Sometimes, on her way home from school or after running Saturday errands for Mama, Vera catches a glimpse of him spilling through the streets with his gang of no-goodniks. Kicking up dirt on the unpaved lanes, darting between horsecarts, dashing past fruit stands, snatching an apple or banana then securing the purloined goods under cap or in pocket, scooting away before the peddler even has a chance to holler for a cop. Here on the steps or out there in the streets, though, she can't really blame him for his wise-guy ways.

He's not a bad kid. Just energetic, cunning, confident, and the combination serves him well. To be honest, Mickey has out-done Vera in that department—fitting in, that is, finding his niche. Right from the start, when raw panic at how to manage the strange ways of this new place sometimes gripped her, there was Mickey, plowing ahead, plunging in, plucky, cocky. Un-afraid, even as a small child. Now that he is halfway grown—bar mitzvah age, and the family is relieved that Papa seems not to have noticed, or perhaps he's given up on this godless crew—Mickey has sewn himself tightly into the fabric of Passaic. Every-one knows him. And judging by encounters she's witnessed in school and on the street they all like him too, teachers and mill hands, boys and girls alike: even the peddlers whose goods he pilfers don't seem to hold it against him, the Yiddish or Italian curses they hurl at him too half-hearted to elicit any retort except his great, gleeful grin cast backward as he hastens on.

Of course, he's a boy. He can get away with all sorts of things that are outside the restricted rules of behavior to which Vera must adhere. Sometimes it bothers her that so many more possibilities seem available to him. So much more in store. It is as if they're rushing upward toward a hallway where several doors beckon and while he has the keys to all of them and the time to stand there and decide, one of the doors opens and strong hands reach out, grab her and pull her in, no volition of her own, no time to choose, no chance to resist.

Now Mickey flings open the door to their apartment. Vera takes Mary's hand, they exchange a shrug and a raised eyebrow —one of many amused looks they've shared today, their superiority to the uncouth urchin a distinct pleasure—and follow him over the threshold. He bursts through the front room yelling. "Mama! You'll never believe it!" and explodes upon Celia sitting with Gussie Lovdozo in the kitchen.

They're at the table, books laid out, notebooks in front of them, pencils in hand, doing their figures together. As she has before, Vera marvels at Celia's perseverance. Five years ago, forced by financial necessity to leave school after finishing the ninth grade as Vera and Mary soon will, Celia and her near-sighted chum Gussie had vowed to keep up their studies somehow. They have stuck to their plan, even though it means trading away Saturday sunshine on their day off from United Dye Piece Works for the gloomy environs of the Resnick apartment, in nearly perpetual shade from the buildings that surround it. They practice their sums, correcting each other's errors—Gussie correcting Celia's, that is, for she is sharp as tacks when it comes to numbers and, surprisingly for someone so seemingly meek, she has ideas about getting the two of them out of the sweated shops. So she doesn't let up on Celia. No matter what else they do during their Saturday sessions, they never skip arithmetic.

Celia, meanwhile, insists that they write book reviews. It will help Gussie polish her English, she says. Vera considers this a lost cause. Gussie arrived from Lithuania in 1906, only a year after the Resnicks got here, yet she retains a comically thick accent. Mama is always scolding Vera about teasing Celia's friend, but Gussie herself takes it well, even occasionally poking fun at her own linguistic inadequacy. And she does keep trying. Together, Gussie and Celia read fiction and write about what they've read. Sometimes it's the latest dime novels, sometimes the higher-brow if slightly out of date titles they find at Passaic's little lending library.

Celia and Gussie also read the newspaper together. Although these sessions are supposed to be devoted to English, they generally devolve into political debate over the issues of the day, conducted in rapid-fire Yiddish and inevitably drawing in whoever else is at hand. Two weeks ago, for example, the whole household ended up in a free-for-all over the march on Washington led by suffragist Alice Paul. Not that there is any dissension over whether women should get the vote, not in this family whose socialist leanings crossed the ocean intact even if the will to action has since weakened. The issue is not the right to enfranchisement for half the population, but whether that right has any relevance, whether women voting will have any bearing on their conditions of life. Mama for one has her doubts. "So I go vote," she'd said to Gussie, who, all flushed and earnest, had made a stirring little speech about what a great event the suffrage march was. "I mark an X next to the name of Mr. Smoothtalker-owned-by-John D. Rockefeller who treats the miners in Colorado worse even than you are treated in the mill? Or I mark an X by his esteemed opponent Mr. Niceguy-owned-by-J.P. Morgan. Tell me if you please what it could possibly matter which one is elected. Your boss maybe will raise the piece rate? The landlord, he'll lower our rent?"

Today, though, is a mathematics day. Celia and Gussie are deep in their calculations. Now they look up, their concentration broken by Mickey's noisy arrival.

"Where's Mama?" the boy asks again. "She has to hear about this!"

Celia looks at her friend, who folds her hands in her lap and waits, then at Mickey. Something in her look stops Mickey. He turns uncertainly toward Vera.

She smiles at her older sister. "He's right, Celia. Mama will love this. Where is she?"

"Mama is lying down. You shouldn't bother her right now. After supper, maybe."

"Why? Why is she sleeping?"

"I doubt that she's asleep, Vera. But let her rest."

"Why already? She's so tired?"

"Not tired."

"So nu, what's the big mystery? What's going on?"

Celia gets up from the table and walks into the front room, gesturing for Vera to follow her and the others to stay in the kitchen. Celia opens the top drawer of the tall wooden secretary. She takes out a tattered, dirty envelope.

"Why are you getting out old letters?" Vera asks.

"It isn't old, Vera. It just arrived this morning. It was all torn up like this when we got it. Thank god it wasn't any worse or it would have never made it here at all."

"So who's it from?"

"See for yourself."

Celia hands the letter to Vera, who can't tell anything by the block printing on the envelope. Then she looks at the stamp. Her heart jumps.

Vera sits down hard on the straight-backed chair where Mama counts out rent money. She looks up at Celia quizzically. Celia smiles, nodding her head and wringing her hands as tears start flowing. Vera opens her arms. Celia folds in to her embrace. They hug tightly, rocking. Vera starts to laugh. Celia soon joins her, sobs hiccupping into hilarity just this side of hysteria. After a few minutes of this Vera pinches her sister's cheek and pushes her slightly away. Holding onto Celia's hands she says, "Sha now. Is it really from him?"

"Yes, Veraleh. Hersh it's from. He's alive."

He's alive, Vera repeats to herself. Or at least he was two months ago, she thinks as she notes the date on the stamp. She doesn't convey her caution, though. It would be too cruel. Look at Celia, how she quivers still.

How she had shook, how she had sobbed, how inconsolable she was that July morning eight years ago on the Odessa dock. No one else made a sound, Vera remembers, after Mama read them Hersh's note, delivered by one of his comrades. Mama stood stock still, stunned, clutching the slip of paper in her left hand, digging nails into her palm with her right. Papa paced the pier, his limp more noticeable than usual, looking at the sky, working his jaw, swiping at the tears leaking down his cheeks. Vera, Sol and Mickey barely breathed. But Celia. How she howled. How she bawled. "How can this be?" she wailed. "How can we leave without him?"

Hersh, her hero, her brave, handsome brother, would not board the ship. He could not abandon the workers' struggle in Odessa. He broke Celia's heart.

Vera still recalls that note. Word for word. Seared into her memory by Celia's screams.

"Mama," Hersh wrote, and this is part of Celia's pain, Vera knows, her exclusion from his final thoughts. "Because I am a coward I am sending this note with a comrade. I am afraid to hug you goodbye. Afraid you will try to take me with you. I have to stay. The moment is critical. The rising I think will come soon. And then, justice for the masses. For the Jews even. For Freydeleh.

"Please help Papa see. For him it is different. He can rejoin the Bund in America. But I am a Bolshevik. You go. Keep the children safe. I stay.

"Do not worry about me. I will write, or send word through Bubbie or the comrades. Kiss the kinderlach. I love you all.

"For peace and socialism, Hersh."

All through the long voyage—overland, in carts and trains and sometimes on foot, to Libau on the Baltic where they boarded a cattle boat and squatted belowdecks retching at the reek of the more lucrative bovine passengers that snorted and stomped above them, finally stumbling off onto the London docks, huddling there for three days waiting for the ocean liner, then eleven miserable days and nights packed with scores of others in the windowless lower hold, the stink and sickness worse than their briefer time beneath the cows, as the great ship traversed the Atlantic—everyone in the family was subdued. Two years after leaving Kishinev for Odessa, the family was headed toward exile once again. Reduced by one again, and again the eldest vanished from their midst. Mama staggered, silent, unapproachable again, as she had been after Kishinev.

From then until today, they had never heard directly from Hersh. Eight years, Vera calculates—he must be twenty-six now. Fully a man. Is he hurt? Has he hardened? For the first year after coming here, they had received brief updates from their Bubbie, the grandmother in Odessa. At first, briefly, Hersh stayed with her. He was, as he wanted to be, in the thick of the revolution. He led a strike at the jute mill. He helped organize the leather workers and stevedores. When an Odessa soviet—a workers' council—was formed, he was named third secretary. So of course, when the terror came and the revolution was crushed, Hersh was a target. He is in jail, Bubbie wrote in November 1905 after the pogromists swept through Red Odessa. Four months later she informed them that he had been sent into exile in Siberia.

Once more only they had received word. It came in the form of a rumor, in June 1906, carried by an old acquaintance of Papa's who arrived in Passaic with the latest wave of immigrants. Hersh had escaped, the rumor went. No one knew where he was, only that he was no longer the czar's prisoner.

And now, finally, this. Hersh lives. Vera lets go of her sister's hands, unfolds the letter and begins to read.

After finishing the letter Vera goes back to sit at the kitchen table with the others. Celia is completely ferklempt, veering from laughter to tears and back, hopping from foot to foot like a madwoman. An expectant, nervous silence emanates from Mickey, Mary and Gussie. The one who barely remembers his brother, the two who never knew him, all three aware that in this household Hersh's name is spoken with reverence, his absence a permanent void. Then, around six o'clock, Papa arrives. As soon as she hears the doorknob turn Vera realizes this is what they've been waiting for. As soon as he steps into the kitchen she sees he is shikker.

He sometimes ends up this way on a Saturday when, after shul, he spends the afternoon downing a few. Papa may have passed the time with his buddies at the landsmanshaften, the social club for Litvak Jews, toasting to the good health of their families and reminiscing about the old country. Or perhaps he's had some shnappes while debating politics with his cohorts in the Bund. Either way, he's definitely wet his whistle. She can see it in his gait, a little too loose, in his arms, swinging a tad too wide, as he makes his way around the kitchen table hugging everyone hello. She smells it on his breath when he gets to her. She cringes and tightens her lips disapprovingly, then feels a quick flush of shame as Mary frowns at her.

After Papa sits down at the table, Celia hands him the tattered envelope. Vera has always thought that Hersh staying in Russia hurt her sister the most. She thought that leaving for America without him was hardest for Mama. As Papa takes out the letter and begins to read Vera watches his face collapse and realizes that with Hersh gone her father has been loneliest of all.

When he finishes reading, Papa folds like the crumpled envelope he drops. His hands fall to his sides. He slumps in the chair. His head droops onto his chest. When his shoulders start shaking Vera realizes her father is weeping. She purses her lips again, and again is instantly ashamed of her lack of compassion.

She doesn't know what to do. The air in the crammed kitchen is stale, thin. Celia and Mickey look locked in panic. Gussie seems close to tears herself.

Mary's head is cocked. She stands a little to the side, watching Papa. Then she steps over to him. She bends and wraps her arms around him. Papa grabs onto her with a desperate lunge and sobs loudly against her.

Finally Papa's tears subside. He pulls back from Mary and wipes his face with his shirt sleeve. He pushes his chair and stands up shakily. He tilts a bit, then rights himself. Standing with one hand on the chair and with the other making little raking gestures in his beard, Papa speaks, low, halting. "I am sorry, kinderlach. All day at the Bund we've been arguing about what's going on in Russia. Some of these cowards are turning Zionist. They want the Jews in Russia should run to Palestine. They forget that we are workers, they forget that our task is to fight for socialism. Not to flee to some fekokteh desert." He inhales in a long, raggedy gulp. "Oy, such a fight we had. And then I come home and what do I discover? A letter. From Russia. From your brother the Bolshevik. Who used to argue with me better than anyone. Who"—his lips quiver—"if you want to know the truth, who I had given up for dead."

"No, Papa!" Celia gasps.

"Yes, Chaya. So I find out my boy is alive, and this makes your crazy papa cry, and I apologize that you should have to see me in such a state."

Mickey says, "But isn't it wonderful, Papa? That Hersh's alive? And he's so strong too, and he outsmarted the czar's police."

"There is no question that your brother is smart, Mendeleh." Papa speaks louder now. He starts swaying again, in what looks to Vera like a loopy replication of the rocking that accompanies his morning prayers. Still he grasps the chair and combs his beard. He looks at his children and their friends. He blinks several times. He looks down. Vera starts to relax. If Papa is abashed at his behavior this scene, thank heaven, must be over. Then Papa straightens again and Vera shudders. He whips his head back and forth, his eyes unfocused. "Brilliant even." Louder. "A brilliant boy, my Hersh. But oy Gott"—Papa's voice rises to a higher pitch, his words a jagged screech—"oy Gott, it would be better never to get this letter!" He cries out, "Better not to know! Better not to start all over again the wait for the news that the czar has killed him. Shot down like a dog he'll be! Oy Gott! Oy Hershel!" And Papa weeps again, this time in a full-throated bawl. He releases the chair and staggers around the kitchen, draping himself around each of his children in turn until all the Resnicks, and Gussie, too, weep with him.

Like castaways, set adrift by Papa's storm, they cling to each other, wet-eyed, wild. It lasts long minutes, everyone uncertain when it might be safe to try their footing again.

Vera notices that Mary is not crying. Her friend stands with her arms crossed, a small smile playing across her face—and winks. A split second of outrage grips Vera. Then, just like that, calm. Everything will be all right. Vera doesn't like extravagant scenes—to witness them or take part in them—but Mary's wink reminds her that flamboyant shows of emotion don't bring the world to an end.

Mary walks over to Papa, now wrapped around Celia, pries them apart, and says, "Stop already with this nonsense about Hersh dying. You should be celebrating he's alive, you should be kvelling how proud you are of your beautiful boy who fights for freedom." Mary hands Papa over to Mickey and tells him to go clean him up. To Papa she says, "Gay shlafen." Go to sleep, this girl tells him. This grand girl who always seems to know the right thing to do.

Papa obeys meekly. The minutes pass, then hours. Mama never emerges from the bedroom. Vera and the others sit around the kitchen for a while, then throw together a supper from left-overs and eat in silence.

Vera looks at Mary asleep next to her. She lets her hand graze lightly against her friend's. Vera herself is only now getting sleepy. Remembering how Mary stopped Papa's tears relaxes her jaws. In a rippling, easy flow from there down her body, each of Vera's muscles unknots itself in turn.

Lids lying heavily on her closed eyes, Vera's thoughts return to Hersh. Yes, it's wonderful to know he's alive. But he must never get enough food, enough rest, peace, safety. He sounds happy, though, it's undeniable. He sounds like himself still. His letter spills off the page, and she thinks that's how she remembers him talking, always in a rush, words tumbling, all zeal, all verve, all single-minded commitment to the cause. Living for the struggle. Never changing in his determination to change the world.

Her thoughts aren't coming in words anymore. Her mind wanders, mixing hazy memories, modern art, fear and fantasy. Bustling Odessa, the Libau boat with its cow stink. Icy Siberia. The Armory, cool, crowded. Kishinev, a man's awful final breath, her father's strangely angled leg. Hersh. With them and alone. No, not alone, he says he works side by side with "my comrades who would die for me."

And how will that change the world? Who will it help if her brother and his comrades die? Vera sees Hersh, handsome with his black curls and dark eyes, tall, raising a flag with a red star, the masses following behind him, then Hersh huddled, thin, starving in the Siberian prison, then moving again, but alone, skulking through a dark forest in his solitary trek into hiding. "I do not doubt your bravery, my son," Papa says. He is drinking from a bottle of shnappes. He and Hersh sit beneath a leafy tree. Vera's heart pounds. Papa is weak and lonely and he's liable to muddle Hersh's head. "Hershl," she whispers from a low branch of the tree where she hides above them, "I wish you were devoted to us like to the masses. We are poor. Mama has shrunk. Here too there's danger. I don't know if Mary can save me. How will we know when it's time to go into hiding? And then, Hersh, when will it be safe to come out?" Shapeless fear surrounds Vera as she sleeps.

Sunday morning, as Mama's piano students come and go, a queer kind of pall holds the household in its thrall. Nothing is really out of the ordinary. Traffic in and out. Papa to the corner store for his Sunday paper and again a half-hour later to buy cigars. Vera and Mary drag two sacks down to the courtyard where they wring, rinse and hang the family's laundry. Much moving among rooms. Much opening and closing of drawers, doors. Mickey accounts for half the racket, though what exactly he's doing no one can ever pin down. Mama's prodigies play their infernal scales. Wrapped around it all, though, a silence louder than the noise shrouds the scene like a chill morning mist.

By early afternoon, when the last of the piano pounders has left, the quiet deepens. Frozen fog, too thick to traverse. Words won't penetrate this. Vera has a sudden image of the carrier pigeons her school friend Dora Silvano's brother trains. She imagines sitting at Mama's secretary and writing a little note to Papa—don't worry, no one will mention how you were shikker and said startling things—then tying it to a twig-thin leg. But a pigeon would never find Papa in this haze.

Vera sits in the old brown armchair holding the Tolstoy she's reading for school. She can't concentrate; her mind keeps wandering to Hersh. Fiction or fact, she can't get away from Russia. She wishes Sol and big-bellied Yetta would arrive. They're bringing bagels, cucumbers and tomatoes, herring and cheese, for Sunday dinner—lunch, but Vera cannot break the family of calling it dinner, another emblem of their low-class ways. Lunch or dinner, surely when her brother and his pregnant wife get here and everyone convenes to eat, the customary chatter will quickly refill the rooms, words rising into the air like balloons, bobbing against each other then floating away. She can't wait to see Sol's face when he reads Hersh's letter. Celia will hand it to him, she'll get that honor, and then will he laugh or cry? Vera has given up on trying to predict anyone's behavior around here.

A series of notes sounds from the piano. Vera looks up from her book. Mama still sits at the keyboard. Idly fingering the keys, staring into space, a tiny smile lifting the corners of her mouth. Vera wonders what her mother is thinking. After yesterday's letter, is Hersh on her mind? Is she remembering some happy scene when he was a child—happy scene where? Surely not Kishinev, where he grew up. Memories of that place never make Mama smile. By the time they were in Odessa, for two years after the pogrom, staying with Bubbie and Zaidy above the tailor shop, saving for passage to America, he was no longer a boy. Does the past, then, allow Mama no easy, airy recollections of him? And how much harder must it be for her to think of Freyde? Mama never speaks of her eldest child. Has she banished her from memory? More likely, Vera thinks, Freyde is always with Mama. That would explain a lot.

With a chance glance at an almost invisible smile, has she just resolved the enigma of her mother? Mama takes fierce care of them all. She is smart and sharp, and funny, too, the kind of mother who makes your friends jealous that theirs aren't like her, Gussie, for instance, who, Vera thinks, hangs around as much to be with Mama as with Celia. Her beauty starting to fall away, Mama is still luminous. But even with Mama's laughter, her loveliness, and even though Vera remains her favorite, she always feels her mother is only partly here.

Maybe a piece of Mama is in Kishinev, with Freyde. Maybe there's another part roaming Russia with Hersh. Which means I can never have her, whole, here with me. I'm more on my own than I ever understood. At the thought, Vera feels a tiny chunk detach from her own innards.

Mama is playing now, a full-bodied piece, head thrown back, eyes closed. Vera closes hers as well. Careful of the newly empty small space inside her, she breathes around it. Once, twice, now steadily over and over, until the procedure is in no way out of the ordinary, until she breathes past the hole automatically. So this is how it's done, she thinks. This is how you train yourself not to touch what has been torn away.

She looks from her mother, features crinkled in concentration on her music, to her father, reading his Daily Forward, deep bags under his eyes. Such a strange morning, at once loud and leaden. It weighs her down. She rests her head against the back of the chair. She listens to her mother play piano.

Two hours later Vera's stomach is growling loudly. It's two-thirty. Where is Sol? Papa puffs his cigar, pretends to peruse the newspaper, but his free hand worrying the curls of his beard gives away his anxiety. Maybe this is the day, Celia suggested when she got back from a stroll with Gussie to find no lunch yet, no Sol. Maybe Yetta's having the baby. Too soon, Mama replied, her eyes narrowed. If her daughter-in-law is in labor, four weeks early, she is in trouble. But if Yetta were in trouble, Sol would have sent for his mother, wouldn't he?

Vera eyes the front page of Papa's newspaper. It features a drawing of a tumultuous scene. People holding signs and running. Police chasing them, clubbing them. A man bleeding. A screaming woman clutching a child. This was last week in Paterson, where police attacked striking silk workers.

With twenty-five thousand people on strike, the situation two towns over is extremely tense. Vera knows the cops could easily go berserk again. What if they do—today? Workers might not get off so lucky this time. A bloody lip is nothing compared to a bullet in the gut.

Stop already, Vera tells herself. Curb your propensity for dramatics. She pleases herself with this directive and repeats it in her mind, elongating the delightful word at the sentence's peak. A propensity to embellish, that's what she has. Sol is simply late for lunch. Maybe the streetcar isn't running. Or he was delayed by new neighbors moving into his building maybe, Sol the mensch pitching in to help carry furniture. There can be a hundred reasons Sol hasn't shown up yet, not one of them connected to the

Paterson silk strike, none involving picket signs or crowds, police or bullets. Why is she even thinking along these lines? Sol lives in Paterson, but he works in Lodi. In a dye shop, for Pete's sake, not a silk factory. So what does this strike even have to do with him? Nothing. It's just a coincidence that the family hasn't seen or talked to him since earlier this month, when the walkout began.

For another hour, Vera expends considerable mental effort along these lines, convincing herself that Sol is safe and the strike irrelevant. When she thinks she'll go mad from the tension she suggests to Mary that they read aloud to each other. Mary agrees. They retreat to the bedroom. Taking off their shoes, they plop down on their backs and lie on the narrow bed, taking turns with Tolstoy.

An hour of that and they've had it. Tedium. It's four-thirty. Nearly time for dinner—supper if you're a hick, Vera snickers to Mary—so to fend off intensifying hunger pangs she gets them each an apple from the kitchen. They lean back on their elbows, chewing noisily, not talking. As she bites into her apple Vera tries to picture the scene of Napoleonic battle she just read. Hersh marches in. A hundred years later, and still Russia is embattled. Class war, her parents call it, and apparently they agree with Hersh that it is his fight. It seems there's a class war going on in Paterson, too. Vera hopes it stays put, right where it is, two towns over. I guess I should admire the strikers, she thinks. They are brave. Personally I prefer peace. Sure, the silk bosses are unfair. They're money grubbers, anyone can see that. But going out on strike means you don't get paid—and how can that make your life better? You're the one who gets hurt. It's as if you started paying extra rent to the landlord to punish him for how high the rent is. Sure, he's a greedy gonif how he holds back heat on the cold winter nights, but you're not going to improve the situation by making yourself poorer. Which is what the strikers in Paterson are doing, as far as Vera can tell. Making themselves poorer. Piling suffering on top of suffering. Not to mention getting arrested, getting beat up, getting in all kinds of trouble and I frankly do not believe for all their trouble they are going to change things one bit. Thinking such thoughts gives Vera a guilty thrill. If she spoke them out loud Mama and Papa would be horrified. But, she thinks, don't we have it bad enough around here? Why would anyone volunteer to make things worse?

I would rather be like those ladies at the Armory show yesterday. Je prefer le plumage. Going on strike won't buy a single ostrich feather. Hmm … I wonder how much a single feather costs. Maybe once Mary and I start working we can pool our paychecks and save enough to buy a feather at a time. Ha! Won't everyone be surprised when one day we have enough to purchase a splendid spring hat.

Vera is so engrossed in her thoughts that she doesn't notice Mary shift her position and creep around behind her. Suddenly Mary grabs her from behind and yells, "Boo!" Vera screams in fright and jumps. When she lands back on the bed they both burst into giggles. Vera says, "I'm going to get you now," and starts tickling her friend.

Struggling, tickling, grabbing each other, they maintain the hilarity until, their sides splitting, they finally flop backward once again. They lie next to each other and wait for the silliness to subside. Slowly it does.

Still giggling a little, Mary sits up, bounds off the bed, pivots and goes down on one knee. She reaches for Vera's hand and tugs so Vera sits up facing her. They grin at each other. Mary strikes a melodramatic pose, both hands clasped to her heart, head tilted up at her friend.

She starts singing, "You made me love you, I didn't want to do it," her arms thrusting out as if to embrace Vera, "didn't want to do it." Vera, grin now a bare nudge at the corners of her mouth, joins in, but softer: "Didn't want to do it." She slides down off the bed and onto the floor, easing into Mary's arms. The room goes quiet. Vera reclines into Mary, looks into her glowing green eyes then quickly down.

Mary taps Vera's chin with two light fingers, lifts it back up. She whispers, "You know you made me love you," and touches Vera's lips with hers.

Lips lightly pressed together, Mary's fingers trembling on Vera's chin. A still and silent kiss. The world stops.

Then, "Veraleh," Mama yells from the front room. "Sol and Yetta are here. Come help me set the table, dear."

Vera gasps, pulling back from Mary. She grabs the bed and rises. Without looking at her friend on the floor, she stumbles out of the bedroom.

Sol and Yetta have indeed finally arrived—no food in hand, but Mama has foreseen this and spent the last hour piecing together a dinner. As Vera steps falteringly out of the bedroom the two are apologizing to everyone for being so late.

It couldn't be helped, Sol explains as he kisses his sisters and brother hello. They have been at a strike rally in Haledon, just outside Paterson. There, standing with thousands in a grassy field outside the house of Pietro Botto, one of the strikers, they listened to a series of speeches "like you never heard, Mamaleh—"

"—And from such a leader!" Yetta breaks in. "Elizabeth Gurley Flynn, oy, you should have seen her standing above us on the balcony. Have you heard of her, Mama Resnick?"

Mama nods. She smiles as she starts laying out plates on the kitchen table. "Hey, watch yourself, what a klutz you are tonight," grabbing the pan of noodle kugel that is about to drop from Vera's hands to the floor. "Yetta, come sit down; Vera, give Yetta a kiss hello and a glass of tea."

Vera is glad to be ordered around. She's a bit shaky. She glances through the bedroom door to see Mary still kneeling on the floor. Mary looks up at her with a small, shy smile. Vera feels her face burn. She turns away. Striking a match to heat the water for tea, she sets her mind to pay close attention to Sol and Yetta's tale of the strike rally.

Mama asks what Gurley Flynn said in her speech. Solly answers, pacing and gesticulating as all the Resnicks do when they talk politics. "Mama, she was magnificent. She said the silk bosses are thieves. She said they steal three million dollars from us workers every single month. Three million! That's the difference between what they pay us and what they get in profits. And that's just in a single month. Can you imagine?"

"Of course," Mama says. "She is quite correct. This is the surplus value created by the workers. The bosses rob it from them and get rich off it."

Vera looks at her mother in surprise. It's been a long time since she's heard Mama talk Marxism. She thought her mother had given up on all that. It's Papa who goes to union meetings. He's the one who's always getting worked up as he reads the Forward, or after spending Saturday afternoons embroiled in debate with his Bundist buddies. He comes home red-faced and furious if anyone has started in with any of "that idiocy about Palestine." On and on Papa goes, each time the subject arises getting red in the face and waving his arms around. He has such vociferous opinions everyone knows not to say a word at such times. Except Mama—for now that she thinks about it, Vera recalls that Mama generally joins in with Papa's anti-Zionist outbursts.

Mama's reference to Marx's theories of labor value shouldn't surprise Vera, she realizes. Just because she rarely hears her mother's political opinions, that doesn't mean her mother doesn't have them. You don't always have to say everything you think.

Papa is looking at Mama. A mixed-up look full of love and longing, guilt and resentment. Vera feels embarrassed at how transparent his feelings are, how they march across his face like that. She hopes her own emotions aren't as easy to read. Mama gives Papa a look in return but Vera cannot decipher it. You don't always have to show what you feel either.

Papa turns to address Sol and Yetta. "So nu, who else spoke at the rally?" The afternoon's worry, the hours waiting to eat, are forgotten. "Was Tresca there? What about Haywood?"

"Yes, Papa, Tresca was there. He gave a grand speech. And so did Hubert Harrison, a shvartze—"

"A colored person, Sol," Yetta corrects him. "Don't say shvartze."

"Why not?" Papa asks. "It just means he's black."

"Because they don't like it. Louie Kupfer told us. They don't consider it respectful. It sounds ugly, like when the goys call us kikes. They want we should say colored." Yetta turns to her husband. "So say colored, Solly, and go on."

"Yes," Mama interjects before he can. "I see. That's right, Leib. It's not so different, the Jews and the coloreds." Then Mama shakes her head as if she's disagreeing with herself. "No. Tsuris we've had. Troubles. But slavery—this is something else altogether. This is why they're so poor, poorer than us even. The colored people were slaves."

"So were we, Lena," Papa says. "Our people were slaves in Egypt. The shvartzes—the coloreds, I mean—they know. All those songs they sing in church, aren't they about Moses leading us out of bondage in Egypt?"

Mama waves her hand lightly as if to swat this point away. "Fine, Leib, you want to believe your Moses story you go right ahead, that's very nice how your god parted the waters and so on and so forth. However, even if that were true, it happened five thousand years ago, and in Egypt."

"So?"

"So think about it, Leib. You too, kinderlach. The colored people were slaves fifty years ago—and right here in this country. Fifty years! That's only yesterday. This colored fellow who spoke at the rally, what's his name again, Solly?"

"Hubert Harrison."

"So how old is he, would you say?"

"I couldn't see him that well, Mama, we were way in the back of the crowd. But in his forties maybe."

"In his forties. So this Mr. Harrison, his parents were probably slaves. His own dear parents, bought and sold like cattle." Everyone is quiet for a minute. Mama looks at each of them intently. She says, "Marx wrote about it, you know," and goes silent.

A small smile alters Papa's face. Again Vera reads a funny mix, this time pride and shame. He brought Mama here and she never got to do any of the things she'd dreamed of, and here in these rooms she has aged, but all along she stays stalwart, stays true.

Sol looks at Mama cautiously for permission to go on. She smiles sweetly and says, "So what did our brother Mr. Harrison have to say?"

"Well, he travels with Tresca and Haywood. He's a fine orator, like them, and he's with the IWW too."

"Ah," Mama says. "So it's the Wobblies leading the strike?"

Sol looks uncertainly at Yetta. She lifts her eyebrows and shrugs. He says, "Wobblies? I don't really know, Mama. In the newspaper they called them reds." Mama laughs. "Well, they're for the workers, I know that. Right, Yetta?"

"Oh, and how! Miss Flynn said the bosses should be put on trial for how they treat us. She said we should get a minimum wage of twelve dollars a week, and no speed-up like they're trying."

Celia, with apologies for her rudeness, asks what Yetta is paid.

"Nothing!" Yetta laughs. "Once my tummy got big the silk macher kicked me out just like that. But when I was working, on three broad looms I made seven dollars a week. That's for six days a week, ten hours a day, you know."

"And the bosses wanted a speed-up," Sol says. "If we hadn't walked out, they would have made the girls work four looms for the same pay."

We, he said. Vera had thought this strike was in Paterson. "But Sol," she says, "You work in Lodi, at the dye works."

"I do—or I did, before the strike." He and Yetta laugh.

How can they laugh? Vera herself is knotting up with worry. "So how come you're on strike too? Who's going to feed the baby?"

"You are!" Mickey, quiet until now, takes up his role as Vera's tormentor. "You have to stop school early—next week—and start working at the shop with Celia to make up for the pay-checks Sol and Yetta aren't getting. What's the matter? Don't look at me like that. Don't you want to do your part for the revolution?"

Some such scenario had been flickering behind Vera's fears. Not even to finish out her final school year. But Papa shushes Mickey and makes him apologize for teasing his sister, so she realizes this worry is unwarranted.

Everyone slides over the invisible boundary from the front room into the kitchen and starts taking their seats around the table as Sol explains that the entire silk industry is on strike. Silk is centered in Paterson, yes, but it includes the dye works in Lodi.

What about the wool houses of Passaic, Vera wonders. Are they next? What a worrier you are, she tells herself. Everyone else seems quite jolly. Well, they like this sort of thing. Contention. Struggle. Mary and I are meant for finer things.

Mary and I. Suddenly they're touching again, sitting in their usual positions next to each other at the table. It seems to Vera that the chairs are jammed closer to each other than usual. She is uncomfortably aware of Mary next to her. The strike talk continues but she loses track of the flow. Dinner on the table, the smells pass over her. She is trapped next to Mary. She senses Mary's skin as though it were touching hers. Mary soft and warm, red with a blush running along her body, inspiring an answering bloom on Vera's face. Cut it out, she tells herself. Mary is in fact encased in clothing, untouchable across the great divide the impossibly distant chairs seem to create, and if her skin seems warm Vera must be imagining it. Then she feels something press against her foot and she presses back. She feels the blush deepen on her face and is afraid to see if her friend's face is redder yet.

The meal goes on and on. She chews. Tastes nothing. Waves of heat undulate toward her from Mary's body. She wants to ask her, what are you, an oven? Stop torturing me, she wants to tell her. But she can't speak. She hopes no one tries to speak to her because she hears nothing. There is only this overwhelming sense of Mary next to her, touching her, not touching her.

This is unendurable, she thinks. I cannot endure this. Then, passing the boiled potatoes to Mickey, she tells herself it's lucky that Sol and Yetta are here with such big news, dominating the table with talk of weighty matters. Otherwise she's sure Celia would notice. Not much gets by her sister. If Celia weren't so engrossed in the conversation about the strike, and clearly dying to break in with what she sees as her own news, the news of Hersh, she would surely see what is going on between Vera and Mary.

After a while someone does see. Mama studies Mary, who is unusually quiet for a renowned wiseacre. Mama asks her if she feels all right. Mary nods, but Mama touches her forehead and says, "You're feverish. And look at your cheeks, like they're on fire." At that Mary glows redder.

"Maybe I should go to bed," she says.

"I agree, it wouldn't kill you to get some extra sleep," Mama says. "You too, Veraleh. The way you two girls stay up half the night reading and talking, I'm not surprised you're exhausted."

Vera feels Mary take a quick look at her, then shrugs and says, "OK." She looks at Celia, who must be disappointed that Vera is leaving before the big moment when she shows Hersh's letter to Solly. She blows her a kiss and shrugs again, then she and Mary head out into the hall to await a turn in the water closet they share with the other three families on this floor.

Once in bed they do read—or at least they lie there, stiffly, side by side, with their books open. Finally Mary asks, "Shall we go to sleep?"

"All right," says Vera. "Goodnight."

She unscrews the light bulb, wraps the blanket around herself and lies on her back. She soon gets hot and throws the blanket off. She shifts around trying to get comfortable. She feels Mary doing the same. After a half-hour of this Vera gets up and goes back out to the bathroom. When she returns to bed she lies on her side, facing the wall, her back to Mary. She closes her eyes. She tries to will herself to sleep. But she can hear Mary breathing. She can feel Mary facing her. Vera has left her hair pinned up and Mary's breaths float across her neck. She feels each exhalation settle against her skin, sink down her back. Breath after soft breath slipping down her neck, along her spine. Vera clenches her fists. This is unendurable. I cannot endure this. Another wisp of air on her neck. Vera feels it all the way down. Mary, please stop breathing. But she doesn't stop.

Vera's vertebrae are tingling. How will she last through the night? Then Mary sighs—a fuller, longer, lingering breath that smacks Vera with the impact of a hot wind. Vera feels her skin open like a flower to the sun. Her whole body trembles.

"Are you cold?" Mary whispers.

"I—no—" Vera tries to clench herself closed. She can feel Mary's body right behind her. It feels as if Mary's body is drawing closer and closer, as if Mary's breath is a hot, howling storm. She can't stop trembling. She knows Mary isn't actually moving, she knows Mary is actually breathing slowly and softly, she knows that there is Mary's nightgown, and hers, between them, and there are inches between them on the bed, which means they are not touching at all—but the quivering shudders through her. And then Mary touches her shoulder and Vera falls backward, into her friend.

Mary turns her so they face each other. Moonlit, Mary's eyes blaze darker than usual, the pupils expanded into deep black circles surrounded by the flickering hazel flames of her irises. Vera is mesmerized. A liquid fire seems to flow into her. The heat calms her quivering but fills her with another, more intense sensation. A new feeling. Molten. She stares into Mary's eyes. Mary stares back.

They finish the afternoon's kiss. And follow it with another, and another.

VERA'S WILL

Hours later, Vera has not yet slept. She doesn't mind. She's waiting to unmelt. And for her frightened heart to steady itself. As she has so often since her first days in this country, Vera feels two things at once. As if she's sliding uncontrollably toward a steep and scary precipice. And as if she can't wait to leap across to the other side.

Vera turns her head slightly and looks at Mary. Her friend's breathing is steady and soft. As dawn starts to break, Vera squints in the slight hint of light. She can just make out Mary's pulse pumping through her neck. Steady and slow. Mary never seems torn, never seems shaky. She never looks as if she wants something and is afraid of it at the same time. She's more solid than me, Vera thinks. She's braver. Maybe after what happened to her mother nothing can frighten her. Still, watching her friend sleep, Vera feels a surge of protectiveness. She resolves to be brave too. Don't worry, Vera thinks. Nothing bad will happen to us, sweetheart. Ever so gently, she squeezes Mary's hand. Sweetheart, she thinks again.

Vera watches her friend sleep for a while longer. She waits for more light to flood the room. It's morning already, she realizes, and I haven't slept at all. It seems like some sort of milestone. She thinks about telling Mary when she wakes up. I was awake all night, she'll whisper. Sweetheart. It's a wonderful way to spend a night, she'll tell her.

Celia stayed up talking with Sol and Yetta into the wee hours. When it's light enough to make out her outline, sound asleep in the next bed, Vera eases out from under the covers. Carefully, quietly, she steps into the front room. She tiptoes past Mickey on his cot in the corner and heads to the piano.

She sits on the brown wooden bench and faces the keys. Perched on its stand peeking out from under the scales exercises Mama uses with her students, there is sheet music. "You Made Me Love You." Music by James V. Monaco, lyrics by Joe McCarthy. She and Mary must have left it there the other day when they were goofing around after dinner. Despite Mama's best efforts, and although Vera diligently practices the classical pieces Mama assigns her, she keeps gravitating to Tin Pan Alley, the lively, popular tunes with words you can remember and melodies you can sing along to. To Vera, these new songs sound more like real life than the beautiful but distant works of the great classical composers.

The piano bench feels firm beneath her tushy. So you're back, I see, she says silently to her body. I'm glad you didn't dissolve into thin air. Although I have to admit there must be worse ways to go. Vera yawns, stretching her arms out in front of her, then laying her fingers softly on the piano keys. She's luxuriating in the feel of herself, the different feel of herself this morning— although she knows she couldn't explain how different, why different, if someone asked.

No one will ask. No one knows. Not in all the world. No one but Mary and her. Vera feels strong, vital, alert with the power of such a secret. Yet even as this power thrills through her, tingling her fingertips as they sit silent on the keys, it is matched with a dread that rumbles up her spine and ends in a shudder that spasms her fingers. The silence breaks as dissonant notes ring out where she inadvertently hits the keys.

Mickey starts, and shifts, but luckily he doesn't wake up. Vera wills herself to take a deep breath. Think about something else now, she tells herself. If you keep thinking about this you'll end up waking the whole house with some crazy symphony.

She pulls the lid closed over the piano keys. She lays her left arm down on it, and puts her head on her arm. She slides her right hand along the side of the piano. As she feels it, careful not to catch her fingers on the splinters of the old wood, an image of Bubbie comes to her. The night before they left Odessa for the journey across the world, her grandmother had sipped tea with Vera and told her to be unafraid. Ever since, whenever Vera clashes with Papa or Mama she invokes Bubbie. Feh on your silly old traditions, she says. Bubbie told me to break away. Be brave, Bubbie said, do something new.

"Well, this is certainly new, bubbeleh." Vera has fallen asleep. She dreams her grandmother's voice. "I'm not entirely sure I was referring to something of quite this nature when we had our little talk before you left Odessa."

"I know, Bubbie," Vera responds. She's surprised she can still speak Yiddish. She takes a sip of tea from a short glass. "But not even you could have predicted what things would be like here. Remember, I was just a little girl then. Now I'm almost grown up. Everything is very different here."

"About this I believe you," Bubbie says. "And I have no complaints about who you have become." Vera glows. "But Vera, what you are going to go through—this I cannot pretend to be happy about." Vera shivers. "Didn't I tell you I didn't want you to suffer like your mother did?"

"Yes." Vera looks down.

"So nu, Veraleh, look at me." Vera does. Bubbie's eyes are tender and sad. She's been dead seven years now; the piano arrived three months after her death, shipped with money she'd set aside to provide music for her daughter. She says, "Don't you know what you are going to face?"

Vera hesitates. "I—I'm not sure. But it isn't the same, Bubbie. This is America. There are no pogroms. I won't go through what Mama did. I'm safe."

Is Bubbie still here, sitting on the piano bench sipping tea with her? Does she kiss Vera on the cheek, or is that just a soft slip of air brushing by? Vera's throat constricts. Is that still Bubbie's voice she hears? If not, whose? "Pogroms, maybe not. But safe? Oy, Veraleh, I don't think so."

In Flew Enza

1918

JULY

It has been a grand day. All afternoon at the Weehawken waterfront. The sun sparkling off the Hudson. Vera and Mary strolling. Waving at straw-hatted passengers lolling their way upstream on expensive pleasure boats festooned with brightly colored paper streamers that catch the breeze and dance in each vessel's wake like frolicking sprites endowed with the power of flight. Shouting encouragement to the flotilla of rickety rowboated anglers who stick closer to shore trolling for bass and pike.

At the height of it, in the heat of the day, watching as Mary trips gaily ahead, chats across river traffic, negotiates crowded footpaths, Vera falls back. Her dear one seems something of a sprite herself. So much energy in such a small person. And awfully fetching in her blue and white dress with the sailor collar. As if she's read Vera's mind, Mary spins round to face her. Visage backlit by glimmery golden afternoon rays, river's mist frizzing her thick brown tresses into a humidified nimbus about her head, she appears for an instant otherworldly—and then she sticks out her tongue.

A wallop of arousal plows through Vera. It starts below, races upward, gallops across her heart, paints her neck scarlet. Gee whiz, she thinks. Five years, and still she clobbers me.

Vera wants to kiss Mary, hard, right here. Instead she grabs her hand and pulls her toward a bench. Mary resists.

"Wait a minute, Vera. How about if I—"

"No, come here. Sit down with me a little."

"Sure, honey, but first how about some"— Mary grins. Sticks out her tongue again, wicked girl, and licks her lips. The two look at each others' faces slick with shvitz and wordlessly agree: ice cream. Mary saunters off. Again Vera is seized by the sight of her. Her posture. Her fingers trailing in the air as she approaches the ice cream stand. The way she cocks her head as she counts coins into the vendor's hands. Something as simple as that sets off a fever ache that Vera finds hard to contain. Mary brings the treats. They sit on a bench and share cones, Vera's vanilla, Mary's strawberry, licking dripping goo from each other's chins, laughing at every little thing. Linking fingers flat against the seat where none can see.

They linger longer than they should, unwilling to let go of each other, this day. Trying not to think of tomorrow, ten hours, the dye, the stench, the endless sweat, Passaic River stink.

They have to head home, however, for the Sunday supper— Vera long since gave up on uplifting Resnick household lingo— they know Mama has made. They lean against each other, softening the long ride on the streetcar's hard wood seats.

After the meal, Mary entertains. For Mama and Papa, seated on the davenport, she replays the day. Madcap gal makes them laugh. Even Papa. Curly tendrils of beard fly out from his mouth, hinting at a hearty chuckle. Mary acts out everyone she and Vera have seen. How this one rushed, that one strutted, how those promenaded. She grabs Vera and makes her march rigid beside her, imitating the stiff gait of a pair of soldiers. "Poor boys," Mama mutters, smile faltering. Mama spent much of last month—nineteen days as battle raged at Bellau Wood—in the next apartment, worrying with old Mrs. Milstein about her youngest boy. She came home each evening muttering about imperialist war, workers as cannon fodder, wishing out loud for some force in this country to do what the Bolsheviks did in Russia. The Milstein boy is due to muster out soon, but any military reference still ruins her mood. She glowers. Mary glances from her to Papa, then at Vera, claps her hands and announces in florid tones, "Kindly return your attention with me, if you will, to the Weehawken waterfront. I shall now perform a pantomime of the passing fashion parade."

She does, so effectively that she seems to doff and don each outfit, running the gamut from shmatte-headed yentas and cowlicked country bumpkins to fresh-bobbed pretty young things strolling beside best-Sunday-suited beaus. Soon Mama grins again.

By the end of Mary's impromptu show, all four of them are howling so hard—well, not Papa, they can't hear him, but they can see, eyes crinkling, puffs of mirth blowing his beard, hands slapping his knees—that sour old man Milstein starts pounding on the wall. He yells, "A little peace, please, some quiet on a Sunday evening, you should be so kind, what's the matter with you in there anyway, sha already." Papa starts shushing them. When the other three keep laughing he ousts them.

"Leave now," he says. "Go outside until you are fit for human company." He whispers the command, unable to look them in the eye, still in the grip of merriment himself.

Vera, Mary and Mama stumble down the stairs. Helpless with laughter, eyes running, they stand at the curb holding the lamppost and each other until the paroxysms subside.

August

Again with the laughter. Only this time it's not fair, it's mean, they're making fun of Mary's cousin Peter Steiner—gevalt, what a putz he is—still no, it isn't right. They've got to stop. But it's hard when Mama herself is biting her lips, struggling unsuccessfully to prevent little snorts escaping. Too bad Papa isn't here to take the three of them in hand. He's spending this Sunday reviewing reports of the Russian civil war, shnappes with his Bundist buddies, toasting the reds, cursing the whites their heads should sprout underground like onions. Without his pacifying presence, Vera, Mary and Mama egg each other on.

Well, and who could blame them? After what Peter just said? Perspiring! Perspiring—and now he's the one, poor Peter nervous, flustered, sweat beading his forehead, dripping down his neck.

Things had started out all right. They always do. No one can say they don't try to be kind when he descends on the household on a Sunday afternoon. They never set out to laugh at him. He forces them. The things he does. Says. So solemn, always, so painstakingly proper. Nodding, spewing please and thank you at every little thing. He sits here making small talk, smoothing the crease in the pants of his seersucker suit, pushing his glasses up his nose, adjusting his collar, plumping his bow tie. A fussy, prissy sort of fellow. Still, he means well and he's all alone in this country and they put up with him, even with his wearisome ways—but if only he didn't make it impossible to keep a straight face.

Just now the talk had turned to their jobs. Mary mentioned how awfully early she and Vera have to rise each work day, clearly hoping her cousin would get the hint and skedaddle. Hoping Mama wouldn't go soft and invite him to stay for supper. At talk of the dye works Peter had said that he hates to think of Vera and Mary there. He turned toward Vera, his words sputtering out in a self-conscious stutter. "Y-you are altogether too f-fine—too r-refined, that is—to work in such a p-place." Vera and Mary looked at each other. Hardly giggled at all. Gee, in fact, Vera thought, he's got a good heart. A guy like him, with a little cash in his pocket, you wouldn't expect him to have any feeling for what it's like for us in the sweated shop. Not to mention recognizing that we're cut out for better things.

Mary looked pleased too. She leaned in and patted Peter's arm. "I couldn't agree more," she said. "We're too good for that hellhole."

He flushed, as he always does at the straight talk this household dishes out. He shifted his weight. Warming to his subject, his lids fluttering like shy butterflies, turning again toward Mama, German accent thickening as the words rushed out, "Yes indeed. Young ladies like these—like your daughter and my cousin, I mean, Mrs. Resnick—these are educated ladies, cultured ladies. This is clear." Mary mouthed "la di da" at Vera behind his back. "Therefore no, I must say again, they should not be perspiring in that place."

And that did it. Mary and Vera burst out laughing. Mama tries to stop herself, raising her hand to her mouth but succeeding only in jolting her teacup and splashing lukewarm liquid into her lap. Peter jumps up, whips out his handkerchief and leans over her, making ineffectual helping motions and snuffling embarrassedly in some indecipherable mix of languages. Mama takes his handkerchief, pushes him back toward the couch, busies herself patting the spilled tea off her blouse, desperate to hold down the rising tide. She loses the battle. A great guffaw explodes.

And the three of them are swept up as a tidal wave of laughter washes over them, Vera and Mary collapsing against the davenport, Mama gasping oy oy. Perspiration shop—oy!

Vera knows she should stop. Raised in a starchy Dresden household, Peter can't speak any normal language—first Jew Vera ever met who came over with less Yiddish than English. So he mixes up words a little, so what? The tiny tug of conscience, however, is no match for the mad, surging giggles that have hold of her.

Eventually, of course, they calm down. Speaking of sweat, Vera realizes she's drenched. She fans Mary with her hands. Her friend returns the favor.

"You must forgive us, Mr. Steiner." Mama's voice is a little shaky still; when Vera looks she won't meet her eye. "I am so terribly sorry—"

"Oh no, Mrs. Resnick, there is no forgiving needed, don't be sorry, no, no indeed. I understand perfectly."

"You do?" Vera blurts.

"So okay already, maybe not perfectly." Peter mops his forehead with his monogrammed handkerchief, pushes his glasses up his nose, smiles at Vera, shrugs. "I must admit that my English is not yet completely polished." He turns his smile toward Mary. "I am quite sure my cousin would agree. No, sha, Mary, don't apologize. Sometimes I make a joke without intending to. But I must say, I am glad. If it means I have the privilege to sit back and listen to you the most lovely ladies laugh, then this makes me the most glad."

The friends look at each other. It would be so easy to proceed at his expense. But no, each seems to conclude simultaneously, it isn't fair, so, "That's very nicely put," says Mary. And from Vera, "Peter, would you like some more iced tea?"

Taking turns at the kitchen counter chipping at the big block of ice they work off straggling shudders of silliness. After, in the front room, sipping, sighing in delight as the chill slides down their throats, the four of them fall silent. Only Peter's frequent throat clearings and nose blowings interrupt the stillness. After a time their visitor takes his leave.

They listen to him descend three flights of stairs, open and close the entrance door, whistle as he walks up the street. Once he's well gone Vera says, "What is that, the third Sunday in a row?"

"Fourth, but who's counting," says Mary.

"Enough, you two," from Mama. "Mary Freundlich, he's your blood relation—I know your father, may he rest in peace, would have wanted you to be polite."

"Polite, yes," says Mary. "A saint, I don't think."

"No one is asking you to be a saint—"

"But he's so, I don't know, so—"

"Dull?" Vera grins at her friend.

"By gum, I do believe that's it." Mary chuckles against Vera.

"So you're cracking up again? So you're thinking you're a couple of regular Fanny Brices?" Not if Mama's going to lecture them they're not. Vera straightens up, squeezes Mary's hand in a silent signal to do the same. "Laughing at a poor lonely man, making faces behind his back. Complaining he comes here too much. You should be ashamed of yourselves, him alone in this country, where else he should go? No one he has, only you, Mary, and that means us, which, believe me, the Resnicks are not such a shiny gift package ourselves, did that ever occur to you, Miss Vera High-and-Mighty, that maybe he's just as unhappy he has to put up with us as you are about him?"

No, that hasn't occurred to her. Vera mulls it over.

Peter Steiner had appeared at their doorstep one Sunday afternoon late last month. Papa had answered the knock and let in the stranger who introduced himself as Mary's cousin. Peter wore a suit finer than any she'd seen. With his bowler hat, his squinty eyes magnified behind thick lenses, his pinched lips and thinning sandy hair and stiff carriage, the skinny, sallow fellow reminded her of Woodrow Wilson. Not the gladdest association in a household whose shorthand for the president is "warmonger."

Mama and Papa's attempts to engage him in conversation about current events quickly revealed that Peter hasn't got a political bone in his body. In fact, fish as they might, they failed to find out his views on any topic—"I hate to say it about your relations, Mary," Mama clucked over dinner after he'd left that first Sunday, "but your cousin is a bissel a nebbish, no?"—any topic, that is, except his joy in finding Mary and the Resnicks and his plans to improve all their lives. On this he waxed eloquent. His eyes misted as he held Mary's hands and said, "I am so magnificently apologizing to hear of the death of your dear mother. Since I have heard this most horrible information, it has been my mission to find my orphan cousin and make everything the most better for you it is possible I can."

Frail and fidgety as he appears, Vera has begun to conclude, there may be more to the fellow than at first there seemed. For one thing, he's persistent. Since he found them last month, he has latched on. A regular Sunday afternoon caller.

After Peter arrived in New York early in the spring, he had spent several months setting himself up in a small jewelry shop on the Lower East Side established with a stake of gems and capital from his father, a prosperous jeweler in Dresden. All the while, he searched for his late uncle Wolf Freundlich's widow and daughter. Days he dickered with wholesalers; evenings he scoured the city in a determined search for family. On Grand Street, the last address he had for his Aunt Bella, he was told of her demise in a fire at the shirtwaist factory where she worked. All anyone remembered of Bella's daughter Mary was that she had moved to New Jersey with some distant relatives. No one knew the name of the adoptive family. But Peter was determined to make the connection. So in the midst of everything— renting an apartment and then a storefront, navigating the rock business and the weird ways of a new land, learning the ups and downs of New York's streets, working on his English while straining to make deals in his severely limited Yiddish—through it all, he kept looking for his only living relative in the United States. When he found her, he resolved to do what he could to help her and the people who had taken her in.

He'd told them this tale during that first Sunday visit, concluding with a request to call on them again. When he did, the very next weekend, it was with all manner of gifts. A box of fine Cuban cigars for Papa. Sheet music—classical for Mama, "For Me and My Gal" for Mickey. Sol and Celia live with their families, and he had yet to meet them, but he brought them presents too: passes to the Palisades, everyone's favorite amusement park. As Vera and Mary shook their heads in astonishment—"This guy must be loaded," Vera hissed, and Mary whispered back, "I know, be nice to him"—Peter handed them each a pair of fine kid gloves, white with a line of mother-of-pearl to the elbow.

Now Mama peers at Vera. "So? You're thinking about what I said?"

"I am, Mama."

"And?"

"And I see the error of my ways."

"Ha!" Mary slaps her thigh, starts chortling again. "I bet you do!"

"Wait a minute, girly," Mama says, sharply, and Mary's chuckles cease. "Maybe you can take something a little serious for once in your life. Vera is maybe starting to?"

Vera returns Mama's look. "Actually, yes, Mama, I am. Mary, we should be nice to him. What's the harm?"

"You're just falling for his flattery, Vera Resnick."

"What? Since when has he flattered me?"

"Maybe not you directly." Mary points to Mama. "But you. All that folderol about your beautiful deep dark eyes, my goodness Lena Resnick, you ought to be ashamed of yourself, a grandmother, letting him ooze all over you like a snake-oil salesman."

Vera gasps. Mary can get away with a lot, but ...

"Hoo ha!" With this too, apparently. Mama shakes her finger back at Mary but it's fake, accompanied with a fond gaze. Vera lets out her breath. "And again hoo ha I say to you, Mary Freundlich. Your cultured continental cousin thinks I'm the pretty one? And since everyone knows my Veraleh looks just like me, this is a compliment to her too? And you're jealous maybe?"

"Jealous! Why, that's just—"

"Fine, I'm ridiculous. But you know what else? You are right that I should be ashamed, and I am. Ashamed only because I'm not nicer to him. Always with the snickering, the three of us, the snorting, and him a poor immigrant."

"Not so poor, though, I don't think." Mary says. "Him with the gifts all the time. Maybe today it was only flowers, still yet."

"True, even if he buys them from some hondler on the street, a flower costs." Mama nods thoughtfully. "You're right, Mareleh. Your cousin must be doing good. Who knew? Money in the family, girlchik, hey? Not that I want anything to do with him if he's some kind of a big boss, but a petit bourgeois—"

"We're not too petty to accept his gifts, right, Mama?" Vera smirks. "Maybe Mary's rich cousin Peter will save her from—"

"That's right!" Mary's voice rises to drown out her friend's. "He'll maybe save me from a life of—"

"From all this shvitzing!" Vera shrieks, and they're hooting again, all three.

OCTOBER

Vera kneels by the chaise longue. She holds Mary's left hand in both of hers. Hot. Vera looks at her friend's eyes. Closed.

Vera lays her head lightly on Mary's breast. Her friend's breathing alternates between harsh, tortured rasps that rock Vera, leave her gasping for breath herself, choking with fear— and short, shallow intakes of the merest slips of air, surely not enough to fill her lungs, so that "breathe, sweetheart, breathe," Vera silently urges. The fact is that Mary's lungs are filled with fluid. This flu is drowning her.

A few feet away, Mama plays the piano ever so softly. Each gentle note barely sounds before it slips away. She plies the keys lovingly. Lullabies. Ballads. Sweet, solemn, simple songs that subtly mesh with the hush of the sickroom.

It had been Mama's idea to bring Mary out of the bedroom and here into the front room, where a bit of light sneaks past the sur- rounding buildings and ducks in for a quick visit late each after- noon. "Let Mary feel the sun a little," Mama had said yesterday. "Don't you want to feel a bissel sun, Mareleh?" Mary had smiled and nodded, and with Vera and Mama supporting her on either side she'd risen slowly from the bed she and Vera have shared for seven years and traversed the miles from there to the chaise longue waiting for her all blanketed and pillowed in the front room. She reclined on the longue and smiled again, looked up at Vera fussing, adjusting. Vera asked if she was all right and yes, Mary nodded, she was. Then she sighed deeply and closed her eyes. She has not moved from the chaise longue since. She can no longer take a deep breath. She opens her eyes less and less often.

Mary is sinking. Falling away. It is clear to Vera that no matter how tightly she holds her sweetheart she is going to lose her. How is this possible? Vera would not have thought anything could be worse than last month ... Papa, how the flu stole him away in four horrible days … Now, although she knows this is terrible to think, it seems to Vera that Papa's death from influenza was but a dress rehearsal for this. She loved her father. She misses him. But at least he lived a life. Mary is twenty. She is ending before she barely begins. Before she and Vera barely begin. Vera wishes her father had bequeathed her some of his outmoded old-world faith so she could curse at his god.

"Vera."

Her gloomy musings vanish at Mary's voice. It sounds a little stronger, doesn't it? That's a good sign. Isn't it? Vera lifts her head and sits up to see her friend.

One look and she can't kid herself.

Mary was small to start with. There is very little left to her. What there is does not resemble Mary Freundlich. Her skin is translucent, tinged with the pale blue hue of oxygen deprivation. Her hair—formerly so lustrous, thick, the auburn waves careering in a kind of corona around her face so that sometimes Vera looked at her and thought she was an angel, with a halo yet, which tickled her, how she called on ridiculous Christian imagery to characterize Mary's beauty—now her glorious mane hangs limp in loose, thin, dull strands.

A sort of steam seems to rise from her skin. The fever's vapors. It is as though Mary's innards are dematerializing. Her essence evaporating—Mary turning to mist, rising, drifting away. Vera wants to jump up, swipe at the air above her, grab it, deliver Mary back into her body. Prohibit this process from proceeding.

Unbidden, unwelcome, that terrible rhyme, the one she's been hearing the children sing as they play hop-scotch on the sidewalk, tears through her mind. *I had a little bird, her name was Enza. I opened the window, and in flew Enza.* Vera shudders. Then the bitter ditty is banished as Mary's voice breaks through again.

"Veraleh."

"Yes, dear?" Against all reason, despite the fever, Mary's bright hazel eyes are clear. Mary inhabits them still. She is still herself. And her eyes still shine with love. It takes Vera's breath away. Her own eyes start to overflow. She turns away.

"Nu, don't cry, sweetheart."

"No, all right, I won't." But she keeps blubbering.

"Vera, look at me. Veraleh. Come on."

Vera looks. She sees—wisdom? Yes, it has always been there, she thinks, hidden behind the laughter. A wise and funny girl. What a woman she would have been.

Vera is cracking from love of her. From Mary leaving her.

Since the night five years ago when they had first acknowledged their love—communicating in thrilling, shocking bodily terms—they have shared a passion that seemed to grow more profound with each new effort to conceal it from public view. They have both known it is aberrant. The world, they've surmised, does not welcome them as they are. So they have worn their best-chum disguise in daylight. In the dark, every night Celia a bed away, they have lain in love's true dwelling place. Skin in mute motion against skin, hushed malingering tongues, fingertips telling silent truths. Alone in the knowledge but not lonely. It has seemed, in a way, that their love has blessed them, in the sense of setting them apart. Binding them together.

She stops crying. She looks at her sweetheart. Mary returns her gaze. Lifting two quivering fingers to her dry, collapsed lips, she blows a kiss toward Vera and manages a little wink. With the same two fingers she motions Vera to bend toward her, then whispers, "Sweetie-pie, send Mama out. So we can talk."

Vera nods. She walks over to the piano and tells Mama that Mary is thirsty. Would you believe she wants a soda pop all of a sudden? Would Mama mind going down to the corner and splurging on one for her? Vera would go herself but—

"That's all right, Veraleh," Mama says. "You two talk. I'll go." She kisses Vera's cheek, retrieves her coat from the closet, glances back at Mary on the longue and leaves.

Vera returns to Mary's side. She kneels next to her again.

"Can you get up here with me?" Mary asks.

"Oy—I don't want to hurt you. Your skin is so tender."

"Vera. Hold me. There's no one here to see. It's safe."

Vera is stung. "That's not what I'm worried about. I'm afraid I'll—"

"—You'll what, dearie? Kill me?"

"Mareleh!"

"Better I should die from love, isn't it, Vera?"

"Mary! Stop saying these things!"

"Oh, you stop it. You're being silly." Mary pauses, out of breath. Vera digs her nails into her palms as her friend struggles for air. Mary whispers, "I just want you to put your arms around me—"

"Mary—"

"Your arms around me, Veraleh. Now." Her gasping subsides. Her breaths resume a quiet, shallow rhythm. Her face opens.

Vera reads fear, anger, despair. Then, as she watches, the features rearrange and something like peace replaces the pain. Mary opens her arms, inviting Vera in. Gently, Vera climbs onto the longue. She eases Mary back a bit, slides her right arm under her back and with her left pulls Mary in toward her. She locks her in a careful embrace. Fighting her own fierce emotions, pushing down rising panic, she focuses on comforting her darling girl. Calm, she tells herself. Just hold her. For a little while yet.

Mary's eyes are closed. Vera caresses her. She grazes some sweaty hairs back off her forehead. She lays her left palm lightly on Mary's cheek.

Mary opens her eyes and locks onto her lover's. They gaze at each other for a moment. Mary whispers something.

Vera can't catch it. "What?"

"Tell me you love me."

Vera swallows. She forces a smile. "Oh, Mary." She kisses her forehead.

"Do you, Vera?"

"I do."

Mary lets out a small sigh. Vera kisses her, this time on the mouth. She fills with wonder at how sweet Mary still tastes. She holds the kiss. She doesn't breathe.

Mary has entwined the fingers of her right hand in Vera's left. She clutches tightly as they kiss, her little silvery ring with the monogrammed M, the one Vera bought her at the five and dime, pressing against Vera's skin. Then her grasp slackens. Vera pulls her lips away. She feels the heat from Mary's fever. Mary's eyes glow strangely. She is in the grip of it now. She is looking at Vera and her lips are moving but she is not saying anything. Then her eyes close. She sleeps.

Vera closes her eyes too. Lying there holding Mary, feeling each wheezing breath, each straining beat of her darling's heart, she falls into a few minutes' half-doze. She sees the two of them splendidly dressed. All done up in silky, feathery finery. Standing under a canopy. Holding hands. Above, a starry sky. Behind them Mama, Papa, all their friends and family, the girls from the dye works, the streetcar conductor even. Everyone they know. Then, from before them: "Do you, Vera, take this woman, Mary?"

Oh, I do.

Mary coughs. Vera starts awake. I would have, she thinks. If we could have ... Stop, she tells herself. Just hold her.

Soon she starts to worry that Mama will return and find them here like this. She pulls herself away. She walks over to the piano. She sits, hands in her lap, staring at the keys.

November

She moves so slowly lately. Vera knows she is alive, knows she breathes still, works, still she eats and sleeps, knows it is herself, still, who sips tea these quiet nights sitting with Mama. But how slowly, with what effort she does all that used to be automatic.

Startled by the quiet around her, Vera looks around. It seems she is alone in the dye works. Has everyone gone already? So quickly? She and Mary used to be among the first to rush out when the work day ended. Her friend would be shocked to see Vera dally. It is not because she likes this place. When work is done she wants to get out of here as much as she ever did, needs to escape the noise and heat, to straighten her back after 10 hours bent over the piece table. Something compels her to join Mama each evening, to sit in the fraught silence they pull around themselves like a tattered old blanket they never knew they'd need again.

A new girl works beside her. Vera can't remember her name. She has a sweet smile. Sometimes Vera wants to slap her. The girl goes quickly when the work shift ends.

Vera looks up at the big clock on the wall. Five-thirty. She has been standing here, poised to leave, sweater over her shoulders, lunch sack in her hand, since her shift ended at five o'clock. This happens often now. Time disappears. Each moment without Mary, unaccountable.

Mama will be worried, she tells herself. I really must go. She puts her arms into the sweater sleeves, reaches into her coin purse for trolley fare. She inhales deeply. But the breath only brings another set of paralyzing agents.

During the day the bosses keep the shop doors closed so the workers won't be distracted by a whiff of fresh air. Now, after hours, with only Tulio the janitor still here sweeping the bosses' offices upstairs, the doors are open to the late-autumn world. From the back rolls in the reek of the Passaic River, its muddy banks clogged with soggy dead leaves, its slow, sad waters rank with the effluent expelled from every silk, wool, linen and dye shop from Paterson to Union City. Mary and Vera used to eat their lunch standing by the river, joking about the smell but still eager for the outside air. From out front, beyond the shop's main door that opens onto Atlantic Boulevard, the five-thirty trolley bell rings. An automobile horn honks repeatedly. Doors slam. A woman scolds her child. Mary and Vera used to stroll the street by the trolley stop after work, so engrossed in talk that more than once they didn't hear the bell and had to wait for the next streetcar.

Somehow, she wills herself home. Later, after she and Mama have eaten, and sat, and sipped, as Mama sleeps, Vera stands on the fire escape searching for stars in the midnight sky.

Everyone loved Mary. Who wouldn't, with her grand energy, her stinging wit? Her unruly brown hair she was forever flinging out of her face. Her flashing hazel eyes. But no one knows how Vera loved her.

I will never love again, Vera thinks, staring at the sky's sole star. Okay already, Mary, I sound ridiculous. Like a dreary character in some dreadful melodrama. You'd have laughed at me if I ever uttered anything so trite. But Mary, she whispers to the star, I think it might be true.

Now she lies in bed. The dark eases itself against her, insinuating itself around her as love once did. The night's cold caresses her. She presses her legs tight, remembering their nights. Surging, urgent, flowing into each other. Lovers. Without a word for their love.

November's breezes brisk across her. Vera shivers, yet the feeling is closer to fear. She forgot to be afraid when her friend was here. What next, alone?

Naming Names

Everybody knows me as Randy but my given name is Mary. I was named, I was told, for my paternal grandmother's sister who died in the flu epidemic after World War I. This Mary was no sister, I now know, but her death was a great sadness in my grandmother's life, and thirty-five years later, when I was born, she insisted I be named Mary.

My mother, as she would tell me when I was a teenager, balked. Mary? As in Jesus Christ's mother? Aside from being an old-fashioned and terribly conventional name in this all-new era of power steering and polio vaccines, it was irretrievably goyisheh to my mother's way of thinking. Her mother-in-law argued, however, that it was a perfectly good old Jewish name. Her mother-in-law won.

Me, I now feel fond toward the name on my birth certificate—even if I haven't gone by Mary for some forty years. There's something so retro about it, so soft-focus, that it has an almost other-worldly feel to me. Of course I know Mary is also the name with which one popular religious cult camouflages the great goddess who has been worshipped in her various guises in thousands of cultures over thousands of years. And I know full well that this female deity, whatever her name, is as imaginary as any other divinity humans have concocted to soothe and succor them on the transit toward death. Still, goddess worship—hey, okay. I can live with that. The whole world longs for mommy? Fine, that's me, mother earth containing the whole world. All-knowing, all-powerful, my monthly menses transmuted from the messy, inconvenient cramp-o-rama they really are to some ultimate mystery containing life and death and whatever other mythic uses anyone thinks up for the sloughed-off uterine lining. Mary. That's my name, don't wear it out.

But if I take a good look at those ancient images of the great goddess whose likeness appears in every civilization until the tragic triumph of patriarchy, I see that she doesn't resemble me at all. I mean, come on. The goddess is not some bony jittery myopic nerd. The goddess is—good god, look at her! The goddess is the spitting image of my mother, Ruby. She's Mom all over! The vast pendulous breasts, massive padded hips, the lush rolls of fat that undulate down her abdomen until they meet the sweet, salty source of life at the Venusian mound where, omnipotence aside, modesty prevails and the adipose waves dip down to bashfully obscure the hairy entryway to eternity.

Jesus. (So to speak.) Why did it take me until now to realize this? I wish I could tell her. "Mom," I'd say. "You're beautiful." I'd show her the pictures, the figurines unearthed in Iraq or Congo, every ancient goddess a perfect body double for Ruby Schumacher Steiner, my mom who would never let me take a picture of her because she hated her overflowing physical self. "Look, Mom," I'd say if I could. "You don't have to be ashamed of being fat anymore."

Look. Mom. You are to be worshiped.

Well. Be that as it may. Mom isn't here anymore. And I'm not Mary.

Whatever flights of fancy it inspires in me now, when I was little Mary seemed like an unbelievably square name. Each time I was introduced to someone I couldn't stand it. Kids automatically thought I was some kind of goody-goody just because of my name. I even got into a couple scrapes over it, fisticuffs with boys on the block who knew they could get my goat by calling me Maryhadalittlelamb, singsonging my short, sensible moniker into an elongated, babyish epithet that drove me bonkers.

By 1961, when I was eight, I'd had enough. It was time to act. President Kennedy, after all, wanted us all to have vim and vigor. I resolved to show mine (well, my vigor, anyway; I still have no idea what vim is) by changing my name.

There was no great mystery over what my new name would be. My absolute favorite person in the whole wide world was Rowdy Yates, the young Clint Eastwood's character on the TV series *Rawhide*. Rowdy was rugged, laconic, had a wry sense of humor and a terrific understated way of dressing. He was who I wanted to be. Rowdy. That would be me.

What do names signify? Who we are? Might have been? Could never hope to be in our wildest dreams? I wanted to be Rowdy but I certainly wasn't very rugged. I was actually kind of a klutz—had, and still have, a tendency to bump into things and shriek. I did play outside with my friends a lot, but with my hay fever I always ended up sniffling and sneezing. Was never into smelly animals either. Can you picture me on a cattle drive? I'd never even been camping. We weren't exactly outdoorsy folk. And laconic? Ha! I'm the kid whose elementary-school report cards always said things like "Mary's advanced verbal skills tend to dissolve into silliness; talks too much."

I did have a robust sense of humor, although to call my eight-year-old wit wry would be stretching things. And I did dress well, I thought. Pretty much how Rowdy Yates would have dressed if he were a suburban tomboy. I tended toward man-tailored shirts, pedal pushers and gymshoes.

All in all, it made perfect sense. I would be Rowdy. So I told Mom. Which is why I'm known as Randy.

She didn't hit the roof, exactly. But she did lay down the law. The "you're a girl" law, to be precise. Which she had invoked before.

Mary," she sighed, standing at the kitchen counter spreading cream cheese and laying thin slices of belly lox on a Sunday onion bagel, "you are a girl." I shifted, set my jaw, tapped my foot. Stood my ground. Waited. Mom laid down her knife. She looked at me for a moment as if she were calculating some difficult sum. "I don't know what your grandmother's going to say if we announce that you're not Mary anymore, but I do know that it'll go a lot easier if you have a girl's name." I stopped tapping. She sounded like she and I were changing my name together. "But we'll deal with her later, okay?"

"Okay." What was going on here?

"I love you and that won't ever change even if your name is Tuchis McGee. Your name isn't Tuchis McGee, is it?" I couldn't help it—I started laughing. Mom grabbed me and hugged me, then she spun me around and lightly slapped my bottom as she slipped into some sort of deranged hotel bellhop persona and yodeled, "Calling Tuchis McGee, is there is a Miss McGee in the house?"

She shook with laughter. Then suddenly she stood straight, passed her hand in front of my face like a hypnotist and stared at me with an expression I couldn't read.

"You shall be called Randy," Mom intoned.

And Randy I was. She was right, I knew it right away. A piece of me—my lower left intestine, which clenched—wanted to hold onto Rowdy. I closed my eyes for an instant. In my mind I saw Mr. Yates himself shrug, tip his hat, turn his back and walk away, his image fading to black as a background chorus of rueful cowboys hummed about rolling doggies ... I swallowed and opened my eyes. Mom was waiting.

I blinked. Murmured, "Randy's okay? You'll tell Dad for me?"

"Ah shorely will now, Miz Randy, ah shorely will." She winked, pivoted into a John Wayne turn and John-Wayne-walked out of the kitchen. My mother could imitate all sorts of famous people really well, even their body language, even thin ones, even men.

Expectation

I don't know if you can call this a life, exactly, Vera thinks. It's neither one thing nor another. "If you want to be accurate," she adds out loud, impelled by a vague notion that her voice will provide a cogency her thoughts have lacked of late. Yes. Accuracy is good. "To be valid and expressive, words should clearly and accurately convey the dimensions or actuality of an object, event or concept." There. It helps to recite the ninth-grade speech and elocution lesson. To focus her mind. Which would be a good thing. "I suppose," she sighs.

Vera sets her swollen feet on the floor to steady the rocking chair. She leans to the side and looks out the window. She pulls the shawl closer, its soft fringe tickling her earlobes as she tries to make out the objects, events or concepts below. Six flights down, lower Fifth Avenue is a dreamscape this morning. Everything indistinct. Everyone enshrouded in flurrying white clouds of snow.

She sits back. Her thoughts start to float away again. She lays her hands on the distended bulk at her midriff. Her eyes close. Effort at mental clarity tapering like a spent candle sputtering out, her brain returns to the vaporous region where it mostly seems to reside during these final weeks of waiting for the baby.

Peter has expressed concern about her strange lassitude. He cannot engage her in conversation, he complains. He has a point. Still, he must prefer this drifty stranger to the snippy harpy she'd shown signs of becoming.

He likes to talk when they sit together in the evenings after dinner. His bride had liked it, too, at first. Peter is a congenial companion in his way. Considerate, soft-spoken. Vera had found him charming, a year ago. Him and his shy glances. She had looked forward to their post-prandial tête-à -têtes.

Peter rescued her. Or so it had seemed at the time. After Mary. Limbo of pain and paralysis. Peter quiet, solicitous. Always there, whichever way she turned. Eventually she had turned to him. And discerned, behind his squint, through those comically thick spectacles, hazel eyes, like his cousin's. When he pressed her, when let me take care of you he said, let me take you away, she had let herself be persuaded.

She has in fact found a sort of ease here with Peter. Respite. From physical labor, material want. Love? She has tried— is trying still—but she can find no love for him.

And so what she had first experienced as his charming solicitousness had quickly come to seem unctuous insincerity. His quiet talk a droning bore. How much can a person say about the rock trade? Plenty, it turns out. On and on, every evening, Peter talks of his business. Which is going very well. Vera has nothing to complain about, she lives better than she ever did, better than anyone she's ever known, and it's all due to the success of Peter's jewelry store, expanded to two stores now, so she had tried for a long while to exhibit at least a little interest in it. But every night? Prices and tariffs, deals and bargains, karats and cuts. Commerce.

One evening last spring, back when she still paid attention, Peter had mentioned the Clayton Antitrust Act and its potential effect on small concerns like his in the face of the new trend toward huge department stores. Now that people moving into the middle class could spend their cash on anything from unmentionables to engagement rings in one big building, some pundits were saying little shops like his would die out. Vera recalled Papa railing against monopoly, Mama cursing companies profiting from the Great War, Celia and Sol debating union tactics in the face of industrial titans' plans to combine.

"Maybe you should get together with the other store owners," she'd said. "Make a plan to combat the—"

"Together? Combat? Compete, you mean. This I must do as a single entity. The big fellows may have more capital, but I am quick, I am smart, I have the many connections. I understand it, the market. I will undercut them. Offer cheaper merchandise. Better deals. I might commence to advertise. I am at all times on top of my toes, you see. This is what is required. Maybe customers will go to Klein's for shoes, if Moe Luzkow on Allen Street cannot be bothered with modern methods so maybe he will go underneath, this is his problem, this I cannot affect and therefore on this I do not dwell.

"But marriages, anniversaries, you will see, Vera, for jewels they will still come to me. Soon, three stores, maybe four, who knows?" He reached for her across the lamp table between their matching wing chairs. "Do not worry about it, my dear." He smiled. "Leave the diamonds to me. Everything will be fine. You will see." He stroked the back of her hand, scraping her skin with the pad of his thumb ridged from loupe and chisel. Her return smile was thin. After a minute he said, "Come here, Vera." She suppressed a sigh, rose and let him pull her onto his lap. Really, she told herself. Why should she mind that he doesn't care to hear her ideas? He kissed her. "So pretty." She's not, she's always known. Too many angles to her face, too sharp. Still, Mary used to say she saw something in her eyes. "My Vera." He drew her against his chest. He nuzzled her neck. He held her tighter. He fumbled with the buttons on her bodice. She felt him stiffen below and she fought her body's impulse to resist. By this night last spring she had known how to yield, to make it go quickly. She had not known on her wedding night. No one had told her what to expect. She'd been shocked, which he'd assured her was normal, and repulsed, which surely was not. He'd whispered that he'd show her what to do. He went slow. He wasn't rough, but he persisted. Then, and since, he has wanted her to welcome this thing, its intrusive, painful thrust.

A few weeks after that night last spring, they'd found out she was expecting. Peter, ever sensitive, hasn't tried anything since. He still tries her patience, however, every night, with ceaseless boring talk. She tries forbearance. Reminds herself of his many sweet deeds. How he brings home flowers, little treats for her, once, twice a week. A dear, kind man. And what are his words about, after all? Grand plans. The world for her. Nevertheless, as time and her pregnancy progressed, she'd become less tolerant, until, somewhere around the sixth month she'd shocked them both one evening by snapping, "Oh for heaven's sake, Peter, enough about Steiner Gems. Please. Enough." He went quiet. She gloried in the silence momentarily. Then she saw his fallen face. "Forgive me," she said. He gladly chalked it up to her condition, poured sherry, toasted the child, led her to bed, and the next night was at it again.

They've repeated the scene frequently since. Peter's palaver: profit, loss, property, leases. Vera, driven to distraction by the endless recitation of minutiae, spitting out a dismissive riposte. Peter stunned. Vera stricken with remorse. Her apology, his indulgence. A kiss on the cheek, she's tucked in, all is forgotten. Until she lashes out again.

It is a difficult dance they've been doing, improvising moves as they go along. If asked who leads, who follows, Vera couldn't say. They are mismatched partners, this much she knows. Ill-suited for each other, but there is no option for either to sit it out, and so they go on, doing the best they can, trying to stop stepping on each other's toes.

She'd wanted to say something along these lines to Celia the last time she took her sister to a moving picture show. She'd have given anything to talk it out. Something had stopped her and instead she'd played complaining wife, making fun of Peter's single-mindedness.

It was a November Saturday. Celia had come in to the city, leaving their two children with her husband Louie. For a lark the sisters had lunch at the Automat on 42nd Street. After the fun of pressing buttons and picking plates out of mechanized slots, after eating their sandwiches and pie, they strolled. Vera made light of her stunted life.

"I have tried every topic under the sun with him. I point out newspaper articles—remember in June, the League of Nations, how Congress refused, wouldn't you think that would interest him, doesn't his whole family still live over there, after all? Celia, you wouldn't believe it, he just clicked his tongue and went back to reciting the week's receipts. Okay, so maybe he has no interest in world events, not everyone is like Mama and Papa. I tell myself surely he has an eye for beauty and art, after all he's a jeweler, every day he works with fine things, so I get him to take me to the theater—don't worry, nothing highbrow, I figure he'll maybe enjoy some nice song and dance, I get us tickets to The Gold Diggers—"

Celia gasped and grabbed her hand. "With Ina Claire and Ruth Terry? I'm so jealous I could spit!"

Vera nodded triumphantly. "Exactly! Everyone was talking about it. But don't envy me. If you went with Louie he'd have a ball, he'd be clapping and laughing—"

"You're telling me! I'd have to put my hand over his mouth to shut him up. Sometimes he gets so loud."

"Well, no such problem here. Peter sat stiff as a soldier through the whole thing. And what did he say afterward? 'Very nice'—"

"No! That's it? 'Very nice'?"

"Wait, I'm not finished. 'Very nice,' he said, 'but a little loud to my taste'."

Celia shrieked a laugh. "A little loud! Oh my god. So how does he have fun?"

"Fun, shmun. Don't ask me."

"Well, what makes him laugh? There must be something."

"My thinking exactly. I would love to laugh with the man. He does accompany me to a picture show now and then. But Celia,

I swear to god, Buster Keaton is falling over on the screen and in the theater everyone is falling over laughing and what do you think Peter is doing?"

"What?"

"Sleeping. Every time we go to a movie show he falls asleep." Celia shrieked again. An unexpected twinge of protectiveness made Vera defend her husband. "You know, he works terribly hard."

"Sure. Like a dog. But even dogs relax."

"He relaxes, Cel."

"How?"

"We have tea, and we talk every night."

"Well, that's nice." Celia smiled. "I always said the guy's a mensch." Vera nodded. "Even if he does belong to the wrong class."

Vera shrugged as they reached the theater and stepped up to the ticket booth. "Two, please." Grand to be able to pay. She has Peter to thank. Luxuries like this were a rare occurrence in the old days. As they'd taken their seats and watched the pianist spread the music sheets, Vera had wondered why she'd lied. Telling her sister of tea and talk every night, as if hers is a model of contented married life. When in fact the nightly routine makes her want to scream. The kind man a stand-in, a marker for the void Vera's life has become.

She does have things. Fine things. Vera is living the sort of life she and Mary used to dream about. Furthermore, she likes it. She sometimes thinks she must have been a foundling, adopted by the Resnicks but not of their blood. How else explain her fondness for creature comforts?

Peter's money has not bought Vera happiness, but it has kept her occupied, at least until these last few weeks when her swelling belly and the new year with its wintry weather halted all that. If the evenings have been a dud, the days of her newlywed first year were anything but. She'd dashed among shops, pored over catalogs, spent Peter's cash. Selecting furniture, appliances, linens. Learning how to work the gadgets in the fantastically up-to-the-minute kitchen. Learning as well the mores and ways of life among the small-business class, the obligations, the behavior expected of the wife. A machine she plugs in to burn Peter's morning toast—deliveries to sign for—answering to "Mrs. Steiner" from the doorman, the greengrocer, the newsboy—mastering the electrical iron for Peter's collars—shopping for readymade dresses on the Ladies' Mile. Custom ordering Peter's wedding gift to her, a beautiful baby-grand piano, from the Steinways out in Queens.

Sometimes, those first months, this new world had flustered her. Sometimes pangs of homesickness for cluttered, noisy Passaic had shocked her gut. Mostly, though, she was glad to be busy. Not thinking, Vera has found, becomes habitual. Which is not necessarily a bad thing. Her jaw, for instance, stopped aching some time in the fall. Until then she'd awakened each day to a throb. The soreness would ease as the day passed. Then Peter would arrive, they'd eat, and after dinner as she endured another excruciatingly dull evening she'd tighten her lips and grind her teeth, only realizing that that's what she must have done when next morning the pain began again. Then, around the end of November, her sour comments ceased. Her jaws unclenched. Lips relaxed. She had lapsed into a torpor in the final stage of her pregnancy.

She braces her hands against the arms of the chair and makes another effort at rising. This time she manages the feat. She waddles around the parlor. Breathing in the rich scents, polished wood of the furniture and floor. Touching surfaces textured and smooth, damask curtains, brass lamps. Staring at the piano's shining ivory, so unlike the yellow, chipped keys she grew up with. Marveling for the millionth time that this fine apartment at this swank Manhattan address, 43 Fifth Avenue thank you very much, is home. One circuit about the room, then she returns to the window. Drops into the rocker, plopping herself down with an "oy" and a sigh, and resumes her roost. She rests her head against the chair's back, wraps the shawl around herself, and gazes with glazed eyes at the snowy scene outside.

If this languor is passing strange, it is pleasant nevertheless. She has settled into it, as a sleeper sinks dozily into a soft mattress, relieved that the being in her womb no longer swims in a sea of unease. She's content now to wait. She finds the silence of this richly appointed room, broken only by the timid ticking of the pendulum clock on the mantel, soothing. What a lovely way to pass a winter's day.

Peter, in contrast, is on edge. Her lethargy has even supplanted his stores as a subject of conversation. This morning he was at her again as he dressed for the day. She had not yet risen from bed. As he stood at the mirror working his bow tie he looked at her reflection in bed and asked, "Why are you so indolent, Vera? Are you ill?" She shook her head. "Do you think something is wrong with the baby?"

"No, Peter."

"Well then, perhaps we should call the doctor?"

"Why?"

"I am saying perhaps just to check."

Her husband is very big on doctors. A believer in the science of modern medicine. It is one of the benefits of his business success, he says, that they should have the best that money can buy. So Vera has been examined several times. She is to be the first woman in their acquaintance to have a doctor deliver her baby.

Nothing is wrong, she assured him this morning for the thousandth time. Mama concurs. She has explained to Peter that sometimes a woman in Vera's condition gets this way. Especially after all she has been through. The last year and a half have been very emotional for her, Mama has reminded him more than once. "Just let her rest. A roller coaster she's been on, like at Coney Island."

It's more like shell shock, Vera thinks, marooned in the rocker, grateful for the layers of glass and brick between her and the glistening haze beyond. I've become like those Great War soldiers, hollow and dazed. Would Mary even know me now?

The morning inches on as she sits in sublime slothfulness—can that be a word, she wonders, then answers herself, why not?—not exactly snoozing but not exactly awake, a blissful state in which she would be happy to remain.

A long, loud, insistent buzz snaps her out of it. Her eyes pop open. It takes her a minute to leverage herself out of the rocker. The buzzing continues. Whoever it is is holding the button without letting up. Whoever it is got past the doorman.

She shuffles to the door and opens the peephole. Oh—that explains it. Mickey has a way of evading every obstacle. Not that the doorman would have objected, he's seen her brother many times, but even if he had Mickey could have oozed his way up, flashing his goofy smile with those jumbled teeth of his, letting fly a little jazzy patter, heyhowyadoinbuddy, somesnowwe're-havinghey, shmoozing until the fellow would have sworn they'd known each other for ages.

She's smiling as she opens the door. "You nudnik, you couldn't take your finger off the buzzer, you thought maybe I didn't hear you? People in China heard you already—"

Her baby brother does not return her smile. His big, hooded eyes dart around the room as he stamps the snow off his boots and takes off his gloves. Always prominent, his eyes are bulging as they tend to on those rare occasions when he's tense or angry. She regards him as he unbuttons his coat. Mickey isn't the good looker he used to be, not since he broke his nose at 16 in a street fight—the only fight he was ever in and wouldn't you know it, it ruined his face. Since then, his countenance is like a cubist painting: the features don't fit together.

She knows not to rush him. He always has to go about things at his own tempo. Finally, coat off, gloves gone, snow stamped from boots, finished with his jittery survey of what he can see of the apartment, he looks at Vera.

"Is Peter here?"

"Peter? Of course not. It's the middle of the day. He's at the store."

"Oh, right, sure, gee, I don't know what I was thinking. I should have gone straight there." He turns toward the door and starts to put his coat back on.

"Wait a minute, mister." Vera grabs his arm. "Are you out of your mind? You think you can show up here all wild-eyed like a meshugeneh, ask for Peter who you know perfectly well is at his store, and then turn around and leave? Do you want me to have this baby right here, right now?" She reaches up to pinch his cheek. "Spill the beans, buster. I mean it. What's up?"

"Okay, okay, but listen, Vera, don't get excited. Everything is going to be fine—"

"What is it? Has something happened to Mama? Why are you telling me don't get excited—"

"Mama's fine, Vera. Although she's probably going crazy with worry." He puts his hand on her shoulder. "Look, a few more minutes won't matter and I should be careful with you in your condition, so let's sit down and I'll tell you all about it and then we'll figure out together what to do."

She takes his hand and starts toward the kitchen, thinking to make them each a glass of tea.

"No," he says, and pulls her the other way, toward the parlor. "The telephone's in here, isn't it?" Vera nods. She follows him to the front window and watches him look down at the street, now completely obscured by the thick swath of snow. Presently he turns to her and asks, "Veraleh, have you heard about what happened last night?" She shakes her head. "Palmer? The raids? None of it?"

"I haven't read the *Herald Tribune* yet," she admits. "Palmer who?"

"Mitchell Palmer, the attorney general. It didn't make it into today's paper anyway. Okay, listen, Vera, we're going to need

Peter's help—his help and his money." She waits. "To get Sol and Celia out of jail."

Oouf! She yelps and claps her right hand to her midsection. Mickey opens his mouth to start calming her down, but, "Wait," she says and holds out her left hand to stop him. "Wait a minute." She lets out a rush of air. "Ooosh. Whew. Oh my."

"Oy vey, Vera, calm down, they'll be okay—"

"No, it's only the baby. Such a bunch of kicks." She backs into the couch and sits. "I'm all right. It's very soon now—don't look so scared, I don't mean today, just soon. So tell me already—Celia and Sol in jail? What's happened?"

"Okay, look. Last night, in New York, Boston, Chicago, Detroit, and who knows how many other cities, Vera, with a thing like this you never get all the details until later, federal goons arrested hundreds, maybe thousands of workers. Said they were acting under the authority of Palmer and some aide named Hoover. They rounded people up at union meetings, pulled them off the street, even grabbed them out of their beds."

"And Sol and Celia?"

"Yeah. Them too." Vera looks at Mickey and for an instant sees him as a toddler. A fleeting image flashes—the four of them in huddled terror, a whiff of foul air—and an instinct to flee grips her. Just as fast, the moment passes. He says, "Sol's in the Tombs." She shudders at the name of the jail under police headquarters in lower Manhattan. "I heard they nabbed him at the ILWU office. Celia I'm pretty sure is in the Jersey City lockup. That's where they took everyone from the Amalgamated meeting in Passaic."

"But why, Mickey?"

"Palmer says they're illegal aliens. He wants to deport them."

"Illegal! Why, Sol and Celia have their papers, we all do. Don't you remember Ellis Island, everything we went through to get in here?"

"Of course I do, but—"

"As a matter of fact, they're citizens. Yes, I'm quite sure of it. All of us are now, only Mama never did, but you are too, aren't you, Mickey, didn't you take the citizenship oath—"

"Yeah, yeah, I took the goddamn oath and so did Celia and Sol, for all the good it'll do them now."

"Don't talk like that, as though they have no rights."

"For god's sake, Vera, I'm not the one trying to deport them. It's Palmer. And to him they're Bolsheviks. Reds."

"But poor Mama's the only Bolshie left. She calls Celia a soft-headed social democrat."

"Don't be so literal. Use your noggin." Mickey pauses. "Look, Vera, I know you've lifted yourself above the fray here in your nice new life." She stiffens. Mickey's tone softens. "I know you've had other things on your mind, Veraleh." He lays a hand lightly on her abdominal expanse. She lifts hers to his head and fingers his light brown waves, cold and wet from the snow. He never wears a hat. Such a kid still, ranging around the city digging up the latest dive with a piano for him to pound on. "Look, frankly, so have I. You've got your life, I've got my music, neither one of us is the comrade Mama wanted us to be." They exchange rueful smiles. "But just because we're not paying attention doesn't mean nothing's happening, Vera. The Great War veterans, they want jobs, and the unions have been getting—you know, this big garment strike and all—so Palmer and his henchmen, they're trying to make a scare, a panic, like the reds are taking over."

"Is it against the Jews?"

"Partly. But plenty of others too. They picked up Italians, Greeks. Poles, Puerto Ricans, Chinese—you name it. Palmer doesn't care where they're from. He says he's going to get rid of every goddamn red in the whole goddamn country. Send them back where they came from. That includes our sister and our brother. And—no, now, don't start bawling, Vera, I shouldn't be going on like this, we'll get them out—"

"I just thought of Mama. Oy, she'd die, she'd just die if she lost two more of us."

"No one's losing anyone, they'll be fine, they'll be swell, we'll take care of them, that's why I'm here."

"It's the baby, Mickey, I cry at the least little thing."

"Sure, sure, kiddo, I understand." He reaches into his pocket and pulls out a handkerchief for her. "I shouldn't have even come here to get you all worked up, I wouldn't have except I was playing down on Greenwich Street last night and then this morning I stopped in at the Ansonia Pharmacy to have some coffee before heading back uptown, and Sam from the old band was there and he told me about the raids. And I figured that since I was so nearby, and what with you having a telephone and all, I'd come over and we'd maybe get Peter to help."

"Yes, we'll call Peter. He'll know what to do." She reaches to the side table.

Mickey takes the earpiece from her and replaces it in its cradle. "Wait a minute." She watches his crooked features. "What I'd really like to do is get Mama's thinking first."

Well I would too, Vera thinks impatiently, but there's no telephone in Celia's apartment, where Mama lives with Celia, Louie and their two kids. Another reason Mama should reside in fine digs here with me, instead of crowded together in a crumbling tenement in Jersey. When Vera had agreed to marry Peter and he'd found them a Manhattan apartment to be close to his business, she had assumed Mama would make the move with her. Mama had said no. She said she should give Vera and Peter their privacy. Vera knew what that meant. Though Mama never expressed disapproval of Vera's marriage, it was obvious that her initial sympathy for Peter had waned. She was polite with him, correct, the way she was with police or landlords. Once, when Vera asked, "What do you have against him," Mama had said simply, "He's not like us." Dumbfounded, Vera said, "He's Jewish, isn't he?" Mama looked at her evenly and said, "He's a capitalist, Vera." Vera snorted. "Two lousy jewelry stores don't make him J.P. Morgan, Mama, for goodness' sake." "Okay, Vera, he's only a petty. Don't ask me to live with him."

So fine, Mama, Vera thinks, you took a stand on your communist principles, and where does it get us? Into this predicament. Two of your children in jail and the other two sitting here across the Hudson River unable to ask you what to do. She gets up to ward off the familiar lonely ache, toddles to the window for another look outside, turns to her brother who sits lost in thought.

"Mama's not here. The snow's getting worse. The longer we wait the harder it will be for Peter to get them out. If it's about money—"

Mickey nods apologetically. "I'm sure if we show up with enough cash—bail, bribes, who knows, so yeah, Peter came to mind."

Vera doesn't know what kind of cash Peter has on hand. Maybe he'll have to go to the bank. Then there's the problem of what he'll do about the store—lock up for the day or leave it in his clerk's hands. And what about the second shop, up on Fourteenth Street? His usual routine is to go there at six o'clock to pick up the day's revenue and receipts. Then he returns to the Delancey Street store to close down that register, enters the figures in his records and totes up the combined total, which he brings home and takes to the bank the next morning on his way back to the store. All that will be thrown off.

Vera and Mickey look at each other. Time is flying. "Because don't forget," Mickey says to her as she reaches for the telephone, "this isn't just an uptown-downtown operation, either."

"I know." Vera takes a nervous breath and lifts the earpiece with her left hand. "It's a two-state procedure." She holds it to her ear and leans down toward the mouthpiece on the table. "And there are just the two of you to do it all." It goes without saying that Vera can't go out in this weather, in her condition. She crosses the first two fingers of her right hand and Mickey does the same. Then she uncrosses her fingers and reaches down to dial.

❧

Vera looks at the clock. An hour has passed since Mickey left. At least she hasn't lapsed back into woolgathering semi-consciousness. Mostly she's been looking out the window and worrying. The snow has let up a bit now that it's done its worst. Down on Fifth Avenue a sole woman struggles against the wind. It has started to howl. She touches her fingertips to the window. Its rattle travels up her arm. She shivers.

She turns for the hundredth time toward the telephone. Mickey promised he would call from Peter's shop. He hasn't. Fifteen minutes ago, when she couldn't wait any more, she dialed the number. No answer. She can just imagine Peter, efficient and brisk once he understood the situation, bustling Mickey out the door, insisting that there was no time to call.

This cold is really too much. She steps away from the window and goes to stand by the fireplace to warm up. The gas fire gives the room a nice glow. It's the latest thing, a modern device that, with one match, provides an old-fashioned fire—not that she's ever lived anywhere with an old-fashioned fireplace, but she loves the idea, so continental somehow, loves to stand at the hearth and look around the parlor. She read last week in the Ladies Home Journal that people are starting to call it the living room. She must mention that to Peter. He's quite willing to follow her lead in these things.

It is a fine room. She developed exquisite taste in the course of picking everything out. "If I do say so myself," she murmurs. Diverting her thoughts from Celia and Sol and jail, Vera runs her hand along the wood of a Chippendale chair—not real Chippendale, but a pretty good replica, one of a pair they had shipped from a specialty company in Grand Rapids, Michigan, along with a colonial-style sofa and loveseat. The matching maple of two lamp tables glows nearly red from the fire. She rubs her slippered foot against the Turkish rug that peeks out from under the baby grand. She bought the rug in March from a pair of very young, very charming merchants on Tenth Street after spending a delicious afternoon drinking strong, thick coffee with them. Peter had been shocked when she told him. He scolded her as though she might have been in danger. But she had felt perfectly safe, surrounded by so many exquisite things and listening to the brothers' stories of how they had found each one. "They are not brothers, Vera," Peter had said. Apparently he knew their shop. He'd looked at her sternly. "They are—well, just be careful." Brothers or not, he'd had to admit they gave Vera a fair price for the rug. Its muted colors, taupe and green, work with the fireplace to warm the room. Especially on a day like this.

She turns to look at the clock above the fire. Why, it's three o'clock already. She is suddenly ravenous. She heads into the kitchen.

When they first moved here she was intimidated by all the contraptions. Now she doesn't think twice as she reaches into the electric icebox and takes out the soup Mama brought over a few days ago. She ladles some into a small pot, places it on the range's pearl gray porcelain surface and reaches for a match. She turns on the gas, lights the flame, puts the pot on the burner and sits at the table to wait.

Celia and Sol in jail. It's cold, she's sure. And dirty. Dark. Vera is certain they're all right, though. She probably would not do as well.

I've grown used to all this, she thinks. She looks at the stove, the icebox, the gleaming stainless steel sink. What if Peter's business suddenly failed? I'd die if I had to leave this apartment. What if Peter dies? Let's hope he's taken care of everything. The husband I could do without. The nice things I'm not so sure.

What a monstrous thought! She laughs out loud. What a fiend you are, Vera Steiner! She cranes her neck to check on whether the soup has started to boil yet. Catching sight of her reflection in the shiny steel of the toast maker on the counter next to the range, she screws up her face in make-believe shame. Then the baby lets loose with another series of kicks and she laughs again.

What—is it morning already? Peter usually doesn't make much noise on rising, his movements in the morning even more measured than at other times. Now she hears him cursing in the bathroom. He must have nicked his cheek shaving. But the sun isn't out yet, it's too early for him to be getting up, in fact she doesn't remember him coming to bed. With a grunt of effort, Vera braces her elbows against the mattress and pulls herself up to a sitting position. She looks at the electric clock next to Peter's side of the bed. Five thirty-five. If he just got back this has been a very long night for him.

She pulls the cord on the lamp next to the clock. Reaching to the chair next to her side of the bed, she grabs her beige satin bed jacket and slips it on.

"So you're up." Peter is knotting his tie as he steps out of the bathroom. "I'm sorry. I was trying not to wake you. It is very important that you get your sleep."

"For heaven's sake, Peter, I stayed up nearly all night waiting to hear from you. Why didn't you call? What happened? Is everyone all right?"

He steps back into the bathroom. He returns, holding a monogrammed brush in each hand, stands in front of the big mirror atop the dresser, and brushes his hair methodically, alternating strokes, two on the left then two on the right. He holds the brushes lightly and applies them delicately. He believes that brushing with just the right amount of pressure stimulates the hair follicles.

From the bed, behind him, Vera watches his face in the mirror. Jaws clenched. Finally he lays the brushes down and turns. He adjusts his eyeglasses. Puts his hands in his pants pockets, jiggles coins, stands there looking around the room.

"Peter?"

"Yes, Vera. Everyone is all right."

"Oh, thank goodness." She sighs in relief. "So they—"

"So they are safe and sound now. Sol on East Fifth Street and Celia back with your mother in Passaic. Snug in their beds."

"Mickey?"

"Mickey too is home by now, asleep also I should imagine—"

"So you've been here since when, Peter? I didn't realize I had fallen asleep, but I must have, I never heard you come in—"

"I have arrived only fifteen minutes ago. After everyone else is paid for and sent home, then only I can come to my home. Do you expect I can go to sleep? I have a business to run. I never even tallied up yesterday's receipts. So, although your family perhaps think the purpose of my business is to bail communists out of jail—"

"Oh, don't—"

"Don't?" He looks at her for the first time. He takes a deep breath through his nose, and smoothes the material on his pant legs. "No, very well. What is the point anyway?" He takes off his glasses, sits down on the bed next to Vera and peers at her. "Now only it is left for me to get back to business. But first tell me, are you all right?" Vera nods. "The baby? No trouble?" She shakes her head. He puts his glasses back on and straightens up. "Good then, fine, I am going. I wish that you should not have further fright on the account of your family. Now you should please go back to sleep. It is not good they kept you awake all of the night."

"Peter, it's not their fault—"

"Certainly. In any case, I am relieved that you are well." He pats her on the head, twice, stands up and walks out of the bedroom.

Vera drops back onto the pillows. She lies there, catching her breath, waiting for her heartbeat to slow. It's amazing after nineteen hours—and those begun only hours after the sleepless night as her husband bailed out her brother and sister—but now that it's done she doesn't feel tired.

Celia wipes the sweat from Vera's face with a cool, wet cloth and kisses her on the forehead. Vera smiles as she props herself up on her elbows. She sees Mama heading to the living room and strains to hear her tell Peter he has a son. Then a tiny sound tugs her. She snaps her head back the other way just as the nurse, an Irish girl in a tidy white uniform, hands the baby to the doctor.

Dr. Dunda speaks. He is measuring and inspecting the newborn and dictating his findings to the nurse. The nurse writes down the numbers. Eighteen inches, seven pounds six ounces.

Vera pulls herself fully upright and scoots back against the headboard. The baby begins to cry. Eighteen inches! My god, she thinks, he must have been twisted and stuffed inside me like a sausage. Immediately this thought is displaced by another. Give him to me.

Vera swallows. She licks her lips. "Doctor," she says. Good. Her voice sounds calm but forceful.

Cradling the newborn, Dr. Dunda steps toward her. "Yes, Mrs. Steiner?"

She holds out her arms. "Give him to me, please."

Her son on her chest feels like a soft, squirmy hot water bottle. She lays a hand gingerly upon him. A wee fist wraps around her little finger.

She eases his head up to a nipple, urging his mouth toward her. Wisps of light brown fuzz tickle her skin. She feels his tiny tongue against her, warm, wet. Her eyes close. Then she gasps and opens them as he tightens his hold and starts to suck.

She looks at her child. Not a half-hour old. He has claimed her.

JUNE 1920

This I can live with. This is a life.

This is what Vera told herself yesterday morning, and the morning before. The thought comes to her again, tonight, as she bathes her baby boy.

"Only you," she murmurs. "More than enough." She cups Willy's head with her left hand. The baby looks up at her, dazzling with those impossibly long brown eyelashes. "Yes, you, dollface." She smiles, quickly dodging her head to avoid his fingers reaching for her hair.

She sloshes suds over his silky belly with her right hand. His fat little legs wiggle in the water. Giddy gibberish burbles out from between his impossibly luscious lips. She plants a big, noisy kiss on each of his impossibly rosy apple cheeks. He squeals with delight, slapping at the water and splattering his mother.

Laughing, Vera leans over him, letting the water drip off her face onto his shoulders. He squeals again and splashes her some more. She moves in for another quick peck, then another, on his elbow, the soles of his feet, his tushy.

The water is cooling. She should take him out, dry him so he doesn't catch a chill. She lingers, kissing, splashing, her laughter mingling with his. Then she lifts him out of the tub. Kneeling on the bathroom rug, she wraps him in one of the thick cotton towels Peter's parents sent from Germany after Willy was born. She dries her tousled cherub, amazed as always at the intense love surging through her.

A swift frisson of fear sweeps away her smile. She pulls her boy close against her, stands and carries him into the nursery. She sits down. She rocks.

Why does she always feel things to extremes? With Mary she was all the time ecstatic, the world sweet as if spun with cotton candy. When the flu took her friend, a miasma of gloom descended. This last year, Peter driving her to distraction with his nightly monologues. Disappointment might have slid into bitterness. She doesn't like to think about the person she might have become.

Then Willy arrived like Moses in the bulrushes and delivered her. She lays her chin against the top of his head, breathing in his sweet smell. "My hero," she whispers.

II

God of Vengeance

"Go on, get out of here already, Vera. Quit making such a fuss. A person would think you're going to Timbuktu. Isn't that right, Leonard? Wouldn't you agree?" Mama pulls her head back and waits for a response from the grandson squirming in her arms.

Lenny doesn't disappoint her. He nods furiously, maintaining a stern expression only until the grownups start laughing. Their chuckles trail off as Lenny's older brother grabs their attention with a shouted "Hey!"

"Hay is for horses, young man." Celia pinches both Willy's cheeks until he pulls away and leans up against his mother.

"Yes, Willy?" Vera pauses, one glove on, and puts her other hand on his shoulder. "What can I do for you, sir?" She knows he loves being addressed in adult tones. But he's a child, and here she is, his mother, going off to gallivant about all day without him. How can she? Look how he clings to her. Now Lenny, as long as he gets plenty of attention he doesn't much care who it's from. But Willy—

"—I said enough already, Vera." Mama puts Lenny down and tugs Willy from his mother. "Vey is mir, at this rate the boys will be in long pants before you leave. You'll only be gone a few hours, I assure you I will let no harm befall them, now get going or you'll miss the curtain."

"Thank you, Mama." Celia grabs Vera's coat from the back of the sofa where it has lain throughout this long leave-taking. She throws it over Vera's shoulders and turns her toward the front door. "Girlchik, I'll never forgive you if we're late to the theater." She opens the door, blows kisses to the boys and Mama, and bustles her sister out into the world.

Vera stands to let a couple get to their seats further down the row. A handsome lady of middle years, well turned out in a burgundy suit with a slight fringe at the hem, a careful nod to the trend but not too garish, the rather dowdier gentleman leading the way obviously her husband. Gentiles, Vera thinks, and with plenty money: the lady probably never even sets foot below 14th Street. Yet this play, all the rage, has drawn them. There's a sprinkling of their sort in the matinee crowd. Also a good helping of younger people, jazzy, the smart set, some of the women in skirts that barely reach their knees.

When she sits back down Celia grabs her hand and squeezes. "Isn't this grand, Veraleh? Can you believe it? I don't know how I can ever thank Mickey. I mean, it would have been enough he got us matinee tickets right away the second week after it opened, but such seats!"

"I know. I'm in heaven." On the aisle, eighth row. As soon as she and Celia had walked in to the Apollo Theater, right here in the heart of things on Forty-Second Street, Vera's guilt about leaving the boys for an entire Saturday afternoon had dropped away. She runs her free hand along the velvet on the seat beneath her thigh. She inhales. Bodies, breaths, stage boards waxed, musk of young actors' nerves. The air quivering as curtain time nears.

This is where I belong, she wants to tell her sister, but she doesn't, it wouldn't sound right, as if she doesn't belong in the life she has. She is Mrs. Steiner with a successful husband, beloved children, fine home. So why does it seem as though she is miscast, playing a role meant for someone else?

Five bells ring. The lights dim. People rush to settle in their seats. A queer flutter of anticipation flitters through Vera. She takes one last look at the program. *The God of Vengeance* by Sholem Asch. The play received raves in Germany, Russia, Italy. Years ago already it was mounted at the Yiddish Art Theater on Second Avenue, starring the great Maurice Schwartz and newcomer Stella Adler. Finally last fall an English-language version opened in the Village. Mickey went, with his gang, musicians, writers, actors. He called Vera the next morning to rave about it. He wouldn't tell her what it was about, just kept saying, "I really think you should see it, Vera, I really think you should see it." He wasn't the only one talking about it. Word spread. Tickets sold out. The producers moved it to a bigger theater. That one drew standing-room crowds too. So *The God of Vengeance* is now here, on Broadway. The day after it opened, before Vera could broach the subject of tickets with Peter, Celia had called from a booth outside her building in Passaic, nattering madly about the great Saturday to come when she and Vera, just the two of them, would go see the most talked-about show in town. Mickey had presented Celia with two tickets as a thirtieth birthday present along with the strong suggestion that she take Vera.

So here they are—oh, there go the house lights, Celia grabbing her hand again, Vera, tickled to death herself, squeezing back—and they are to top off the day with cake and ice cream back at her place on Fifth Avenue. Celia doesn't know it but Louie and their kids Estelle and Bernard will also be there to help her blow out the candles. Last she heard, Sol wasn't sure if he and his family could make it but they'll try. The plan has been for Mickey to come over after she and Celia left. Right this very minute, while the two of them sit like royalty in these plush red seats, he is minding the boys while Mama cooks a birthday feast. "Marie Antoinette I'm not," she had laughed when Mickey and Vera had gone over the day's arrangements with her. "The whole family together for once and you think I'm going to let them just eat cake?"

The curtain rises. Celia's hand is still in hers. Vera pecks her on the cheek and turns her attention to the stage.

Gasps from the audience. The curtain falls on the first act. A pause, then long applause.

The house lights come up. Vera sits. She can't move. All around her people are talking, a furious rush of conversation, but the sounds are muffled, distant, as if she's underwater.

She should look away from the stage. She should maybe close her eyes. It won't help. She'll still see the scene as act one ended. Two women embracing. Kissing.

"Penny for your thoughts." Celia is squirming in her seat, leaning in toward Vera. Vera slowly turns to face her sister. Again that aqueous sensation. As though she's moving through a viscous medium, thicker than air. "Nu, what do you think so far?"

"I—well, it's—"

"—I know! Wow!" Celia stands. She pulls Vera's arm until she rises too. "Let's go to the bathroom. We can talk while we stand in line."

"You go." Her legs are pudding. She sits back down.

"But—" Celia tries to pull her up again.

"I'd rather not fight the crowd. We'll talk afterward."

"Oh, all right."

Now Vera does close her eyes. She sees them again. Rivkeleh, whose father Yekl runs a bordello but is bent on keeping her pure. And Manke, a beautiful prostitute. The women are drawn to each other. Or Manke is defiling the younger girl. Which is it? Love or corruption?

Vera swallows. It's like a desert in here. The air so thin and dry. I've got to drink something, she thinks. She stands slowly, testing her legs. Shaky, but they support her. Around her, laughter, conversation. No one else looks ready to topple over. No one notices the fear in her eyes.

Somehow she sits through two more acts. The temperature in the theater veers, their boiler must be on the blink, now she's sweating, now she quivers in frigid air. During the second act's climactic scene she tries to will herself numb but when the women clinch onstage something inside her stirs. Manke strokes Rivkeleh's breast, they kiss, lying together they speak sweetly of love. Vera sits rigid. She makes an effort to avert her eyes but they return to the stage, just yards away. The lovers are so close she hears their hearts pounding in her own ears. At the end when Rivkeleh is cast out by her family, Vera reads the desperation on her face and slumps in her seat, defeated.

"Ma! Ma! Hurry up! I have to go really bad!"

"All right, Willy, I'll be out in a minute." Vera is relieved her voice sounds even. She finishes drying her face, replaces the towel on the rack, runs her hands through her hair. They come out damp. Her scalp is still sweaty after her panicky retreat from the dining room. She washes and dries her hands, hangs up the towel. She steadies her breath and wonders how to explain why she ran out on Mama's good food, Celia's birthday cake and ice cream.

She takes a long breath and faces the modish young woman in the mirror. Brown hair cut in a stylish bob. A string of brightly colored baubles looped long round her neck dips into décolletage. The necklace's many colors are a gaudy contrast to the muted gray of her dress. Silk, it has a sleek line, hanging straight over her slim figure, cut to the knees, with a trim of tiny silver beading at both the hem and the plunging V neckline. The delicate silver watch on her left wrist reflects silver glints inlaid on her gold wedding ring.

Tuning out Willy's steady tapping on the bathroom door, Vera searches the mirror. Everyone says she has sad eyes. Deep, they say. The taller Turkish brother in the Tenth Street shop where she bought the living-room rug had called them smoky that day three years ago when they first met. "Full of mystery," George had said. She'd laughed and pointed out that the air in the little room at the rear of the store where they sat drinking strong coffee was thick with white tufts rising from the cigarettes he and his brother smoked one after the other. He couldn't even see her eyes through all that smoke, she'd said. He'd smiled and shrugged and kissed her hand and looked up at her, his own eyes shadowed by something familiar she couldn't quite make out.

She still stops at their shop every now and then. Not to buy. Just to sit and chat in the back room. Separated from the store by a curtain of black wooden beads, dimly lit by a single standing lamp with a beige-and-black Indian-print cotton throw hung over the shade, it is supposed to be their office and is also their storeroom but mostly it is a sitting room, crammed with a desk, three chairs, shelving, cluttered with books, framed prints and engravings, theater programs. The detritus of men who read, men who think, men who, though barely beyond their teens, observe and consider and seem to somehow know the world. Men who, while merchants like Peter, see beyond commerce. Men in whose company she can breathe. If they have to attend to a customer she leafs through back copies of *Harper's Bazaar*, pointing out the cartoons to Willy who pretends to grasp the irony. The brothers serve her tiny cups of thick, sweet Turkish coffee, talk with her of the theater, of books, fill her in on the latest Paris fashions. They are cultured, and oh they are charmed by her boys, they sit them on their laps and pass swatches of expensive material across their necks, tickling them, yet none of this is why she is drawn to them. She cannot account for the affinity she feels with the two "men of the Mediterranean." That's how George, the tall one, referred to his brother and himself the other day, ducking his head shyly as he always does when he speaks. Wally, a little shorter, a little chubbier, but with similar thick black hair, strong nose and broad forehead, shares George's enchanting accent and softly apologetic tone of voice. "Oh come now, dear boy," he'd said with a small smile at Vera, "nothing nearly so grand. We are not even Greek."

Now she wonders what they would make of the play she saw today. When she'd told them she'd be going to the matinee they'd been quiet. Wally had simply said they would look forward to hearing about it.

She does not mention her occasional visits with George and Wally to Peter. He does not care for the brothers. They are too refined for someone like him to appreciate. Or perhaps he's jealous. Well, Peter isn't here. Having boarded the train last night after closing the shop, he is in Detroit helping his brother Ernest, just arrived from Dresden, settle in, open accounts, furnish his jewelry store and so on. Her husband will not return for several more days. Perhaps tomorrow she'll take the boys on a stroll to Tenth Street to talk to the Turks.

The woman in the mirror looks less agitated. If her eyes hold a secret they hide it well. Vera turns, opens the door, and stands aside to let her little man rush in.

Three hours later she sits at her vanity. She does not look in the mirror as she brushes her hair before going to bed. For once her mind is quiet. She's too tired to think. She runs her hands up and down her arms. The skin is tender, as if bruised.

She stands and steps to the bed. As she sits she is startled by two light raps on her open bedroom door. She turns, tightening her bed jacket around her, expecting to see Willy rubbing his eyes. Instead it's Mickey standing there sipping from one of her china teacups.

"Oh—I thought everyone had left."

"Everyone else has. I made myself another cup of coffee. You don't mind?"

"Of course not." Mickey is leaning against the doorframe. She pats the bed next to her. "Come sit down and talk to me."

"First let me make you some coffee too."

"Oh no, Mickey, I don't want any. I'm going to bed."

"Maybe not. The night is young." She regards that lopsided grin of his and raises her eyebrows quizzically. "I'm going up to a club in Harlem. There'll be great music. Why don't you come with me?"

What on earth? She has two children sleeping in the next room. Mickey has thought of that. He says he thinks Izzy the doorman would be willing to come up when his shift ends at eleven and stay with the children until Vera gets back.

This conveyor belt of a day has dragged her far enough. No, she tells Mickey. It's sweet of him to think of her, but not tonight.

"Okay. One of these days, though?" She nods. "Soon, Vera?" Fine, she says, soon. Maybe Mama would be willing to spend the night taking care of the boys some time soon.

Mickey puts his cup down on Vera's night table and sits beside her. Her baby brother smells of gin and coffee and cigarettes. She leans against him. He puts his arm around her. Yawning, she snuggles into him. A volley of automobile horns rises from below, the room rocks with syncopation like a speakeasy, then there is silence.

Before she hears Mickey's voice again she feels it. His ribs vibrate. She smiles sleepily.

"So what did you think of the play?" Like a leash pulled taut, his question jerks her awake. She doesn't move. He nudges her, a soft elbow to her side, and says more quietly, "I've been waiting all night to hear." Her head stays down. He ducks his so he's in front of her face and she can't avoid his eyes. "Hmm, Veraleh?" He's insistent but now it's a whisper.

"I don't know what to think, Mickey." She's whispering too. "I—" It's all she can get out.

She feels Mickey's hands on her shoulders. Slowly, lightly at first then applying more pressure, he kneads her muscles, moving in tight, careful circles around her upper back, working his way up her neck. The piano player's fingers work at the knobs at the base of her skull. He is loosening something thick and solid, a lining like the cement shell she and the boys watched being poured on a Third Avenue construction site yesterday. If it cracks, what then?

"Let me tell you what I think," he says. The massage doesn't stop. His whispered words seem to enter her through his fingers. "I think they are very brave."

"Who?" She is so tired, propped against him.

"The women." He no longer whispers. His voice is low but sure. "In the play." He pauses. His fingers stop moving but he tightens his grip on Vera's shoulders. "The lovers."

A small sound in her throat, a shudder. Mickey wraps an arm around her chest, turning her and pulling her against him. With his other hand he lifts her face.

Like a terminal patient appealing to her doctor for a little more time, Vera looks at her brother. He's holding her so strong, so safe. Maybe he knows the way out.

"What do you mean ... lovers?" The word comes out in a choke but she pushes on. "Mickey, what are they?"

"They're people." He searches her face with his honest eyes. "Just people, Veraleh. Like you."

Like me, she thinks, and she's in the tunnel again, dizzy, queasy, jostled by unseen forces, lurching forward against her will, as her brother surrounds her in a bear hug and she smothers in his speakeasy smell.

November 1923

This argument they've had before. And, Vera thinks, I'll be damned if I'm going to let it spoil my mood tonight. Her lips tighten. She slips earrings—lotus flowers of fake lapis lazuli and gold plate—into her recently pierced ears. Celia had been scandalized when she got the holes made. Like a shiksa she said Vera looked. Don't be silly, Vera had laughed. It's the style, that's all. Tut tut. Get it? She bought the earrings, cheap imitations of the riches in King Tut's tomb, at a little store on Eighth Street, enjoying a guilty thrill at the act of disloyalty to her jeweler husband. This is the first time Peter has seen them.

She is aware of him behind her but prefers not to look at his reflection in the mirror. She knows what she'd see. He stands there, head thrust forward like a chicken, hands clasped at his back, staring at the sparkly, dangly evidence of her treachery as he tries to maintain an even tone that will win her over to staying home tonight.

He hasn't much of a case. The children are sound asleep. Well fed. Bathed. Snug. She'd put them to bed an hour ago. She sat between them and held their hands and sang "Yes We Have No Bananas," transforming the silly song into a slow, soothing lullaby. She watched them watch her, sleepy little tykes struggling to stay awake, greedy to keep the beloved one in sight. She'd finished the song, kissed Lenny, kissed Willy, turned off the light and said goodnight. And now she's supposed to stay here, for what?

Peter catches her eye in the mirror. "Vera," he says, clipped, precise as always, exasperated too. Poor Peter, she thinks, how I try your patience. She swivels on the vanity stool. She gives him a smile that is all limits. Still he tries. "Vera," again. His face is stiff too. His smile strained. "I do wish you would stay in this evening. You go out too often. It cannot be good for—"

"Good for whom, Peter? The children are asleep, they don't even know I'm out. And often? You consider four times in six months often? Really, Peter—"

"Yes, all right, perhaps not often but the children, it is nevertheless not good for the children that the mother is not in the home on the Saturday evening. I cannot think it is a good thing for these boys … "

He trails off. What case can he make after all? That Vera neglects Willy and Lenny? Nonsense. They are a mutual admiration society, she and her boys. A team. Vera and Willy especially. Sometimes lately he finishes her sentences for her. Or reads her mind. She'll start, "Willy, would you please—" and he'll dash to the kitchen drawer for the carrot peeler or run to drag Lenny from his games for lunch, in a rush to complete, to please. Of what can Peter possibly complain? That she has no energy for the children after an occasional Saturday night out with Mickey or the new friends she's met through him? Nonsense again. Come a Sunday morning after a Saturday night out the house awakens to the sounds of Vera skipping about the kitchen whipping up grand breakfasts, humming one after another the

VERA'S WILL

hopped-up songs she's heard uptown. On those mornings she is alive in a way she rarely feels on other days. It communicates itself to the kids, too, Lenny grabbing his momma's hands and squealing as she dances him around the room, Willy grinning, tapping his feet against the legs of his chair as he sloshes syrup onto a stack of flapjacks.

Vera looks at the window. It's a clear night. There is air out there. She stands abruptly, reaches for her handbag, moves toward the door. Peter will have to get out of her way.

"What are you doing, Vera? Where are you going?"

"I told you already, Peter. There will be tea, there will be cakes, we will read the poetry of Edna St. Vincent Millay." She just won the Pulitzer Prize; how can this be too bohemian for him? "You are welcome to come, I told you that." She pauses. She looks at his fish eyes swimming behind the thick eyeglass lenses. "You still can if you'd like. Mickey volunteered to stay with the boys. I'll call him if you want." Please no, she silently pleads, proceeding out the bedroom door and heading up the hall to the living room.

"This of course is ridiculous. Mickey is not at home on the Saturday night. He of course is in some terrible basement room playing this shvartze music—"

"Peter, I've told you, it's jazz, and don't call them shv—"

"It makes no difference what I call it. I have no time for poetry, Vera. You know this." She puts her gloves on, grips the back of the living-room sofa and releases a grateful breath. "So okay already, I give up, go, but please at least, do not stay late into the night." He moves quickly toward the front door as she buttons her coat. Reaching into his pocket, he holds out two coins. He grabs her hand, pulls it open and smacks the money into her palm. He takes a slow breath, presses his hand over the cash, gives a light squeeze. "Vera my poor dear, you are right. Just because your husband is a philistine this does not mean you must suffer without culture. Here is for the taxicab." He leans into her, kisses her cheek. "Have some fun with the poetry."

The soiree is at George and Wally's apartment on Thirteenth Street, all of two blocks from here, but Peter insists she get Izzy to hail a cab for her. Vera doesn't argue. She takes the two half-dollar coins, returns his peck, steps from the apartment and waits for the elevator. When she gets to the lobby she passes one of the coins to Izzy, a tip for his silence about her walk up Fifth Avenue.

At Twelfth Street she stops for a red light. She's flown the first block, flinging herself forward like a stone sprung from a slingshot.

She breathes a deep rush of chilly air. She tips back her head and gazes at the sky, just able to make out a star or two. What a sparkly, crinkly night. Crisp. She'd like to bite it. The traffic light clicks green and she steps off the curb.

How did she get here? Vera throws back her head and laughs. Florence looks at her quizzically. Vera laughs again, but quieter, as Florence takes her hand and brushes her lips across its back.

What else can she do but laugh? She cannot blame this on the sherry. Not three little sips, a thimbleful, spread out over the course of an hour, finished an hour ago. No, alcohol didn't do this. She did it herself. Dropped herself onto this woman's lap. And here she sits, holding this woman's hand. She feels light-headed, but it's not due to the demon drink.

Yet she has been drinking it all in. The poetry, the music, dancing. And the talk. It swings all over the place. From Freud and his latest theories to the death of Pancho Villa to the Yankees and their World Series win over the Giants in their new Bronx stadium. At this last, mentioned by George, someone had yelled out, "No, do not tell me—I believe I shall be ill if you tell me Babe Ruth is your hero. That brainless ball of blubber. I thought this gang was more enlightened than that."

George had pulled himself up to full, willowy height and said, "Pardon me, but if the Babe is a brute"—tossing his head toward Wally as his friend passed with a tray of petits fours—"well, you know I have a weakness for brutes."

"Watch it," Wally retorted, continuing with his rounds. "Your id is showing." That brought a big laugh all around.

Yes, it all tastes delicious. And yes, Vera supposes she is drunk on it. George and Wally. The people she's met the last few months. And now Florence. On whose lap Vera finds herself perched. As though, long ago cast into outer space, she has at last returned to the earthly atmosphere and breathes rich, intoxicating oxygen again.

The party is winding down. Vera isn't tired. She doesn't want to leave. Earlier, she'd danced and danced, the Charleston, the new craze flinging her across the floor as Wally kept cranking up his old Victrola, playing the song over and over. Each time more people got up, until everyone was dancing, faster and faster. Kicking up her heels, bending backward, forward, twirling, an ecstatic swirl of bodies, sweat, release.

It had been after that, elbows, heels, hips still tingling, when Vera spotted a short, plain-faced woman with light brown hair pinned back in an old-fashioned bun heading in from the kitchen, carrying a sherry. "Florence!" Vera cried out, crossing the room in one long lope. "Florence Silvano!" The woman had settled into a deep brown leather chair, set her sherry on the side table, looked up at the sound of her name—and Vera had launched herself on top of her.

"You're crazy!" Florence laughed, giving Vera a hearty hug. "And how did you even know who I am?"

"Well, do you know me?"

"Of course. I'd recognize you anywhere. As soon as I saw your eyes I knew." Florence pinched Vera's cheek. "Not to mention that laugh. Boy, does that bring back memories."

"So you do remember me. Probably as that annoying friend of your annoying little sister Dora."

"Yes, something like that."

Now fifteen minutes have passed. Here they sit, talking a little, mostly not, nodding to the music's jazzy beat, Vera's weight not seeming to bother Florence at all, the oddness of this scene prompting neither to make a move to alter it. So Vera laughs.

Then she stops, the laugh catching in her throat as Florence takes hold of her other hand. Florence's thumbs, small and soft, move in small, soft circles against Vera's palms. Vera looks down, then up at Florence's face. Florence lifts Vera's hands, lays a light kiss inside each palm, then places them against her cheeks. She puts her own hands on Vera's face. Vera starts at the touch, then releases a sigh. She and Florence hold each other's faces. They look into each other's eyes. In a moment they kiss, this time lips on lips. Once, quickly. Vera begins quietly to cry.

She takes the long way home, walking arm in arm with Florence. The night air nips at her, drying her tears. Florence is silent, squeezing Vera's arm. It feels good, leaning on Florence. She is shorter than Vera, and thin, but she seems sturdy. Rooted, like a wind-stripped tree unafraid of the season.

They walk over to Broadway, then down to West Fourth Street and toward the southern perimeter of Washington Square. They turn in to the park. It's deserted. Yet Vera feels safe, holding on to Florence Silvano.

An empty walkway echoes to their footfalls. At its end they find a bench. They sit. The chill brushes Vera. She shivers. Florence puts an arm around her, pulls her close. The quivering stops.

They talk. Small things for a long while, catching up. The old hometown, teachers, shopkeepers, Florence's big Italian clan, "and speaking of big Italians you ought to see Dora," she laughs. "Believe you me, Vera, you wouldn't recognize your old chum. Four little ones later—"

"Four! No!"

"Yes, four, and a fifth on the way."

"Poor thing. She must be exhausted."

"Oh, she's okay. Even if she is twice the gal she used to be." They both smile. "And you, yours?"

"They're grand, Florence."

VERA'S WILL

"Little Einsteins, I suppose."

"Yes. Willy, anyway. He'll do something big. Cure diseases, discover new stars. As for Lenny, what a charmer. I wouldn't be surprised if he ends up a movie star."

"Oh boy. Oh boys, I mean. You've got yourself a pair of paragons."

"All right already, maybe I'm gushing—"

"Don't mind me, Vera, I'm only teasing."

Florence lifts her hand to brush back a wisp of hair and Vera catches a glimpse of her wristwatch. Nearly one a.m. She must get home. She cannot move. She is home.

Silly thought. A park bench. Late. Cold. But it's too soon, she thinks. Let me stay a while.

Peter has probably been asleep since soon after she left the apartment. He retires early and sleeps hard, never moving until the electrical alarm rings on the bedside clock. Can she count on him sleeping so soundly that he doesn't know she isn't there? That he won't know how late she returns, even if she returns at two, three, four o'clock in the morning? She tenses up as she calculates the risk.

"What is it?" Florence asks.

Her voice brings Vera back. "Nothing," she says. She squeezes Florence's hand. "Tell me again how you know George and Wally?" Florence explains that she met them at a dinner party about a year ago. "And whose dinner party was that?" Before Florence can respond, Vera blurts, "Don't answer that! How rude of me. What a question—whose dinner party indeed. Why, it's none of my business. Honestly, Florence, what an impression you must be getting of me. Jumping into your lap, laughing, crying, and now I'm interrogating you. You must think I have no manners at all—or else that I'm as nutty as a fruitcake. Why, you must wonder why my keepers let me out into polite society."

A chuckle from Florence. "I think you are honest, and I find it beguiling. The dinner party was at the home of my friends Michael and John. Michael teaches with me at P.S. 110."

"And the Turkish brothers were there?"

"Yes, George and Wally were there. Although you know those aren't their real names." Vera raises her eyebrows quizzically. "And of course you know they aren't brothers. Or Turkish, for that matter."

"Not only rude—you must think I'm terribly naive. I did believe they were brothers. Until I ran into them uptown. Well, even the first time I didn't catch on, but I finally did the second or third time I saw them, I think it was at Small's Paradise."

"The Harlem clubs? Then you're not as naïve as all that. Small's Paradise—très chic, no?"

Is Florence making fun of her? "I went three times. My brother Mickey took me. He's a pianist, he plays jazz, places all over town, up there too."

"So he introduced you to the fast crowd."

"Fast, slow, I don't know. It is a different world, though, you're right about that. The music, the booze—they act as though there's no such thing as Prohibition—"

"They get away with it, too. Pay off the police and the profits keep rolling in."

"Exactly. And there's something else. There we were, up in Harlem, colored people on the streets, colored people in the band, colored people waiting on us—"

"But no colored people sitting with you. Only serving, never being served?"

"So you've been to the clubs?"

"I don't have to. I know how the world works."

"I'm ashamed to admit I was oblivious to it at first. With Mickey it's different, he jumps in with the band, he sits with his player pals, he never settles at a table."

"But you noticed?"

"Not on my own. I might have stayed oblivious, but I told my mother about my Saturday night out last month. Did you ever meet my mother, Florence? Back in Passaic?" Florence shakes her head. "Do you know what a Bolshie is? That's what Mickey calls her." Florence perks her head up. "Well, that's Mama. A Bolshie to the grave, god forbid."

"Good for her. So she—"

"So she pointed out to me, in rather strong terms, I might add, that something is wrong with traveling into a colored neighborhood and patronizing an establishment that colored people can't patronize. And for what? For Dutch Schultz to make money off the sale of bootleg liquor. Slumming they call it. Mama said it's a terrible word."

"A terrible concept."

"Yes."

"You haven't been back."

"No, I haven't. But don't call me honest, Florence. Please, I'm not. I stay out of Harlem so Mama won't think ill of me. And—"

"Is that such an awful reason to do the right thing?"

"And I'm dishonest in so many other ways."

Florence is quiet. She sees, Vera thinks. How I only pretend to be a normal person.

It's why Vera hated that game they'd played at the party tonight. Why she'd hidden in the kitchen until it was over. The Truth Game. Whatever anyone asks, you're supposed to answer honestly. No matter how awful the truth is. How can they find that fun?

"Vera," Florence says. "Dear, look at me." Dear, she calls me? Vera doesn't look. She mustn't know what a liar I am, she thinks. What a fraud. "Vera, I know."

Vera's chin suddenly lifts, held in Florence's grip, and then Florence's lips are on hers. This time the kiss isn't quick. It's long. Hard. It doesn't end.

Florence's mouth presses against hers with such force it almost hurts. Vera pushes back against Florence, just as hard. She clasps her hands behind Florence's head and pulls her closer. She can stand no space between them. She parts her lips. Their tongues do a steaming dance. Behind the sweetness of sherry still on her tongue, there is a hint of a lemony flavor to Florence. Tasting her, tart and sweet, running her tongue along her teeth, savoring her, Vera's chest compresses.

Florence explores the insides of Vera's cheeks with her tongue, bites her bottom lip lightly, lays her face against Vera's face. She holds Vera tighter. She kisses Vera again, gently this time, slow and tender. She's saying something, low, shaping the words against her lips. It's her name. "Vera Vera Vera," she whispers as she kisses her. The Vs vibrate down Vera's spine, each one followed by the warm wet pillow of Florence's lips, the repetition calming her, arousing her. Her tears stop. The pounding of her heart slows. Her chest swells. It opens. It fills with air.

Their kisses turn urgent again. Vera's pulse picks up speed. She throbs in a part of her she'd forgotten could fill with such feeling. Kissing without cease, she climbs onto Florence. She clamps Florence's legs between hers. Florence rises up to her, moves against her as Vera bears down. She rides. She can't contain this. She starts to explode. She honestly does.

Vera studies the pulse in Florence's throat as it slows and steadies. Part of her notes the strangeness of the scene. Two women. On a park bench. In the dead of night. Sprawled on top of each other like lovers. What if someone passes by?

The thought floats idly away. No one will come. There is a zone of protection around them. They're free as birds. She feels as though she and Florence could lift right up and flutter away, land in the leafless treetops and nestle there until daybreak. Vera pictures herself as a bird—like the doves Florence's brother trained, she suddenly remembers. Her homing instinct has brought her to this place.

"It's awfully late," Florence whispers after a while. She nudges Vera off her lap. "Let me walk you."

They rise. "And then come in," Vera says. "I'll make hot chocolate." She grabs Florence's hand to cut off any objections. "It'll be all right. Peter will sleep through it, I assure you. And the boys too. No one will hear us."

"Hear us?—"

Vera looks at Florence's tired eyes, and the bashful blush across her face. "Oh, you wicked girl." Vera grins. "I have no further designs on you this evening."

She can't believe she's talking like this. Vera Steiner, you have surely lost your marbles, she tells herself, but then Florence returns her grin, still blushing furiously, and her next thought is that yes, she would indeed like to touch her again, really touch her this time, skin to skin. Inside, where it's warm.

They sit in the kitchen sipping cocoa. Vera is still wide awake, but she can see that Florence is drooping. She yearns to lead her to bed and curl against her in sleep. She sighs deeply.

"What is it?" Florence's head is propped against her hand on the table.

Vera doesn't want to cry any more. She smiles, waves "nothing" with her hand, and returns to an earlier subject. "So George and Wally aren't brothers. But they're not Turkish either? And their names?"

"Wally is from Egypt." She glances at Vera's scarab brooch. "His father is a pretty successful merchant over there. When Wally decided—actually, I think his father decided for him— anyway, when Wally left for the States, his father paid for his berth and gave him enough money to buy the first shipment of Turkish carpets and cover a year's lease on the store."

"And his father thought up the name too? I can see why he's so successful."

"No, 'Magic Carpet' was Wally's idea. He figured he'd never overturn all these ridiculous images folks here have, so he might as well market to them. And according to George, they'd be more likely to buy Turkish carpets from Turks."

"Instead of Egyptians?"

"George isn't from Egypt. He's from Palestine. Jaffa."

"So he and Wally are Arabs."

Florence nods. "And he says Americans are afraid of Arabs. They think they're sinister, they think they'll cheat them."

"Sounds familiar."

"Right. So they say they're Turks. And Walid becomes Wally."

Vera thinks of her brother Mendel who became Mickey. She closes her eyes and a fuzzy image of Hersh appears. Hersh who became—what? Perhaps a nom de guerre. Did he die with that name? Does he live with it?

She opens her eyes at the touch of Florence's hand on hers. "And you?" Florence asks. "How did you become Mrs. Steiner?"

Vera swallows down a sour bubble. Hesitating, searching for a way to explain, to herself as much as to Florence, she taps into something dammed up inside her, and it spills out in a barely audible flow. Especially the loneliness.

When she finishes she finds herself on Florence's lap again. Her head on Florence's shoulder. Florence's arms around her. I really am loopy, she thinks. What if Peter comes in? But he won't, she is sure, and the worry wafts away in a whiff of Florence's neck, a warm, clean smell mixed with a little chalk dust. Vera breathes her in, Florence's voice vibrating against her cheek as she in turn tells how she came to the city. By herself. To be herself. Even if it meant being alone.

"So here I am, the spinster schoolteacher." Florence's throat vibrates in a different rhythm. Vera lifts her head. Sadness tugs the corners of her friend's mouth downward. Florence has a blunt face—you might even think it dull, until it is animated by emotion. Then her visage brightens or dims as feelings march across. Here is an honest person, Vera thinks. She tells the truth. Right there on her face. How could I have thought it a plain face? It is emphatic. Why, she's been lonely too. Maybe more than me. At least I've had my boys to love. Vera lays a light, tiny kiss there, and there, at each edge of Florence's mouth.

So here we are, Vera thinks, opening her mouth to say it but an electric jolt of love shocks her speechless as she takes Florence's hand.

Love? Okay, now it's definite: I have completely lost my marbles. Vera reaches this conclusion as she lies next to snoring Peter at four a.m. Florence left an hour ago. Vera went down to the lobby with her, walked her past Franco the midnight-shift doorman, thanked heaven that he was fast asleep at his desk, stepped outside, helped her hail a cab, passed her Peter's fifty-cent piece, pressed her hand urgently as they said goodnight. She watched Florence drop her head against the back of the seat as the taxi pulled away. She returned to the apartment and stood at the living-room window looking down at the avenue until her arms and legs grew heavy and she decided she was at last ready for bed. But sleep does not come. Something impossible does, flowing through her, with every breath.

This cannot be, Vera thinks. We only just met. All right, that's not precisely true. I knew her fifteen years ago. Dora's big sister. So now? We meet again, and—what? We fall in love? Like in a fairy tale? It can't be.

There is no fairy tale like this. Two women. Not something you tell your children at bedtime.

Willy and Lenny. A sick feeling grips her. They must never know. She promises herself that they will have a normal life.

Their mother may be abnormal, but after this last year, Vera knows she is not the only one. The play, then the clubs. The soirees at George and Wally's. Their big apartment overflows with paintings, hangings, art from around the world, and it's crammed with furniture, a mad melange of authentic and ersatz, the place throbbing with the same vitality that brims from their wild mix of friends. This is what they call "the life" in Harlem. Now she knows more about it, the life these people actually lead. It is errant. It is forbidden. Yet she sees now that it does not have to be empty. And it does not have to be lived alone.

She had always thought she and Mary were unique. That what they had, what they did, was nameless, new, unheard of in all the world. Instinctively they'd hidden it. They touched only in silence, or when they were alone. But there had also been a sense that they were special. Lucky. It was as if they had discovered a private dwelling place, precious, privileged. And though they were its only denizens, though they should have felt isolated, afraid, instead they felt secure, sealed inside secret walls of love.

In the five years since Vera was cast out from that magical place, she has been in exile. Compelled to play Mrs. Steiner as best she can, her boys the consolation prize. There is no alternative, she has thought. And now?

She is not the only one. The knowledge, acquired over these last months, has spun her round. When the dizziness had passed, a new sensation arose. She was voracious.

I've been starving, she thinks, heavy with the sleep that finally folds around her as after a fast-breaking feast.

FEBRUARY 1924

The sun peaked some time ago yet it slides down slowly, stubborn, as though stuck in another season. It glimmers against brittle blue. Vera narrows her eyes, skull nudging the back of the bench, and lets the warmth shine on her face. It is much warmer than a winter's day has a right to be. The squint blocks her peripheral vision of the birch trees spaced along the little park's perimeter so she can imagine them in full blossom— not as they are, spindly, flailing bare, soot-blackened branches.

Sitting in the playground on Delancey and Columbia, kitty-corner from P.S. 110 waiting for Florence to emerge, she is not being selfish. Rather, she is treating her boys to a rarity, a winter's day posing as spring.

Head on her lap, legs akimbo, lying half on and half off the bench, one thumb in his mouth and the other gripping his blanket, Lenny is fast asleep. He naps as well here as he would at home, and the fresh air is good for him. As if in instant rebuke to the thought, a gust of automobile exhaust gushes toward them from the line of cars ascending the Williamsburg Bridge. This morning's *Herald Tribune* said Henry Ford will soon sell his ten millionth Model T: half of them must be on that bridge. Vera lays the blanket lightly over Lenny's face before the gray plume of greasy fumes reaches them.

She leaves a hand on his head and works her fingers through the sweaty tangle of fine sandy hair. It's amazing what a good sleeper he is. He and his brother both. They inherited this gift from their father. Nothing budges the slumbering child. The noise from the bridge is constant. Its steel skeleton rattles as elevated trains rumble across. Screeching brakes. Honking klaxons squeezed ceaselessly by truckers pushing empty rigs to Brooklyn, heavy canvas covers flapping up top. She watches Lenny's face as another swell of sound arrives. The school bursts like a dam, releasing a flood of children. Shouting, laughing, clapping. Shoes slapping against pavement, they spill toward the playground from across the street. Still her little one sleeps, the merest shadow of a frown slipping across his forehead as a girl bumps the bench on her way to the merry-go-round.

Vera tracks the girl's progress toward the spot where Willy has been entertaining himself for the last half-hour. He's a bit put out with his mother. She'd promised to play with him while they waited for Florence. But Lenny parked himself on her lap and fell asleep as soon as they got here, and she's been stuck in this spot ever since. Willy whined once or twice until she gave him her "knock it off, buster" look, pulled him close and whispered a suggestion. He is fascinated by trains, so Vera pointed out how the merry-go-round might serve as a make-believe locomotive. She tipped his cap up and flipped it backward and told him it looked like a conductor's hat. Then, with a tap on his tushy, she sent him scooting off to ride the rails.

She has been observing Willy while his little brother sleeps. The way he moves. Meticulous. Calibrating each act. It makes her want to laugh and cry. He is such a person already. So utterly himself.

He looks like Vera—dark-haired, dark-eyed—but there is a lot of his father in him. His carefulness. The way he assesses each situation instead of just plunging in and having fun. He's thorough. He's neat. Dislikes loose ends. On Sunday afternoons he kneels side by side with Peter and they shine their shoes. She hates to see it. A four-year-old shouldn't be so fastidious. She tries to accommodate his need for order, for she wants him to feel secure, but she also steers him toward the carefree, childish side of himself as much as she can.

He does want to have fun, she can see it, yet it takes coaxing. In the last year or so she's discovered that he loves demonstrating his advanced knowledge about things to Lenny. So she'll use the pretext of enlisting his aid to trick him into letting go and enjoying himself. "Willy, would you show your brother how to put that puzzle together?" Or, "Explain to Lenny how a train runs, would you, Willy?" Once she gets him settled at some activity she loves to watch his face. He's so smart she can practically see his brain bulging. His little forehead ripples with concentration as he puts together the pieces of a puzzle or draws a picture or pushes his wooden train pieces across the living room floor.

Lenny's smart too. But there's more of the good-time guy to him. And he takes his mother more for granted. Once he's playing nothing can distract him. It brings out the devil in Vera. She has to constantly hold herself back from swooping down, making him shriek with surprise, rolling around the floor with him, luxuriating in exuberant silliness until he's hiccupping, gasping for breath, climbing all over her out of control with glee.

With Willy such a thing would be difficult. He is ever alert—especially to his mother. Exquisitely attuned to the air around her. Every nuance of Vera's thought or emotion creates a shift in the atmosphere that he detects.

She'll be watching him, as now. Something will cross her mind or draw her attention—as now, watching the little girl skip toward the merry-go-round where Willy has been playing alone. He'll sense the change—there, he looks up, gives Vera a small smile. Then he waits, watching her face for a cue to what comes next.

His sun rises and sets with her. What power she has over this little boy's heart. It frightens her sometimes.

Sometimes, though, like now, it thrills her. The muscularity of it. As if she could move mountains for him. She is invincible, because he needs her to be. His champion.

Vera smiles at Willy, waving gaily. Signal received, his own smile broadens, and he reaches toward his new playmate to pull her up onto his train.

Sitting on the bench, the weight of the little one across her legs, the sight of Willy playing, awash in sunshine and his mother's love, Vera gives a sigh of contentment. Then a new note sounds.

"Good afternoon."

She jumps. There's a half-second lag before the words register. Then an electric zing. Florence's voice. Suddenly limp, she clutches a handful of Lenny's loose curls to steady herself.

Where's Willy's strapping hero now? One minute stalwart, and the next? Why, Vera Steiner, your heart is going pitter-patter like some pitiful weakling tied across the railroad tracks simpering to be saved. And all because—

"I'm here."

"Yes you are." Oy. It's not bad enough she's splayed like a feeble heroine in the clutches of an evil mustache twirler. Has she lost the power of intelligent speech as well? Lenny starts turning his head about, trying in his sleep to escape Vera's grip. She releases his locks, he goes slack again, and she looks up at the smiling schoolteacher. "Nu?"

Wonderful, she thinks. Now I'm down to monosyllables. This is ridiculous. Why do I still fall apart at the sound of her voice, the sight of her smile? It's two months already. I should be getting used to this.

Yet how can she? Get used to this thing between them that has no name?

Florence sits down on the next bench over. Come to think of it, she appears not altogether in command of herself either. In fact, she seems to have gone speechless. Vera regards her. What a prim schoolmarm she looks with her sensible gray wool coat, stubby black shoes all laced up, brown hair braided like a challah and pinned atop her head. In muted colors, all contained, how proper she appears, how stern. Only the roseate glow on her cheeks giving away what lies beneath.

The sun sparkles in Florence's eyes as she returns Vera's gaze. There's a greedy gleam in them. Another zing shoots through Vera. She starts to reach for her friend but stops herself.

She's having trouble with her hands. They've come unmoored without Lenny's hair to hold onto. She might float off. She concentrates on squeezing them together, willing away this sense of displacement that descends when she's with Florence.

It is as if they have stepped outside the world, the two of them. Together they drift. Vera is at once fully present—here, in the flesh, prisoner of sensation—and entirely apart. In her own world, hers and Florence's. Lost, found.

It is a fearsome feeling; it pleases her too much. If only she could remain dislodged like this. If, like magic, this could be the world. This golden anomaly of a warm winter afternoon with her boys and her—

Sharp pains needle her arms, pushing up from the hands pressing each other. She returns to earth, brought back, as always, to wedge herself into place. It has to be good enough, the real world. She glances down at Lenny, asleep, then at the merry-go-round where Willy plays, then to her side, at Florence. She unclasps her hands, lets one reach, makes contact with her friend's cheek. The pads of her fingertips tingle.

The voluble world—its patter of automobile traffic, clattering pushcarts, laughing children, Florence's heartbeat, Willy's voice—rolls over her. Flattened by its volume, she can barely breathe.

"Why did they name that school after you?" She hadn't realized Willy's voice was right here. He stands between the two benches, his back to Vera. Hands clasped behind him, neck muscles working as he thrusts his head forward to speak to Florence. His stance, so like Peter's, sets Vera's teeth grinding. Willy waits a second or two, reasoning, she knows, that this is surely enough time to answer a simple question, then addresses her friend again. "How come it's named after you when you're not even dead?" Her jaw relaxes. Her son whips around at the sound of her laughter, than back to her friend who has joined in. "Hey—what's so funny? What did I say?" His fists clench at his sides.

"You asked quite an acute question." Vera marvels at the way Florence reads Willy. Ever eager to hear his intelligence praised, the boy cocks his head. Vera can't see his face but she knows exactly what expression he wears: eyes narrowed, nostrils flared, mouth open in the look of yearning, hungry concentration that comes over him when he's learning something new. "But before I answer it, may I ask you one of my own?" Florence the teacher, Vera thinks. Willy nods. He shifts his footing, spreading his feet a bit more widely apart, centering himself like a boxer awaiting the next parry. "How did you know the name of my school? Did your mother tell you?" Willy shakes his head silently. "One of the schoolchildren, then? Sylvia over there, the girl you were playing with? She's one of my first graders, you know. Did she tell you?" Again the head shake. Boy, he's enjoying this, Vera thinks. Maybe too much. Her son is awfully sure of himself when it comes to brains. Florence folds her arms and feigns exasperation. "Well then, I do not understand how you know the name of the school." Eyes twinkling, she glances over his head at his mother.

Oh I love you flares through Vera. Straight away, like a clairvoyant, she hears her friend send the same sentence back. She goes all liquid. A puddle on a park bench.

When Willy answers Florence, his voice is quiet, shy. Vera strains to hear.

"I read it," he says.

Love blows in again, this time like a hot wind from a bellows, and then as she looks at Willy and Florence the feelings merge, the heat and the wet, and she is at the mercy of a single flow of feeling, unstoppable, relentless, terrifying. Her child and her— her what? Why is there no word for what Florence is to her?

The conversation to her right has become quite animated, Florence and Willy moving on to a spirited exchange about his precocious ability to read. He taught himself, he says (Vera not- ing that he has excised her role from the tale), he learned how to recognize the letters on Poppy's newspaper. And your first name, he points out to the woman he and his brother know as Tanteh Florence, I've seen it a hundred times. When Willy says his mother scribbles it everywhere, the schoolteacher blanches.

"Don't exaggerate, Willy." Vera looks at her friend. "Maybe on a grocery list once or twice. I probably made a note to myself to tell you something."

"Oh no, Ma, a lot of times. You write her name a lot." Vera looks at him. He's right. She hadn't realized. She'd better be care- ful. For Flo is not—can never be—she'd better watch herself.

Meanwhile, Willy has moved on. He is an honest fellow. He confesses that he cannot read the second part of the school's name.

"Nightingale?" Florence prompts. He nods, shakes his head, nods. Yes, he guesses that's the name. No, he cannot read it. Yes, although he hates to admit it, all those letters strung togeth- er confound him. "Try saying it, Willy. Nightingale. Florence Nightingale."

He does, then asks who that is. Florence rises. Taking him by the hand, she says, "Let's cross the street and take a closer look. There's a plaque on the wall that we can read together. Then you will see why Florence Nightingale deserves to have a school named after her. She was an altogether grander, braver person than I."

Vera watches them as they approach P.S. 110. Holding hands like mother and child. If only ... oh well, she thinks. We must live

136   VERA'S WILL

in the world as it is. But you are wrong, dear. There has never been anyone grander than you.

It is a long walk back to Ninth Street as afternoon falls to evening. Vera is anxious that they won't arrive in time for her to prepare dinner, feed and bathe the children and get Peter's food on the table before he gets home. She keeps trying to speed the boys up. Their short legs can walk only so fast.

They should have left earlier. But Lenny slept so long and Florence and Willy had so much to talk about and she herself would have been happy had the afternoon never ended. When finally Lenny awoke and they did exit the playground, perhaps she should have hailed a taxicab. The driver might have let the boys sit up front with him, bounce on the padded wood bench, tootle the horn. She could have paid the fare with her mad money, kept folded away in the little change purse inside her handbag.

That would have stolen six splendid blocks strolling Florence home up Essex Street. Vera smiles at herself. This by you is splendid? Tenement-crammed slums? You see what love does to you? But I'm not just being selfish, she argues back for the second time this afternoon, it's good for the boys, too. They are far too sheltered up there above Washington Square. Let them see how the other half lives—how their own mother used to live.

On Essex Street men in great flowing beards gesticulate and debate. Women lift long dresses from the muck of the gutters. Dirty dogs run loose. The scent of frying onions wafts from windows where people lean and shout in strange languages. Lenny and Willy gawk, kicking at pebbles on the broken-up sidewalk. Willy shrinks against Vera as a ripe-smelling rag peddler touches his face with a swatch of velvet, spitting out an incomprehensible sales pitch. Lenny lights up as he examines a scissor sharpener's cart laden with knives, pots, pans, and unfamiliar, exotic contrivances designed for hearths left behind in another world. Flo seems to know half the neighborhood. Of course. She has been teaching here for ten years. Boys and girls, teenagers and young mothers, so many people wave or call out to Miss Silvano that Vera feels as though she is in the company of someone famous.

Six blocks and before she knows it they say goodbye. "You live here?" Willy asks. That's right, Florence says, pointing. Right above Zlatkin the kosher butcher. "Talk to us from the window," Willy demands. All right, Florence laughs, so after she kisses each of them goodbye, Lenny, Willy, Vera, light pecks on the cheek for one and all, the women assiduously avoiding each other's eyes but at the last minute Vera can't resist grabbing her friend's hand and pressing it tightly between hers, only for an instant, surely no one notices—after Florence says her goodbyes and steps over the clumps of clucking yentas sitting on the steps to her building, she reappears on the second floor.

Framed by the window and lit from behind by an electric light, she has the aspect of an apparition. Her disembodied face seems to float, pale, expressionless, like a specter summoned from the ether at one of those séances Harry Houdini has been exposing as frauds.

Down on the sidewalk looking up, the three of them are spellbound by the eerie effect. Holding hands, sons on either side of their mother, they stare at the face in the window. Vera glances at each boy. Willy looks perplexed, as if he's trying to solve a puzzle with too many pieces. Lenny is rapt, but fear starts to play across his features and he creeps closer to her.

Vera returns her gaze above. Tries to find her feet. To keep them on the ground. And her hands—she focuses on the sweat, the grime, the gummy, gritty texture of the boys' skin against hers. Let them hold her here. So she won't drift away again.

For the world has gone quiet again. Quite a trick for Essex Street. Vera has become a spirit medium. A receptor for the silent communiqué Florence sends from above. It enters through her pores and she casts it upward in redoubled intensity. Back and forth between them as the day grows dim the message plays.

a secret source of light that might be strong enough to stop the darkness about to fall.

A messenger boy on a bicycle swerves up onto the curb, ringing his bell and yelling at them to get out of the way. Lenny yanks his hand and leaps to safety. Willy tightens his grip on Vera. She can't move fast enough. The bicyclist rams into them and they topple onto the pavement.

Willy scrambles up quickly, red-faced but apparently unhurt. Worry knitting his forehead, he peers at his mother. She straightens to rise, smiles at him, then follows his eyes to her knees. They are pinked and torn, with specks of scrabbled concrete stuck into the flesh, but they're not bleeding. She wipes her skinned hands against her muddied skirt. "Would you be so kind, young sir?" She reaches for him. Five tiny fingers tremble into hers.

Another pair of hands grips her elbows. Soft, but strong: Florence must have flown down those stairs. Fingers still entwined with her son's, Vera leans on Florence, who pulls her upright. She looks up along Florence's arms into eyes brimming with suppressed laughter and lets loose a low hoot at her own clumsiness. Assured that she's okay, Lenny grabs her other hand and starts laughing. So does Florence, and finally Willy. Soon the four are raising such a ruckus that Zlatkin steps out of his butcher shop to check on the commotion. Florence waves him off: everything is fine.

Bundle Of Happiness

I was a fifties kid growing up in Northdale, just over the Eight Mile Road city line from Detroit. I pattered around our backyard, played in the basement, ate dinner from tray tables in the living room watching *My Little Margie* and *Love That Bob* on a black-and-white TV set whose staticky reception had Daddy constantly jumping up to adjust the rabbit-ear antennae. I liked Velveeta and Wonder Bread, swanky frankies and cracker jacks. A white kid in the suburbs, my nineteen fifties weren't about wars or witch hunts, though by decade's end I was worrying about the bomb and civil rights.

Actually, I worried a lot—mostly about how to fit in. I couldn't get the hang of who I was supposed to be and it made me feel like a big weirdo. I spent those hours in the backyard pounding nails into two-by-fours or digging tunnels to China instead of on the sidewalk jumping rope or playing jacks or struggling through any of those other girly games that made me feel all awkward and inaccurately attached. In the basement with Steven Bergman from next door I would only agree to play house if I could be the dad. Then I'd endlessly replay the single scene of myself coming home from work, asking what's for dinner and ordering him, my wife, to bring me a beer.

Mommy was always trying to doll me up in lacy, frilly dresses, uncomfortable, itchy and impossible to play in. I preferred jeans and flannel shirts. I wore my favorite jacket, reversible, red on one side, black on the other, well into summer no matter how sweaty I got. I felt dashing in that jacket.

I didn't know how to answer when anyone asked what I wanted to be when I grew up. Trying to picture myself as an adult, I'd get a foggy feeling in my head, shrug and smile and feel stupid. Mommy stepped in. Ballerina, she said, which I found ridiculous, especially since my one and only venture in the field, the after-school ballet class Mommy and Daddy had forced me to take when I was five, had ended in a humiliating fiasco: me flailing about on stage, miserable and out of place as a sugar-plum fairy in *The Nutcracker*. Later she'd started saying I wanted to be a teacher. Although I really couldn't see myself spending my life in a classroom like both my parents, the idea of it didn't violate something inside me the way that ballerina business had, and it was good to have an answer when people asked, so we stuck to the teacher thing.

Everything was a little off. At the same time, everything was all right. My brother Elliot could be annoying. He was awfully stuck up about his cranial capacity, which was how he insisted I refer to his famous intelligence. And I didn't really like wrestling with him because even if he let me be Dick the Bruiser he always ended up hurting me but since I had a rule against crying in front of anyone I had to just take it. Yet at other times he was fun. Like the springtime Saturday mornings in the new decade, the year I was seven and Elliot ten, when we'd read together.

At eleven o'clock Dad was long gone, at the research library as usual, working on his doctoral dissertation as he'd been doing my whole life. Mom was still in bed. Saturday was her day to sleep in. Out on the big screened-in back porch, Elliot and I leaned into each other on the wrought-iron loveseat Mom had painted fire-engine red the summer before. Elliot was crazy about science fiction. My taste ran toward *Mrs. Piggle Wiggle*, but El kept interrupting me to read me sections out of Heinlein or Asimov. At first I clucked my tongue and acted annoyed but then I got caught up in his tales of strange beings in distant galaxies.

Soon he closed his book and began weaving his own yarns of danger and intrigue in the vastness of space. I joined in, contributing peculiar names for the characters he made up, names that sounded very smart and science-fictionish to me. This was the best part, because El surprised me by accepting the names I submitted, and so we climbed starry stairs together in a true artistic collaboration. There was Yeoman Cyclopsoid, originally a dastardly one-eyed space villain who over time developed into a nearly human mutation more to be pitied than feared. Other characters I named included Portia Poundaflesh (not the sole creation cribbed from the Shakespeare readings Mom staged for the household every few weeks), Leech Loppaloppa, Freon Freonforce, Pituitary Gland-o-war, Spitfire Rohobish, and Jigwamp Kartacca of the legendary planet Kartacca Oyveydom.

Elliot and I ended our science fiction session when Grandpa Ben and Grandma Gussie came over in the early afternoon. The four of us went into the backyard. We fed the birds together, Grandpa Ben demonstrating how to entice the robins to come close enough to peck bread crumbs right out of your hand. I loved how he did that. I couldn't manage the trick myself no matter how gently he urged me on. Just as the bird was about to alight on my hand I faltered, stepping backward several steps and sitting down, thud, on the grass. The bird quickly flew up into a tree branch. Grandpa Ben looked at me. I don't know, I just could not let that bird peck at my skin.

Soon we were back inside, sitting at the kitchen table playing gin rummy and listening to the Tigers game on my transistor radio. Even though it was a hot day, Grandma Gussie put the kettle on and made cups of Sanka. Instead of just lifting the coffee cup and drinking like normal people, she and Grandpa Ben poured a little bit from the cup into the saucer, blew on it to cool it, and then sipped from the saucer. I couldn't believe how queer this was but Mom had told me never to say a word about it or I'd make them self-conscious about being immigrants and never having gotten the hang of how to be normal Americans. So I just looked away when they did that. I concentrated on drinking my chocolate milk properly, as Tanteh Vera had taught me, without slurping or smacking my lips. I wondered what kind of country Grandpa Ben and Grandma Gussie came from where people didn't know the difference between saucers and cups, and how far their country was from my other grandmother's, the one we called aunt, Tanteh Vera.

My actual aunts, Rose and Bud, showed up around the time Mom got up. Mom's sisters were ten years younger than she was, so when I was seven the twins were barely out of their teens. They cracked me up with their silly jokes and the kooky friends they brought around. Man, their pals were a blast. Especially Auntie Bud's, gals who wore flashy clothes and leather jackets, Madge, Peaches, Red. Bud and her girlfriends were really nice to me, lifting me up and spinning me around until Mom told them to stop if they didn't want me to throw up. Auntie Rose was great too. She kissed and hugged me about a thousand times. Mom said she was wild, pointing as proof to Rosie's marriage to Uncle Ibrahim, a Ford assembly line worker with a big black mustache and crinkly eyes who smiled a lot but rarely spoke.

"An Arab," Mom said, shaking her head.

"So what?" We were in the kitchen getting lunch. I dished fruit salad into a bowl as Mom laid out strips of cold cuts and cheeses, slices of pumpernickel and challah, tomatoes and cucumbers.

She looked at me and shook her head again. "Oh, Mary. Rosie should have married a Jew. It's best to pick someone from the same background. Let alone—look, just remember, pick someone like yourself if you want to be happy."

As Mom and I carried the food out to the picnic table on the back porch, I looked at Uncle Eeb, trying to figure out how he was not like us. I watched him pile salami and Swiss cheese onto bread. My uncle, the only Arab I knew, seemed to like the same food as us Jews. He got along with everyone in the family, playing Parcheesi with Elliot and me, helping Grandpa Ben with heavy household chores, contentedly eating Auntie Rose's famously bad cooking. What was it that Uncle Eeb didn't have in common with us? All I could come up with based on family Saturdays was that, unlike Jews who talked a lot, and loud, Arabs were quiet. It seemed to me that Uncle Eeb should get a lot of credit for putting up with the constant yakking.

As for me, I was at my ease. School days were an endurance test. Stomach ceaselessly knotted, uncomfortable but unable to identify why, I felt like a clenched fist jammed into a stiff, tight glove two sizes too small. On weekends, and all summer, at home with my family, reading, listening to the ballgame, playing cards, eating, goofing around, I forgot to feel like I didn't fit.

One Saturday a month, Dad would swing by the house at two or three o'clock, after he'd finished his scientific research for the day. He'd honk the horn. Elliot and I would yell goodbye, run out to Dad's car, and he'd drive to Tanteh Vera's. We were in for a dull afternoon, sitting in our grandmother's small, stuffy apartment, watching the TV turned low or hunched over a checkerboard, careful to stay quiet while Dad, Uncle Lenny and Tanteh Vera played cards and, in occasional short-lived conversational spurts, talked in low, stilted tones.

On this June Saturday, though, Tanteh Vera was to meet us at Uncle Lenny's. She was much more modern than Grandma Gussie. She drove, she smoked, she lived alone. Uncle Lenny also lived alone, in the next suburb north. His house seemed bare to me, used as I was to the clutter of end tables crowded with glasses, cups, dishes, notebooks, pens and pencils, crossword puzzles, books, newspapers, magazines, junk mail, the refrigerator and cupboards bulging with edibles, the couch piled with clean laundry waiting to be folded. Uncle Lenny's tabletops were free of debris. There was nary a scratch nor watermark on the gleaming teak surfaces of his Danish Modern furniture. His fridge was almost empty. I guess today you'd call his style spare, but back then, to me, it seemed barren, spooky. There was a hush to the place, too. No TV blaring in the background—he didn't even keep one in the living room, just a small set atop the dresser in his bedroom.

Without that, or the din of constant chatter, laughter, bickering that created the white noise of home, Uncle Lenny's house gave me the creeps. Uncle Lenny did a little bit too. With his stuttering, it was agonizing waiting him out whenever he tried to say something. Then there were his sad eyes, hooded and deep like Tanteh Vera's. And the small smile he fabricated once in a great while. I'd once overheard Mom call him "tightly wound," and I did have a sense of closely coiled springs that I did not want to burst.

Funny, though: I was also nuts about Uncle Lenny. I'd bring him a bottle of pop without him asking, or I'd force myself to go sit on his lap to try to cheer him up, and even though it was a little bit frightening, I was never sorry because his face would open, bright as any star I'd ever seen, and he'd give me such a squeeze I'd shriek. I'd heard Dad tell Mom Uncle Lenny was weak, but I thought Dad was just confused by how his brother never raised his voice or pumped his fist or issued scary threats.

I also liked it on Tanteh Vera's lap, especially when she had a cigarette because the smoky swirls settled into such odd, fascinating shapes before they dissipated in the air. That Saturday, I remember, Uncle Lenny asked Dad and Elliot to go out back with him and check the septic tank. The idea of any one of those three knowing anything about plumbing or underground pipes cracked me up, and then Tanteh Vera caught my eye and winked and I knew she was thinking the same exact thing, though we were both too smart to say a word. We just waited till the three he-men left, then she slapped her thighs inviting me to climb on board. She was sitting in front of Uncle Lenny's big picture window in what he called the family room even though there was only him in that house. The glass framed a view of the big backyard. As Tanteh Vera smoked she watched Dad, Uncle Lenny and Eliot walking around, kicking clumps of grass, consulting. I watched her. Following her gaze, pondering what she saw of such interest out there, sneaking looks into her deep brown eyes. Wondering what I might find inside.

❧

That night, back home, I dawdled, trying to put off bedtime. After I brushed my teeth I stood in front of the bathroom mirror looking into my own eyes, wondering if they'd ever be as deep as Tanteh Vera's.

I felt unsettled. Also mad, because Elliot got to stay up another hour after me. I always resisted bedtime, begging to stay up a little longer. But Dad was a stickler for getting enough sleep. He himself often went to bed as early as eight or nine o'clock. He was up and out of the house early too. What with his sleep routine and his long hours in the research library after school and on weekends, we didn't see him very much at all. Except that one Saturday afternoon a month when he took Elliot and me to see some Steiners. And except bedtime, when he was always present to send me off to sleep.

I knew if I exited the bathroom it would signal that Dad had once again defeated me in the battle to stay up another half hour. He'd already announced, "You brain will not grow to its full size if it doesn't get enough oxygen, and it can't get enough oxygen if you don't get enough sleep." Now he shouted, "Mary, out of the bathroom and into bed right now!"

"Okay! Fine—I'm going!"

Suddenly Mom's voice filled the air: "Bundle of happiness!"

A thrill rushed through me. I looked up. Mom was standing right there in front of the doors to the three bedrooms. She had a stack of clean towels in her arms. She stepped into Elliot's bedroom, laid the towels down on his bed, picked up the whistle from his nightstand and stepped back out. She winked at me, lifted the whistle to her lips and blew two long, loud blasts. She reached over and grabbed my hand.

"What the goddamn hell!" My father came pounding up from the living room.

"Hey! Who blew my whistle!" Elliot, following right behind.

"Bill, please," Mom said. "I said bundle of happiness. And Elliot, you know the rule, don't you?"

"Yeah, I know. When anyone announces bundle of happiness we drop everything. Bundle of happiness takes precedence."

"That is correct, boychik." Mom reached for my brother, meanwhile pulling me close by her side. She turned toward Dad. "Honey?"

"Okay, everybody, your mother has decreed a bundle of happiness," Dad said grumpily. He took a step, and the four of us huddled close together. I had to hand it to Mom—she'd sure come up with the perfect end to the day.

Yay! Bundle of Happiness! That's how I thought of it—capitalized, like a holiday, or the title of a play—but it actually wasn't any big thing. Just a family hug. The four of us standing up, embracing each other. Mom had named it, and she usually initiated it. It was sort of like a fire drill. I mean in the way it would happen suddenly, announced with no notice, and everyone would have to jump up and follow the routine. It gave me the same sensations as when the fire drill buzzer sounded in school: scared, nervous, overwhelmed and excited all at once.

Elliot and me in the center, Mom and Dad on the outside, we hugged and hugged. This must be what it's like for baby birds in the nest, I thought, when the mother and father birds cover them with their wings. It was the best feeling in the world.

Like a glass of milk as chocolate sauce is pouring into it, a sweet, giddy bubble started to rise up through me. I yelled, "Bundle of Happiness!" in a high, excited voice. Then Elliot yelled it too. Mom sang it, twice, in her goofy opera-singer voice, making everyone laugh. And then Dad shouted it, in his silliest mock-German accent, and I could hear from his voice that he wasn't grumpy anymore. He was really happy, just like me, I could tell. We were a Bundle of Happiness, and we were home.

Rooms Without Windows

MAY 1924

Ah-choo! Ah-choo! Ah-choo!

Gevalt! Three times in a row, and the last set was five. Dusting always does this to her. Yet she does it every day. She cannot abide grime—neither the great balls of fluff that agglomerate on the wood-plank flooring of Mickey's tiny uptown rooms, nor the minute particles that infiltrate her spacious Fifth Avenue home, insinuating themselves against polished surfaces, between parquet tiles, along woodwork, lintels, beams. Vera and dust are constant combatants. And gorgeous days like this are the worst. The sunbeams that shine through the windows spotlight thousands of motes. They seem to taunt her, dancing about, giggling you see, we're still here! Not for long, she thinks, scooting down to slide beneath the piano so she can skim a rag along its exposed underparts.

She bounds back up and grabs the broom. What a mood she's in! What a day lies ahead! She sets the Victrola to full blast and starts sweeping to the beat of her new record. "Down Hearted Blues." Maybe there's something wrong with Vera, how the music zooms her spirits, swivels her hips. The way Bessie Smith sings doesn't make her feel blue at all. Downhearted? Her heart is in her mouth. And soon her mouth will be—okay, now stop that, she tells herself, giving a little shake. Cool off. Or you'll plotz before the day has even begun. This time when the song ends, she decides, she won't turn the needle back to the beginning to play it over again. She really must cool off.

It's all Mickey's fault. As usual. Moving to the music, she sweeps and smiles. He has a knack for—well, what his knack is for besides music who knows, but whatever it is it comes in handy. This record, for example. She'd been fretful as she woke up today. Not sure this whole plan was such a good idea. Since the music started, however, she has found the pulse of the day. Now she's well ahead of schedule. Not calm, true, but it's a good kind of not-calm. The house clean, she will soon start to ready herself.

She wants everything to be perfect for Florence. She must look perfect, smell perfect, taste perfect—she feels a blush rise on her cheeks and thighs—and she wants to be perfectly at her ease. The perfect hostess. Maybe when Florence arrives Vera will turn the record on again. Maybe they'll dance. She wonders if that will turn Flo on. The blush burns anew—honestly, what vulgar thoughts she finds herself thinking lately. That's Mickey's fault too, she decides. What a bad boy he is. How she depends on him.

He knows about them. When Florence had realized she'd been alarmed. Vera had watched her friend's eyes cloud with fear. Over time Flo relaxed. Now she trusts Mickey. For Vera, it is a relief that someone in the family knows. And loves her anyway. He doesn't think she's sick—he's actually told her so. He'd asked her how love can possibly be sick. The way he put it, it sounded so reasonable.

She'd brought it up again this morning. With Peter at the shop, while the boys finished their breakfast, she'd sat Mickey down on the living-room sofa and asked for a way out of the day's plans.

All her doubts had been rising again. Was she crazy, letting him cook up this scheme for Florence and her to steal an afternoon alone? How could it be the right thing, what they were doing? What they would do, finally, today. What kind of depraved mother would send her children off so she can surrender to forbidden feelings? Shouldn't she have been fighting them instead? Shouldn't Mickey have helped her resist?

Eyes on the floor, voice quavery, swallowing down some sour taste, she'd reminded Mickey that what she and Florence want to do is known to be a sin. A crime. What she and Florence are. A sickness.

Mickey rolled his eyes. He asked, "Which one?"

"Which what?"

"Which is it? Sin, crime or sickness?" He pulled a toothpick from his pocket—" And where'd you get this sin business from, anyway? What are you all of a sudden, religious?"—and he started a tussle with his crooked teeth. When he finished he pocketed the pick. He looked at Vera. He dropped the snappy tone. He said quietly that it couldn't be all three, that he was pretty sure it isn't a single one of those awful things. Damned sure that Vera isn't any awful thing. With a wave of his hand he dismissed every doctor, priest and rabbi, every psychologist and schoolmaster—every expert, all the world that would brand her a pervert.

He'd rolled his eyes and waved his hand and pronounced his Sapphist sister decent, upstanding and fit. Then he'd said, "Now come see what I've brought you. This is hot stuff."

In the kitchen they'd found Willy making a big show of waiting for Lenny to finish breakfast. He jiggled his legs against the chair. He twiddled his thumbs. He was whistling, in Lenny's ear, loudly, as his mother and uncle walked in.

"Stop that, Willy," from Vera.

"Well, he's procrastinating." Willy looked over his shoulder to check that his use of a big word was noted. Vera watched him pause, tip his chair, and decide to do it again. "If you ask me," he said, dropping the chair back down and facing Lenny again, "you should be arrested for loitering."

"No one asked you!" Lenny yelped, pointing his spoon at Willy. "And talk English!"

"Ha—that's a riot, you little ignor—"

"Come on, boychik." Mickey ruffled Willy's hair. "Be nice. Let your brother eat."

"But Uncle Mickey, we've got to get going! He'll ruin—we'll miss everything!"

"No, we won't, I promise. It's early yet. You'll get onto all the rides you want to."

Lenny laid down his spoon and turned. "The boats that go around?"

"The boats, and the bumblebees—"

"And the carousel?"

"Certainly, of course the carousel, I guarantee it." Mickey kissed the little one's cheek. "Only do me a favor, Lenny, eat your eggs before your brother explodes."

"Okay."

"And make it snappy!" Willy tipped his chair again. Mickey righted it. He reached toward the chair next to the boy, picked up a sack and pulled out the Bessie Smith recording. Turning to Vera, he said, "I've been meaning to give you this for a while."

She kissed him and tasted sugar. "Mickey, why didn't you have breakfast here? Look," she said, pointing to the boys' dirty plates. "I just made a million eggs."

"I ate first so you shouldn't have to make 2 million."

"Very funny. It wouldn't kill you to have something besides donuts and coffee every morning."

"Yes, mother. Anything else, mother?"

"I suppose not."

Not long after, the three of them had left, Mickey ushering the boys out the door, Vera listening as they shifted from bickering to excitement, their voices echoing down the hall and then up the elevator shaft, laughing, interrupting each other, vying for their uncle's attention, until she heard no more. That was it, then. Everyone off to Palisades Park, across the river in Jersey.

It is to be a grand family Saturday at the amusement park. Mickey, Willy and Lenny are to meet up with Celia and Louie and their two, Estelle and Bernard. Mama will be there too. The boys have been beside themselves with anticipation. It's not only the prospect of riding the terrifying roller coaster with their cousins, but also how they're getting there. Riding with Uncle Mickey in his car, the battered black jalopy he shares with the other fellows in his band, the one they pile their instruments into for gigs uptown, in Brooklyn, Jersey, Philly.

It had been assumed that Florence would be part of the Palisades outing. Mama would have been tickled pink. Vera's spinster friend shares her mother's political inclinations. Sitting and watching the children on the rides, they'd talk, Mama giving Flo the latest news from Russia where a better world's in birth, Flo filling Mama in on fundraising efforts to defend Sacco and Vanzetti. Meanwhile, Vera would sit on Flo's other side and chat with Celia. It would have been a wonderful day, a good time, with her laughing boys and her chattering family and her special friend.

It would not have been enough. What she has of Florence, when she sees her, what they do together, none of it is enough. Not any longer. She only gets Florence when Peter is at work. With Willy and Lenny. After, before. Crowded. Underneath. A stray touch, a finger graze, stolen split seconds, that's all.

Somehow, Mickey understands. He had a brainstorm about the great outing to Palisades Park. At the last minute, Vera would have a headache. An awful one—a migraine. She'd have to bow out. Florence would have to stay with her, sit with her in a darkened room holding a cool cloth to her forehead. Mickey would take the boys by himself.

An hour ago, as Lenny had finally finished eating, when it was time, Vera had had no trouble going pale. Remorse and fear drained the blood from her countenance. She swallowed down a sudden urge to take it back, cancel the plan, say she felt fine. She realized she had been dreading this day as much as dreaming of it. She really did come close to swooning. Dizzy, woozy, gritting her teeth against the work crew drilling behind her eyes, she could only nod as Mickey sat her down, hushed the boys away from their stricken mother and said he'd call Florence. He got off the phone, reported that Flo was on her way and took the boys away.

After they'd left Vera sat a while, until the blood stopped thumping in her ears. Then she rose. Surveyed the room. She'd spied her nemesis—dust—and gotten to work.

Now the record ends, and she lifts the needle arm to close the top of the Victrola. She looks at the clock above the fireplace. It's ten-thirty. An hour from now, Florence will be here. What will they do?

Vera's conscience makes another grab but she slithers out of its grip. Heading to the bathroom, she slips off her clothes and steps into the shower. The hot water pummels her back. Guilt drips away. She gulps the steam into her lungs. They expand.

For blessed hours she and Florence will be alone. And not on a park bench.

In bed. Dampness tints the sheet's cotton roses a darkening hue. Florence lies prone, twisted slightly, facing away. Vera watches the last drops of sweat tiptoe down her friend's back. They fall from her shoulders into the curving arc above her buttocks, then, one by one, like condemned prisoners walking the plank, the liquid beads slide single file across her hip, descend her luscious lowered cheek and plunge onto the sheet.

Vera extends a finger. She touches the spot where the droplets fall. Her nail skims Florence's skin while her fingertip meets the moist sheet. She brings her finger to her mouth. She tastes Florence's sweat, and with it the other, deeper taste still lingering. Reaching forward again, she takes hold of her friend's hip and pulls until Florence is nestled back against her. Vera bends her knees into Flo's. She reaches her arm over Flo's side and feels two hands encircle hers. She leans her face against Flo's neck.

Spoons. They lie skin to skin. No space between them. At last.

"Mmm." Flo's voice jerks Vera awake. She'd dropped off for a minute. Amazing. She hasn't a thought in her head. So peace is possible. She lets out a lazy "mmm" of her own as Florence flips over. Their breasts touch. Vera bites her lip, releases, its corners lift. Flo eyes her for a moment and asks, "What are you smiling about?"

"All the trouble I went to."

"Trouble?"

"Making myself beautiful for you."

"You did." Florence moves a hand along Vera's neck. "You are."

Vera kisses Flo's hand. Holds it against her cheek. "Thank you. But I mean my dress, my shoes. The earrings I picked out especially to please you. My makeup—a little powder applied just so, two subtle circles of rouge. For heaven's sake, you never even noticed my Clara Bow lips. Positively beestung. I must have spent twenty minutes refining them."

"But I did notice."

"You did?"

"Of course."

"Oh come on, you barely looked at me when you got here. You hardly said two words before you—"

"Before I bussed you right where the bee stung you." They laugh. They kiss. Florence leaves her lips there so Vera feels her next words on her mouth. "I'm sorry if I seemed a boor, dearheart. Believe me, I saw how swell you looked. In fact …" She pauses, breathes. "Well, if you want to know the truth, you looked so smart you scared the living daylights out of me."

"You, scared?"

"You'd better believe it. For a second there, I almost turned right around and ran out the door."

"No." Vera laughs again. "Not my brave Florence Nightingale, heroic survivor of a hundred battlefields."

"No, not the hero. Plain old Florence Silvano from Passaic. The schoolteacher. Who saw you and got scared that she was in over her head." Florence pulls her lips away and looks at Vera. "When I looked at you I felt … so much …" She closes her eyes. Vera presses her forehead against Flo's and waits. Her friend's pulse ticks in quickening tempo against her brow. Her friend's short, shallow breaths rustle down Vera's chin. When Flo speaks again her voice trembles. "It felt like too much. Like this— you—might be too much to face." A drop hits Vera's collarbone. She lifts her head. She's never seen Florence cry. Florence's body goes rigid and she presses back against Vera's. "Don't look at me," she whispers. A lasso wraps tight around Vera's heart. Lying silent as Flo's tears soak her neck, she caresses the back of her friend's head with her left hand and moves her right hand in slow, soft strokes along her back, her tush, her thighs, her arms, shoulders. The tears taper off as, limbs loosening, Florence yields to her touch.

Vera presses her palm into the small of Florence's back. Her friend's body ripples into hers. In a supple sliding motion Flo slips downward and takes Vera's nipple into her mouth. Vera breathes in sharply, struggling to maintain control. Easing back up, Florence kisses Vera lightly on the shoulder, the neck, the earlobe, the cheek. She finds Vera's mouth. Soothing, tender, dreamy, they smooch. Flo opens Vera's lips with her tongue. Limbs entwining, their bodies urge into each other.

Vera feels the weight of her friend's body on top of her. She feels Flo everywhere. She is no longer aware of the sunbeams spotlighting the bed, the hot, wet sheet, her own gasping breaths deepening into groans that grow loud, ragged, raw. She feels only Flo, and the fever throwing her open at every point of contact: Flo's hair tickling against the hollow of Vera's hip, Flo's tongue tasting Vera's breast, Flo's fingers feeling their way into—suddenly Florence pulls her head away and looks in Vera's eyes. She says something but Vera can't focus, not with this throbbing all through her. She grasps the back of Flo's head, reaches, bites, jams herself against her. Flo makes a sound as if to speak again but Vera permits no further delay. No words, her finger on Flo's lips says, then it lowers to the wet heat between Flo's legs.

Two o'clock. I guess I shouldn't have wondered what we'd be doing in an hour, Vera thinks.

It has been everything she longed for. Everything she'd forgotten, and feared.

The physicality. Was it like this, so full, with Mary? It did not advertise itself so loudly, she knows that. Not once were they alone. All they could ever do, for five years, was fumble under the covers. They'd moved sparingly, covering each others' mouths, stifling every sound. She'd never realized how it held them back. How limited their love was. Never knew until today. She's surprised she's not mortified at the racket she has made. Wailing, calling out. But she feels no shame. Only wonder. For now she knows how it can be. Love roaring through you—and you, letting it roar out in your own voice!

"Flo." The sound of her own voice speaking softly jars her. She didn't know she was ready to talk.

"Hmm?" Her friend's eyes open. She hugs Vera, who lies enfolded in her arms. Her voice is husky. "How long were we asleep?" She yawns.

"You've been sleeping for almost an hour."

"Not you?"

"No. I've been watching you."

Florence reaches up to the back of her head, pats the place where her bun long ago came unknotted. "I must look a sight."

Vera smiles, kisses her on the cheek and takes her hand. "When you were crying before—"

"Oh, I'm sorry, Vera, I don't know why I got so—"

"No, don't be sorry. I understand."

"You do?"

"I think so. I've cried too. Remember that first night, in Washington Square?" Florence nods against Vera's head. "I've been thinking about it." Florence doesn't say anything. "Flo?" The syllable comes out thin, tentative.

"Mm?"

"Flo?" Vera snuggles in closer.

Florence holds her tighter. "Yes, my love?"

Her love. Lying against her breasts. How long is left of this afternoon? Don't be a fool. "Nothing. I just like saying your name."

Florence laughs a little. They kiss. They lie still a bit longer. Then they rise.

Vera runs a bath. They soak in it together, talking quietly, a low running murmur punctuated by tiny kisses. They wash each other. They step out of the tub and pat each other dry.

Vera swathes Florence in her long satin bathrobe. Florence is too short for it. It drags on the floor. She starts to step out of it but Vera insists, saying, "So I'll wash it," retying the sash around her friend's waist, then standing there holding her fists tight around the knot. She leans her chin against Flo's head. The wet hair against her brings Flo's earlier tears to mind again, and with them the question Vera stopped herself from asking.

We are in love, she thinks. It is beyond denying. They have held each other, kissed each other, only twice. The first night, fully clothed, in darkness, in the park. And today, flesh to flesh, in the sun's rays slanting through her own bedroom windows. The first night there were fast moments of euphoria. Today, extended hours of joy. And yet.

Both times, one or the other has wept. Why do the kisses always begin with tears? This is what she'd wanted to ask Florence. And when will we kiss again? How can we go on until we do?

They stand next to the bed. Vera leans into Florence, hands still holding the front of the robe, head bowed atop her friend's. Flo's arms are around Vera's waist, head against her shoulder. They stand there, holding each other, and rock.

They have to let go soon. They must dress. Maybe Vera will give Flo a bite to eat. Then her friend must leave. They lean into each other, rocking.

"Flo," Vera whispers into her friend's hair. She can't tell if Florence hears her or not. "What are we going to do?"

"Pardon me? What did you say?" Vera twirls the kitchen faucet off and turns toward Peter. She must have heard him wrong. He stands in front of the living-room fireplace with his back to her, hands gripped behind his waist.

"I am going with Wilhelm and Leonard out for the fresh air. We are together walking to the river."

Usually a walk is part of the Sunday evening routine. It's barely ten a.m. Will wonders never cease.

Wait a minute. She has an idea. Her heart speeds up as she dries her hands on the dish towel. She can finish the breakfast dishes later. If this really is what it sounds, a father-and-sons stroll in the summer sun, maybe there will be time for her to take a walk too. To Essex Street, maybe. To Flo.

She'll need a fast shower first. Rinse off all this shvitz. The heat of the day hasn't even hit and already the air in the apartment is heavy, thick. That's okay. She can be ready in no time. She steps out of the kitchen and turns into the hallway, toward the boys' room.

"Where are you going, Vera?" Odd question. To help the boys get dressed, she tells Peter. "There is no need of that. I have already laid out their clothing. Wilhelm can aid Leonard to put it on." What has come over him? Whatever it is, she's glad. Soon Flo. Alone. An ache of anticipation runs through her. She heads toward her bedroom. "Please just a moment, Vera." His voice sounds peculiar. The words clipped as usual but the timbre a little off.

"Yes, what is it, Peter?" Oh, of course. "Would you like me to make you some sandwiches?"

"No, this is not necessary." He turns to face her. His expression sends a warning tingle down her craw. "Please come into my office." It is barely more than an alcove, the little space off the living room with his desk and shelves of accounting records. This is where Peter usually spends Sunday afternoons, going over the stores' books for the previous week. He turns his back on her and moves into the doorless room. "I have something I must show you." In a low tone, as if he doesn't want the boys to hear.

He stands by the desk. Upright. In a business suit as always. Every day a perfectly folded bow tie, matching handkerchief, white collar that she has starched to his specifications. He gestures to her to join him, pulling back the desk chair so she can sit.

He has asked her to stay out of his office. Now he wants her at his desk? Something is wrong.

She edges onto the chair. He stands beside her, against the desk. One of its drawers rattles as his knee jiggles against it. He opens the drawer. He pulls out a sheaf of papers. Why do his fingers tremble? The pages titter against each other. He drops them onto the desk in front of her, lifting his hand quickly as if from flame.

A dozen or more scattered sheets, not the tidy stack this desktop expects. They seem heavy. Weighted down with words, some typed, some crowded with Peter's neat handwriting. On the top leaf she makes out the doctor's name, Eduard Dunda. His stationery. Is Peter sick? She tries to swallow. She starts to ask, "What is—" but just then he clears his throat and backs out of the office.

Vera hears his tread on the living room floor. She listens to him pace the length of the room, once, twice. Then he is back, standing behind her chair.

She has the feeling she should sit very still. She stares straight ahead. She hears a muscle twitching under Peter's collar. Is that possible?

She sweats. This office is the hottest spot in the apartment. Cut off, a tiny niche with no windows, no breeze. Instinct: fling the pages in his face and flee.

"Vera."

She jerks. "Yes?" She's bitten her lip. She tastes iron.

"I take Wilhelm and Leonard out now. Please read these matters. This evening—"

"Why are you whispering, Poppy?" Suddenly Willy is at her side. "Is it a secret? Momma, is it a surprise?" He leans against Vera, his hot little body coiled for fun. "Because I'm all ready to go, Lenny too, let's go, let's go, come on."

He tugs his mother's arm. Vera kisses his forehead. She reaches to hug him, but Peter pulls her child away from her.

Her husband's voice is back to its usual volume. "This is good. I too am ready. Let us go. We shall watch the boats sail on the river."

"But the surprise, Poppy? The secret?"

"There is no surprise, Wilhelm."

"Momma?"

"Come along, Wilhelm." Quick, sharp, a trigger being cocked. "Your mother also is not speaking of surprises. Get Leonard. Meet me at the front door." Willy darts back for his brother. Vera feels empty air where he stood. Despite the sweat on her neck, she shivers when Peter whispers again. "This evening, when the boys sleep, we will speak of these things. Kindly be prepared." Then he's gone, without the usual gentle shoulder squeeze.

At first she is perplexed. Peter knows she doesn't read German. If he has something important for her to review, why give it to her in a language she cannot fathom?

She strains to understand. Peter must be ill. Apparently he has consulted Dr. Dunda. A Hungarian Jew, Dunda trained in Berlin. He is fluent in German, as is any doctor who wants to keep up with advances in science. Perhaps he had his clerk use a typewriting machine to reproduce passages from medical journal articles. She glances at the handwritten pages and nods to herself. At least those are in English. Peter must have translated the German passages, or taken notes directly from others in English.

He is unwell, she tells herself, and too reserved to present the facts to her directly. How like him, dear man. She clasps her hands together and thrusts them forward, at the same time straightening her legs and stretching them out in front of her, releasing some of the tension that has held her body tight since he called her from the kitchen. She sighs, swallowing down the guilt that accompanies her sense of relief. Her husband is sick, perhaps very sick: she shouldn't experience this realization as a reprieve.

I'll put the pages in some sort of sequence, she decides. That way I can read them through and then we'll know what we're facing.

Once they're in order, she runs her eye along the first two pages. Typed on Dr. Dunda's letterhead, a list of titles and authors. Journal citations, she assumes. Articles on Peter's mysterious syndrome. She glances at the authors' names. They mean nothing to her. Westphal. Moll. Montegazza, an Italian. And Charcot—French, this one. Then more Germans. Von Notthafft, von Krafft-Ebing. The names blur into each other. Ulrichs, Magnan, Adler, Hirschfeld, Braunschweig, Freud, Sadger, Stekel.

Wait. She looks back. The famous Dr. Freud? Why would Dunda refer Peter to his writings?

She turns to the first page again. This time she looks at the titles rather than authors. Starting to feel queasy, stalling, expecting the German to be impenetrable. It is not, entirely. *Die Contrare Sexualempfindung.* Some are in Latin. *Psychopathia Sexualis.*

She is getting the drift. The sheet shakes in her hand, as it did in Peter's. She drops it, as Peter did.

She forces herself to go on. Lifting the pages again, she turns to Peter's notes. She skims. Looks away, then again pushes her attention back to the papers. The words.

Oh god. The words do not diagnose Peter. The pages are a study of his wife's pathology. She is reading about her own diseased self.

So many terms. She had not known. She is an Urningin, elsewhere an Urnind, Uraniad. Unwomanish woman. Intersex. Invert. Homosexual. Tribadist.

She is tainted. Congenitally depraved. Hereditary degeneracy. So say the esteemed doctors of Vienna, Berlin. Neuropathic disorder.

Peter has marshaled the words and they march across the pages like the numberless troops of an unconquerable army.

Vera and Peter sit at the kitchen table, teacups in front of each.

It is too hot for tea, she thinks. She takes a sip. It singes her throat. She swallows several times then sips again.

The soapy smell on her hands from the boys' bath. Peter's fingers tapping on the tabletop. Sweat above her lip.

She can't wait forever. "I have read your notes," she says.

"Pardon me? Speak up, Vera."

"I said I read it."

"Ah. All of it you have read?"

"All of it."

"Therefore you understand my predicament." Low in her body a pain erupts. She shifts in the chair. "Please respond to me, Vera. I have no wish to prolong this."

The air is soupy. It is a miserable struggle to see through it. "I don't know what to say, Peter."

"I would like you to address this situation. I am concerned to act correctly. For this I must allow you to speak your piece."

"My piece?" All she can seem to do is echo him, feeble-voiced, clenching against the growing pain low in her gut.

"I had hoped not to have to be crude, Vera. You are a refined woman, sensitive, as indeed I now understand is not unusual in these cases. And I care for you." He pauses, again, staring down at his teacup. He looks up, past her left shoulder. "Very well. I will present you with my assessment."

Stabbing, twisting, something tears in her lower abdomen. She jumps up, runs out of the kitchen and into the bathroom.

How did he know? What has he seen? She hadn't thought she'd been so transparent. She has been a fool. Mistaking his reserve— his fear, his pain, confusion, she now sees—for obliviousness.

Hunched on the toilet, she groans. He knows. He sees. What happens now?

*

"It does not matter, Vera. None of these details is germane, you must understand this. It does not matter if it was once only, an accident, somehow, or a hundred times with a hundred accidents of nature like yourself." She gasps, staring at him and his drumming fingers. He has never been cruel. Look what I've done to you, she thinks. He returns her look, gazing directly at her finally, and sighs. "Forgive me. I do not wish to speak harshly." He pauses again, picks up the papers from his lap, shuffles through them. "Frankly, however, this is the crux of the matter. It is not a question of fault, not a question of frequency—"

"Peter, please, I didn't intend, and I do not intend, I assure you—" What is she saying? That she will never see Florence again?

"It is not a matter of intention, not at all, Vera, this is what I explain to you. Do you intend to look again at your friend in the way I have seen, the way I have waited and wished for you to look at me? To whisper her name in your sleep again?"

"I—what—"

"Yes, often, in the morning as I dress and you are yet in bed, Vera. Years ago it was my cousin Mary's name, but I forgave you, I made allowances for your grief, I instructed myself to be patient. In time, I believed, you would turn to me."

"Oh, Peter—"

"Now it has been for some time another name, and I have listened to you speak it for too long, and I see her name, you write her name over and over, yes this is correct that I have looked in your night table drawer, the fine stationery I bought you, ruined, all over it her name. I have also reports, this is correct, Franco, you think he cannot use a little extra, he won't take five dollars from me he should do a favor before he starts his shift, watch you, follow, see where you go in the afternoons, you think he doesn't tell me, always to the schoolyard, to her, always. You think I am so foolish, you think I never know all these things?" Peter's voice has risen. He's breathing hard. He stops, squeezes his eyes shut, takes a long, deep breath. He reopens his eyes and when he speaks again it is with an evident effort at control. "No matter. I am ...

I had hoped it would not … but now I understand that we must face facts. I understand now that it is in a way not your fault. Not a matter of intention. Even if you have an iron will you cannot control this disease." He pauses again, briefly. "Yet still, I thought, perhaps there is a cure. But Dunda shows me, no. About causes there are differences. Is it an abnormality of the brain, or a failure of psychic differentiation? Learned men disagree. Much research remains until complete answers are found. But on one thing there is unanimity, or as near to it as there ever is in science. This I must reiterate. The experts agree, Vera: You cannot change. I am sorry to say it, believe me, for you are my wife, the mother of my sons, but I must face the facts. What you are, you are."

What I am. The humid air swirls. She closes her eyes to stop the spinning. She pictures herself with Flo and the boys on Delancey. From where did Franco watch? How often? What did he see? A look, a touch? Crazily, she thinks of the lost child Dorothy clicking her heels three times in Willy's book *The Wonderful Wizard of Oz*. What I am. I am. What I am, I am. What I am, I am.

A mistake of nature. But I am an intelligent person. A lover of art and literature, of the theater. A mother, a daughter. I am— there's more, I know it, there's got to be more to me than a genetic defect, an anomaly. I am better than this, I swear I am. I will tell Peter. I will persuade him. He need take no action. He need only let me … let me …

Vera opens her eyes. Peter is leafing through the pages. Preparing the rest of his presentation. Making an obvious effort to stay calm. An unexpected shaft of anger spears her. She straightens in the chair. Let me abase myself. I suppose that is what I am supposed to do next. Humble myself before you and beg forgiveness. For love. Forgive me, Mr. Steiner, forgive me for loving someone who is a finer person than either of us.

A person. Just people, Flo and me, that's what Mickey thinks, and George and Wally too, she reminds herself. She looks at Peter. Let us be, she pleads with her eyes. But he doesn't meet them. Still she stares. Please, please, why can't you let us be?

"Peter." Her voice, back to normal volume, even, calm, surprises them both. Now he looks at her.

"Yes, Vera. Please say what you wish."

"I will." She takes a deep breath, then goes on. "I can't argue with your experts, Peter. I'm no doctor. But I don't believe they are as fully agreed as you make them out to be." He raises his eyebrows. "If I understand your notes correctly, Dr. Havelock Ellis does not consider inversion to be a disease. He sees no need of treatment."

Peter waves his hand as if wiping away a cobweb. "Immaterial," he says.

"Why?"

"Please proceed," he says, pursing his lips and peering at her. "I will explain it all when you conclude."

"Well, all right, then there's Dr. Hirschfeld." Peter snorts. She hurries on. "He says inversion is a natural aspect of—of human feelings."

"Anything else?"

She has never heard this tone from him. She is being dismissed. Anger spurts up her spine. She flashes on Flo's face, her lips, the tingly touch of her fingertips. She rises. "Yes, Peter." She lunges toward him over the table, grabs the papers from his lap. She rifles through them until she finds the one she's looking for. Straightening back up, she remains standing. She can't stop the sheet from flapping in her shaking hands so she concentrates on keeping her voice clear and steady. "Dr. Freud. I believe he is now recognized as the world's foremost expert on human psychology." Peter nods, a tight little smile disfiguring his face. "Well then, your Dr. Freud—"

"Freud says it is impossible—" Peter jumps up and grabs the page out of Vera's hands. Voice rising, he waves it in her face—"it is impossible, says Dr. Freud, impossible to convert, to cure, to change—"

"But—"

"Because it cannot be done. You cannot overcome this, Vera. I am patient no longer. It does not matter whether it is only a neurosis caused by your envy of my—or your neurotic wish to marry your mother—"

"What on earth—"

"Yes, this is the benign explanation, but the explanation does not matter." His voice lowers into a snarl. "You can choose any one you like. Yes, even Hirschfeld's, a renowned degenerate himself but I do not care, you like his account, fine, take his account." Is he going to spit at her? "The point is," and he sneers, as with a flourish he tears the page into pieces, letting them drop onto the table, "you are as you are. On this everyone agrees. There is nothing I could have done. This Dunda has explained to me." Abruptly he sits. The chair slides backward at the impact. Vera winces as she hears it scratch the linoleum. He pauses for a moment as his breath slows. When at last he speaks again, head down, it is in a whisper. "You are as you are, Vera. And as you are, you will not raise my sons."

Vera doesn't like rooms without windows. She doesn't realize she's asleep, that this square space in the dream is a prison cell, and she wonders why Celia is not here. Surely Celia has heard what is happening to her; why no word from her at all? And Sol? In Celia's absence he could have come. Celia doesn't speak to him since he went over to the other side. He's a boss now, an owner, a *macher* in the garment district here in Manhattan. Mama is cool to him but she hasn't broken completely because she wants to see her grandchildren. Where is he? Why doesn't he offer some sort of help?

It's like one of those books by Agatha Christie. The case of the shrinking family. Hercule Poirot she's not, but this is no great mystery.

At least she still has Mama, who has rallied behind her, not merely in this dream but in real life. Vera knows she shouldn't be surprised that the old red, the quoter of Marx, reader of Engels, rejecter of bourgeois norms, is not scandalized by her daughter's Sapphism. Still, theory is one thing and practice another, as Papa used to say, so Vera had expected the worst. After Peter had confronted her last week, after he'd laid down the law as to how she would be permitted to proceed, she had shrunk from telling Mama. She pressed Mickey to be her surrogate. Two days after the scene with Peter, Mama showed up at her daughter's door and gathered her into her arms. It stunned the sobs out of Vera. She cried for a long time. Mama never let go. Afterward, sitting with glasses of tea in the kitchen, hoping Lenny would keep amusing himself in his room with the toy truck Mama had brought, they talked.

Mama has always known. "A thousand times I've kicked myself, Veraleh, for letting you marry him. You had just lost Mary. You weren't thinking straight."

Vera's lips shaped a small smile. "You tried to make me wait."

"A bissel, but I held back. You didn't want I should interfere. And you thought I didn't know about you and Mary." Vera winced at the old pain. "You didn't want me to know, so all right, I thought, I don't know. I won't advise her not to make any decisions until the grief eases up. You went ahead like a meshugeneh. And I let you. Bubbeleh, I'm sorry."

"Well—"

"You're right, well at least I got two gorgeous grandsons out of it." At Vera's grimace Mama had said, "Veraleh." Held steady by her mother's dark eyes, by the bottomless depths beneath the heavy lids, Vera had listened. "Veraleh, they are still your children. Peter can't change that."

But here, in the dream, he already has. This windowless room, Vera now understands, is a prison cell. Four walls, and they enclose—nothing. Only Vera, and barely enough stale air to sustain breath. Suddenly, the nightmare's cell door flies open. Dark-suited men surround her. "Come with us," they say, and now she is in a courtroom. On trial. She sits, hanging her head as Dr. Eduard Dunda stands before the jury box holding up an X-ray image of Vera's abdominal cavity. The jurors gasp, some turning away from the sight of the twisted creatures writhing in her viscera. The X-rays emit a foul odor. The jurors—oh god, Celia among them—cover their mouths in disgust. Their eyes dart between Vera and the horrid images that reveal what she holds inside. The verdict is preordained. Guilty. Guilty. Guilty. The men drag her down a long, dark hallway. From behind doors on either side she hears Willy's voice, and Lenny's. "Momma! Momma!" She grabs at doorknobs but the men slap her hands away. They throw her back into her cell. They slam the door.

Vera comes abruptly awake as the apartment door slams shut behind Peter, entering with several workmen. As he directs them toward the little cluster of cartons and luggage in front of the fireplace, she rises from the rocker where she'd drifted off as she watched Fifth Avenue.

Peter bustles about, supervising the movers. He doesn't look at Vera. She stands still. She tries not to think and realizes it isn't difficult at all.

In fact, she finds, she is calm. She yawns. She'd like to go back to sleep. That's how she'll get through this afternoon: stay focused on the bed waiting in her new home.

You can't fight City Hall. Mama, Mickey, Flo all wanted her to try. But Vera knew that Peter—the world—had erected walls too high for her to scale. She faces solitary confinement. A life sentence. She can't think about that now. All she can think is that soon the turmoil will end. Soon she finally can rest.

Exile

Now that her money has run out, Vera stops searching. No more bus trips to Muskegon or Port Huron. No weekends in Ann Arbor, staying at the Y for two days prowling the campus, showing Willy's picture, checking bulletin boards, trying to catch the dean of students who has become adept at avoiding her visits.

No more lunch-hour stops at the Free Press and News buildings to place another personal ad. If anyone in Detroit has seen Willy these last four months there's no chance now to find out.

Reluctantly, she faces facts. The pursuit, the tracking of Willy's movements from point A to point B, is over, exhausted along with her funds. There are no options. She knows it. She stops.

She cannot call off her heart, however. She is so used to it, this quest, that sometimes she thinks it has infected the organ itself. Lying in bed nights her pulse beats out their names. Wil-ly. Len-ny. Wil-ly. Her boys in her veins coursing like a fever.

Vera stands at her little desk tapping her foot. She glances out the narrow attic window at the sun, slowly lowering in the early evening sky, then back at the desk with its neat stack of papers and single snapshot tacked to the wall. Mother and sons. So long ago.

She has been seeking them, one way or another, for seventeen years. She never missed a visit, never skimped an allotted minute. Four o'clock to six o'clock the third Sunday. Every month for fourteen years, until Willy entered the University of Michigan three years ago.

Tote it up, then. The measure of her motherhood: 348 hours. The sum total since her exile began.

That includes five months subtracted from 1930—ten precious hours Peter stole when he moved west without warning, uprooting the boys and joining forces with his brother Ernest in a discount jewelry business after the stock market crash cramped the style of his fershtinkeneh-rich customers in New York. He jerked Willy and Lenny away, put six hundred miles between mother and children, and it took her five panicky months, working extra shifts in the fourth-floor filing room at Carl Fischer's sheet-music company on Cooper Square, borrowing, scrimping until she had pulled together the money and made the arrangements and managed to follow them to this city of auto plants and alleyways. Perpetual cloud cover, abounding lack of grace. Christ what a hard-muscled, uncultured numbskull of a place. But she came. And she stays, day after dismal Detroit day.

She has tried to keep clear sight of her boys. She has concentrated so hard that sometimes she couldn't see anything else. But her vigilance has made no difference. Her sons have been like passengers on a fast-moving train, rushing from her as she stared, arms outstretched, left behind. As they grew, Willy and Lenny shrank further and further from her. Until there she stood, lone figure by the tracks, straining to see, their faces in the window diminishing to pinpoints as they sped away.

Vera thinks back to the April afternoon when Willy's roommate had called Peter and Peter had called her to report that the brilliant physics student had gone missing just before taking his junior year final exams. She was shocked, and frightened, and she was horrified as Peter ticked off the possibilities—abduction, murder, he didn't even consider that this was Willy's own doing, he expected ransom calls, a bloody trail, he was after all a prosperous man—she shook as the scope of the thing revealed itself. Yet instinct told her that Willy's vanishing act was of his own volition. Sudden? No, it was more like the grand finale to the magician's trick where the assistant fades in stages, first her legs, then her torso, one arm, then the other, until only her ripe red smile hangs disembodied in the air, then—whoosh!—it's gone too.

Sometimes, convinced he is alive and well and basking in his accomplishment, she thinks she ought to just sit back and applaud. Bravo, Willy, she should shout. Well done! It took you and your father a while, but you've managed the trick now. You're out of range. I can't get to you. Can't touch you. Not even the quick tousle of your black curls you used to grudgingly allow me on our monthly visits.

Still I can't stop dreaming of caressing those curls, stroking the skin on your shoulder. Is it still as soft and smooth as when you were a baby? When I was your mother?

On the ground, however, the search is over. Everything she has is spent. She will do as Lenny suggests. She will suspend the quest.

"W-w-wait t-t-till he g-gets in t-t-touch, M-m-m-a," Lenny had advised last week. "I'm sure h-h-he's all r-r-ight." She'd nodded, relishing the feel of him standing beside her at the bus stop, savoring this morning's fading after-shave scent layered atop his lifelong Lenny smell. Wondering at her luck, at least with this one.

Maybe he forgives her in a way Willy won't, maybe he forgets how he felt in a way Willy can't—all Vera knows is that lately, since her younger son moved out of his father's house and into a small apartment with three fellow Wayne University students, he has allowed her a closer approach. He meets her for lunch sometimes before a class, or after work she walks with him to the library. Little talks as they munch or stroll. Sometimes he even asks her advice, about a report or book. She can't believe her good fortune—has to clench her fists to keep from clutching at him, grabbing his hand, refusing to release—can't believe he is here, beside her, the two of them appearing for all the world as though they are an ordinary pair, middle-aged mother, college-man son.

Her heart tightens with joy at his little confidences— unreasonable professors, charming coeds—but the tortured staccato of Lenny's stutter stabs. Vera remembers his fast, free chatter as a tyke, contrasts it with the effort he now expends to express himself, and yearns to give him back his early ease. She can't replace what she herself erased.

"L-l-let it g-go, M-m-ma," he'd said last week. Wait for Willy and, you'll see, he'll turn up soon. A postcard from, who knows, Chicago, or New Orleans. Even if he doesn't write, Lenny said, give up. You won't find him if he doesn't want you to. Stop.

She won't make any more phone calls. Gussie and Ben are too kind-hearted to charge her for them, but with what they bring in from the little corner grocery downstairs Vera knows they can't afford to subsidize her daily calls to Peter. Useless, frustrating, infuriating calls. Her ex-husband acts as though she has nothing to do with it, no right to know if there's any news of their son.

So it is to be another solitary evening here at home. Home. After all this time she still can't think of the hot little attic room that way. This is temporary, Vera had assured herself when she first moved in, and she still clings to the designation.

When she arrived here seventeen years ago she thought of the Schumachers' attic as a sort of emergency shelter to which she'd had to evacuate after a terrible storm. And wasn't Peter's whole stunt, whisking the boys to Detroit, like a tornado? A vortex that rages through and leaves your life a flattened, featureless landscape. A second squall, after she'd barely survived the first. Well, she landed here, and musty cell though it is she is grateful. The room is clean and cheap and it came to her through the good graces of none other than Gussie Lovdozo, Celia's poor-as-a-dormouse, meek-as-a-lamb best friend from the old days in Passaic.

Gussie, who Vera and Mary used to find such a figure of fun for her greenhorn accent, her old shoes full of holes, her perpetual good nature. So many years later, the tables are turned. Vera's the charity case. Begging at Gussie's table—Gussie Schumacher now. In dreary Detroit. On Dexter Boulevard. A boarder in the house above the deli Gussie and her husband Ben own and run.

Another night in the attic, then, without even the futile busy-work of the Willy search's calls and letters. Vera resumes her foot-tapping. She picks up a pack of cigarettes and shakes one out. She pauses before reaching for her lighter and breathes in deeply, salivating at the rich smells of Gussie's cooking rising through the floor vent. It's not as though she's a prisoner up here. Not as though the Schumachers wouldn't love for her to sit and eat and shmooze with them around their kitchen table. They've made that clear. Invited her to join them many times over the years. Really, they couldn't be more gracious.

But Vera cannot. She is not part of their happy little family circle. She has her own family, goddamn it. Her sons. No matter how hard Peter has tried to erase her from their lives like a misplaced digit in an otherwise perfect equation. Why should she take part in some sham? Why can't she live her own life, a complete life, like normal people?

Why is there never an answer to that, and why can she never stop asking?

She steps to the window and cranks open the louvers, inviting in the evening air. She lights her cigarette, looks down at the street. The scent of newly mown grass pushes past the kitchen aromas and tobacco. For an instant she's back … Florence … their single afternoon in the Fifth Avenue bedroom. Vera bites her lip, brushes a wisp of hair out of her eyes, sighs.

As she watches out the window Gussie comes down the porch steps, cups her hands to her mouth and calls the girls in for dinner. Soon they appear, rowdy Rosie racing around the corner, red curls flying about her face, barking orders back to pudgy, pale Bud who, as usual, lags behind. Bud comes skipping along, a dreamy smile on her face and a clutch of dandelions in her hand. She reminds Vera a little of herself at that age, while Rose is like Mickey when he owned the streets of Passaic. Rose and Bud. Can you imagine anything more ludicrous? Vera cannot fathom what Gussie was thinking when she named her twins. Really, she is a lovely woman, no twit, yet in some ways a hopeless hick. It's as if she just got off the boat from Lithuania yesterday instead of forty years ago. And still with that embarrassingly thick accent. Honestly. Well, at least her older girl, Ruby, seems to have plenty on the ball. A twenty-one-year-old graduate student in drama at Wayne State—a grown woman, Vera realizes, which brings home how her years in the attic add up—Ruby is probably either burrowed studying in the bedroom she shares with her eleven-year-old sisters or down in the store helping her father.

The twins rush up the walk, headed, no doubt, toward one of their gushing, overblown, slovenly embraces with Gussie. Vera quickly closes the window and turns away. She leans her back against the window frame and smokes. She reaches over to the night table and turns on the radio to drown out the Schumacher noise as Gussie, Rose and Bud come piling into the house, the crash of silverware accompanying the girls' jabbering laughter as they set the table. Vera savors her cigarette and tries to shut out everything but the sounds of Duke Ellington riding the A train.

Closing her eyes, she sways slightly, still leaning lightly against the window frame. The music makes her think of Mickey, of home, for the second time tonight. She wonders where her brother is. He tries to keep her informed of his schedule but she loses track of where he's playing.

When she finishes her cigarette, Vera goes in to her little bathroom to wash her hands before dinner. She looks at her face in the mirror. She hadn't realized she'd been crying. That's how used to it I am, she thinks. Good lord. Pretty soon I'll be weeping in public. I've got to snap out of it. She stares at her reflection for a beat, then sticks her tongue out. She turns on the faucet, fills the sink with cold water and dunks her face in.

Bud will be bringing her dinner soon. She's surprised at how the thought cheers her. The kid dotes on her. Finds Vera glamorous or something. Why disappoint her? After she dries her face and hands, Vera walks across the room and opens her pocketbook, which she'd flung on the bed when she got in after work. She takes out her lipstick and goes back into the bathroom. Peering at her face again, she applies the lipstick, then blots her lips with a square of toilet paper. A little powder, too? No, let's not get carried away here.

Vera recognizes the shy knock, goes to the door and opens it for the child. Bud grins up at her. "It's chicken paprikash," she says. "Your favorite." Vera smiles, takes the plate and puts it on her desk. She turns back to Bud, who hands her a napkin, knife and fork, says, "I'll go back for your seltzer."

"And ask your mother if you can bring your dinner up and eat with me."

What the hell did she just say? Vera has no idea where that came from. Too late now. Bud beams with pleasure, nods her head vigorously, and shoots out the door and down the stairs.

"You ask her. If you're so nosy about it."

"I would, but you're the one she—"

Children's voices, lighthearted squabbling. Vera smiles in her sleep.

"I said no." Still asleep, Vera tenses at the new tone.

"Please? Come on, she likes you better."

Oh, that's Lenny, then, in the dream. Curled up in a corner, every third Sunday, convinced Willy is their mother's favorite. She grits her teeth.

Voices rise through the vent, entering the attic from the kitchen two floors below, pulling her awake. She resists, watching the dream-Lenny unfurl. He's tall, loose-limbed. He grins. Brilliantined brown curls spill across his forehead. Her baby nearly a man now. Safe after all. But the smile— something wrong with his mouth when he opens it to speak— gaps between rotting teeth, red gash of flapping scabs for a tongue—she can't hear him. Behind him, a shadow. Where is Willy? Her baby boy mute, her first born lost.

Exile   179

"She is not mean."

Children's voices draw her up from the old ache. Pushing against the pain in her jaw joints, her fingers rub her awake.

"Okay, okay, maybe not mean exactly, but she's mad all the time. I'm scared of her."

It's Gussie's girls, she realizes now. Her dream made them Willy and Lenny, but these are not her children. She opens her eyes, blinks at the ceiling cracks white against the morning gloom.

"Well, you're just a scaredy-cat—"

"Oh yeah? Everybody knows you're the big baby. Buddy Baloneyhead!"

"At least I'm smart enough to know that Tanteh Vera isn't mad. She's just sad. Why can't you tell the difference?" Vera feels a queer pull in her chest. She sits up, swivels, touches her feet to the floor, feels for her slippers, steps into them. Carefully, noiselessly, ears cocked. Reaching for the bedpost, she puts on her bathrobe. The girls' voices come through clearly. She pictures Bud peering at her twin who sits in insulted silence. "What? Why aren't you saying anything? Rosie? What?"

"I don't know what I'm supposed to say since I'm too dumb to know the difference between mad and sad."

"I—I didn't—"

"Well, isn't that what you said?"

Ten minutes older, yet Rose is years ahead. Poor Bud. Vera stifles the urge to run downstairs, get a look at the girls' faces. Tell the truth, she chides herself. It's Bud you want to see—how she lights up when you enter the room.

She's missed something. Their voices lowered for a minute there. Now a third person has entered the conversation. A young woman: "You're sure you want my opinion?"

"Yes, please!" Loudly, in unison.

"Okay then. My opinion is that, as usual, you're both right. Hey—stop with the groaning, Roseleh. I mean it, you both have a valid position here. Buddy, I agree with you that Mrs. Steiner is sad." A pause. "However, Buddeleh, I also agree with Rosie.

Maybe it's not such a great idea to ask her about her sons."

"No, Ruby, I didn't say we shouldn't ask her. I only said I shouldn't ask her. Bud should, because she won't get mad at Bud."

"I don't think she'd get mad at anyone. But I think she might get sad."

"Even sadder? You think so?" Bud's voice small. Vera strains to hear, chest taut again.

"Yes, I think so. And you don't want to make her even sadder, do you?"

Vera can't hear Bud's answer but she can picture her, a shadow falling across that little potato face, appalled at the thought that she might cause her upstairs friend pain.

Tanteh Vera. Sad aunt in the attic.

In an abrupt rush to fill her lungs, she lunges for the pack of cigarettes on the nightstand, grabs a fag, lights it. She sucks in a deep draft of smoke. Sitting on the edge of the bed, hands flat against the mattress, cigarette tight between flexed fingers, she taps her foot on the linoleum and holds the smoke inside. She lets it possess her.

It had suddenly felt so close in here. Stifling. Better now. She releases the smoke into the air, watching a thin line ease out of her. Satisfied, she picks a fleck of tobacco from her lip, stands, takes a shorter drag, releases it. She goes to the window and cranks it open. It's drizzling. That explains why the kids are still inside this Saturday morning. She tilts her head back. Purple bruises smear the sky. The babble downstairs has grown louder again, Gussie and Ben have joined in, they're on to other topics. Vera smokes and watches the rain.

"Where are your folks?"

"They're both in the store, Mrs. Steiner. Do you need anything?"

"No, just wondering. And please, Ruby, enough already with this 'Mrs. Steiner' business. I know you're too old to call me auntie anymore. So make it Vera."

Sitting at the kitchen table, Ruby looks up from her notebook and smiles. "Well, I'll try."

"Good."

"Oh—Ma said to tell you there's a fresh pumpernickel in the breadbox. And she made gefilte fish. She said you should help yourself."

"Thank you. That'll be lunch. I think I'll just make some coffee for now." Vera steps to the sink, fills the percolator with water. "And the twins? I heard their voices. Thought they'd be down here."

Ruby's cheeks go pink. She drops her pencil and lifts her eyes toward Vera. "Oh gee, did they wake you? I should have sent them to the bedroom sooner. I had to run them out of here so I could get some studying done—I needed the table to work at— they get so noisy—I'm sorry—we were thoughtless—"

"No, no, please, Ruby, relax."

Vera takes the can of coffee out of the icebox. She measures a scoop into the metal filter, replaces the top of the percolator, sets it onto the burner, lights a match, turns on the gas. The flame rises. She blows out the match. She leans back against the kitchen counter, facing Ruby.

The girl fiddles with her pencil, flipping it back and forth, watching her fingers. Vera hears steady drizzle from the open window behind her. A misty hint of it brushes her neck. She shivers. Yet it's hot. More like steam. No relief. She listens to the rain dribble down a drainpipe, piddle into the broken pave- ment of the driveway. She smells worms. She wishes the coffee would start to perk. She must have left her cigarettes upstairs. Summer is such a slow season here.

Ruby has stopped fidgeting. Vera regards her. "I appreciate your courtesy, Ruby, but you really don't have to start treating me like a guest."

"No, I know, but—you're not—"

"I know I'm not family, but—"

"Oh no, Mrs.—Vera—that's not what I mean at all. Sure you are—family, or practically. That's just it. You're so much a part of us that I'm afraid we crowd you too much. I started thinking about it because lately, this place has started to feel so crowded to me, I mean sometimes I think I'll just go nuts if I don't find a spot to be alone, and then there's you, cooped up in that attic room, and Buddy always barging in on you or Rosie making a commotion so you can't sleep, and it dawned on me that maybe a loud, messy family spilling over onto you during your precious hours when you're not at work isn't what you need. So I told everybody to start being more considerate of you."

"You what? Then that's why—"

"That's what Buddy and Rosie were arguing about before. I'm an idiot. Or maybe it's hopeless with this crew. I mean, I try to get them to take more care and what happens but— oh, brother. Look, I'm sorry. I did mean well."

"I know you did. I'm not surprised. You've always been a sweet girl." Vera smiles, but she's suddenly uncomfortable. She turns toward the stove, fusses with the percolater for a moment before facing Ruby again. The girl is smiling back at her, an embarrassed blush spreading just beneath her strawberry-blonde hairline.

Vera nearly jumps at the shock of pleasure that pumps through her. Something sharp in this one's eyes, something alive.

Vera sits in the straight-backed chair at her desk sipping from her second cup of coffee. The ashtray in front of her is already half-filled with butts. Bud made it for her in school. Vera touches the cool, lumpy clay. It's rough, unglazed, marked with little depressions where the child tried and failed to smooth the edges. Bud's fingerprints like an abstract design. It should be named, Vera thinks with a small smile, this masterpiece. Study in Gray.

Like this day. The rain has picked up. It drums against the attic roof. She drums her fingers against the desk in unconscious rhythm. She takes another drink of coffee.

Ruby. Not the type you notice right off. Still, she's grown up to be a good-looking gal. She seems soft—wisps of hair framing her face, zaftig form contained in quiet clothes—but that is an illusion, Vera thinks. She suspects there is steel underneath.

She's a good girl, her mama's pride and joy. For ten years an only child. All-A student. And such a help in the deli after school. Then, out of the blue, the twins. They came early, they were sickly, it was hard. What would I have done without my Rubeleh, Gussie often says. A living doll how she helped with the babies. Never jealous of the lost attention. So mature. And practical too. Gussie was overwhelmed—impossible to care for Rose and Bud and follow all the religious laws—so Ruby went to Ben. She persuaded her father, and since then no more kosher kitchen.

A modern girl. And a scholar. When she was accepted into graduate school last year, oy how Gussie kvelled. "The first in the family to go to college, we were so proud, that was good enough, you think? But not for this one. She wants her master's degree." Gussie blushed, and Vera was amused at how she was embarrassed to brag but couldn't stop. "Her master's yet, can you believe it, Veraleh?" Gussie the only one left who still calls her that. "To tell you the truth, I'm not so sure what it is, even. But she's so smart, and she wants it, and such a good girl, why shouldn't she? She works for every penny, believe me. Whatever she wants to do, it's all right by me."

Vera drinks the last of the coffee. She glances out the window. Still with the rain. She wonders if it's wet where Willy is. Whether he has an umbrella. She shakes the last cigarette out of the pack. She lights it. She stands and smokes, one hand mechanically delivering nicotine like a widget slapping bolts against a flange, the fingers of the other rat-a-tat against the chair's back.

Her eyes graze the walls. Bare except for the single photograph above the desk. Relic of what was lost. Tears well up.

No. She shakes her head. Not today. I'll take a walk, she thinks. Maybe the rain will wash it away.

She's at the tall pine closet in two strides, grabs her galoshes, steps into them. Where's her pocketbook? She takes in the room again. Austere. As if I'm cloistered in here, she thinks. Like a nun. No life.

It's all wrong. Anger tastes like iron. Her hands fist against her hips.

An old feeling tries to rise. Habit—reflex—to push it back. She lets it lift, a kite testing the sky. Oddest sensation ballooning inside her. Guilty, almost giddy, picking up her keys, she opens the attic door.

"Nu, are you nuts, going out in this rain? Gussie, what do you think, have we got a meshugeneh for a boarder?"

Ben beams at Vera. Behind the meat counter she can see only his top half, chest barreled against stained white apron, bald head shining atop his tree-stump neck.

"Enough already, leave her alone, Mr. Knows-What's-Best-for-Everybody. It's a free country. She has a right to take a walk." Gussie is at the cash register next to the door. "Only Veraleh, come here, we don't want you should get your hair wet, so put this on top." She's pulled a plastic shmatte from a drawer. She flaps it in the air. Vera takes it and puts it on her head, tying the ends beneath her chin. She reaches into her purse to pay. Gussie waves her money away. "Please, don't insult me, just keep your head dry. And here is a pack cigarettes, you should smoke them in good health."

Ben has come out from his station amid the salamis. He points at the pickle barrel. "You want one?"

"Is that supposed to protect me from the rain too?" He shrugs, chuckling. "Thanks, anyway, but it's too early for pickles."

"Pardon me for the contradiction, but it's never too early for pickles."

"I'm not going to try to debate you in your area of expertise, Ben. I'm just going to take a nice little walk and come back and have some lunch. I heard a rumor Gussie made gefilte fish."

Now that one grins, a fine netting of wrinkles gathering at the corners of her mouth. It's a funny thing, Vera thinks, how Celia's pal has aged. She's not so much older than me, yet her hair has gone gray and there are lines all over her face. Laugh lines. She had a rough time as a kid but now things are going her way. Don't be jealous, she tells herself as a green twinge pings.

She'll walk a few blocks. Have a smoke, and return. Read after lunch. She waves at Gussie and Ben and steps through the door into the wet world. She opens her umbrella under the awning. She sniffs the steamy, wormy air, detects another layer, something fresh moving in. Takes a deeper, longer breath and sets off at her standard brisk pace.

"Slow down! Vera, wait a minute!" She turns. Why, for heaven's sake, it's Ruby, rushing out the side door, sloshing down the driveway toward her. Laughing, hair windswept, squinting into the wet. "Wow! It's coming down harder than I realized." Vera has nothing to say. How lovely Ruby is, how alive. The girl takes her free hand. Vera stiffens. Ruby lets go. "Oh, I'm sorry. I'm such a nudnick. Plowing you down when you were looking forward to taking a nice walk in the rain all by yourself. I'll leave you alone."

Vera finds her voice. No, she says, please join me. Walk with me, please.

Vera managed to snatch this new novel, *Mildred Pierce*, from the library the day it arrived, but she puts it down now. She can't concentrate. She stretches, arching against the headboard, flexing her arms, pointing her toes. She yawns. Relaxes back against the pillows.

This rain. Strange day. She keeps expecting a knock at her door. Any minute now, Bud, with some offering. A finger painting for Vera's wall. A snack. A question, about New York maybe or her momma in the old days in Passaic, or she'll ask for a book report suggestion or help with her penmanship. There has been a breach, lately. People entering, after all this time.

So Ruby. They had chatted, the girl explaining her studies. She's in love with the theater. She's writing a play for her master's thesis, and on the side she's learning to stage manage with a WPA theater group—"sort of an informal apprenticeship," she calls it. She dreams of moving to New York. "I'll take Broadway by storm," she'd said, laughing at herself, rolling her eyes. "Well, maybe you will," Vera had replied, smiling but serious, and Ruby had looked at her, skeptical, grateful, locking her arm through Vera's, kicking through the puddles. They walked like that, far longer than Vera had planned, block after block in the pouring rain, turning into the little park at the end of Yellowstone.

Circumnavigating the soggy baseball diamond, talking. Ruby mostly, cheeks ruddy with rain and gusto, a rush of words, explaining her idea to Vera, her effort—"I'm probably crazy but I've got to try it"—to meld comedy and drama. In May, after the semester ended, she'd gone to New York with two chums. They stayed two nights at the midtown Y, took in a comedy, *Arsenic and Old Lace*, and two dramas, *Watch on the Rhine* and *Native Son*. Why can't a playwright use both, she asked, why can't the genres be combined? "That's what I'm trying to do," she told Vera. "Oh, not combine themes—come on, you can't compare *Arsenic* to *Native Son*, they're like two different worlds—I mean, not content but form. Play with form, play with means of expression, but what you express, well, it's got to matter, doesn't it? It's got to mean something." She's writing a farce, complete with mistaken identities, missing persons, slamming doors, "the whole megillah," she said, but somehow with a serious theme. Vera couldn't quite get it straight, there was an awful lot to it, the Spanish Civil War, lynch laws, the Battle of the Overpass, Hitler, Father Coughlin, somehow all connected. The play takes place in Detroit "but it takes in the whole world," Ruby said, then she stopped, and smiled, glowed redder yet, looked down but turned her eyes up to Vera. "Oh boy, you must think I'm full of beans—I just heard myself—takes in the whole world indeed—sometimes I get a little carried away—"

Vera touched the girl's chin, quickly dropped her hand but kept her eyes on Ruby's. She shook her head. "Full of ideas, maybe—"

"Crazy ideas. Who do I think I am—"

"Maybe you're the next Shakespeare. You never know, Ruby. I used to go to the theater in New York, I've seen hits and I've seen flops, and listen, kiddo, I wouldn't bet against you."

Ruby radiant as they walked on. When was the last time Vera walked like that? When was the last friend?

When was—when did—oh god—Florence—with a start, Vera sits up straight in the bed and whips her head toward the desk. A glance at the standing calendar confirms what her gut knows. August. Her exile began seventeen years ago today.

Ruby, rain, walk forgotten, she's underwater. Submersed in the old torment. Her chest heaves—she'll drown—this flood—this fetid, endless grief. She clasps hands over mouth to muffle the gathering bawl and lows like a lost beast.

Eventually the weeping stops. Teardrops sprinkle her calves. Her legs plop back down. She stays like that, half-lying, half-sitting, budged against the headboard like an animal dredged from the depths and washed up against a piling. Washed clean. That's one thing to be said for these scenes. Less frequent now, but when the storm does come it empties her. She relishes the numb exhaustion that follows. She can be dead again for a while.

This is the time to talk to Florence. Like she talked to her that first time, seventeen years ago. With a pen. On paper. Letters she never sends. Ridiculous ritual, yet relentlessly it rears its head. Every year on this day. First the tears, then the words.

No—no! Why write to a ghost? Face it, she tells herself, that's what Flo is to you. Let her go. Maybe a friend again now … not like that, never again like that … but someone to talk to, someone present, in the flesh.

It's an old tug, though. Not easy to resist. I won't write, I won't, she promises herself, but let me look, I'll just look at what

I wrote before, it'll be like a goodbye. And she's up, she's at the desk, then she's down, on her knees, jerking drawers, ransacking, scouring her files. A paper minefield. Divorce proceedings, custody agreement. Don't look. Mama's last photo. Clippings, records from the Willy search. Avert your eyes. A matchbook—what's that doing in the drawer?—Baker's Keyboard Lounge, eight months ago, Mickey, with Dorothy. Vera wonders when she'll see her brother and his new wife again.

She can't find what she's looking for.

Then she remembers. It's not in the desk. She shoves everything back in, slams drawers, and she's at the closet, crawling toward the back, flinging footwear. There it is.

A shoebox, a big one that long ago held a pair of high-button shoes. Now it's—what? A box of excuses? Seventeen letters explaining away her disgrace? Seventeen years of apologies, never delivered.

She takes the box to the bed. She squats next to it. She lifts the lid. Inside, a neat pile. In order. How organized I am, she thinks. One of my few virtues. She picks up the top letter.

She wrote it on a day like this one. Nineteen twenty-four, an August Saturday. It was raining, she remembers. She was glad, she remembers. She could not have borne another day like the one before, could not have done it in such awful sunshine. The drear suited the task at hand.

To tell Florence goodbye. The day before, she had tried. Mickey had carried the message: Florence would meet her in Washington Square after school. So Vera had gone. She had waited at the northern boundary. She had seen Florence approach. But she had stayed hidden behind the arch. Florence did not see her. Vera watched her friend look around. She watched her wait. She watched her, finally, leave, and then she did too.

The next day, Saturday, a hard rain. Willy and Lenny playing in their room, subdued, as if they knew. Vera at their father's desk. She wrote a letter. She reads it now.

Florence,
Forgive me.

Is that all?

Three words. It was all I could manage, she remembers. I was splitting in two. Heart cleaved clean through, one half clinging to Florence, the other to her boys, all of them slipping away like blood sluicing from sliced arteries.

She remembers sitting at that desk listening to the rainfall as love slid away. A spasm rends her midsection. She bends into it. Kneeling on the bed, folded over herself, she rocks until the cramp subsides.

Forgive me? Her lips tighten. It would have been asking too much. She's glad she never finished the letter, never sent it. She wrote three words, she folded the paper, she put it in a box and there it sat, a single sheet, until the next year when she took it out and read and wept and wrote another.

She folds the first letter and lays it next to her knee. She takes out the next sheet, from August 1925, and reads.

Florence,

Well, she thinks, at least I wasn't verbose, dropping the page with its single word and turning toward the window. She closes her eyes and listens. Dinner hour approaching, the downpour has abated to a mizzle, tittering softly at the open louvers. She looks out. The clouds are breaking up, parting ways and rushing off like a crowd leaving a Saturday matinee. High and far away, the sun peeks forth. Happy ending for a rainy day. High and dry, that's how I left her, Vera thinks. She gets up and steps to the window, on the way sweeping her cigarettes and lighter from the desk. She lights a cigarette and watches the lavender sky brighten into a luminous blue. After a year all I could write was her name.

Vera can't seem to picture that day. She can see her room, all chintz, the bedspread, the wallpaper, good taste according to the Christian Women's League or whatever those goddamn biddies called themselves, can you imagine Peter putting her there, among the old maids, shiksas no less. She can nearly smell the place still, floor wax, boiled potatoes. Daily maid service, tasteless dinner served at six o'clock sharp, nine o'clock curfew, visitors in the parlor only. She had no visitors. Except for meals she stayed in her room on the third floor. She was lucky, supposedly. She was supposed to be grateful for Peter's largesse, settling her there at Roberts House on Thirteenth Street, just blocks from the boys, paying her lodging for the first two years.

Lucky. Vera tastes salt. She lifts the cigarette and takes a quick, hard drag. She rubs her forehead with her other hand, runs it through her hair, along her scalp, pinches the back of her neck, returns to her face. She swipes it across her eyes and pulls again on the fag. There. She's collected herself. Enough with the crying. Why can't she remember the day she wrote the letter? Tried to write, that is, managing only Florence's name. An August day, today's date, one year into exile. One empty year completed. Maybe that's why she can't call up the day. That first year a blank.

At least the previous August she'd thought to ask forgiveness. That was before she knew what a year was.

She knows it now. Fast, short puffs, shaky fingers, she spins away from the window, picks up the ashtray, grinds the butt into it, hard. She leans back over the bed and, leaving the second letter lying there, reaches into the shoebox to pull out the third.

August 1926. Ah yes, here's the prototype. As she lifts the thick sheaf a gorgeous, disgusting sensation like picking a bloody scab spikes up her spine. She gives herself a shake and, holding the letter, starts to pace.

No masterpiece of brevity, letter three. All—what is it, eight? nine?—pages a slobber of suffering. A mad, lachrymose, protracted howl of anguish that became the model for all the letters to come.

She is serving a life sentence. For the first twelve months she'd been numb, but two Augusts into it she was coming undone. Spilling her guts in ink and tears. That went on for years. Funny, Vera thinks. I guess I've finally poured myself out. Lately the letters have been succinct. No more water left in that well.

She won't write again. She braces herself to read this one from August 1926. She paces. Window, desk, bathroom, bed, window. Desk, bathroom, bed. She reads.

Dear Florence,

How you must hate me. Well, join the club. Willy won't even look at me, the one Sunday a month I'm allowed near him. He shakes my hand, takes my coat, hands it to the housekeeper. Talk about hate, the sight of this Katie with my boys makes my blood boil. Peter has her all uniformed of course, all starched and stiff. And her voice, shrill with that Irish trill—I know, Mama says she's just a poor worker, an immigrant like we were, I shouldn't take my anger out on her, that would be your line too. But Willy is so proper, so distant. He calls me "Mother," for heaven's sake. And he smiles this awful little smile—you haven't seen it, it's new this year—his eyebrows lift in the middle, his face like a question mark, as if he's never felt a real smile rise out of him and he's asking if he's got it right. A facsimile.

You might think I'd be relieved. I might be expected to prefer this to how he was at first. Clinging to me each time, pleading, wailing, "Please, Ma, please, don't leave, why won't you stay; why don't you love me anymore?" That's what he asked me. Why I don't love him. He shrieked it the day I moved out, and over and over at the end of each visit for months. Can you blame him? No one ever explained. Peter wouldn't let me. One day he informs me I'm to leave, the next I'm sitting at his desk trying to write you, the next, he takes the boys to the zoo and suddenly his hired hands are here, in my own home, grabbing clothes from my drawers, throwing them into trunks. And just like that I'm gone. Except Peter's timing was off. He and the boys returned as those momzers were hustling me out. The look on Willy's face. Shattered like a china doll. And his cries, and Peter pulling him away, blocking his sight of me, hurrying his hired hands. He wouldn't even let me hug my children. Lenny went silent, huddled in the corner.

Both of them bereft and all I could say was "I love you" as I left, I love you, I love you, over and over, hoping to be heard over Willy's screams, inside Lenny's bad dream. But if I loved them I wouldn't leave, would I? This, I know, is what Willy will always believe.

And what did Peter say to them? How did he explain their mother moving out? He says he did not tell them the truth: expelled for crimes against nature. He says he never will tell. I believe him. Some Teutonic code of honor. So he told them nothing?

Now we occupy the same territory, my children and me, but there might as well be mountain ranges between.

The next thing I knew I had been installed in a third-floor room in Roberts House. Maybe I should have done something, used the telephone in the foyer, called someone. Do you think so? Who, Flo? Who should I have called? Mama at Celia's, out in Jersey; no telephone. Mickey who knew where. You—but I couldn't—I don't know why—so I sat on the bed in that room all afternoon. Then, around four o'clock, a knock on the door, one of the matrons saying I had a visitor down in the parlor. I rose and went down the stairs. I don't know what was with me, Flo, what do you think was with me that I did whatever anyone told me to? I was moving like a robot, I stumbled coming down the final flight, and Peter grabbed me. He pulled me upright and stood at the foot of the stairs staring at me. What was he doing there? Who was with Willy and Lenny? Staring through those thick eyeglass lenses as if they gave him X-ray vision. I stared back but his face was indistinct. It kept breaking up and reassembling.

He steered me by the elbow into the parlor. We sat by the garden window, in two wing-backed chairs angled toward each other with a tiny occasional table between them. The sun beating against my neck surprised me. Up in my room, the curtains closed all afternoon, I had thought night had fallen, but there were still many hours left to this day.

You always stuck up for Peter. It used to annoy me no end. He's not a bad person, you'd say; he is courteous, and kind, you'd say; and he cares for you, and for the boys. And oh, I'd think, there she goes again, blocking my way when I want to blame him for this impasse we find ourselves in. I knew you were right. He was a good man. Perhaps he still is, at base. If he's done wrong—and can I really say he has?—it is my fault. Having an invert for a wife contorted his heart. What did I expect? Could it have happened any other way? I don't know. One more thing I do not know. I do know that that afternoon he seemed to think he was being kind.

"Vera," he said, "you must sign some papers." I had to lean in to hear him, his voice was so low, the words coming out so slowly as he pulled an envelope and pen from his breast pocket and handed them to me. I opened the envelope and took out several pages of legal documents. "Read them," he said in that strange, strangled voice he was using, but I couldn't, the letters wouldn't adhere to the paper or maybe it was written in a foreign language, so I whispered, "Just show me where to sign," and I laid the sheets on the table. No, he said, you must understand, and he grabbed my hand that was poised over the papers. Sitting so close, our knees were nearly touching. His fingers were trembling against mine. He covered them with his other hand and wrapped it around mine. "You must understand," he repeated, and squeezed. My hand was starting to hurt, the pen trapped inside pressing against my palm.

"Understand?" I mumbled. Was he going to explain why he was doing this to our children?

"Understand what you are signing," he said. He sighed deeply, laid my hand in my lap and let go of it. "Understand that you are not their mother anymore."

I had been sitting with my head down. We hadn't made eye contact since the stairs. Now I looked at him. His face was swimming in and out of focus. I squeezed my eyes to flush away the tears. I was trying to clear my head, Flo, I was telling myself to stay calm. And then I looked at him again. He seemed composed, and I resolved to match his demeanor.

I felt we had entered the final stage of a contest that I must not lose. Yes, my darling, I was deluded, it seems, even then, still not taking it all in.

I said, "I will always be their mother, Peter." I was relieved to hear my voice hold steady.

"Biologically this is accurate. But you will sign these papers and the meaning of this is that you relinquish all legal rights with regard to Wilhelm and Leonard."

"All legal rights," I said, and again I was pleased at my even tone, and as I looked at him and did not weep it came upon me that this was all I would accomplish. I would comport myself well. I would behave with dignity. I would not blink as I signed away my sons.

Peter said he would pay my Roberts House room and board, as well as incidental expenses, for two years. After that, he might also lend a hand, he said, if I needed help finding work. Where I lived would be up to me, but it must be above 14th Street or below Delancy. In fact, he said, Brooklyn would be best. I started to ask why but stopped myself.

He made me a deal, Florence. He actually put it like that. As though our children were—what? commodities? property?—yes that's it, as if they were his property, to which I could have access, but only on his terms. "This deal I make with you, Vera. You sign the divorce papers. You sign the custody agreement. You agree to all the conditions

I have specified. In return, I will allow you to visit with my sons in my home on the third Sunday of every month for two hours. I will even remove myself from the premises during these visits."

And if I did not agree? If I rejected his magnanimous offer? Oh, Flo, come on. I didn't even bother to ask.

I did ask if that was all and he nodded and I lifted the pen to sign but he stopped me again. "Wait a moment, Vera." I looked at him wearily: What more could he possibly want? He turned away and gazed out the window, head tilted upward, squinting into the light. He seemed to falter for a minute, then he said softly to the sun, "You have no right to hate me. I protect my sons only. I loved you. You deceived me—and now this ... situation ..." He was pronouncing his words carefully; the way he used to when he first came from Germany; when we first met. Then he finished: "I will care for my sons. I do only what must be done. The blame lies with you."

No tears! No tears! Stop, she orders herself, and drops the letter onto the desk. She continues pacing. It's 1941, she tells herself, this is a different kind of day. Don't look back. Resist—don't read the rest. She lifts the letter, neatens its pages into an ordered pile and replaces them in the shoebox. She picks up the other two, the first and the second, from where she'd left them lying on the bed and puts them back on top. Funny, she thinks. For two letters I had no words. After what Peter said. She resumes pacing.

By the time she'd written this third letter she was in her own place, a fourth-floor walkup in Hell's Kitchen, two rooms, two windows onto a shaftway. That's when the words came. Once a year from then on, she had opened the floodgates and out flowed torrents. Annual missives of misery, written oh so faithfully to the one I love.

The one I loved. "Past tense," she says out loud. "Loved." She will not write today. She picks up speed, moving back and forth across the floor, pumping her arms in rhythm. I loved her.

I love her not. Loved her. Love her not. Was Flo riven too? Did she ever glue herself back together?

Vera stops short. She sits on the bed beside the shoebox. She closes her eyes and sees Florence again. As she saw her the last time, in August 1927, left arm around Mama's shoulder, right fist thrust high. Flo and Mama jammed among the thousands in Union Square. Crammed at the edge of a crowd of thousands, and somehow Vera spotted them as her bus passed.

She should have been there, she knows. One more failure. The week before, Vera had turned down her mother's request that she take her to the rally. Mama had appealed to her. She'd even invoked Papa. He would have gone, she said, he would have wanted us all to go, and Vera nodded, yes, it's true, but still she shook her head no. Mama made one last stab: "Sacco and Vanzetti, they're just like us, Veraleh." The old woman peered at Vera, her eyes aflame at the frame-up of two immigrant workers, their death sentence meant as a lesson to the rest. Of course she was right, Vera knew that, it was unjust, horrible, of course they should not die. She's wrong, though, Vera thought, looking away. We're not alike. I too was accused. Convicted. Condemned. But no one will ever march for me.

She still would have gone, just to stand beside Mama for an afternoon. But the protest was set for August 21—the third Sunday of the month. Her time with Willy and Lenny. Vera would not yield it for any cause. So she had passed on a bus as the masses rallied. She was heading to Klein's for its school-days sale on boys' wear; then she planned to walk to Peter's for her two hours with her two little strangers.

She was sitting on the left side of the bus next to the window. Just as she reached up to pull the cord for the next stop, she heard the chants and looked out at the crowd in Union Square. Suddenly she saw Florence, and next to her, Mama. Their backs were to the street. How she made them out she does not know to this day. Something about Flo's stance, she supposes, the angle of her head. Maybe she recognized her summer shift, a riot of violets plastered against her sweaty skin. Standing there in the sun. Mama wore a hat but Florence's head was bare, her hair twisted and pinned on top, her neck exposed.

Then they were gone, the bus moving along. Vera swiveling to see. Her heart hovering at the edge of Union Square, beneath her breast a vacant cavity.

SEPTEMBER 1941

Vera sees the candle as soon as she enters the house. A squat white wax cylinder beyond the archway in the kitchen, thin flame sucking dusk's lengthening shadows.

As she steps into the living room, shaking red-orange leaves off her feet onto Gussie's floor mat, closing the door, shrugging off her sweater and dropping it onto Ben's rocker, she wonders if the candle is part of some religious ritual she's not familiar with. The high holidays have begun. Ben must be down Dexter at B'nai Moshe for the second night of Rosh Hashanah services with the other god machers, as Mama used to call them. Maybe tonight he's got Gussie and the girls with him. Yesterday he had come back from shul alone, sat at the dinner table and seethed. Gussie had bustled, piling plates with brisket and steaming potatoes, bristling but obviously intent on ignoring his ire. The twins squirmed. Ruby shot warning looks to silence them. The awkward scene reminded Vera she is an intruder. It stirred queasy memories of the family following Mama away from Papa's beliefs. She should never have started eating with these people but they'd worn her down.

Vera drops onto the couch, thighs squeaking against its thick plastic sheath. She plunks her handbag down next to her. Sits still for two beats. Appreciates the hush, something this household usually achieves only in the dead of night. She twists the watch off her wrist and tosses it into her purse. She reaches for her feet, removes her shoes, throws them toward the stairs. Then she unhooks her garters, stretches her gams and, one at a time, carefully rolls down her nylons, gathering each around an ankle and pushing it off with the other foot. She runs her hands up and down her legs. Skin smooth, tight. Not bad for a middle-aged dame who sits at a desk day after day punching numbers into an adding machine year after year. All for the profit of Sam Pleck. She should be grateful, she knows. Mickey's connections got her the job as soon as she got here in 1930. She's kept it all this time. People hungry, desperation all around but platters keep spinning so Pleck's record store keeps selling and Vera is kept busy entering the figures. His modest riches pay her modest wages. Desperation all around; she can't complain.

Firm calves. Every noontime she walks. Pleck's is on Bagley, smack between Wayne University and downtown. The streets are alive there. Students, shoppers, workers from offices, restaurants, stores. All sorts of people—well, not like New York, but better than the monochrome sameness of Gussie and Ben's neighborhood, the thick, placid stasis that makes her want to scream. Eleven years and she can't find the life here. Except during her lunch-hour walks. Blocks comprising the university, library, art museum, school board headquarters, opera house, theaters. Woodward down the middle like a syringe shooting Vitamin B into Detroit's distended bulk. The area takes up all of what—one square mile? Pitiful, really. But she's thankful it's here. When she catches sight of a woman professor, say, or a Negro family, or someone in foreign garb, or an arty-looking type with beret and beard, it gives her a queer kick. Company, echoes of home, signs of life. All she can find, a few disparate faces on a midday walk—except for the nights out when Mickey's in town.

He swoops down like her fairy godmother, sweeping her from Dexter and the deli, the safe, quiet, cozy corner in which Gussie and Ben have swaddled themselves and their kids. Mickey has shown her what else Detroit is made of. He has pals everywhere, and nobody minds if she tags along, so she's made the rounds a few times. After gigs, he treats her to after-hours chow-downs. Some of the musicians, barely scraping by, double up in tiny, run-down third-floor flats where they heat red beans and rice on a hot plate. Others have real homes, and wives, and some of the wives don't mind when a motley crew descends deep in the night. Stoves are fired up. Feasts materialize, and booze, and Vera has found herself almost relaxed once or twice, at the kitchen table with a Gladys, Lorraine, picking at a peach cobbler's remains, washing it down with the last rum of the night.

Mickey hasn't played Detroit for a while. Vera hasn't heard jazz or Alabama accents, wolfed down ham hocks and collard greens, in quite some time.

Sitting on Gussie's couch, still gripping her calves, she sighs. Then she straightens and tosses her stockings toward the staircase. They lie balled up on the rug. Luxury: pretending this home is hers. But she's hungry. As a boarder she's come to expect a hot evening meal. She sniffs. None seems forthcoming this holy evening. Is this the one when they fast? If I were religious, Vera thinks, I'd certainly prefer feast days. Doesn't life take enough away? Why devote special days to doing without?

She'll have to scrounge around in the kitchen. Throw together a sandwich or make a plate of cold leftovers. She stands, cringing as her skin sticks to the plastic then pops clear.

Moving into the kitchen, she gets a kick out of her bare feet slapping the linoleum. As if I own the place, she thinks. A thrill like thievery. Though all she's stealing is this moment, and it's not even necessary at that. They give her privacy, these Schumachers. Every line she draws, they respect. Still. This is not where she belongs.

She listens to the wind chasing leaves across the backyard. Funny how you can be lonely for so long yet when you find yourself among people it still seems wrong.

She opens the icebox, locates a platter of tongue. Mustard from the pantry, a couple slices rye from the breadbox. As she puts them on the counter and reaches up to take a dish from the cupboard the candle catches her eye again. It sits on a chipped saucer. From the look of it—a deep well burned down the top, great gobs of melted wax along the sides like congealed lava flow from a volcanic eruption—it has been burning for many hours.

She wonders why. She notices a slip of paper wedged under the saucer. She slides it out. A few words and some numbers. Yiddish, or maybe Hebrew. Must have something to do with the holiday. She makes her sandwich, sits at the table, chews. When she's finished she washes the plate, dries it, replaces it on its shelf and finds herself standing there staring at the candle again.

Vera jumps at a tap on her shoulder. She spins around. It's Ruby. "Sorry" from the young woman to Vera's "Oh!" Then they both laugh.

"Sorry," Ruby repeats. She's wearing what Vera recognizes as her studying outfit: an old robe of Ben's, thick men's socks, house slippers. "Don't mind me, just getting a ginger ale." She grabs the green and gold bottle from the icebox, digs in the drawer for a bottle opener. "I'll be gone in a sec."

"What's your rush? You startled me, that's all."

"I don't want to—"

"I didn't think anyone was home."

"Yes, this quiet is amazing, isn't it?" Ruby smiles. "Daddy mooned around so much Ma gave in—"

"Closed the store?"

"For the whole day, can you believe it? Went to shul, and they even dragged the twins along."

"And you?"

"Daddy knows better than to start in on me. Or else Ma held him off, I don't know. I'm not interested in that mumbo-jumbo."

"That's what my mother used to call it—well, she said it in Yiddish, mishegoss."

"She wasn't old-fashioned, then?"

"Mama? Not a whit." Vera sits, pulls out another chair, and Ruby joins her at the table.

"You're lucky. A woman ahead of her time." Ruby pauses. "Really ahead. Born in 1867, right?"

"How did you know?"

"Ma was telling me about her, this morning, when she lit the Yahrzeit candle."

"Yarhz—?"

"It's for your mother. You didn't know?" Ruby's eyes open with the question and Vera sees herself reflected in them. She winces, looks down, stands up, starts to leave, but Ruby stands too, touches her shoulder and says, "Vera." Next Vera's face is on Ruby's shoulder. Ruby holding her as tears fall. Only a few. Vera cuts off the flow. She swallows. She pulls away. She wipes her eyes. They sit back down. Ruby says, "Your mother is the only non-relative Ma lights Yahrzeit for."

"I'm not surprised." Vera dabs at a stray tear. "Gussie adored her." She glances at the candle, then back at the girl. "But Mama died in October. I don't get why the candle today. For Rosh Hashanah?"

Ruby shakes her head. "I know September's not over yet, but today's the anniversary if you go by the Jewish calendar."

"Which Gussie does? I thought she'd dropped all that."

"This one thing only, lighting candles for the dead. Don't ask me why." Ruby shrugs and smiles. When Vera returns the smile she says, "I'm sorry."

"Oh, well, she's gone a long time already. Thirteen years." After a minute she adds, "You get used to the losses."

"You've had—" Ruby stops in mid-sentence. Sips her ginger ale.

"I've had what?"

"I was about to cross over into nosy." Vera lifts her eyebrows. "Should I go ahead?" Vera waits. "I was going to ask—when you said you get used to loss—I was going to say you've had your share, haven't you?"

Vera gets up from the table. She's at the back door in two strides. She opens it. Inhales the early autumn air. Is someone burning leaves already? Little cyclones of them eddy on the lawn. A breeze twirls into the house—it feels clean, she closes her eyes as it brushes by her—then Ruby's voice: "Oh no!"

Vera turns. Her eyes follow Ruby's. The swirling air has snuffed the candle out.

Vera looks at Ruby. The girl averts her reddening face. She's afraid I'm going to cry again, Vera thinks. Over a candle. Oh brother. Her lips compress. I've had enough of this. She lifts her wrist, then remembers she took her watch off.

"What time is it?" she asks Ruby.

"Six-thirty"

Still early. Vera is at the archway in three steps. "Let's get out of here." Ruby, perplexed, doesn't rise, so Vera returns, takes her hand, tugs her out of the chair. Delighting in the new bloom on Ruby's round face, Vera aims her toward her bedroom with a push on her shoulders. At the stairs she picks up her stockings and shoes and heads up. "I'll be back in a jiffy. You get dressed and leave your folks a note."

"Where are we going?"

"Where else? To the movies."

Riding home not two hours ago, who'd have thought she'd be back on the bus again so soon? Then it was packed: she'd had to stand. Every day it's the same, going and coming, the bus always jammed. Force your way in, flex your knees so you don't drop during the turn onto Grand Boulevard, suffocate amid all the bodies packed against yours. No room to lift a book, no chance to retreat into a daydream, not with the other passengers jabbering block after block. Tonight is a nice contrast. Heading back downtown—same driver, his loop coinciding with my loopiness, Vera thinks, how crazy am I going to an eight-thirty movie when I have to get up at six for work tomorrow—the bus is nearly empty. The seats a treat, and next to her Ruby Schumacher.

Neither woman speaks. An easy silence. Going to the movies with a friend. Vera marvels. She feels a sense of release, as of bunched muscles loosening.

They get off at Grand Circus Park. Eagerly taking Vera up on her movie idea, Ruby had said she'd been dying to see *How Green Was My Valley*, playing at the Adams. Now they're here, over an hour early. Should they sit on a bench and chat? Take a walk around the circle? Window shop?

"I know," says Ruby. "Let's go get a sundae at Sander's."

This one has some sweet tooth. "Do we have time?"

"Sure."

"Then why not?"

They walk down Woodward. The setting sun tints Ruby's hair russet. The stiffening wind blows it around her face.

At Sander's, there's not a table to be had. And the racket! Clatter of spoons clinking against frosted glasses and gleaming goblets filled with gorgeous multi-colored goo. The after-work crowd gabbing madly as they dig in. Mothers with chattering tykes gorging on tall, sugary concoctions. Two seats open at the counter. As she and Ruby move to grab them, they pass some women Vera recognizes as secretaries at Detroit Bank and Trust. Three others at a nearby table obviously came straight from a Crowley's sales floor, still with the name badges on their chests. Ruby takes a stool to Vera's left. To Vera's right sit a thin, tired-looking girl in a Kresge's cafeteria uniform and two small children. Neither kid can be over five. Vera watches their eyes glow as their sundaes arrive. She catches their mother's eye and smiles. She wonders where a gal like that gets money to treat her kids to ice cream. Who takes care of them during the day. What they talk of as she tucks them in.

For that matter, who would have expected to see any of these women? On a work night, and with money so tight? But then, she thinks, I wonder what they see when they look at me? Tall, slim, carefully groomed, sharply turned out in a tailored navy suit. Glints of steel streaking her hair, grim-lipped—only she isn't, not tonight, she's smiling, slurping her Boston cooler and grinning at the gleeful little strawberry-sauce-streaked faces to her right, smiling to her left, too, at the bubbly coed downing spoonfuls of hot fudge and ice cream with greedy abandon.

All these ladies enjoying an after-work splurge. And Ruby and me. What must they make of us? Spinster aunt treating her niece? Teacher and student ... girlfriends ... but she's so young ... Ruby goes on plenty of dates, Vera knows. She's seen some of Ruby's beaus. Gawky fellows, not in her league, nowhere near. Of course Vera keeps her opinions to herself. It's not her business who Ruby sees, where she goes when she gets all dolled up. Last Saturday, for instance, in her green dress, the color perfect against her hair, padded shoulders, scoop neck, the waist cinched and belted, skirt lying in demure folds against Ruby's thighs, but Vera can picture how it flares out when she hits the dance floor, how it flounces when she jitterbugs, an emerald aureole around a rosy center. Those callow boys can't possibly appreciate—

"Vera, did I tell you—" Vera jerks her head—where had she gone—good heavens—what was she thinking—her breath catches and a gulp of Boston cooler goes down wrong. She gags for a few seconds. Ruby pats her back. "Are you all right?"

Vera nods, clears her throat. "Did you tell me what?"

"But are you all right?"

Vera nods again. "Yes, really." She covers her chagrin with a thin laugh. "Please, what were you going to say?"

Ruby proceeds to fill Vera in on her academic progress. Soon she's impersonating her snooty British thesis advisor, chortling between spoonfuls of ice cream and hot fudge. Ruby's verve stirs Vera. The girl reminds her of someone. She's not sure who. Then, a memory. Mama and Mary, laughing.

"My mother would have liked you," she says. Ruby's face, so open a moment before, seems to shut. "Ruby? Did I say something wrong?" Ruby shakes her head. "I meant that as a compliment, you know."

"I know." Ruby shakes her shoulders as if to throw off a cloak. "So?"

"So it's the anniversary of your mother's death and we Schumachers spend the entire day reminding you of her. Bringing you sadness when we should be helping to lift it. First Ma with her ferblunget candle—"

"She meant well—"

"And now me, blathering on about my silly project—"

"It's not silly—"

"But I reminded you of her again—"

"Yes, and I'm grateful—"

"Grateful? For more hurt?"

Vera thinks for a minute. "Sometimes it's good to remember."

"You don't have to make me feel better."

"I'm not. Believe me. It's fine."

Ruby takes a deep breath and sends Vera a subdued smile. They sit in silence. Vera watches something else play across Ruby's features. Ruby catches her peeping: Vera flinches, then looks at the girl head-on and says, "Penny for your thoughts."

"No, that's my line."

"What?"

"I was just wondering what you were thinking." Ruby swivels toward Vera. She grips Vera's stool and twists it so they face each other. Ruby folds her arms in front of her. "I wonder that a lot, actually. What you're thinking about. How you keep your spirits up."

Vera snorts. "I don't. Haven't you noticed?"

"Oh, you're not such a wet blanket. At least not with me." Ruby unfolds her arms, takes Vera's hands in hers and holds them in her lap. Vera clenches but she doesn't pull away. "Listen, Vera, we're friends. Aren't we?" Vera nods stiffly. "I know Ma thinks it's kind of funny, I'm so much younger than you and all, but I have no patience for the college crowd and I really don't give a damn what anyone thinks. You—I —we have a lot in common, don't we? The same interests, and you lived in New York and all. And you take me seriously, you listen to me. I really appreciate that. But there's one thing. You don't talk. Now I will gladly blab till I'm blue in the face, I will if you let me, and you're kind enough to let me, and it's great to have your ear, but Vera, if we're really going to be friends I've got to let you get a word in edgewise. Don't you think?" Ruby cocks her head. Her eyes drill into Vera's. "How about it?" Ruby squeezes her hands. "Do you understand what I'm saying?"

Vera squeezes back. "You're saying it's not enough that I'm your friend. You want me to let you be my friend too."

"Aha!" Ruby whoops, a wide smile splitting her face. Vera grins too. The waitress leans to refill their water glasses. Still smiling, Vera swerves toward the counter, covers hers. "No thanks, we've got to run." To Ruby, "We almost forgot about the movie. Can we still make it?"

"Is that a joke?" Ruby snickers. "Or do you mean the ten o'clock show?"

"No—we've missed it? Talked right through it?" Ruby nods, tittering. "What time is it?"

The girl bends, covers her mouth, lifts the other hand in a "wait" gesture, gives in to a round of giggles. Her stool wobbles.

The fit passes. Ruby looks sheepish. "So much for being too mature for people my age."

"Grownups laugh." When Ruby reaches for the bill Vera grabs her hand. "Let me pay. No—don't argue. Better you should spend it on books."

"Okay. Thanks. So do you? Laugh?"

"I suppose that's your subtle way of dragging me back to your earlier point?"

"I suppose it is."

"All righty, I suppose I'll tell you whatever you want to know. On one condition."

"And that is?"

"We come back to the Adams this weekend."

"It's a date! After all, we can't keep Roddy MacDowell waiting forever."

Instead of catching the bus in front of Hudson's, they stroll up Woodward a ways and end up sitting in Grand Circus Park. The subject, at first, is Welsh miners. Ruby wants to see *How Green Was My Valley* to compare it to *The Proud Valley* from last year. "I can't imagine how this one can come anywhere close," she says. "Showing what people face. What the mine owners do, the way they destroy lives. Movies made in this country are never that honest—"

"What about *The Grapes of Wrath*? That was last year too."

"True, true. Okay, maybe sometimes—but you see, that's another reason I want to see this one, it's made by the same director. Can he get the vocabulary right in such a different setting?" Rollicking laughter ten minutes ago, and now such earnestness. Running underneath, Vera's sure, passion. Like Mama had. And Flo. "Regardless, this one can't possibly measure up to Proud Valley. You know why, don't you?"

"Tell me."

"Paul Robeson. Singing 'Deep River,' that's what everybody talks about, and that was beautiful, inspirational, but it's his acting I'm talking about. So stirring. When he speaks it's as though you're hearing the truth for the first time." I should play her my record, Vera thinks, Robeson singing a Yiddish workers' song. "Oh, I'm sorry. Do you know who he is, Vera? I'm in school, it's what I study, but I shouldn't assume—"

"Of course I know Paul Robeson. Do I seem such a philistine?"

"I—well, Ma never heard of him, and Daddy, forget it—"

"I like to think I'm a little more sophisticated—"

"You are, you—"

"Oh lord. Now I sound like a stuffed shirt."

"No you don't. I was condescending. As if your generation is all ignorant—"

"My mother was a classical pianist. She gave lessons. And my brother is a musician—"

"Assuming you're prejudiced, too, oblivious about the Negroes, discrimination—"

"She made quite a speech about that once—"

"Who? About?"

"My mother. About the Negroes and how they were slaves. They have it worse than the Jews, she said."

"They do."

Vera nods. It's been nearly a year since she met her brother's wife. She should write. Ask them to stay an extra day next time.

Mr. Right

On slow, silent Sunday afternoons ours was a haunted house. Mom was not a specter, no, she was blood and plenty of flesh, but she haunted the place nonetheless, insinuating her sense of injustice, of lost opportunities, into the ceiling beams and carpet fibers.

Mom spent Sundays reading the New York Times that Dad brought home in the morning along with fresh bagels. She loved the Sunday Times. She took hours to read it. She didn't attend all that closely to every single section. But when she got to Arts and Leisure in mid-afternoon she settled in for a long, wistful session reviewing developments in the New York theater scene. That, she felt, was her natural habitat, and she was forever perplexed about how her life had come to this instead. She belonged in the world of lights, ideas. Brilliant words, stirring songs. How had she ended up shut out? A big flat blob living a blasé life in a bland, blah suburb, a world away from all she'd dreamed of? She'd get a fresh bagel, her second or third of the day, slather it with butter or cream cheese, prepare a cup of Sanka, ease her bulk down into one of the two big brown easy chairs that flanked the living room couch. Sometimes before she picked up Arts and Leisure Mom looked out the big picture window for a while. She sighed.

I knew what she was thinking. She'd told me often enough. "I should have trod the boards. Or travailed backstage, at least. I trained in the arts, you know."

I knew. She held a Master's degree in drama from Wayne University. She had nearly followed up with a stint studying with Stella Adler in New York. She had written a one-act play that was nominated for a prestigious amateur award. Had she gone to New York, who knows, it might have been produced. She might have made her name.

She'd stayed in Detroit. Gotten stuck here, teaching—and now, back at work after the years at home with Elliot and me till I started school, she wasn't even teaching high school drama, now it was fourth grade—instead of there, acting or writing. Here, she was wasted. Her talent shelved. Forgotten. Except by Mom herself, especially on Sundays when she tore through the Times and misted over about what might have been.

One April Sunday in 1962, when I was almost nine, Dad had delivered the bagels then driven to the library before the skies cracked open. I sat on Mom's lap in the living room, watching the pounding rain. I was in a pensive mood. Couldn't decide what I wanted to do with the day. Call my best friend Karen Kornblatt and ask her to come over, spend the afternoon with her in my room making up superior plots for Nancy Drew books or in the basement rummaging through boxes of my grandparents' old seventy-eights and pretending to be gay sophisticates from the Jazz Age. Or stick with Mom, find an old thirties musical on TV and sink into it with her, laughing at Joan Blondell's wise-gal cracks, agreeing that Mom would have been perfect in that role, gasping at lavish production numbers.

Meanwhile the rain was pummeling Mom into a ruminative melancholy about what might have been. "It's not mere drama, what I'm caught up in," she said. "It is high tragedy. In the classical sense. The sense of promises unfulfilled, heroes brought low both by circumstances out of their control and also—I know this, Randeleh, I don't shy away from the truth—by their own tragic flaw."

Hers was Dad, she told me. Her circumstance and her flaw. She'd fallen in love with him. He "was himself a classic case of the tragic hero, you know, he'd been headed for such great things, a math prodigy, track star ... and now, look at him, and look at me. Don't you think it's ironic that the denouement for both of us is in the classroom? Hmm?" Mom paused to sip at her Sanka. "Look, honey, don't misunderstand me. Teaching is an honorable profession. I cannot abide those who denigrate it. Still, between you and me, what they say is true. Those who can do, those who can't teach. Randy, in this life we must look the truth in the face. I've taught you this much?"

"Yeah, Mom."

"Then you see that this saying, cynical as it is, carries the ring of truth. Except that in my case, if teaching is all I can do, it's not because I lack the talent for better things. It's because your father needs me. It's a higher calling, making this man a home." Mom took a bite of her bagel, chewed. I listened to the rain hitting the window in a relentless rhythm. It started to hypnotize me. "And so—" My head snapped up. "—I do what I must. I teach."

Today, I knew, Mom felt especially glum, for the spring theater season had just begun, which made for a thick arts section and a dejected Mom. Even her name, she had once pointed out to me, showed that she was meant for the stage. Ruby. It sparkled, it shone, "as I would have, honeybunny, as yer old mudder would have." Her success in the classroom—she was one of those rare teachers beloved by kids and parents alike, remembered far into adulthood as the one who kindled a love of learning, instilled confidence—was, she said, "no mystery. The reason I'm a good teacher is because I was trained in the theater. Teaching is performing. You are on stage, in front of an audience, every day, all day, for nine months out of the year." She took another sip of Sanka, felt for my hand, squeezed. "You know what they say, Randeleh. The show must go on."

We sat quietly for a little while, watching the rain. Then: "Hey you." Mom wore a pained smile as she rubbed the top of my hand with her thumb. Sheesh, enough already, I thought. What a ham. But then I realized that she really did look sad, and her eyes really were full of love, and a tight feeling squeezed my chest. Poor Mom. I was her best—her only—audience.

She looked at me with that sweet, sad smile, waiting.

"What?" I squeaked.

"Knock knock."

"Who's there?"

"Sam and Janet."

"Sam and Janet who?"

"Sam and Janet evening, you will see a stranger," she sang. With that swiftness she sometimes displayed—sudden mood shift joined with an almost lithe physicality that seemed impossible on her overloaded frame—she let go of my hand and was on her feet, holding a half-bagel to her mouth as though it were a microphone. Mom had become Mary Martin singing her heart out in *South Pacific*. She segued from crooning Sam and Janet's evening into full-throttled washing men out of her hair.

Before I knew it she had grabbed me and pulled me up onto the stage with her. Soon she had me marching in place, belting about the uniqueness of dames. I sang in the mock-Brooklyn accent she'd taught me, swooning over the dustmop that had suddenly materialized as a prop. I flexed my muscles, looking down at my chest and imagining it tattooed with lovely dancing girls doing the hula like Ray Walston's in the movie.

We sang together to a rousing finale and gave ourselves a big hand before collapsing in laughter onto the couch. As I caught my breath, Mom took my hand again and kissed it. "Life up on the evil stage, hey kiddo?"

I knew my line. "It's never what a gal supposed, Mommy."

"Nope, it's not." She squeezed my hand again, then let it go. "It certainly is not." Breathing heavily, she heaved herself up, stepped back to her easy chair and plopped into it, coughing as a wash of dust rose up from the cushions. She looked out the window. The rain had stopped. She picked up the Times again.

I couldn't see her face, what expression she wore, which left me unsure which way my own feelings should swing now. I closed my eyes. I could call Karen. I could go get my Nancy Drew. But, "This is no time for reading," someone said inside my head. "This is no ordinary day."

I opened my eyes. Mom hadn't heard. I smiled to myself. He's right, I thought. "Of course I am. I'm always right. By definition." Well, that bordered on arrogance, but I had to admit it was true. "Put aside your books," the imagined voice told me. "Stop sitting around. It's time for action. Wrongs are being done. Stand up for justice. Do what needs to be done."

"Where you going, honey?" Mom asked.

"Outside, to ride my bike. Look—the rain stopped."

"Just be sure you stay on the block. And come right home if it starts again."

Ha ha! This was an auspicious beginning. Secret agent Randolph Right was on the case, and already his sublime powers of sublimity had pulled the wool over Ruby Steiner's eyes. On the block indeed. Ha ha!

I wheeled my bicycle out of the carport and onto the sidewalk. I pedaled toward Greenbelt, and up two blocks to the parking structure that was always empty on Sundays. I walked my bike up the ramp to the top. I looked at the streets and houses below. There, perched high above Northdale, I became Randolph Right.

He was, I had to acknowledge with all due modesty, the most amazing human being who had ever lived. As Randolph Right, I was a secret agent-businessman-defense attorney-brilliant brain surgeon-Tigers second baseman-engineer-mountain climber-Sears catalog model-firefighter-sculptor-scientist. Alternately, successively, sometimes simultaneously. I thought of Randolph as a true Renaissance Man. When occasionally necessary, he was also a superhero—a modest one, no cape, no superhuman powers except the unique and mysterious attribute "chest invincibility."

I had known of Randolph Right for a long time. He showed up whenever someone needed saving. Most often, that was on Sunday afternoons when the house turned haunted. Mom morose, reading the theater section and pining for the life she might have led. Elliot at a friend's house, working on some nerd project or writing some nerd paper. Dad absent after the morning bagel run and not expected to rematerialize until dinnertime, when he would show up with a pizza or Chinese food. The Steiners atomized on Sundays. Each person floated, separate, complete, like disparate substances on the table of elements Elliot had been memorizing for his seventh-grade science class. Everyone stripped to their primal selves, not reassembling into a familial formula until eight o'clock and Ed Sullivan. Me too. I became essence too. I can't say whether it was my own discrete impulse or I was part of a chemical reaction, a chain begun with Dad's departure, but on Sundays, when each Steiner was a solo act, I summoned Randolph Right.

There wasn't much Randolph couldn't do in 1962. He was at the height of his powers. Riding my bike around and around at the top of the empty parking structure, I morphed the day into Monday because Randolph's real work, the work of righting wrongs, generally began on a weekday. After work he'd drive home from his downtown office in the northbound traffic on Greenbelt, suit jacket hanging from the hook behind him, tie loosened, listening to his car radio. Sometimes an item on the news tipped him off that he was needed. Sometimes he happened upon a crisis situation. Sometimes, although he was not strictly speaking superhuman, mental telepathy would come into play and alert Randolph to a situation.

However he knew he was needed, once he knew he headed straight into action. Whether it was saving nuclear secrets from the Russians or extricating a child trapped in a burning building—or even if it was some less flashy task, like fashioning a favorable defense for a victim of a frame-up or explicating for NASA a complicated law of physics he had just discovered that would permit astronauts to travel to Mars and back without once having to go to the bathroom—regardless of what he was called to do, he did it.

Gazing out at the suburban sameness of Northdale, my eyes glazed over and Randolph Right heard the call to action. A tart-tongued comic actress, a Carol Lombard-Ruby Steiner kind of gal, had been kidnapped and was being held for fifty trillion dollars in ransom. To the rescue! Randolph revved his Aston Martin—I readied my bike's pedals—and sped off—I zoomed down the parking structure's spiral ramp. Once at the bottom I sat quietly for a while, imagining the whole caper then picturing Randolph slipping away.

He didn't care for publicity. He liked things low-key. Perhaps this was part of what made him so attractive to women.

Randolph Right played the field. But he wasn't a crass sort of Lothario. On the contrary, he had a tendency to fall deeply in love in the course of his exploits. He fell for brainy women. Tough yet tender gals, smart and sexy. Love didn't work out well for Randolph and the objects of his affection. In fact, it tended toward tragedy. Brain tumors, cancer and horrifying ends like drowning in quicksand snatched happiness away from him every time. Yet Randolph always bounced back. He shrugged off the sorrow and moved on. Still, as he kept trying to make the world a better place, he couldn't stop trying to find that special someone to share it with. Rita Rath helped.

Rita showed up every now and then, unannounced, often just after Randolph had performed a particularly magnificent act of world-important heroism only to fall victim once again to ghastly personal disaster. Rita knew how to care for Randolph. Her presence alone did the trick. She made him feel settled, less solitary in his solitude. He loved her, but he wasn't in love with her. And Rita, she loved him too, in her own way. She was a little bit Rosalind Russell, a little bit Tanteh Vera, a little bit Our Miss Brooks, and a little bit Miss Murphy the music teacher. Also a little bit Randolph Right himself. Sometimes they were twins, devoted sister and brother. Sometimes bosom buddies.

Their precise relationship was unclear, but clearly they complemented each other somehow. Right needed Rath. She made him vulnerable and kept him invincible all at once.

Miss Rath and Mr. Right. And me, Randy. Together, we could face anything.

I pedaled home.

Hide and Seek

"Nu, Veraleh? You don't want we should be late?"

Should she bother yelling down the stairs that there's no such thing as late when you're going to the Graystone Ballroom on a swinging Saturday night? That the musicians will keep playing, the dancers dancing? And that Leonard Steiner, the illustrious guest of honor, probably won't show up until poor old Gussie and Ben are ready to stumble home to bed?

"A few more minutes, Gussie."

What Vera really wants is to not go. A slight fainting fit would be a welcome diversion just about now. Anything to get out of what promises to be one hell of a horror show. Thanks to Ruby, however good her intentions.

Vera sits on the bed and smokes. She's dressed, all but her boots. Them she just has to slip over her shoes and it's out the door. Ben will get them downtown to the hopped-up corner of Woodward and Canfield in a jiffy.

She can picture the three Schumacher adults waiting downstairs all aglow at their big night out, Rose and Bud having been bundled up and shipped off to spend the night with their friends down the street. Ben's bald pate shining, face red from necktie knotted too tight. Gussie clasping her fancy beaded purse. Ruby in high stepping-out style. One more puff. Two. She descends.

"Hmm?" Vera hadn't caught what Ada Pleck said as she pecked Vera on the cheek just now. Ada and Sam are back at the table after a surprisingly nimble turn round the dance floor. Not bad, Vera had observed, jitterbugging at their age. She'd been watching how they handle each other.

Moving as a unit. The comfort of a married couple.

Not for her.

Sam and Ada here at Lenny's going-away bash. It's bad enough she has to be polite to Peter and the cretinous Mabel. Her boss and his wife too? Honestly. Nice enough people, but who wants to socialize with them? Blame it on Ruby. One day last week she'd swung by Pleck's back office to meet Vera for lunch. When Sam had wandered through Vera introduced them, and as she buttoned her coat and pulled on her gloves she listened to her friend and her boss make small talk. Watched him bask in Ruby's glow. She couldn't blame him. Young, plump, vivacious, skin afire from walking Woodward facing down the frigid Detroit River air. The girl is captivating. But infuriating, too, when she steps beyond her bounds. As far as Vera is concerned that's what she did when she invited Sam to Lenny's send-off. "And bring your wife," Ruby had added, without so much as a by-your-leave to Vera. "But Vera," she'd said over BLTs at the Kresge lunch counter, "he's obviously fond of Lenny, did you hear him saying what a good boy he is, how handsome, how smart, and he thinks the world of you. Do you really think it will kill you to share a pleasant evening with him?" Vera had stared at her, not knowing where to start, finally uttering a terse "fine" and leaving it at that. And now Ada twirling on the dance floor and flouncing back to the table to peck at Vera's cheek.

"Hmm?" Vera repeats. "I'm sorry, Ada, what did you say?"

"I said it's a pleasure to meet your friends and family after all these years."

Family? Vera's smile feels utterly fake, but Ada has turned her attention back to the dance floor. Vera does the same. There must be a thousand people here. Lined up along the marble staircases, snapping their fingers and leaning their drinks on the hand-carved handrails, bending over the broad balconies to watch from above, bunched around the fabulous fountain. Everyone moving to the music. Waiting in line for soda pop, sitting at the tables, nobody can stay still.

Don Redman's band swings like nobody's business. And so, somewhere in the midst of that mob, do Lenny and Ruby. They've been at it for at least a half-hour now.

Lenny had surprised her by showing up on time. He's in high spirits. Sharp in a brown pinstripe suit with wide lapels. On good behavior, too. Courteous and shy with the older generation, attentive and gracious with Ruby. Vera had thought he'd agreed to this whole to-do just to please her but now she sees he's glad for the attention. Well, what did he expect? He defied her, defied his father—for once, she and Peter had seen eye to eye—but did he think they would punish him once the deed was done? He's in for plenty of punishment where he's going.

Lenny off to war. Vera has never known such fear. Even Willy, the not knowing, it's not as bad as this. Yet how can he think she is angry? How can he imagine that his rash decision to enlist—what Peter called "a foolish, childish display of bravado," lashing out when Lenny announced he'd signed up with the Army Air Corps and would ship out in three weeks—how can he think this would make his mother turn away?

On the contrary. She can't get enough of him. Heartsick, but she understands. He's swept up in war fever. After Pearl Harbor last month the whole country is. He sees his chance to become a man. Unfair, Vera thinks. I've barely had a chance to know the boy. He's barely known a mother's love.

Since she heard the news she has been frantic to make up for all he's missed. Somehow, miraculously, Lenny lets her. He's just as hungry as she, it seems, or else her panic has rubbed off. In any case, her baby boy, the one with the perpetual devil-may-care pose, has spent most of his last two weeks as a civilian with his mother.

Vera sees what else draws him to these daily swings by the deli on Dexter Boulevard. And it ain't dill pickles. She knows too well what an attractive girl Ruby is.

"Look at those kids go!" Ada points to the dance floor just as Lenny dips Ruby into a deep back bend. He pulls her up, snaps her hard against him, holds her there for a beat, then flings her outward for an extravagant twirl. The girl throws her head back and laughs. Her eyes sparkle. A spark escapes, alights on Vera's spine. A thunderbolt of emotion rips through, as if summoned by these dancing Dr. Frankensteins to jolt her heart back to life. Ruby's exuberance, Lenny's elan quicken in Vera's veins. She might combust. She stands. She grabs Ben.

"Let's dance!"

"Who, me?" He laughs and tries to resist as Vera lifts him to his feet.

Gussie potches his tush and says, "Go on already, have some fun!" Laughing, clucking, oy-oy-oying, Ben makes a big show of being pulled onto the dance floor.

Where he proceeds to cut the rug like nobody's business.

"Whoa—what the—" Vera is stunned. Who'd-a thunk it? Take stumpy, steady old Ben out from behind the deli counter and look, my gosh, he's light on his feet, he's Fred Astaire, he's James Cagney. She tries to keep up with him but she isn't sure how at first. She hasn't danced since heaven knows when, and then nothing like the jitterbug. What in the world was she thinking getting up here with him? She feels foolish, exposed. Then Ben slows down and shows her the steps, holding her two hands in his. It's simple, really, one-two-three four-five-six back-step. She starts to get the rhythm. They speed up bit by bit and soon they're swinging to beat the band, all around this big, beautiful ballroom.

How about that, Vera thinks. After a blue moon, dancing. She glances at Ben, sweat glistening on his hairless dome, pot belly bouncing yet he doesn't seem to give a damn, he's a slim, lissome boy again, weightless, free. She wishes she could let go like that. He catches her eye and winks as he guides her into a series of dips and turns. Not exactly my prince charming, she thinks, but then again who is? She smiles at her own joke. Ben takes that as permission to pick up the pace even more. She catches a quick glimpse of Ruby and Lenny, her hair flying, his head thrown back at a jaunty angle, then they're lost in the crowd as she and Ben spin on.

Vera and Ben stomp and twirl through three more numbers. He makes a jesting feint toward starting in again at the opening notes of the next song but when Vera shakes her head and leads him away he sounds a loud, comical "Whew!" He whips out a hand-kerchief and mops his neck as they head back toward the table.

Vera is shvitzing too. Her body feels strange. Limbs loose. As if dancing really has reanimated a deadened, dismembered corpus.

I should do this more often, she thinks. It would keep me young. Instantly she chides herself. It's a little late in the day for that. Where would I go, anyway? Nowhere I could really lose myself. Come fully alive.

She sits down to a silly round of applause. Ben jumps up and bows. She looks around the table. Ruby and Lenny lead the pack, she clapping, he whistling the way Mickey used to at the head of his band of street hooligans, two fingers between his lips. Tears streak Gussie's face. "Oy, I'm going to pish in my pants," she shrieks between guffaws. Vera's boss is grinning and nodding and pounding the table. Her boss's wife claps rhythmically. Peter offers Vera a mock salute, a strange expression on his face as he turns back to his wife. Mabel smiles vacantly, taps her spoon against her glass, pats her peroxided, permanent-waved locks.

Everyone is coupled up. Two by two. How splendid for them. How fortuitous, should there be a flood. Her mouth tightens. All the normal people, ready to carry civilization forward should an ark beckon. God she'd like a drink. What kind of dance hall only serves ice cream and soda pop? Hasn't anyone told these people Prohibition ended years ago?

Boy girl boy girl. Neat, nice pairs. All but strange Mrs. Steiner. Odd man out as always. Mrs. Steiner the first, that is. She tries not to look at Peter and Mabel. Let's not dwell on all that, not tonight, she tells herself. It's supposed to be Lenny's night, and look, he's having a ball, isn't that marvelous? The thought of what comes next ... she looks away, and there is that vapid Mabel person again. Her sons' stepmother. Ludicrous word. She happens to be married to their father. Yet she is the one they lived with, ate with, she's the one who put them to bed, bathed them, tended their scrapes. Vera knows little of their daily lives. So many topics they skirted in their monthly rendezvous. So often those Sundays had a furtive feel. As if she were an interloper or a spy—or, the way Mabel looked at her, as if she were carrying in contagion from a quarantined precinct. So much they couldn't touch, she and her boys.

With an abrupt snap of her head, Vera cranes her neck and looks toward the entry hall. The rest of the party should have been here by now. Where are they? What if they changed their minds?

As if summoned by her thoughts, her brother appears. Mickey! Oh, he's here! A rush of heat, a clicking into place along her ribcage. She watches as he takes a few steps into the ballroom then scans for her table. He sees her. He waves. She stands. He's hesitating. His smile is small.

"Ma, there's Uncle Mickey, do you see—"

"I know, Lenny—"

"I'll go bring him over—"

"You stay here. I'll go." She practically pushes her son back into his seat. She rushes past him, past the whole table of gibbering couples, bosses, ex-husbands, landlords, strangers one and all. Toward the only one who knows her. She runs along the perimeter of the dance floor, dodging bodies. She flings herself into Mickey's arms. Outlandish behavior, they're sister and brother, not star-crossed lovers, but oh hell it's so good that he's here.

Mickey hugs her. He's shivering. Snowflakes on his coat. "Sheesh, it's freezing out there." Vera steps out of his embrace and grabs his hands. Gloveless, as always. She rubs them, looking at his face. What's wrong? "Vera, Dorothy—"

"Where is Dorothy? Is everything—I so wanted to see her, I want—"

"I know, I know, only ..." Mickey pauses. "Vera, you didn't realize, I guess, but—"

"But what?"

"Dorothy can't come in here."

"Why on earth—"

"It's Saturday night. They only allow Negroes on Mondays."

She looks around the ballroom—suddenly sees that the only Negroes are in the band—and back into her brother's tired eyes. How could she not have noticed? "I ... it never occurred to me ... I didn't—"

"Sure, sure, who knew, who'd think to ask? Only, see, she's waiting outside in the cab and I've got to go, Vera. I won't stay without her—"

"No, of course not—"

"I only came in to tell you. The bouncer—"

"The what?"

"See that guy in the tuxedo, Vera?" She follows his gaze, and nods.

"You think he's the doorman?" She nods again, hesitantly. "That's the guy in charge of keeping people out." Oh god. Her stomach turns over. "He turned Dorothy away."

"How awful. She must be—just wait one second, I'll grab my coat—"

"Oh, no, Vera, we don't want to break up your party."

She looks at her brother. "Mickey. I ... just get in the cab with Dorothy, and wait for me. I won't be a minute. Please?"

Mickey nods. She kisses his cheek and dashes back to get her things.

I didn't belong there anyway, Vera thinks. Surrounded by the sound, the sane, the Adams and Eves. In the Schumachers' vestibule, Vera waits while Mickey helps Dorothy out of her coat.

She hangs it up as Dorothy steps out of her boots. "Can I take your hat?" Dorothy unpins it and hands it to her.

They've barely made eye contact. Vera had apologized, repeatedly, as she'd gotten into the cab. Dorothy had just said, "Okay then." She'd looked out the window the whole ride back to Gussie and Ben's.

She must hate me, Vera had thought as the taxi skidded along Grand Boulevard. She must think I have no idea what she faces. All those people in the Graystone Ballroom. Inside I'm completely unlike them. Yet it's her they won't let in.

Now a coil of shame twists in Vera's gut as she puts Dorothy's hat on the closet shelf. Her brother's wife cast out and she didn't even see. What would Mama say? See it all from now on, she orders herself. Don't be part of it.

"Would you like something to drink?" Vera asks Dorothy. "Ben keeps some shnappes, and I've got a pretty good bottle of brandy up in my room."

Dorothy looks at Mickey. He's got an arm around her shoulders. He pulls her closer and says, "Whatever you want, baby."

She turns back toward Vera and says, "I guess I wouldn't say no to a brandy." She lifts the corners of her lips a smidgen. "Take the edge off of this chill."

Vera lays a hand lightly on Dorothy's shoulder. "Sit," she says, aiming her onto the couch. "Relax." She steps toward the attic stairs, hesitates, turns back. "I'm so glad you're here." Dorothy's eyes meet Vera's for the first time. Still guarded, and sad, but the anger seems to be seeping away. "Grateful, really."

"Grateful?"

She thinks I'm a phony, Vera tells herself. She walks back toward the couch. She sits beside Dorothy. "What I mean by grateful," she begins, then pauses as Mickey sits on his wife's other side. As if to catch her. "When we met, last year?"

"Yes?"

"I should have said this then."

"Said what?"

"Thank you. I should have thanked you—"

"For—"

"For marrying Mickey." Wait. That came out wrong.

Dorothy chuckles. Mickey too. "Gee thanks, sis," he says.

"I meant—"

"I know I'm not the catch of the century, but jeez Louise, Vera, you make it sound like Dorothy's doing her Christian duty or something!"

"Come to think of it, Mick, you were a bit of a charity case—" Dorothy's eyes twinkle.

"Hey!"

"Mismatched socks. Eating cold beans straight out of the can." Dorothy pinches his cheek. She turns toward Vera. "Still, it was my pleasure. And you're very welcome."

"Okay, you two, quit teasing me. You know what I mean." Vera takes Dorothy's hand, reaches across her lap and grabs Mickey's too. "He's my little brother. He's been alone. I'm just so glad—"

"Oy, Veraleh, don't go all mushy on us here." Mickey pulls his hand away then yelps, "Ouch!" as Dorothy gives his palm a little slap. "What's that for?"

"For sassing your big sister when she's trying to say something nice. Now apologize."

"Okay, okay. Sorry, Vera." That crooked grin of his. Grand. But she isn't done. "So why do you still look so serious?"

"I'm the one who owes an apology." Vera faces Dorothy again. She'd like to take her hand again, but she isn't sure she should. "For tonight." Dorothy waits. "I wanted you ... to be part of the family. So I invited you. And you were treated horribly." Silence. "I don't know which is worse. Them keeping you out, or me not knowing that they would." Vera bites her lip. "I ... I don't know what else to ... " Still Dorothy says nothing. Vera looks down. "I'm sorry." She jumps when Dorothy touches her hand. "Oh—"

"Hell, it's a physical reflex, woman. You were startled. You jumped." Vera waits. Dorothy peers at her shrewdly. "Maybe we should all try to relax."

Vera hears car doors slam, voices approaching outside. At the Graystone, when Vera had gone back for her coat and told everyone about Dorothy being barred the party had quickly broken up. Ruby nearly apoplectic with wrath and remorse, her parents shamefaced. Peter, Mabel, Sam and Ada seeming sympathetic, the men nevertheless saying they and their wives would stay a while—until Lenny left them all dumbfounded. Snatching coats, pulling back chairs, gripping his father and Vera's boss by their starched white collars and practically lifting them into the air, he'd announced that the party was officially over. "Th-thi-this is a g-g-goddamn d-d-disgrace," he'd said, not yelling but managing to make himself heard over the music. "Wh-wh-what the hell are w-w-we s-s-s-sup-p-pposed to be celebrating, anyway?" Vera saw Gussie gulp at the bad language but she herself was thrilled. "I'm l-l-leav-v-ving to f-f-f-fight the g-g-goddamn Nazis! B-b-bomb those b-b-bastards b-b-back t-t-to k-k-kingdom come—f-f-for what?" Face flushed, he turned toward Peter. "And my own aunt can't c-c-c-come to the p-party?" Where did he get the backbone? He rarely speaks three sentences in a row. "It's a g-g-god-d-damn d-d-d-disgrace—" Peter's high, lined dome of a forehead bobbed in a placating half-nod. Vera caught Lenny casting a glance toward Ruby. Oh. It's for her. No matter, she was glad her son was taking a stand. "A goddamn d-d-disgrace, and w-w-we're all g-getting the hell out of this st-st-stinking place. You t-too, P-p-p-pop." He leaned toward his father, stretching his long neck and eyeballing him from above. Peter made a jerky movement, a leg twitched, and Vera thought, why he's scared. How about that. "G-g-get y-y-our c-c-c-coat on and g-g-get out of here." Her boy had looked at Ruby again. The girl's eyes blazed. Lenny had turned back toward his father. "G-g-give me your c-car k-k-keys. I'm sure the P-P-Plecks won't mind driving you home. I'm t-t-taking Ruby."

VERA'S WILL

Now here they come—Lenny, Ruby, Gussie, Ben—and Dorothy's supposed to what? Act eager to be introduced? Accept another round of apologies? Be the gracious one, soothe their embarrassment?

Vera looks at Dorothy's face. Lined. Tired eyes. No spring chicken, her brother's bride, or maybe whatever she's endured has aged her beyond her years. I know something about enduring, Vera thinks. I've got to let her see. That I understand, at least a little. That I won't be a part of anything like this, ever again. That I'm sorry. That I want her for family. Sisters.

I do. I won't. We will be.

Their second brandy. Dorothy takes Vera's hand and for an instant Vera remembers dreams she never lets herself have, someone on her bed, touching her, and she nearly laughs that this is how it finally happens. Not a sweetheart but a sister. Not squalid, not the dirty stuff of the longings she's suppressed, but decent. Clean. Sitting on my bed with the woman of my brother's dreams. Holding her hand. Becoming friends.

"You mean it took him three years?" Vera asks.

Dorothy nods. She smiles. Her face glows. "That is exactly what I mean." Dorothy pats her forehead and her cheeks.

The glow, Vera sees, is a slight sheen of sweat. "Are you too warm?"

Dorothy shakes her head. "It's all right." She takes a sip. "The brandy, I think."

"I ... we probably shouldn't have anymore."

"Why not?"

"I just mean, shouldn't we get back downstairs?"

Dorothy listens to the sounds from below. Voices. A Benny Goodman record. "I'm fixing to stay up here and talk a while. They're having a fine time."

"But Mickey—"

"Oh, don't worry about him, Vera. He can entertain himself, I'm sure I don't have to tell you that."

"He might be worried—"

"About what, for heaven's sake? That you'll try to—" Dorothy stops mid-sentence and looks away.

Pricks of shock scrape the back of Vera's neck. She'd like a cigarette. The pack's on the desk. She can't get to it. The moment extends.

Dorothy knows? Squeamish hope sweeps her. She takes a quick swig for courage. "I'll try to what?"

Dorothy turns to Vera. "I didn't mean ... Your brother, he loves you. Part of why tonight turned out hard. He ... look, I've lived in this world long enough, I guess you could say I'm toughened behind all that—"

"The Graystone, you mean?"

"Uh-huh. Like I say, nothing much surprises me. But Mickey, he was shocked—not so much at—we play the clubs, he's seen this stuff—he tries to protect me, and I guess he assumed you would too. He figured if you had a party there, and invited us, you'd know the rules—"

"Oh, Dorothy. I should have."

"Yeah. You should. Got a feeling next time you will. Anyway, when we got turned away, we were standing there outside trying to decide what to do, and do you know what he said to me? Before I told him to go on in and find you, I mean? He said, 'Vera of all people.' He expected better from you."

"When he said me of all people ..." Vera looks past Dorothy, toward the door. What if someone comes in? "Did he mean ..."

"You know ..." Dorothy pauses. "What I'm saying is ... is that you know what it's like to be on the outside looking in." Vera can't speak. "That's what he meant. By saying you of all people." Dorothy fiddles with her wedding ring. Vera focuses on the calloused fingers. She feels as if she's in the bassist's hands, strings being plucked all over the place, low, soothing, lifting to high notes, release. "Oh, lord in heaven, woman," and the sharp tone snaps Vera's head up, eyes off Dorothy's hands and back to her face, where she sees not anger but impatience, swiftly softening into amusement. "I don't know why I'm talking this way, all careful-like and all. We don't have to pussyfoot around this here. Your brother and me, we live a different type of life, you know. Clubs, dance halls, dives. All around, here and there. Our line of work, it doesn't matter where, big cities, podunk, we don't hang around regular-type people too much. It is all kinds. Know a guy in Harlem, Billy Strayhorn, played with him a couple times, you heard of him?" Vera shakes her head. "Wrote that song about the A train."

"Oh! I love that number. It always reminds me of—"

"Of those other times, clubs uptown, huh?"

"Mickey told you?"

"Sure. He told me. Now I'll tell you something, Vera. Listen, I guess maybe you don't know this, but gals like you, they're not so rare. Leastways not amongst the folk we tend to find ourselves amongst." Dorothy chuckles. "Now I'm not shocking you here, am I? I mean, you do know you're not the only one parts your hair on the other side, don't you?"

May 1943

Everybody on the bus is sniffling this morning. There's a scratchy tickle in the back of Vera's throat. Her eyes itch. Her seatmate just sneezed. Her nose drips. Glorious springtime!

She doesn't mind. Detroit in bloom. The season is fleeting: it drifts through after the cold and before the heat. Precious weeks that will be gone in a wink. First rain came, and now, finally, green, to sweep away the grime that legions of auto workers sprinkle like fairy dust across the land. Every day of every year, microscopic particles of steel shavings and god knows what else dance eastward from the River Rouge megaliths, west from the smokestacks of Dodge Main, landing on Bagley, on Dexter Boulevard, on all points in between, an invisible shower of shmutz that insinuates itself into the dank Great Lakes air and clogs every sinus, lingers in every lung–this year more than ever, with Messrs. Ford and Chrysler and their martial rival Gen. Motors stepping up production to fill military orders. Steel must be milled. Tanks assembled. A year and a half into battle, the plants run twenty-four hours. Assembly lines have been retooled, timetables revised. *There's a war on, woman*, as Rosie the Riveter reminds her from ads on the side of the bus. But there are flowers everywhere—from the burgundy and crimson geraniums and petunias encircling the oak trees that march along Grand Boulevard to the apricot tulips and tawny primroses Gussie has planted around the house to catch the rainwater runoff that drips from the roof gutters—and Vera would rather smell them than dwell on all that death. At least until after work.

Tonight, as every night, she will reboard the bus. Watch the blocks pass. Step off onto Dexter Boulevard. Inch up the sidewalk dreading the news that the telegram has just arrived. Every muscle clenched. So far, luck. So far, there is no shiny five-pointed poster, pretty emblem of another soldier dead, plastered to the puny window of her attic room.

Lenny. Her handsome hero of a son. Glamorous flyboy, doing his duty for god and country. Until he dies. I fail to see the glory in that, Vera thinks, reaching for the pull cord as the bus tips toward Woodward. Or what his flights over North Africa have to do with freedom. She opens her pocketbook, pops her compact, inspects her face. Good. Lipstick intact despite her tendency to press her mouth into a tight, thin line. Eyebrows neatly plucked above the deep wells from which Flo used to say Vera's soul peeked. Long ago.

She stands, sighs, eases into the aisle. She smoothes her skirt, rights the line of her blouse, runs a hand along perfectly coifed waves of brown going to gray. Steps off the bus. So, Vera thinks. Irving Berlin I'm not. God bless America? Fine. Great. Yet she's sure it doesn't matter how many torpedoes Lenny drops. Hitler might not like the Allied bombing raids over Tunisia—he wants the African markets just as Wall Street does—but they won't save the Jews of Europe.

So? Her mother's voice fills her mind as Vera begins walking briskly down the block. What else is new? Mama, the old red.

Dead almost fifteen years now, still imparting her Bolshie brand of wisdom. That's not what this war is about, Veraleh, and you know it. What does FDR care from the Jews? So if Lenny dies? It's for nothing? Your boy won't die, Mama whispers. Vera can nearly feel her mother's cool breath caressing her cheek.

Mama's right, she convinces herself. Lenny's fine. He writes her of cutting up with his crew, cracking jokes as they streak through the sky. He'll survive. And the other? Where is Willy? Vera tastes salt as a single tear wets her lip.

Pull yourself together, she commands as she approaches Sam Pleck's Record Shack. She turns at the corner, and again at the alley. She heads into Pleck's by the back entrance.

Vera is lucky in her co-workers. Really, no complaints in that department. Only, must Sam's secretary play the radio quite so loud quite so early in the morning? Must the inventory clerk whistle incessantly? Is it absolutely necessary that the two perky, ponytailed typists smack their keyboards in just that never-ending cadence, clackety clack until the cows come home? And smack the gum they constantly chew, too, the two of them in unison like demented bobby-soxed cuckoo clocks?

Whoa there. It's only nine-fifteen. She's been in barely forty-five minutes and she needs a break. Can she get away with one this soon? I'd better, she thinks, or I'll snap at someone and then this little office will shrink even more.

"Betty," she says to the secretary, "would you cover for me if Sam comes through? I've just got to have a second cup of coffee."

"Sure, hon. You do look a little bleary-eyed. Get me one too, would you?"

"Honestly, I don't know what's wrong with me this morning." To be honest, she does. "Cream and sugar?" Betty nods. "I'll be back in a flash."

Vera pulls her pocketbook out of a drawer, pats Betty's shoulder as she passes her, grabs her sweater from the peg next to the secretary's desk and bounds down the stairs. She leaves the way she came in, through the back door.

The morning air is still cool. The day feels quiet. Slow. The sidewalk is clear, everyone inside offices, Wayne classrooms, the little stores that line Woodward. Vera breathes easier.

Flower boxes flank the curb. She stoops to sniff. Straightening, she reaches into her pocketbook for her little silver lighter and a smoke. She takes a deep draw and squares her shoulders. There. Relax, Vera Steiner. It was only one brief turn on a tiny scrap of a dance floor. No one knows. And it'll never happen again.

It's not that, she tells herself. She crosses the street to the coffee shop. I'm exhausted, that's all. I don't know what Dorothy was thinking, keeping me out until last call. Why, I didn't get to bed until nearly three a.m. Did I sleep at all?

The counterman hands her two steaming cups. She promises to return them by the end of the day and hands him two bits. I hope this props my eyes open, she thinks. A working girl needs her rest. It's easy enough for Dorothy and Mickey. They'll roll out of bed hours from now. Their job—hard to acknowledge that's what it is, that work can be a thing of joy—doesn't begin until regular people are preparing for bed. Oh hell, they'll never understand, crazy way they live.

To tell the truth, though, she can't complain. They drag her to gigs, theirs or their pals', and she has a blast. The jazz is grand. The pulse, on the once-in-a-blue-moon nights when Dorothy and Mickey pass through, feels like life. What's the point in grumbling? I could pick up the phone this morning, she thinks, scold for an hour. Tonight they'd be on the horn again begging me to join them at some hot new spot, promising I won't regret it.

Does she? Regret last night? Back behind Pleck's, Vera stops short at the door, breathing the coffee's steam.

How long had she danced? Four minutes, five, that's all, then it was over and like Cinderella rushing after midnight from the ball she'd tottered to the table without looking back. The song had ended, a slow number, familiar though for the life of her she can't remember it now, the music pausing only for an instant, people dropping coins into the jukebox, one record starting up right after the last one finished. It was in that instant between tunes, as the WAC let go of Vera's hand to brush a stray hair from her face, looked up, grinned and looked away, with the noise of a hundred chattering voices, clinking ice in dripping glasses, laughter, someone clapping to get someone else's attention, the smell of sweat and alcohol fumes and fruity scents from too much perfume—that was when the too-much, too-real feel of the place broke through, broke the spell and Vera pulled swiftly away.

Before that, she'd been bewitched. For four minutes, five at the most. By a short, solid female soldier with brown hair, a baby face and a hand that felt like heaven pressed lightly against Vera's back. She'd danced. Floated, for yes, she'd had a drink or three, and it was a romantic number and it had been forever since she'd felt a womanly palm firm in the small of her back, a warmth radiating up her spine, down her legs. With her other hand the WAC clasped Vera's. She held it tight, up close against her shoulder. Vera's fingers tingled at the touch. She closed her eyes. She glided, surrendering to those hands. Trusting them to guide her in this long forsaken homeland.

She laid her cheek on the WAC's shoulder. The girl smelled soapy, clean. A dreamboat.

Did I put my lips to her skin? Vera swallows, an acidic sting in her gullet as the coffee goes down. Oh god, did I get that carried away? She presses her forehead against the wall. Get a grip, girlchik, she tells herself. One kiss, it's not as though you crossed the River Styx. The slightest little nip on the neck, a split second, that's all, and then the song ended and in the pause before the next one she lifted her head and came to her senses and slipped away. The WAC hadn't pursued her. Vera had caught sight of her once or twice, swinging with younger gals. Probably realized I'm too old. Probably wondered what an old broad like me was doing at Gigi's.

Vera balances the coffee cups in one hand while she opens Pleck's back door. I have no business at a place like that, she thinks. Last night was the second time she let Dorothy and Mickey talk her into it. She resolves to tell them that's the end. Wherever else, she's game. Only not Gigi's. Not Sugar's. Her brother and sister-in-law mean well. They don't see the danger.

Not yet noon. Although she wants only to sleep, hours of work remain. Soon, on her lunch break, she'll get some more spring air. One of Detroit's rare clear days. First, fifteen more minutes here. At her station. Counting Sam Pleck's funds.

Vera is good with numbers. Not a natural adept, but put an adding machine in front of her and she can hold her own. I ought to, she thinks, running a pencil over the column of figures. I've been at it long enough.

She's content pressing keys, double-checking totals, carefully printing them in Sam's green ledger books, one per budget quarter. Maybe content isn't the right word. Settled, then. Vera isn't someone who really fits anywhere, ever, she knows that well enough, but the task of keeping Sam's books suits her. She's glad to have a routine. And this job isn't so bad, what with Betty's radio providing background music and plenty of small talk available from the secretary herself, the typists and clerks. Sam plows through several times a day. Here he comes now, a friendly pat on the back to the boys, "Hello, Vera, how ya doing, my dear" to her. "I'm all right, Sam," she replies. "How about you, Betty, my beloved," as he enters his private sanctum. Cigar smoke wafts through the outer office in his wake. "Just swell, Sam, just swell," Betty yells, for he's already inside, door closed. She winks at Vera, who shakes her head, smiles back, and clasps her nose as a plume of smoke envelops her.

If she has to have a boss, Vera knows, she could do a lot worse. Sam's always asking about Lenny with what seems like genuine concern. Concern you can't take to the bank, of course, and all right it wouldn't kill him to up her pay, especially now with business picking up. Sam Pleck likes to make a buck, there's no question about that. This war has been good to him. The country's gone music-crazy these last few years. Records fly out of here. It's funny, considering that the man has no taste whatsoever. Music? He doesn't know Crosby from Caruso. But he's good at picking underlings. Everyone on the selling floor is hep as all get-out. They move the product, he watches what they sell, they fill him in on trends, he taps the profit. Sometimes Vera wonders if the sales staff resent the way their expertise lines his pockets. She's seen some of these kids, cigarettes and coffee instead of lunch. Does it ever eckle them, his hail-fellow-well-met act, when meanwhile he ducks out at four or five o'clock to drive his Chrysler Imperial to his big house on Outer Drive? Betty has been there at the next desk nearly as long as I've been here at mine. He must have hired her in '32, '33. Yet I'll bet my bottom dollar she hasn't had a raise in at least five years. Does she ever wonder why the guy can't spare her a few more cents?

He's a good boss, a nice man, never harsh, always reasonable, but it does get to you after a while when you sit recording his numbers day in day out and the numbers keep rising and you're still a lousy boarder in someone's attic, the quiet of your cell invaded every night by tinny emissions lifting from Gussie and Ben's big old Philco. When your piano was taken along with your children a lifetime ago, and your fingers' only chance to touch the kind of keyboard they crave is if you walk down to the Grinnell Brothers' showroom after work. If that salesman is on hand, the fey one with the trim gray mustache, if they're not busy and if you catch his eye and he gives the nod, you can sit at a grand piano and play for a quarter-hour or so. When you have to sneak small pleasures like that you can't help but wish for a little cash in your pocket. When Vera looks at all Sam has, summers with his wife and kids at their place on Cass Lake while she can't afford to live in even a tiny studio apartment of her own, it takes a mighty effort to stave off bitterness.

Betty's voice interrupts her reverie. "You are something else!"

"Hmm?"

"The way you keep punching those numbers and pulling that lever. It's like your fingers have a mind of their own. I mean, look at your eyes—flicking between the invoices and the adding machine and I just bet you haven't made a single darned mistake, and yet at the same time I can see your mind is a million miles away. How in the world do you do it?"

Vera shrugs. She pushes her chair back from the desk. She regards Betty and the other girls. We work like dogs, she thinks. No matter how we feel we carry on. Automatons. Extensions of our machines. Betty attached to that switchboard, the bobby-soxers typewriting fiends. All of us cogs in the Pleck money-making machine. Next time Ruby starts in about her beloved CIO, I ought to ask why the unions don't do something for the girls in the back office like me.

"Ready for lunch, Vera?" She nods, but declines Betty's suggestion that they eat together, sit at that lunch counter on Warren, watch out the window as Wayne students rush between classes. "Why so blue?" Betty asks.

"What do you mean? I've got some errands to run, that's all."

Not true. She just feels like eating alone.

She munches grilled cheese at a greasy spoon much like the one Betty'd picked but further east. After a few bites she stops. Smells and sounds perfume the crowded lunch spot, making her queasy. Garlic fuming up from chili someone slurps noisily in the booth behind her. Radio blasting Sam Heilmann's Tigers play-by-play. The joint is none too clean, either. When the cook plops Vera's glass of ginger ale in front of her, it slides along the slick film covering the countertop. Skip it. She rises. She wipes her fingers on a paper napkin. She pays. She leaves.

Ten minutes until she has to go back to Pleck's. She finds a bench at a bus stop on John R. She sits, inhaling May's flowery scents mixed with Motor City traffic particulates. This morning's allergic sniffle recommences. She pulls a hankie from her purse, dabs at her nose.

She was a fool to go to Gigi's. Didn't she know what it would do to her? Stupid, stupid, stupid. How many hours before she can get some sleep? She lets her eyes close. Behind her lids she sees the WAC. Sweet-faced girl. Her hand on my back.

A horn honks. Her eyes open. This will never do.

She rises with a small sigh, recoiling at a popping sound then looking around, embarrassed, when she realizes it was her knees cracking. Jesus Christ. I'm turning into an alter kocker, she thinks.

Forget the girl. The quotidian, though. The day-in, day-out of it all.

The mood digs in. Refuses to release her. The afternoon drags.

After work, at last, back on the bus. When she gets to Gussie and Ben's, she'll yoo-hoo a quick howdy-doo then head up to the attic and go to bed. If her luck holds, they'll keep the radio low and the twins will study quietly. This is all Vera hopes: a good night's sleep.

If she had her own place she wouldn't have to worry. Yep, and if I had a million dollars I'd be a millionaire. She squeezes into an aisle seat as the bus lumbers forth.

She watches Woodward pass. As the packed bus takes a left onto Grand Boulevard, standing passengers grab poles. Vera grips the seat in front of her. That's something right there, she thinks. You've got a seat. She knows what Mama would tell her. Workers and soldiers dying. You have no reason to gripe. So what you're alone. A boarder in someone else's home. At least there's a roof over your head. A job. You haven't starved, you have your health, no one dear was shot at the '37 hunger march.

She pictures her passbook with its pages of minutely multiplying numbers. Now there's a happy thought. After all these years as a boarder, she has managed to save a bit again. She smiles: my hope chest. So what if her hopes have whittled down to the humblest of dreams? Her own place. It would be something, at least.

How lovely to live in Palmer Park. She'd take the Hamilton line after work. And on a spring evening like this, she imagines, she might stay on past her stop, not getting off until Seven Mile Road so she could stroll south through the park itself, smell flowers, smile at picnickers, watch small children feed the ducks before heading home. A little apartment where she could sleep and read and broil a lamb chop beholden to no one for use of the stove. Pull back the curtains and watch the weather and wait for Willy. Lie in the bathtub as long as she wants, unworried whether someone might hear her weep.

A young woman stands next to Vera. She digs into her purse, hands at Vera's eye level. Vera remembers the feel of the WAC's fingers on her back. A twinge of desire overtakes her. She shifts in her seat. Watch out, she tells herself, or you'll miss your stop. Good dancer, the WAC. Vera never even got her name.

One dance, it's all I allowed myself, why can't I have a name to go with the face when I close my eyes at night? It would be little enough.

Off the bus, walking up Dexter. She makes a fist, punches her palm, purses her lips. Stifles the sniveling before it begins. Approaches Gussie and Ben's. And shifts from one emptiness to the next.

Lenny. Stepping along the sidewalk, Vera readies herself to hear he's dead.

She's practiced often enough. With each battle she's tried to prepare. Guadalcanal. Salerno. Dysentery, drowned, shot to bits. Downed, brought crashing to earth or sea. The daily ritual, though familiar, chills her. She shivers. She throws her favorite spring sweater over her shoulders. Pale green cashmere, beaded monogram at the heart. Her blood pumps. Step step. A thudding at her temples. She clutches her pocketbook. He's dead, she tells herself. Give up.

She's at the house. She stands still, eyes the cracked pavement, draws a jagged breath, smooths her skirt with clammy palms. Lights a cigarette. Raises her head. No gold star. She takes a deep draft, releases the smoke along with the dread. Lenny lives.

Vera takes out her keys, heads up the driveway, enters Gussie and Ben's house. It's quiet. Thank heaven. No one around.

She crosses the kitchen. Ascends the stairs. Unlocks the attic door.

She drops her purse, steps out of her shoes, spreads her toes against the cool wood floor. Sits down on the bed. Looks out the window. Watches the sky until stars appear.

IV

Lost and Found

"He was a cook, Vera. A cook!"

"I know."

"Cooks aren't supposed to die!"

"No." Vera holds the handset tight, searches for something to say. She wishes she could hold Dorothy, hug her until the pain goes away, but you can't hug away the pain of a brother's death, and certainly not across six hundred miles of telephone line.

"Cooks feed soldiers. Vera—am I right?" Dorothy rushes on without waiting for a response. "Not that he knew a damn thing about it, believe you me, woman, my brother Curtis could not find his way around a kitchen for anything, I can't imagine he actually produced any edible food. Probably had him peeling potatoes all day, or dishwasher most likely. Be that as it may, his classification was cook. K.P. duty. And cooks don't fight. Right?"

"Right."

"Cooks cook. Or even if they scrub pans. It's soldiers who die." Dorothy draws a raggedy breath then rushes on. "He wanted to fight. I told you, right?" Vera nods, feeling foolish as she realizes Dorothy can't see her. "They told him no. Said, 'stay in the canteen, boy.' You know why?"

"I do, Dorothy. Because he was—"

"Because he's a Negro. None of our fellows, they won't let them get out in front. Clean latrines, make the generals' beds, hell I bet Ike figures those boys sure know how to do that sort of work. Probably scared what'll happen if they give them guns—ha! Stuck Curtis in the kitchen, scrubbing pots and pans, peeling potatoes, day and night, boiling beans. He wrote me. — Remind me to show you. I'll bring it with me next time we're in Detroit. He was sick of it, disgusted, what use is this, that's what he wrote me, just this last letter, last month ... last time he wrote. I have to show you. Wanted to do ... more ... you know? They, well I don't know's I can say they humiliated him, he was so proud, Vera, I wish you could have seen, a proud man, beautiful, really, and I don't say that only because he was my brother, damned good looking, almost pretty if you know what I mean, kind of fellow folks would always look twice. Upright. All the time. So that I don't care what he's doing he is not bowing down. Not Curtis. But still yet. Still yet, just because he could take it doesn't mean they should have done that to him, you know?" Vera nods again, realizes again that Dorothy can't see, wonders what else she can do, but Dorothy is already plunging on. "Stuck him at the sink like that, or serving up the food it may be, slopping it onto the white boys' trays, imagine how he felt, or, hell, serving the generals at their tables, eyes down, yes sir no sir ... like as if he was back home, like as if it was the old days if you know what I mean." Dorothy falters. She may be running out of steam. "And Jesus god, him a beauty, I wish you'd ever seen, a fine fellow, fine fine fine ..." A pause, and Vera pictures Dorothy's eyes. They must be swollen nearly shut now from all the tears. Dorothy starts again—"Still and all"—but slower, quieter—"seeing as how they did that to him ... made him a cook is what I'm saying ... if you're not going to give a fellow a chance to be a hero"—her voice rises—"how in the goddamn hell do you go and let him die?"

How is not clear. The telegram, which Dorothy has read to Vera twice, finesses the facts with standard-issue gloss. "Regret to inform." "In the service of his country." This morning, damning the long-distance expense, getting Sam to say he'd deduct the charges from her next paycheck, Vera had made some calls, hoping to help in some little way from Detroit while Mickey and Dorothy made the trek to Queens to bury Curtis and then back to their Harlem walkup to gather with friends. At least now they know it wasn't a bullet. That would have been grotesque, not allowed to fight but caught in the spray—or a stray mistaken shot—errant unexploded grenade—or a step onto a land mine. It was none of that, the helpful Marine clerk on the phone claimed. Merely disease. Malaria, or dysentery, maybe, or it could have been some sort of foreign germ, you'd be surprised how many fellows it claims, the clerk explained. Conditions over there—but where? Oh gee, I'll have to check, somewhere in the Pacific theater I think, can't tell from his file, security reasons and all—there's a lot of guys get sick. Some don't make it. Cost of war, I guess, miss. Shame, but there it is. Sorry for your loss. He'd managed to be both peremptory and polite, dismissing her but in a sympathetic tone.

Vera wonders if the papers the clerk had consulted showed what shade Curtis's skin was. Perhaps not, or he wouldn't have even tried to be kind. What sort of fellow Curtis was. That he had a sister. Who needs Vera's help. In a practical sense—which Vera gladly gives, this is the easy part, the money, the calls. It's the intangibles that concern her.

Comfort? She's never able to find any herself. How to provide it for her best friend?

For this is what Dorothy has become. They eased into it slowly at first, starting with the night of Lenny's goodbye party two years ago. Each for her own reason cautious. Far from where they started, each, ready to forge a new link.

Letters, the phone when one or the other is feeling flush, fleeting visits when the band makes a Motor City run. Not enough, never enough, yet somehow by now the tie is strong. So when Mickey had called yesterday, Sunday afternoon, when he'd said Dorothy needs you, Vera hadn't hesitated.

The telegram had come a few hours before, he told her. The body was due to arrive in New York the very next morning. But they were, as usual, broke. Would Vera—could Vera—did she think she might be able to spare—to help with the burial and such—

"Of course," she said.

"Really?" Her brother asked. "I know you can't have much. We hate to even ask—"

"So nu, I won't buy those diamond earrings I've been eyeing."

"Seriously, Vera, we're sorry you should have to sacrifice—"

"Come on. You're family."

"Glad you feel that way." Mickey hesitated. "Because this thing is going to really add up. Not just buying a coffin, but hiring a hearse to drive it out to the cemetery in Queens, the burial itself, and the plot. And then afterward, tomorrow night, Dorothy wants to have something, some kind of gathering—"

"Sort of a shiva—or, what is it she—her folks—do—"

"Something like that. Some food, some booze, let her relax, let the band pay their respects, you know, it'll help out. Don't you think?"

"Sure. She needs company. She's lucky she has you."

"And you. Which, so listen, I'm talking a loan here, Veraleh. We'll pay you back. As soon as we can—"

"Stop already with that. I have some savings." There goes her Palmer Park apartment. Silly dream. "I'll get to Western Union and wire it this afternoon."

Mickey must have heard the quiet in her voice. "Oh jeez, Vera." He took a noisy gulp of some drink. "It's got to have took you a long time to save—"

"I said enough already." How easy it was to decide. So she'd stay in the attic. Not so tragic. She'd survive.

"I'd ask Solly—he's got plenty bucks—if he hadn't been such an awful shmuck about me marrying Dorothy. Not that he'd help anyway. But even if he would, I'd never go to him. I hope you understand ..."

"Of course, Mickeleh. What happened to him that he could act this way? Mama would be so ashamed—"

"I know what Mama would say. That it's because he went over to the other side. Because he's rich from the rag trade is why he's a goddamn bigot. I don't know about that, I'll tell you the truth, Veraleh, there's plenty got no dough at all have been just as nasty toward Dorothy and me, Jew and goy alike—"

"It must be—"

"The hell of it is she's forever trying to protect me. She says she's used to it ..." Mickey sighed. "They say slavery ended eighty years ago. For a Negro it's as if it was only yesterday. That's how bad it is, the way they're treated. Well, you know. You two have talked. But about Solomon Resnick I'll say this: nothing is what I want from that gonif. So ... well, thanks a million, kid."

That had been yesterday. Today, as soon as she'd gotten home from work Vera had called Dorothy. Now they've been on the phone for a half-hour. At first she had to strain to catch Dorothy's words. At first Dorothy only answered direct questions. Thus, slowly, Vera has learned about the day Dorothy and Mickey have had so far. Subway to Brooklyn. Bus from the Heights to the Navy Yard. Where they discovered that the ship had already arrived. The coffin was already in the hearse. For a moment Dorothy's voice on the phone rose, high and plaintive. "We were late! Oh god, we were supposed to be there to meet him and instead he was all alone, no one he knew waiting for him, strangers only, strangers handling him, no one who cared, no one he loved." Then she paused, and when she spoke again the panicky note had vanished. "What the hell am I talking about, meet him? Dead—he doesn't know—doesn't care—him?—there is no him. You know, Vera?"

"I know, dear."

Then Dorothy, in a monotone, sketched in the rest of their day. Riding behind the hearse in the Ferguson and Sons Funeral Home's car. Watching as some men pulled out the coffin. Following behind as they rolled it to the gravesite. Standing while some other men worked a pulley dropping the box with Curtis's body into the ground. Riding back into the city, and up to 135th Street. All in a deadpan recitation that gave Vera a tight feeling in her chest.

When Vera had asked who was expected tonight, Dorothy said Mickey'd set all that up but she figured there'd be a houseful of folks. Neighbors, friends, who knows. Vera guessed every drum thumper and horn blower in New York might very well show up, for Dorothy and Mickey are well loved in those quirky circles. Some scene, it would be. Vera wondered how Dorothy would handle it in her muted, numb state. And then, just as it seemed Dorothy was ready to hang up, instead she opened up. She let out with a gasping sob that wrenched Vera's heart. And she cried. For a long time. Vera, helpless, made nonsensical "there there" sounds into the telephone. Finally Dorothy had started to talk.

"A cook," she'd said. "A cook."

It has now been forty minutes and she hasn't stopped talking except to take a quavery breath, blow her nose. "A cook," she says, and again, "a cook." For forty minutes while in the background Vera hears Mickey noisily laying out plates, arranging chairs, Dorothy has talked without pause. So that now Vera's fear is whether her friend will ever stop. Will she never retreat to the internal enclave where she'd been locked before, at least far enough toward normalcy to stand the company that is on its way?

"Goddamn it all. Vera, a cook, and they go and let him die!"

This is more than grief, Vera knows. This is rage. To which Dorothy has every right. But she worries. This kind of fury. This kind of pain. When wrongs are done to you and yours. There is a righteous wrath that picks you up and sweeps you away. Sweeps you clean. And the anger is good, and the anger is true—but it takes you to a far country where no one can live all the time. It isn't easy to return. Yet you have to, leaving the dead, temporarily at least, unavenged.

She realizes Dorothy has gone quiet. "Dearheart," she says, and there is no response. "Dee?"

"Yeah, Vee. I'm here."

"I wish I were too. There, with you. Wish there were something more I could do."

"Believe you me, so do I." Dorothy sighs. She sounds as if she's balancing out. "Truth to tell, though, Vee—"

"Yes?"

"Not so sure as how anyone can really help. Not so long as this world stays how it is."

"I understand."

"Close as you can, anyway." After another short silence Dee says she'd better go help Mickey pour drinks, and Vera says goodnight.

She stays at the kitchen table after hanging up. So here we are, she thinks. Dee and Vee. They're lucky if they meet in person two, three times a year. Sometimes they can grab only a quick clasp on a club floor during a musical break. Other times it's a meal, a picnic, a leisurely getting together when Mickey and Dorothy have managed to tack on an extra day before or after a Detroit gig. The three of them have a blast shooting the bull. After a while Mickey removes himself, listens to a ball game with Ben or climbs a tree out back with the twins, so the friends can gab alone.

The talk goes deeper then. Sometimes, in the thick of it, one grabs the other's hand. At the physical contact a gush of feeling flows through Vera. She loses her train of thought. She strokes Dee's fingers, the bass player's calluses at the tips hard and smooth as a carapace. She has a shell, like me, Vera thinks. She's earned it.

Dorothy has shown Vera her soft side. Her smile, eyes warm, fills Vera with gratitude and something like peace. That smile isn't offered easily, Vera knows, or to just anyone. What Dorothy shows the world is a steely strength. Forged in fire, for she has seen terrible things. The sisters-in-law have exchanged life stories in their monthly correspondence. Dorothy's early letters were funny, full of piquant tales of life on the jazz-club circuit, and Vera replied in kind, concentrating especially on stories of Mickey's exploits as a street kid in Passaic. Then they went further. Vera learned that her friend's grit was acquired at some cost. And when her friend asked more details from Vera, she, to her own shock, complied.

She shouldn't have been surprised. She'd already established, from her years of annual eruptions to Flo, that she can put down on paper things she could never say out loud. But the letters to Dorothy actually get mailed. She has revealed her feelings to someone she didn't know three years ago. Someone nothing seems to faze.

Vera's mad about her, and "so what!" she tells herself. I'm allowed. We're family. It is not romantic love—Vera accepts that this is not an option for someone like her—but slowly and steadily this unforeseen relationship has unlocked her rusty old heart. What a sap I am, she thinks. They write each other, religiously, every month, and when a letter from Dorothy arrives inevitably it chokes Vera up. Just the fact of it. Of her. They've even exchanged pet names. Dee and Vee. How about that.

In a letter Vera received only last month, Dorothy had mused about her experiences in the North and the South. She and Curtis were raised in a sharecropper's family, parents scratching subsistence from a patch of Alabama dirt. When Dorothy was fourteen and Curtis nine, after two lynchings in the next county, their mother and father shipped the children to live with an aunt in Chicago. *But don't you dare think everything's fine up North*, Dorothy wrote. *You think that little thing at the Graystone was bad? Hell, that was nothing, woman. Mick's told you enough that you know the weird ways of life on the road. It's hard. For anyone, I suppose. But for a Negro? Forget it! Hiding on the floor in the back of the car while Mickey gets gas. Waiting while he brings out food because the restaurant won't seat me. And when the band travels by bus, all along the circuit, and this is the North, mind you, I'm talking about St. Louis, Indianapolis, Milwaukee, Chicago, Detroit, we most of us have to scoot down low, hoping we can ease through those speed traps, little towns where if they see our faces in the windows we'll win us a ticket, a night in jail, or worse.*

With all that, Dee's joie de vivre rarely flags. Vera sees how she refuses to be beaten down. Surely, in time, Dee will recover from even this latest excruciating blow. Vera might never entirely understand how. It's something inside her friend, some kind of strength, resilience, pride; whatever name you assign, it defines her, and draws Vera ever closer.

DECEMBER 1944

What a studious household this has become. Now that the twins are sophomores in high school, they've begun to apply themselves academically a bit. Ruby's influence, obviously.

She's been teaching since September, in exactly the spot she wanted: drama coach at Cooley High, where she also teaches two sections of English Lit, two of American, and handles home-room chores. As the semester heads toward its end, to be capped with a production of *The Man Who Came to Dinner* starring her favorite theater-smitten seniors, Ruby's mood is sky-high. And when Ruby soars, she lifts the whole family's spirits.

The whole family. There's that phrase again. Earlier this evening, Vera had excused herself and come upstairs after dinner, as Bud and Rose broke open the books and spread out around the kitchen table. Sometimes she feels almost as though the twins are her own kids ... Ruby sort of a daughter and sort of a friend ... and they love me too, that's the hell of it, she tells herself. Gussie doesn't mind, she started making room the day I moved in. Ben too. Took a while for me to see. I've got my boys, that's what I kept telling myself, they can't make me give that up, I won't let them force me to join them. Then somewhere along the line it dawned on me that I had joined, I was in. And it doesn't take anything from my boys and me. No one is saying that isn't real. Only that this is too. Not just this Schumacher crew, either. There's Mickey, and Dee.

In all Vera's years nothing has gone according to plan. Yet look what's happened. Like some crazy Rube Goldberg contraption, outlandish, improbable, the mismatched pieces clanging against each other but the thing as a whole chugging along. a life seems to have been cobbled together.

It may be the best someone like Vera can hope to achieve.

She bows over the nightstand to grind out the cigarette butt. Then she leans back on the pillow, arms folded behind her head. watching the louver-shackled moonlight play across the ceiling. Not half bad, really, when you tally it up. A brother. a friend or two. Some kids. Some laughter. Every night over dinner she hears accents that remind her of home. If her boys—when her boys come home, it will be a life complete.

And love? The other kind? She swallows. She unlocks her hands, lays them on her chest. Honestly, Vera tells herself. Forty-six years old. Why can't you let it go?

She closes her eyes. Wills herself to sleep. Dreams of sweet forbidden things.

Late the next afternoon. It's dark now. but today the sun was out, none of Detroit's usual December gloom. and Vera is in a mellow mood as the bus approaches home. She wonders what Gussie's cooking tonight. She's looking forward to dinner. but equally to afterward in the attic, a cup of tea. finishing her book. *A Tree Grows in Brooklyn*. She had it on reserve at the library for months before she could get it and now she sees why. So sad, so ... it makes her think of, remember. so many things. Tomorrow she'll start *Strange Fruit*. It'll be another rough read. she knows, but Dorothy's ordered her not to write again until she's read it.

She steps off the bus, placing her boots gingerly against the snow, trying not to slip on the ice. She spies Gussie and Ben and some others standing outside the deli. How those two love to shmooze. Between that and their tendency to extend credit to every shmendrick with a sad story, it's a wonder they keep the store going at all. Vera waves, skidding as she walks over an unshoveled patch of sidewalk. As she rights herself and draws near the house, she notices a big black Packard parked in front. Peter's car.

Stay calm, she tells herself. Lenny's fine. He has to be.

"Veraleh! Vera, dolly, hurry, come on, come here, come here!" Gussie's rushing toward her, she's grabbing Vera's arm, kissing, laughing. "Such news!"

"What is it already?" Everyone's smiling, even Peter. Ruby's here too.

"Veraleh, get ready—"

"Momma, hold on." Ruby grabs Gussie's shoulders. "Let Mr. Steiner tell her."

Gussie nods and gives Peter a good-natured nudge. "Nu then, go ahead."

He clears his throat. He juts his head forward. He gives Vera a weary smile. His eyes are watering from the cold. "It's Willy." Vera freezes. "They've—we've found Willy." She waits. "He's in the hospital."

"No! Where?"

"The V.A. hospital. In Battle Creek."

Half Life

My father was a scientist. He was very intelligent. More than intelligent—he was, I was given to understand, a genius. Like Albert Einstein or Isaac Newton. He would have been the one who came up with $E=MC^2$ or discovered gravity if he hadn't been born too late. If he hadn't been born too early, he might have been first to clone a human being or cure cancer or take a space/time radiospectograph of the Big Bang.

When the TV news announced one night that Crick and Watson had won the Nobel Prize for unraveling the genetic code, image of an eerily twisting double helix filling the screen behind Walter Cronkite's head, Dad looked grim. His jaw muscles bulged as he ground his molars to nubs. He pushed away his TV table even though he'd barely eaten any of Mom's famous brisket, slow-cooked while she was at work.

"DNA—I could have done that," he grumbled.

Mom agreed. "Rah rah rah for Watson the wunderkind. I'm so sick of hearing how young he is. Born in 1928, isn't that great. Well, he didn't have to go to war like you did." Dad grunted. "And that's the way it is," Mom concluded, voice dripping with irony, "Thursday, October 18, 1962."

Not two weeks later, I spent the whole weekend holding open the back door as Dad and Elliot lugged cinder blocks, steel beams and endless crates of canned goods into the house and down the basement stairs. Sunday night as I helped Mom make dinner while Dad and Elliot relaxed in front of the TV, I must have been acting grumpy because she put her hand on my shoulder and said, "Snap out of it, Randy."

"What?"

"I know you're pooped but you should be glad you could help. Glad we're all going to be safe."

"But the atom bombs—"

"If the bombs fall we'll be right here, downstairs, warm, dry, and fed, and for a darned long time if necessary."

"What about radiation?"

"This is what I'm always telling you, kiddo: thank your lucky stars that your father's a scientist. He knows what he's doing. Nobody in this family is getting zapped."

Dad had gotten right to work as soon as President Kennedy forced Kruschev to take his missiles out of Cuba. He was pretty well convinced that the Russians had double-crossed JFK and a nuclear attack was still imminent, so he quickly read up on the principles of home fallout shelters and swung into action. He even kept Elliot out of school for a couple days to help. The two of them built it all by themselves.

Cinderblock walls separated the shelter from the "Institute for Advanced Studies" and a ceiling of steel beams ensured it would withstand the worst bombs. The feature we were all proudest of, and which showed that Dad really knew what he was doing, was the entryway. It consisted of a twisty passage that changed direction three times because, according to Dad, radiation couldn't turn a corner. Now the cozy little room was stocked with cots and books and tons of canned food, a radio and batteries, flashlights, matches and candles, a chemical toilet and a fifty-gallon water tank. Dad had even raided the boxes with his war mementoes, so the shelter also held two authentic World War II combat helmets to shield Elliot's head and mine in case any atomic bomb debris got through the ceiling of steel beams.

As word of Dad's feat spread, it was the talk of the neighborhood. Everyone was in awe of our shelter. People came knocking on the door asking to see it, and Dad led little tours to show everyone what he'd done. At school my friends kept asking me if they could come to my house if there was a bomb. "Well," I'd say, crossing my arms and looking sad but stern, "unfortunately there is only enough space and supplies for four people. Maybe you should tell your dad to build one for your family." I felt quite complacent after these conversations—except for once, when I suddenly realized Dad wasn't planning to save the rest of our family and I got an unsettling image of my grandparents pounding on our door, the neighborhood in ruins around them, a big patch of radiation approaching, Grandma Gussie and Grandpa Ben crying, calling out in Yiddish, Tanteh Vera smoking, staring down the iridescent mushroom cloud.

Oh well. Science is a harsh mistress, as Dad was fond of telling El.

Strictly speaking, my father wasn't a scientist at all. He just chaired the Northdale High School science department and taught earth science and astronomy. I found this funny. The two subjects seemed like opposites to me: rocks and stars. But Dad said that rocks "and everything else on Earth, Randy, you and me and even Tanteh Vera, are star matter." Whatever that meant.

My rare conversations with Dad tended to go like that. Him making weighty pronouncements. Me nodding or shrugging. Him waiting a beat, tapping his foot, grinding his teeth in an obvious effort to give me a fair chance to speak. Each of us peering past the other in search of a rescuer—Mom for me, and for him Elliot would do nicely—someone to intercede, break the impasse, set us free from this excruciating, unnatural engagement. I always got the feeling he saw me as sort of an alien species. Which I did not hold against him, since basically I felt the same way about him. But man oh man I loved the way I could ask him anything and he'd know the answer. The way he always smelled clean. His careful, neat manner, the way he took up a precise amount of space so you knew just where he was when he was there and when he wasn't he left no residue. Yes, that too I loved: the clear delineation between his presence and his absence. It made me feel safe, somehow, not only his solidity but also the vacuum he left in his wake. The empty space I knew he'd fill on his return. I loved how he called me "dear" and patted my head when I padded over to him to say goodnight. He called Elliot "son" but he called me "dear."

He did have a quick temper. But it was easy enough to handle when it flared: get out of the way. The thing was, Mom explained to me often, Dad was frustrated in life. I mean, there he was, for all intents and purposes a walking, talking brain—sort of like this one "Twilight Zone" episode I'd seen where future humans consisted of floating mental essences stripped free of the daily necessities faced by mere physical entities. And then there was me. A girl who the year before had said "cosmetology" instead of "cosmology" in my final fiasco of an effort to be included in one of Dad and Elliot's scientific dialogues. I never did live that one down. Look at it objectively: why should a man like that have to consort with a girl like me?

It was a wonder he functioned at all, Mom felt, given the unfair obstacles he'd faced. Not just the war. It started way before that. "A marvel what a fine family man he is," I overheard her tell Auntie Rose on the phone once. "With his upbringing." She referred, I knew, to his parents being divorced and how Dad and Uncle Lenny grew up with their father. It had warped him, she felt. Between coming from a broken home and losing the momentum of his education when he went to war, "he really does remarkably well," she told Rose.

Mom had told me the whole sad story. How Dad had been an amazing student way back when. How he grasped abstruse concepts in a flash and then, with breathtaking leaps of insight, extrapolated, connected, pushed past, saw further. Great things were expected of Willy Steiner. World War II got in the way.

He enlisted. He was commissioned a first lieutenant. With his brains and his scores on the new IQ tests the Army had started using—Mom said Dad's were the highest yet recorded—he was destined for some special assignment. The sort that would have kept him out of harm's way, like breaking codes or inventing better bombs. But Dad wasn't having any of that. He wanted battle. He meant to kill some Nazis.

He never had a chance. Battle of the Bulge. It went bad fast.

One Saturday night the year before, Mom and I had stayed up late watching old movies and she'd confided in me about Dad's painful injuries and long recovery and how long it had taken him to overcome the resultant reliance on morphine. She made me swear I'd never mention it and I never did, but in my own mind I wondered whether this dramatic secret didn't explain something about the brittle character I knew. Perhaps his cognitive brilliance was locked in constant battle with a persistent yearning for oblivion lodged in some primitive nether region of his brain that remembered the feeling of opiated peace.

I wasn't sure when Mom and Dad got together, but I knew she'd taught drama and literature at Cooley High until she got pregnant with Elliot and that Dad went back to graduate school at Wayne for his doctorate in astrophysics while at the same time taking a job at suburban Northdale High. Teaching was supposed to be an interim thing, until he got his degree and moved up to university-level research. For all my growing-up years, in a small house with a big yard in Northdale where the family moved in 1957 to give Dad a shorter drive to work and therefore more time for his studies, my father was supposed to be laboring on his dissertation. When published, we assumed, it would lift him to the stratosphere of scientific acclaim where he rightfully belonged.

In the meantime, bored and frustrated with high school teaching and concerned that his son get a solid grounding in the sciences so he could go to MIT or some place like that, Dad paid a lot of attention to enhancing Elliot's education. My brother was a chip off the old block, pretty obviously another scientific genius like his father, and all agreed that his thirst for challenging material was not being met in the classroom. "Which is understandable," Dad said in one phone conversation with Uncle Lenny that I eavesdropped on that autumn. "I mean, you can't blame the teachers. What the hell do they know about how to deal with a kid like that? They're just as dumb as everyone else. Dumber, probably. Hell, if they had any other options they wouldn't be stuck in those crummy teaching jobs." I almost spoke up, asking why he was stuck in a crummy teaching job, as were Uncle Lenny and Mom, since none of them was dumb, but I didn't because (a) I was kind of hiding on the other side of the kitchen wall and it seemed wiser to keep quiet, and (b) I remembered that he was different because he was working on his Ph.D. thesis and would soon make the switch to higher education.

Dad had devised a rigorous after-school study program that Elliot had been following since fourth grade. Luckily, nobody expected me to understand science the way a boy like Elliot could, so nobody ever suggested that I should spend my evenings and weekends in the Institute for Advanced Studies. It wasn't really an institute. It was the basement rec room—although even calling it a rec room is stretching things, it was really just the damp, smelly basement but they had set up an old mattress, a bridge chair and card table down there next to the washer and drier and it's where Elliot did his reading, his projects and experiments. Dad got a kick out of referring to it by the name of the Princeton center where Einstein spent his final decades. He said he called it that to inspire Elliot, but Mom had already told me that we would probably be moving to New Jersey before too long because once Dad got his doctorate he'd most likely be offered a position at Einstein's institute.

It was the next spring, another Sunday, seated in front of our tray tables finishing dinner, when Mom turned to Dad and said, "Hon?" He didn't respond. "Bill?"

"What?" Under his breath, "Jesus H. Christ." He'd probably been thinking about a physics problem while the rest of us watched *Wonderful World of Disney*. He hated it when someone interrupted his train of thought.

"Please do not take that tone with me, Bill."

"Whatever you say."

"What I say is are you finished eating?"

Dad finally turned toward Mom. "I suppose so. But Ruby, please." He started to rise. "I'm going to bed." Dad was often asleep by eight o'clock.

"Bill, I know you need your beauty sleep"—Mom winked at me—"but hold on just a darned minute."

"What now?"

"Don't you want to do a final run-through?"

"A final what—oh, that's right." Dad pushed his glasses up, swallowed, sighed. "OK. Won't hurt to go over it one more time. The kids can help."

"Right you are." Mom rose, walked over to the TV and turned it off. "Randy, Elliot." She started taking plates from our tray tables. "You're in luck. I'll do the dishes tonight. You two go downstairs and get the stuff for Dad's presentation." She cocked her head toward the big clock on the wall over the TV. "Synchronize watches, please. We shall reconnoiter here at 1915 hours exactly."

The next morning Dad was to make his annual presentation on geology and evolution to Mom's fourth-grade class. Every year my parents drafted Elliot and me to help them run through it the night before. Elliot made a big show of rolling his eyes. Not me. A science lesson with Dad—and all I had to do was play the part of an ignorant student. This should be a cinch.

El and I ran downstairs to get the props. He headed for Dad's filing cabinets. He pulled the huge fold-out map of the Grand Canyon from a bottom drawer. I went to the bomb shelter to get Dad's dinosaurs.

Whenever I brought my friends down to inspect the shelter, I was particularly proud as they oohed and aahed at the little prehistoric tableau on the top shelf above the canned goods. I had arranged four plastic dinosaur figures there in an artful representation of the moment of their extinction. Now I pulled over the stepstool and took down the dinosaurs for Dad's evolution lecture.

After we brought up the maps and dinosaurs Elliot went to his bedroom. He said he had homework but I knew he wanted it perfectly clear that he had no interest in this elementary stuff. Mom asked me to stay to "critique our technique, Randy. OK?"

Dad talking. Not a very exciting technique, but I knew they really didn't want to hear that opinion so I didn't express it. Pointing at the Grand Canyon foldout, he explained how each layer represented a different time period. "Time passes on a grand scale," he said, or something like that that was supposed to be a pun on the name of the canyon, although Mom had told me last year that her kids never got Dad's joke.

He went on, throwing out a lot of terms. Sedimentary this, deciduous that. Igneous. Crystallization. Then he started talking about radioactivity. This interested me more, because of our bomb shelter and the Russians and everything, so I listened a little closer. Radioactive decay, he said, was how they figured out how old different layers of rocks were. And not only rocks but anything that had fossilized into rocks—like dinosaur bones, which was where my plastic figures came in. Dad picked one up—it was the Tyrannosaurus Rex, of course, everyone's favorite—and stuck it onto the Grand Canyon map with a long pin. I wasn't too thrilled with him sticking holes in my dinosaur but decided to give him some leeway since it was for science. The Rex lying against one of the middle layers of the canyon was supposed to represent the fossilized imprint of a prehistoric creature.

"Now," he said, clearing his throat as he always did at this point, "the question is this: When did that dinosaur live and die? How can we find out?" He paused. Perhaps at this point some of Mom's students would venture some stupid guesses. I hoped not, for their sakes. Dad wasn't too diplomatic with dummies.

He looked at Mom, who was watching his every move, enrapt, as if he were Sir Laurence Olivier playing Hamlet. He winked at her and said, "It's all about the daughter." What? I didn't remember him ever saying that before.

I tuned in more closely. He started throwing out even more terms. Isotopes. Protons, neutrons. Uranium, nitrogen, mass spectrometry. Apparently there were all sorts of ways to trace how many million years old a rock or fossil was, and some of them were very complicated. It was pretty hard to follow, at least for a non-genius like me. But when he went over Carbon-14 dating, which he said was the simplest technique and only usable for less ancient periods, I tried real hard to get the gist of it.

It all had to do with half lives. What a sad concept.

When anything dies, a certain kind of carbon in it starts crumbling down into a certain kind of nitrogen. It takes about five thousand years for half the carbon to disintegrate into nitrogen. That is its half-life. Scientists measure how much carbon has decayed against how long the half-life is and this gives them the age.

The original carbon is called the parent. The daughter is the nitrogen it becomes in death. The waste product, the decay.

I stood up and started walking toward the back hall.

"Randy, wait. Your dad's not finished."

"It's okay, Mom. Thanks. I understand."

"So you got it, Randy?" Dad asked, smiling. "You understand about the half-life?" He turned toward my mother. "I told you, Ruby. I told you I could explain this. Randy's a year younger than the kids in your class and even she got it."

"Yeah, I got it, Dad. You measure half-life by the daughter."

He pumped his head up and down vigorously. "Exactly."

The Lean Years

Vera is mesmerized by Willy's chest. Each breath's pectoral swell and ebb. His skin stretching as the thorax expands and easing back on exhalation. Her tension recedes in these brief minutes when suspiration is all, the rest, the blood, the screams, blunted by the latest dose of morphine. She is spellbound by the fact of his breath, the beauty of his broad, vulnerable chest—why is it exposed? why does the sheet cover only his injuries? why don't they protect what's left of him?—his tiny nipples punctuating each rise and fall. In these intervals, fifteen, twenty minutes at a time, his face at peace, she feels as if she can levitate. As if, lofted by the precious air he breathes, she might enter her son's opiated dream.

He does not twitch. This first stretch after an injection is pure serenity. Until there's a stitch, then another, end to sweet release, his face starting to register pain. Gaps in his breath, groans begin, he sweats. Flaming stakes stab Vera as Willy, still unawake, gasps in anguish. This is the worst. That he should be asleep, unconscious of everything else, only the pain penetrating.

She wipes a cool wet cloth across his forehead.

A nurse comes in. She bustles about, adjusts the intravenous drip, eyes the chart clipped to the foot of the bed. She glances at Willy's face, lifts an eyelid. Vera glimpses the orb, glassy, white, iris rolled up. She feels weak. The nurse lets his eye close. She lifts Willy's wrist and takes his pulse. His hand hangs limp.

Vera feels she will come unhinged. Her boy helpless like this.

Now the nurse is writing in the chart. Suddenly something fetid fills the air. Vera nearly gags.

"What's that smell?"

The nurse looks up, sniffs. "Oh," she answers. "He's—it's the morphine, you know, he's out so cold, he can't control his … well, you know, his functions." Vera swallows a rush of tears. The nurse hooks the patient's chart onto the bed, straightens, reaches over and pats Vera's arm. "Don't worry. Just let me go for supplies and I'll get him all cleaned up."

"No." Vera rises. "Show me where everything is. I'll do it."

Quick, grab the bar at the head of the bed, turn away, bend over, blood to the brain, breathe in. Out. There. All right. She'd almost crumpled but she tells herself she's okay now, straightening, running her eyes along the wall, the window, Willy's face, anywhere but down there, the ruined limbs. Vera has never fainted in her life but just now she damn near did, when she pulled back the sheet and saw his legs and the smells hit her full blast. It's not only that he's soiled himself. A rank odor rises from his wounds, oozing through the dressings laid on his thighs, his calves. Okay now, she repeats, steadying herself, I can do this. Toughen up. Pretend he's a baby again. Do it the way you did it then.

She turns toward his lower half once more, concentrating on staying calm, taking air in through her mouth, releasing it out her nose, telling herself to get used to it for it will be like this for a long while. He needs her. She will not fail him again. This time when she sees his legs—swathed in bandages, gunky with ointment and blood, on his right side pus running onto the sheet, which explains the smell, but she knew this, he's getting sulfonamides to treat the infection in the first surgical site, not unusual, the nurse has explained, no need for alarm—now the

266   VERA'S WILL

sight of his injured limbs fills her with the tenderest sensation. A feeling like falling leaves. A blanket of leaves descending out of season to lay an aromatic poultice, each blade leaching healing herbs into her skin. A strengthening potion. Now, somehow, the sight of his wrecked legs, even the hideous stink of them, braces her. She can do this. She can care for her hurt young man.

But, oh, how to touch him? He is inert yet raw, every nerve alert to the possibility of pain. She must not make it worse.

Vera looks at her son's face, fine, almost pretty in the settled stretches between grimaces. His hair falls in waves off his forehead. His torso is muscled, taut. He is gorgeous. Like Michaelangelo's David, slingshot at the ready in that Florence square. Only, will he ever stand again? He need not face down giants. No one will demand that. Merely stand.

She does not know in any detail what Willy has been through. Where he was before he went to war or how he ended up here, like this. The Battle of the Bulge, she knows, shrapnel, she knows, but exactly what happened she must wait to hear. Both legs are honeycombed with wounds. He may lose them both, although one of the doctors has told her it's too soon to say. She holds to this. She has to. Five years gone and when at last she brings him home will he be halved, a rolling reminder of how she stunted him, a motherless boy unable to rise?

Oh god. This has to stop. Vera didn't shoot him. The Germans did. He is a casualty of war, like thousands of others. She has a chance now. She can do what mothers do.

She puts on the neoprene gloves the nurse gave her, stretching them over her fingers and palms. Then, testing, her hands approaching his hips in a gingerly, deliberate motion, watching his face for signs of pain as she makes contact. Does his brow contract a quarter-inch? No. Her fingers are like feathers. There. He's fine. She rests her hands lightly for a minute to let him get used to it. All right. Now.

Her son is a man. She wants nothing less than to see his private parts. But she volunteered. She pulls his thighs apart slightly. He flinches and she immediately lets go. She watches his face until it relaxes again. She reaches into the basin on the floor beside her, soaks a sponge in warm, soapy water, wrings it out, brings it to his groin. She begins to wipe away the mess.

She must move his legs. Lift them at least a little, tip him first to one side then the other. She starts with his left leg, finding a purchase point under his knee, pulling it up and over with one hand while with the other, quick as she can, she swabs away the filth. As she turns the knee slightly to get at some more of it, Willy emits a loud moan. Startled, she lets go and his knee falls back, hard. He cries out, his mouth open, fists clawing at the sheets. Oh god she's hurt him, and she drops the sponge in the bucket, peels off the gloves, lurches up, leans into him, grabs his hands, lays her face against his. She unfurls his fists by force and holds his hands between hers as she kisses his cheeks, forehead, whispers, "Sssh, ssh, it's okay, sha, Willy, sha, I'm here." Kissing him as his breath slows, holding his hands until they go slack, laying them at his sides, smoothing the hair off his forehead. Whispering, "Sha, sha, baby boy, sha," stroking his hair, slow, soft caresses. She doesn't know until she lifts her face and looks at his that she's crying. She can barely see him through the tears. It doesn't matter. She can bawl now, she can carry on shamelessly, she doesn't care, can't even try to stop it until—

"Ma?"

"Vera." The voice is familiar. An error out of the past. It drags her out of a lustrous dream, Willy and Lenny cuddling on her lap, flannel nightshirts, her face buried in their silken curls, their cumulus-cloud hair, and the heavenly scents, baby sweat, peppermint—"Vera! Wake up!"

Why so loud? And for heaven's sake, why does he have to shake her shoulder? "I'm awake, Peter. You can take your hand away now." Muscle memory. An instant of physical contact and her old tone, curt, caustic, takes over.

Why is he here? They have an agreement. He should have waited his turn.

"Vera. I believe you are perhaps not aware of the time. This likelihood notwithstanding, I must hold you to the procedure we discussed." Pitch perfect. Vintage Peter, stuffy words issued at a staccato clip. The accent has softened considerably—he's worked at it, she knows from Lenny, since an incident soon after the war started when a neighbor called him a "lousy Kraut"— yet close her eyes and they could be back on Fifth Avenue.

She runs her hands over her face, shakes awake. She takes stock of herself, slumped deep into the hard-backed chair at Willy's bedside. So she's been here all night. Oh no—poor Ben. He drove her here and he was to drive her back after Saturday visiting hours ended, with Peter's turn to come Sunday.

Good heavens. It is Sunday.

She straightens in the chair. She stands. She looks at Willy. His eyes are open. They're glazed. Flat on his back, he stares at the ceiling. She doesn't think he's awake. The nurse says the morphine does strange things. He's not in pain, she can see. That's the main thing. She touches his hand. He doesn't react.

Peter clears his throat. For god's sake, Vera thinks. I don't know when I'll be back. I have to beg Sam Pleck and he still may not give me any days. Let me have me another minute, you farbissener ... She glares at him. He taps his watch but then he steps into the hallway.

She stands next to the bed holding Willy's hand. Gazing at his face. He'd been a natural athlete, agile although awkward about the adoration it brought him at Central High. He swam, he ran track because his body compelled it. She remembers him leaping over obstacles at a meet when he was 16. She'd hunched in the stands, afraid to be seen breaking the third-Sunday bounds but driven to witness his speed. His grace, like a gazelle—no, a panther, for if you glimpsed the glint in his eye, the calculation, you saw danger. Lenny had told her once that Willy envisioned the course as a physics problem and that as he ran and jumped he was figuring all the variables. Velocity, force, motion.

He'd run. He'd jumped. He'd been fleet of foot. Now he is this. She thinks of the old nursery rhyme. He will not be nimble again, nor quick. She lays her hand on his cheek. It's warm with the fever of infection. His mouth is slack. Spittle collects at the corners. She wipes it away with a finger.

She kisses him on both cheeks, on the forehead, the chin, the top of his head. "I have to leave, dear," she says, looking into his glassy eyes, relieved, in a way, that he floats. That he doesn't know she's going again.

He blinks. With visible effort, he presses his cracked lips together, swallows, blinks again. "Ma," he creaks.

"Vera, I must insist that you go now. Willy now is with me." Peter touches Vera's shoulders again, pulling her from their son just as his eyes clear. She feels Willy watching her leave.

Ben thinks she's asleep. Even if he knows she's not, he'll let her be, she's sure, won't utter a peep, just drive and watch the scenery until she's ready to talk. What a kind man. She'll have to do something nice for him. To thank him—and make up for the botch she's made of his weekend.

Friday, after Peter had brought the news, Gussie and Ben had worked it out that she and the girls would cover the store so that first thing Saturday morning he could drive Vera to Battle Creek. Then he'd wait while she spent the day with Willy. "Don't worry, Veraleh, I'll entertain myself, you'll see," he said. "Maybe I'll take a tour where they make my corn flakes, who knows? When visiting hours end we'll come home." She'd tried to decline, insisted she could take a bus, but she'd been glad Ben wouldn't budge. It would be good to have his company on the ride there. An island of calm next to a nervous wreck, he'd steady her, get her through the hours on the road until they arrived at the hospital.

Saturday morning, in the car, she had spent the time tearing her cuticles, grinding her molars. Once there, Ben was a darling. Keen to her frazzled state, offering his arm as she edged onto the elevator, sticking with her as she traversed the endless hall to the nurse's station, squeezing her hand outside Willy's room, pulling her to him, holding her until her quivering ceased. Then he'd released her, reached around her to open the door, turned her about and, with a little shove, dispatched her. "Go already," he'd whispered. "Gay mit der boychik."

Now, heading back, she pretends to sleep. Let him concentrate on the road, listen to the radio, resist his fatigue. He shouldn't have to tend to her as if she's the patient. It's inexcusable, how she'd left Ben to fend for himself while she sat with Willy, watched him, washed him, propped open his jaw to drop ice chips into his mouth. She forgot all about Ben as she held her son's hand, chair pulled up against his bed, until her own head drooped and, chin to chest, she fell deep asleep. She forgot everyone but Willy, and the world was nothing else until Peter shook her awake this morning and pulled her away. The next thing she knew she was in the hospital lobby. There was Ben, snoring, shoes off, shirttails out, his thick frame wedged into a Lilliputian seat. The sight of him, knowing that he'd no doubt had a miserable night in this ridiculous little chair and would nevertheless express concern for her, had nearly brought her to her knees.

Five years of fear since Willy disappeared. Somehow she'd endured. Now he's here, and she has been allowed the merest peek before scurrying from the scene. Ben has to get back, tomorrow she's due at Pleck's.

Willy's legs are ravaged. For Vera, for years, it has seemed as though her own ravages would never heal. As if, like a soldier who has taken a bullet to the spine, she would never again rise. Perhaps now ... She will stand with Willy. Walk with him, when he can. And will herself to believe he won't once more walk away.

"Get my son some morphine!" Vera hasn't run since she was a kid. She runs now, to the nurses' station.

"Calm down, Mrs. Steiner."

"Don't you hear him screaming?" Vera jerks her shoulder away from the young nurse's placating pat. "Don't—just give him his shot!"

"He's already had his shot, Mrs. Steiner. Please lower your voice."

"Give—him—another—one," Vera growls. "Is that quiet enough? Or how about this? I'm on my knees—help him, for the love of—"

"Nurse, give me Lieutenant Steiner's chart, please." Vera looks up at the new voice. This woman looks about her own age. She doesn't wear a uniform, medical or military. She kneels next to Vera. She holds out her hand. "Mrs. Steiner, I'm Margaret Lean." A firm shake. Suddenly Vera feels silly. She starts to straighten up—Willy screams again, she can hear him all the way down the hall—and she's back to her knees. She opens her mouth to beg him some relief and finds she hasn't the strength. His torment batters her, and she's bruised already from the last round of wails. When it's like this, endless high-pitched shrieks, and then when it trails off into hopeless weeping, his mouth shaping wet wordless sounds like a mewling newborn, Vera thinks she will go off the deep end. She can't. She has to fight for him. She opens and closes her fists. "I hear him, Mrs. Steiner." Oh yes, a woman beside her on the floor. She's stroking Vera's hands. "I know, dear." Extraordinary, how it assuages the pain. Vera could stay like this—no, no! She has to pull herself together. It's all well for some sensitive stranger to comfort her, but Willy is the one who needs help.

She removes her hands. "Thank you, but I have to—"

"I know he's in pain. But as you can see here on his chart, your son is not due for another shot for two more hours." Vera looks at the folder Margaret Lean has spread out on the floor in front of them. The markings mean nothing to her. Then the woman's forefinger, slender as if she were named for it, points at a line of words. "I'm sorry, Mrs. Steiner, I can see no one has taken the trouble to explain this to you. We're so undermanned, and we're full up with boys back from the front, but that's no excuse. I apologize on behalf of my staff."

Vera looks at the woman's small, close-set eyes, the lines across her forehead. "Your staff?"

"Yes. I'm the chief of nursing administration. And I take full responsibility."

Margaret Lean explains that morphine is an extremely powerful drug. That it must not be overused. It could actually hamper Willy's recovery. He could become addicted. In fact—

"Why can't we worry about that later and take care of his pain first?"

"We're trying."

"Try harder. Please."

"The dilemma the doctors face is—"

"Because it's getting worse."

"No—"

"Yes, it is, that's the awful thing. I'll think the morphine's working, I'll think he's improving, and then he's crying again, and the pain has come back, sooner than last time, and I realize this injection didn't help as much as the last one." Vera turns to the chart Nurse Lean holds open. "Would you check? Maybe the doctor made a mistake. Maybe he lowered the dosage by mistake."

Nurse Lean reads, finger running line by line. When she looks up she wears a sad smile. "No, I'm sorry, the dosage is correct."

"But it's not."

"He isn't getting any less medicine, Mrs. Steiner." Oh god. Now she gets it. His injuries are worsening. Bits of shrapnel digging deeper, festering, that's why he's still on the critical list after a week in Battle Creek, two weeks after he was shot. But this is supposed to be the finest site for treating combat injuries. If they can't save him— "And his condition is not getting any worse." Vera lets out a breath. "The problem is that he's building up a tolerance to morphine."

"What do you mean?"

"His system is getting used to it. Coming to depend on it, and at the same time, starting to resist its effects. The same shot doesn't help as much anymore. He'd need more and more to keep the pain at bay."

"So give him."

"I'm sorry. We just can't. It would kill him."

Must be a tough dame to have made it to this position, especially in a man's world like the V.A. And she didn't get here by being pretty. Pinched look. Lived-in face.

"So …"

"So he's going to have to live with the pain. Until it goes away." Vera's knees hurt against the hard floor. She stares at the chart. When did the head nurse put her arm around her? It's warm. She'd like to wear it, a fleece wrap against winter cold. She's got to shrug it off. Get up, go back to her boy. "You too, Mrs. Steiner." Margaret Lean's tired eyes on Vera. Imagine, she spends every day at this place. "You're just going to have to live with the pain."

Vera nods. And looks away from the careworn face beside her.

"Ma."

She drops her purse on the chair, turns back to his bed. "Yes, darling?"

"Why—" but his eyes close. Thank god. She'd hoped he was still deep enough under from the last shot that he wouldn't notice her exit. She swivels, picks up her purse, tiptoes back to the door. She mustn't look back: she'll miss the bus; she's already cut it too close. "Ma?" Hand on the knob, she stops. Again, his eyes have closed. Just go, she tells herself. Then, half-formed, slurred, discernable perhaps to only a mother's ears, for the first time she hears from Willy words strung together to form a complete thought. "Ma, why are you leaving?"

As if her heart hasn't found enough ways to break.

☙

Ben would have driven her this second Saturday but she'd forced herself to put her foot down. Let him tend to his store, his family. The bus is good enough. So she was up at 4 a.m., took the Dexter line downtown, Greyhound station at five-thirty, on her way by six o'clock. She sprang for a cab when she got to Battle Creek, made it to the VA by ten. She wished she could be there when Willy woke. She'd like to be the first thing he sees. It was not to be, not this weekend at least.

By the time she'd arrived, two nurses were working over him and she had to wait a while in halls awash with activity. Orderlies pushing wheelchairs, the patients' hands trailing cigarettes, ashes falling to the floor laying a soft carpet that cushions footfalls and, moistened by the tread of doctors' and visitors' snow-damp boots, dyes the white linoleum a dingy gray. She leaned against the wall outside Willy's room, tapping her foot, smoking, crossing the hall to tip the ashes into a tall metal receptacle, trying not to contribute to the dross. This is a hospital, after all. Vera is appalled at the low level of cleanliness. Although she can see that they try, a band of bent-over maids in blue uniforms and boxy black shoes coming through twice a day with mops and scrub-brushes and brooms, it doesn't seem to do any good. And you listen to the hacking coughs, and you see the spray flying from soldiers' mouths as they're rolled to X-ray, and you smell them sometimes as they pass. The attendants seem oblivious, some of these boys are stuck in their own stink for who knows how long—she can't think about it, can't think that this is Willy during the week.

How will he get well? Someone must tend to his hygiene when she's not here. Mrs. Lean said the nurses are overtaxed, Vera thinks now as she drags herself up the steps of the Detroit-bound bus. She'll talk to Peter. Get him to pay for a private-duty nurse.

Ten hours ago as she'd stood and waited for them to finish with Willy, she'd listened to the whoosh and hiss of an iron lung machine in the room next to his. She found herself, between cigarettes, breathing in rhythm, her mood spiking and plunging with the machine keeping someone else's unfortunate son alive. Now, as she eases into a window seat next to a young man nestling a cane between his legs, wondering for an instant how badly he was hurt, how long it took him to improve, whether his mother stayed by his side the whole time, as she leans her head back and closes her eyes, Vera thinks of the poor boy who lies immobilized next door to Willy. She pictures him locked inside that grim gray box, and her respiration slips again into the too-even tempo of the artificial breathing apparatus. As they did this morning, in thrall to the iron lung, her spirits rise and drop with the intake and outflow of air. Up: Willy's safe, he'll recuperate, there's a long road ahead but he'll survive. Down: he's demolished, he's destroyed, her ultimate punishment has arrived.

"Don't you think you're maybe being a little dramatic, dear?" You momzer, Vera thinks, hoping her face doesn't reveal how she feels about Sam Pleck right now. "I mean, things come up for all the girls. Like Betty, when her brother died last year. Don't I always do right by you? Didn't she get a day off for the funeral?" One day. Unpaid. I rest my case, Vera thinks. A pain shoots up the side of her face. She unclenches her teeth. Pleck puts his hands on his hips, curls his lip in a stance of mock-reprimand. "Frankly, Vera Steiner, I'm surprised at you. After all these years, you know perfectly well that Sam Pleck Records functions as a team."

"Sure, Sam."

"So why do you come in to my office, nine-thirty on a Monday morning I haven't even had my coffee yet, and make like you're the union and I'm the boss, for god's sake? Presenting a list of demands to me like I'm John D. Rockefeller or something. After all these years as friends."

"Sam—"

"I know, you're going to hurt my feelings again, you're going to say I am the boss."

"Well."

"Well nothing, Vera. If we're friends we talk like friends. Your Willy's in the hospital, you don't think I care? It doesn't occur to you that already, on my own, I'm thinking how can I help, I'm asking Ada what we can do, I'm calling my nephew the big macher at Sinai, I'm asking who's the best bone man?"

"Really, Sam? Oh, I'm so sorry—"

"Sorry, shmorry, you come in here like all of a sudden a chutz-padicker it hurts me. I'm injured. I feel betrayed. And so dramatic, too, a regular Sarah Bernhardt, the tears in the corners of your eyes, the mouth so tight. What, you thought you'd better lay it on thick to get a little something out of Pleck, he's so tight with a dollar?" Sam's executive chair creaks as he sits down, leans back, hands folded behind his head, feet braced against his desk. "So all right, we'll chalk it up to a misunderstanding and I'll tell you what I'm thinking. Okay by you, Vera?"

"Okay."

"You want a cup of coffee, Vera, I'll get Betty to—"

"No, no thanks, Sam."

"Okey-dokey. Now you do know that I can't give you a leave of absence or whatever you want to call it. I mean, you know I can't pay people who are not here working? Don't you? Much as I might like to."

"I wouldn't expect that. What I was hoping was that you'd let me take some sick days, a couple of weeks to be with him. I must have some coming to me after all these years and how many days have I stayed home—three, four days in fourteen years? and none of those with pay—" She stops. Sam's chuckling. "I said something funny?"

"Excuse me, I shouldn't laugh, I know, you're all fmisht, you can't help yourself, but Vera, you're doing it again."

"Doing what?"

"You're making demands again. You started right in again telling me what I should do for you."

Maybe she should leave. Let him stop by her desk later and tell her what he's decided and leave it at that. But—"Look, Sam, can I talk turkey with you?"

"This I like. This is what I've been trying to say. We're friends, we'll talk. This is not negotiations. This is not games." He puts his feet on the floor and pulls his chair upright. "So tell me already."

"I have a little money saved. Almost nothing, a little something that I've been setting aside pish by pish each paycheck. So I wouldn't ask you to pay me if I'm not here, say on Fridays, or maybe Mondays and Fridays."

"What are you talking about?"

"I've figured it out, and with my savings, if I'm careful, find a room in Battle Creek, I think I could swing it. I could afford to work Tuesday, Wednesday and Thursday, and of course be paid for those three days only, and spend Fridays through Mondays in Battle Creek. Just till Willy's out of the woods."

Sam whistles. "Hoo-ha," he says. "Oh boy."

"What?"

"Let me see if I've got this right. Because this is a very complicated plan you've come up with. First of all, you go to Battle Creek right now, for the next two weeks. Am I right?" Vera nods. "And for these two weeks when you are not here doing my books I pay you anyway, since according to your calculations I owe you at least that much even though we do not have any such thing as paid sick days here at Sam Pleck Records. Correct?" She says nothing. "Then, you come back to work, but only on Tuesdays, Wednesdays and Thursdays—"

"I'd work late, I'd stay as long as you need me. I'd do all my work, get everything done just as always."

"Very good you clarified this. So you work until two, three in the morning Tuesdays, Wednesdays and Thursdays and you go away for a four-day weekend, and this is every week until who knows when."

Vera rises but keeps her voice even. "To tell you the truth, Sam, I really don't think it's as crazy as you make it sound. Or an insult to you. But I can see I was foolish to think—"

"You'll sit down, please, Vera."

"What's the point, let me just get back to work."

"You'll sit down. You'll listen. Then you'll work." She can't afford to lose this job. She sits. "You know you're asking me something impossible. Not the next two weeks and not two days a week after that."

That's it then. Bus to Battle Creek every Saturday morning, bus back the same night, for Peter has made it clear she's not to repeat the sleep-over incident and leak into Sunday, his time with Willy. "I understand."

"Not yet you don't, Vera. It pains me now I know you don't think so, but I still consider myself your friend. Ada too. I don't know, maybe you think I'm a rich man, but it isn't so." Idiot, she thinks. I do your books, remember? "I've got a mortgage, a summer house, the kids'll be in college soon, what they call liquid capital I'm not so full of." You're full of something, buster, she'd like to say. She'd also like to go to the vending machine down in the stock room, buy a red pop, get rid of this acidic taste in her mouth. "So I'm thinking. And I'm talking, this past weekend, Ada and me, what can we do to help Vera and that poor boy of hers. Well." Drumroll, please. What'll it be? Dinner at a fancy restaurant? "Cash on hand I don't have. Connections I do. So my connections, this is what I offer you, dear."

Her cue. "I'm all ears."

"Number one, Ada's brother-in-law Sy, the one with the lumberyard? All right, so it's not Sy, but his uncle Nat. He owns a medical supply business."

"I'm listening."

"Sure, now you're listening. Ada called Nat and he's going to donate whatever Willy needs for the next year."

"That's great, Sam. But I believe the V.A. pays for all that."

"Well, check the quality. If the government takes care of it and it's up to par, fine. If not, you'll tell me, we'll call Nat, and he'll get you whatever you need, I don't care if it's crutches, gauze, bedpans you should excuse the expression, whatever the case may be."

"Thank you, Sam."

"Nu, I'm not done. One other thing. Ada and me, again we put our noggins together, how can we help Willy Steiner? And this is our gift: As soon as he's out of the hospital, he's ready for some fresh air, get back on his feet ... er ... you know what I mean—"

"Yes?"

"We would like Willy to accept the gift of one month, free of charge, he should stay at our cottage on Cass Lake. With a nurse, a friend, his brother—when is Lenny getting back? soon, yeah?—whenever Willy wants, even it'll be in the summer months. You'll just let us know when he's ready to go, we'll send out our girl, she'll shop, the icebox will be fully stocked, there's a rowboat, well, you get the picture."

"Thank you. That's very generous." It won't get Willy—or her—through these next grueling months. Maybe it will give him something to look forward to.

If she had her druthers, Vera would be snoozing. Instead, she's spent most of the last hour soothing Ruby's jitters about what lies ahead.

The kid is apprehensive, and Vera can't begrudge her a little attention. She's touched that Ruby offered to accompany her to Battle Creek. Vera saw the pile of term papers Ruby carted home on the last day of school. Yet her friend is giving up Christmas Eve and Christmas day—a full 20 percent of Cooley High's winter recess—to help with Willy.

Typically generous gesture. Ruby has a big heart. If she cares about you she shows it. Of course, she lets you know if she doesn't like you too—Vera's seen her in action once or twice, ticked off by a rude customer at the deli, impatient with a date who couldn't match her wit, and then, watch out, how cuttingly she expresses her contempt—but if you're lucky enough to be the beneficiary of her affection she can make you feel like the center of the world. She hefts you above the humdrum. You bask in her luminescence. And if you're emptied, as Vera has often been, she replenishes you with, let's face it, love. Nothing wrong with love between friends.

The first hour on the bus from Detroit to Battle Creek that's how it had been. Ruby bubbling, Vera captivated. They'd caught up on theater news. Ruby unfolded a clipping and read aloud Bosley Crowther's delicious review of *Harvey*, a comedy that opened on Broadway last month. "We've got to go, Vera, we'll take the train, how about spring break, can you get your vaca—oh—good god, what a dunderhead I am—well, we'll wait till the road company comes to Detroit."

Companionable silence for a short while. Vera watched the scenery. A procession of icicle-hung trees in the forested verge beyond the road. Ruby dug into her purse. She filed her nails. Then sidelong glances. The tactful intermission ended.

"Vera." Tentative, testing tone.

"Yes?"

"Don't you think I'd better get on the ball?"

"What do you mean?"

"Won't you tell me about Willy?" Vera didn't answer right away. Ruby kept her voice subdued. She's trying hard not to spook me, Vera thought. This topic has always been taboo. "After all, I'm here to help. How can I when I know next to nothing about him?"

Vera looked at her seatmate. For a moment she watched Ruby wait. A model of constraint. Dying to dig, a froth of anticipation visible just behind her eyes. "What can I tell you, dear?"

Ruby asked Vera to describe Willy physically. His voice. His vocabulary. "What gets under his skin? What tickles him pink?" She barely waited for Vera's responses before she was off and running again. "Favorite food? What does he read?" It was a relief each time she switched themes, if only because it alleviated Vera's unease at answering difficult questions, which they all were. However, Ruby didn't let up. She veered from one subject only to alight on the next, always circling back to the center, intent on locating the core identity of the mysterious missing son she soon would finally meet.

Fair enough, but fair didn't make it any easier. Ruby's questions reminded Vera that she barely knows her firstborn. She reached for scenes from when he was two, three, but Ruby asked about his high school buddies, whether he'd had a girlfriend, if he liked to go to the beach, and it brought her up short. She'd seen the boys so little. When she had she'd tried to connect, and to some extent Lenny let her, but Willy she could never reach. Especially once she followed the boys to Detroit. When she'd shown up in 1930 after that five-month gap, he'd clammed up tighter than before.

It always comes down to this, doesn't it? The mother who left him. The irremediable breach.

If she has the idea, tucked in the back of her mind, that now she has a chance to make it up to him, Vera admits in more honest moments that this will never be. Abyss too deep to fill. Still, she'll try.

Ruby has finally quieted, mulling over her slim new store of information. The two of them watch the country road widen. The woods give way to farmland, there are service stations, a fresh produce stand shut tight for the winter, then a scatter of houses. Traffic increases. They approach Battle Creek.

And who's to say? Maybe it's the company, Vera thinks, Ruby's optimism rubbing off, but who's to say Willy won't open up to me? He's alone, he's hurt, he must want his mother. And here I am. Caring for him, as much as I can. He must love me a little. His mother, after all.

"No," Willy snarls. He's more with it, as Dorothy would say, than last week. And now that he's fully conscious, he's angry. If she's made him a fallen angel in her mind, mute, feeble as he was, she's made a mistake. His devilish temper is on full display.

Strange, though. Not when Ruby's in the room.

The girl has gone to get ice. His eyes mild as they followed her into the hall. Between shots, the pain is present but not intense—Mrs. Lean was right, he's learning to come to terms with it—and he is clearly pleased at the presence of a pretty, unexpected visitor. He'd seemed to be in a mellow state until Ruby left. Then Vera had asked if he'd like a sip of water and he'd nearly bitten her head off.

The look he gives her. Back off, it says. It says stay away from me, bitch.

Vera reels, reversing until her hips bump against the windowsill. She whirls around and leans her forehead against the pane, hands flat against the frame on either side. The frosty glass chills her pate, sending an ache down the back of her neck. Holding her eyelids apart to stop herself from crying, she pulls an inch or two away and surveys what lies behind the hospital. Rimed fields under cloudless noontime skies. She is benighted by the sun, its rays refracted against the glazed winter vista, obscuring her view as fully as if a howling blizzard blew.

It is a clear, cold day. And she is a fool. After all these years with no access, had she thought that she'd find a secret passageway suddenly exposed and, like Bud's heroes the Hardy Boys, barge in? No, she'd known better.

But that he hates me like this … She closes her eyes against the bright.

She turns to face him again. He's asleep, or pretending to be. A line, worry or pain or ire, cuts across his forehead. He has spoken with the doctors since the last time she was here. He understands his predicament. Can you imagine, she asks herself, how he must feel? No wonder he lashes out. All right, she thinks, wishing he could hear the things he won't let her say. Let me have it, Willy boy.

Put the blame on me if that's what you need. I can take as much as you can dish out, if it pulls out the poison and helps you heal.

But I won't let you forget that I'm your mother. I love you more than you've been led to believe.

Ruby shimmies into the room, on every third count lifting her hand to ring an imaginary bell. Someone has turned up the PA system. It's playing that Judy Garland trolley tune—albeit punctuated by "paging Dr. Davis, paging Dr. Davis" patched through like a bridge between choruses—and Ruby is making like a choo-choo train. Moving to the saucy three-three beat at each "clang," twisting at the waist, jutting her hips, shaking her shoulders, and she's flashing her eyes, and she's singing along with Judy Garland as she dances in. But that's not all. Margaret Lean's hands are at Ruby's waist, and Vera's jaw drops as she watches the chief of nursing gyrate in behind the younger woman, turning out her heel with laughing abandon.

Willy laughs too. Willy claps. Willy snaps his fingers. He braces his hands against the bed and scoots up a bit to see better, wincing at the pressure on his legs but holding the position just the same. Vera can't believe it. She hasn't seen him this animated in years, let alone since he was brought here half-dead.

Once again, ladies and gentlemen, the wonder that is Ruby Schumacher. Vera would like to grab her and plant great big smoocheroos all over her kisser. This gal—if she's not Jesus Christ incarnate she's pretty damned close, raising the inanimate back to rollicking life. Look at him. Laughing so hard tears run down his face.

Suddenly Vera knows: Willy will recover. Oh, Ruby.

But how the hell did she get the nurses to put that record on, and blast it all up and down the surgical hall? And what in the world is the dignified Margaret Lean doing dancing, ditching all decorum, and on Christmas Eve? Doesn't the woman have a family? Isn't this the night of the great goyishe feast?

Vera, chuckling, shakes her head. "Honestly, Mrs. Lean, you could have knocked me over with a feather when the two of you—"

"Peggy."

"Hmm?"

"Call me Peggy."

"Okay, Peggy. Anyway, the sight of you two—what is it?" Vera stops at Margaret Lean's cocked eyebrows.

"You were supposed to tell me that I should call you Vera."

"Please do." Even now, a half hour later, she must be overexcited from Ruby's dance extravaganza. Why else this little tremor of pleasure? Well, Peggy's nice. And it's nice to sit like this, in her office, over tea, poured from water heated on a little hot plate. As Ruby had taken her bows, parked herself next to Willy's bed and kept him laughing with tall tales from the Cooley High front, the head nurse had asked Vera if she'd like to join her for a cup of coffee. When they got to the cafeteria, it had just closed. Now they sit here, two little chairs turned to face each other in front of Peggy's desk.

"He's going to make it, Vera."

"I know. I feel as if I'm breathing for the first time in weeks."

"But it will be a long, slow process."

"How long?"

"Hard to say. And you should really talk to his doctors for the details. I believe he'll need a whole series of surgeries—"

"Oh god—"

"So, assuming they're no longer considering amputation—"

"They're not?"

"I'm overstepping here. Talk to the doctors, Vera, please."

"Yes, but—"

"But I don't believe he's going to lose his legs." Vera can't speak. Peggy waits a beat before she goes on. "However, he'll need several surgeries. Bone work. Skin grafts. After each one there'll be a difficult recovery. It will take him a long time to recuperate. And it will be strenuous, the physical therapy, especially, and there's a lot more pain in store for him."

"Must you sugarcoat it?"

"Well, how about that—you cracked a joke."

"You didn't think I could?"

"I had a feeling. But there'd been no evidence yet."

"I've been ... I'm sorry if I've seemed ..."

"I know."

When they get back to Willy's room it's nine o'clock. He's asleep. Ruby sits at his bedside reading. She raises her finger to her mouth, closes the book with quiet care and meets them at the door.

She elbows Vera with a smirk. "You never told me I was such a colossal bore that I could actually talk someone to sleep."

This is the first time Vera stays over in Battle Creek. She and Ruby sleep in a motor court hotel. Peggy Lean drives them from the hospital, and that is another first—Vera has never known a woman who drives, let alone owns a car. She is dying of curiosity about her, but she is also dying to get some sleep so she resists her impulse to invite Peggy in to talk for a while. When they say goodnight, Peggy offers to pick them up in the morning on her way in to work. Again, Vera wonders about her life, but she just thanks her and steps into the car court. The carefree mood Ruby conjured earlier still holds sway, and neither has ever stayed in an actual motel before, so it is a lark exclaiming over the neatly made twin beds, testing the mattresses, turning the radio on and off, examining the paper-wrapped glass in the diminutive bathroom. Once tucked in, they chatter like schoolgirls.

Tonight, a week later, is different. No more motels, Peggy has decreed. Vera can't imagine why a busy, important woman like this has taken her under her wing, but she's not complaining.

She has a blanket invitation to stay over at Peggy's whenever she's in Battle Creek. Ruby, too, if you can believe the generosity.

It's New Year's Eve. Any merriment being made is courtesy of Ruby. She is still at the VA with Willy. After his eight o'clock injection he'd asked Vera to leave—politely; there have been no repeats of last week's ugliness, Vera almost believes Ruby spoke to him—he just said he'd like to turn in. Vera would have stayed anyway. Pulled up a chair in the hall outside his room, near enough to hear if he needed anything. A tussle might have ensued, Willy fuming, his mother desperate to stay, but instead Ruby told Vera to go. Anyone could see how tired she was, Ruby said, all this bus travel back and forth, three times in the last two weeks, and besides, it was too sad to leave Mrs. Lean on her own tonight. Before Vera could object Ruby took her hand and said, "Please. Let me do this." When Vera peeked back into Willy's room to discover him already in a haze, eyes unfocused, brow smooth, and when Ruby said she'd see the new year in with him even if he was insensate in morphine-induced slumber, Vera gave in. She'd gone home with Peggy Lean.

So now here they sit, in front of the hearth, listening to Guy Lombardo and his Royal Canadians swing them toward midnight. Each time the announcer reminds them that the broadcast comes live from the Roosevelt Hotel in Manhattan, Vera suppresses a surge of sentimentality for her life in New York. She is having a most agreeable evening. She mustn't let herself sabotage it.

After last week, and then Saturday again, and today, dinner together in the hospital cafeteria, then the drive to Peggy's home, Vera knows the basics of the nurse's story. Peggy lost her husband years ago. In the previous war, in fact. She'd been a young bride, married her high-school sweetheart in a rush before he shipped off to the front, and not months later, Belleau Wood, he was gone. A widow ever since, living alone in this big house with an occasional boarder. A couple of girls from the nursing staff, Vera gathers, one who stayed a year, one who stuck around for a few. No family left to speak of. Both parents long dead. A brother who lit off for California years ago.

Vera wonders why Peggy never remarried but it would be too nosy to ask. The nurse is equally circumspect. She asks for no further details when Vera tells her she's divorced.

They greet midnight with an inch of brandy lifted in a toast. "To 1945," Peggy smiles. Lovely full lips. They touch snifters. They sip. Drink's heat, fire's glow.

MARCH 1947

Vera stands at the kitchen sink. She stretches. She glances out the window at Peggy's slush-filled backyard. Wretched weather. It hasn't snowed since she was here last weekend but Peggy says the sun hasn't shown itself either. Each day the temperature rises just enough to penetrate the layers of ice, every night dipping down to freeze them again.

Might as well make myself a cup of tea, Vera thinks. And— I know—I'll write to Dee. Kill two birds with one stone: fill her in and fill the time till Peggy gets home.

Vera sings to herself as she runs water, puts the kettle on the stove, lights the burner. That lovely Rodgers and Hart number, how does it go, something about writing a book. She stops when the kettle whistles, just as the clock strikes three o'clock. She pours. Barring crisis, Peggy'll be here by five-thirty or so. Vera worries about her driving home. Peggy is careful, she knows. But the roads, the dark, the cold, a woman alone.

While her tea steeps she steps into the little office nook. She takes a fountain pen from the desktop and lined paper from a drawer. She feels guilty using Peggy's paper, Peggy's ink, for these things aren't cheap, but she knows Peggy would be offended if she bought replacement supplies. Peggy's generous. I want you to feel at home here, she has told Vera many times.

The nursing chief works long hours. The pressure is intense, and the grief she witnesses every day among the wounded soldiers and their families takes its toll, so she is usually weary and she is frequently subdued. Yet she is always considerate, and with Vera she has been unremittingly sweet.

In fact, the closest to bad temper Vera has seen in her had come two years ago, a few months into their arrangement, when Vera had offered to pay partial rent for the weekends she stays. "How can you even suggest such a thing?" Peggy had asked, and turned away. When Vera said her name and reached for her hand and Peggy turned back, her lips were quivering. She forced a smile, fast, shook her head, said, "This is an affront, I tell you, a true affront," in a self-mocking tone that forced the moment's end.

Vera has never raised the subject again. She does what she can to pitch in. Cooks sometimes, does a little cleaning. She likes to bring Peggy small gifts, silly nothings, all she can afford. Such a treat the way Peggy appreciates small pleasures.

Vera lifts the fountain pen, dates the letter, stops to think about what she wants to write. Images of the bleak early days with Willy here in Battle Creek come to mind. Who knew she'd find something … special. She hums… she really could write the book … about how Peggy talks, and listens, and looks. She writes:

Dear Dee,

When I look back, I imagine I'll think of Willy's time in Battle Creek with its own little title, like a chapter in a book. The Lean Years. Peggy has been so much a part of it. I don't think Willy's aware he's had a guardian angel, checking his chart, riding the nurses, looking in on him although that is not her job. Without her watching out for him, I bet he'd be stuck in that place for another two years at least.

And for me? She's been a godsend. What lean years these really would have been—mostly I mean my morale, but now that I think about it there's probably a literal side to it, too, because you know how I forget to eat, Dee—without Peggy, what a shriveled-down thing I'd be. I'm not, because she's let me lean on her. When Willy—well, you know how hard it's been, Dee, we've talked about how it's ground me down, and you've seen him in action yourself, that time you visited last spring. This battle of wills he's challenged me to, it was in full swing back then, you saw how he wouldn't let me do a thing for him, with me standing right at his side he'd ring for an aide to bring him ice. He's never really let up. Every day, daring me to disappear, doing everything he can to drive me away. Except when Ruby's around, and even then it still comes out, his endless resentment. Saturday last week, for example. Ruby came to Battle Creek with me and we were in Willy's room and it seemed to be going well, chatting, about nothing, the movies, this and that, Ruby babbling away as usual and Willy joining in if you can believe it, Mr. Don't-Waste-My-Time-with-Trivia asking for Ruby's report on what she's seen lately. Anyway, she said something about that Rosalind Russell movie "His Girl Friday" and quick, just like that, Willy made a crack about single women. "They have all the fun," he said. "Ask Ma. Although she probably preferred 'The Gay Divorcée.'" Ruby, the darling, didn't miss a beat. Low, in a sort of disdainful purr, she said, "That's divorcé,—spelled with one e, because the title character is a man. A cad, by the way. Like you." Then all of a sudden she slapped his hand! "Apologize to your mother," she said. And he did. Ruby looked at him, and when he turned to me and said, "Sorry, Ma," he was blinking, and I saw the hidden soft inside, and for a second I heard something sincere in his voice.

Now that I think about it, it's as if I've had a team. Without them I don't know what I would have done. Ruby a buffer between Willy and me. And Peggy my refuge from the rest of the world.

Because, boy, has all this wearied me. Work all week, then every weekend the traveling, then work again. Week in week out, back and forth. On the bus. Off the bus. Plus I'm here my week off in the summer. And holidays. The Detroit-to-

VERA'S WILL

Battle-Creek circuit—hey, I bet there's nothing like it in the jazz-club world. For what is it now, well over two years, right? And Dee my dear, a girl does get worn out. Do you realize it, I'll be fifty years old next January! An old geezer. Yet Peggy has sustained me. She's gathered me in like I'm a pilgrim spent from hard life on the road, and she's offered me repose.

We get along so well. It's the way you and I would be if you weren't always traveling. Do you know that there are weekends I've stayed in Battle Creek just to have a Sunday with Peggy Lean? Ruby often does, as you know—stay over, I mean. She long ago managed to charm Peter, naturally. He's glad to have her there with him on Sundays. So if she doesn't have an impossible load of tests to grade she spends the night on Peggy's couch. Once in a while—well, to tell the truth, almost every Saturday lately—I stay too. I sleep on the daybed in Peggy's sewing room. Once Ruby's up and out, we have a lazy Sunday, Peggy and me. We drink coffee. We sit, we talk. In the warm-weather months I help her with her gardening. Once in a blue moon we go downtown to catch a movie matinee.

Sometimes we're even together on a Saturday. It's supposed to be my one day a week with Willy. But if he's given me too dicey a reception I cry uncle and I'm at Peggy's house by two o'clock. She long ago gave me a key. If she's at work I let myself in and spend the afternoon wallowing in Willy's rejection. If she's home, and she rarely is, six-day work weeks are her usual thing, but if she's here I'm awful company. Or I used to be. The first few times I felt so dejected, I did nothing but mope. She was wonderful. She worked around the house, did some mending. Let me be. One Saturday after several weeks of this, she made lunch, and sitting across the table from me she looked up from her sandwich and said, "You know, it's better this way. Let the young people have their time." That's all. I don't know why, but it did the trick.

Since then, when I give up and retreat from the hospital, spend the rest of Saturday here at Peggy's, I don't feel as guilty.

Ruby seems to be what Willy needs these days, not me. Maybe she can motivate him to make the final push and re-enter the world.

Vera has finished her tea. She looks up. Half past three. A while still till Peggy gets home. She's probably at her desk, filling in the weekly nursing reports. And Ruby is probably perched beside Willy, holding his hand as he sleeps after his afternoon injection. Vera had left a little before two o'clock. He hadn't forced her out. The truth is that when she walks in here, into Peggy's house, she feels, for the first time in years, as if she has come home. Sometimes that tug is stronger than the compulsion to stay by her boy's side.

Vera washes the teacup and leaves it in the drainer to dry. She watches the sky through the window, worrying about Peggy driving home alone. She yawns. She wishes Peggy would walk in the door right now. She imagines them taking a nap together. Lying side by side on Peggy's double bed. Holding hands, perhaps.

Rumors of War

"Sha! Jesus H. Christ!" Dad, in the living room, watching the six o'clock news. "Would you look at those goddamn idiots?" Mom's face, already flushed from the July heat steaming through our cramped kitchen, reddened. The delicate filigree of broken blood vessels that crisscrossed her chipmunk cheeks glowed, reminding me of a filmstrip I'd seen in school about the Mississippi River and its tributaries. Mom and I had just finished rinsing and cutting up vegetables and she'd asked Dad to come dress the salad. Now she stepped to the archway between the kitchen and living room and glowered. Eyes still on the TV, he held out his hand like a traffic cop and said, "Just hold on, would you, goddamn it? Look at those cretins. Jesus H. Christ."

Elliot would be back any minute. Jumping at the chance to get out of the house, he'd gone to pick up a pizza. Mom was already peeved at Dad for not bringing dinner home himself after the library—and for going there at all today. When he got home, empty-handed, he'd mumbled, "Sorry," brushed past, headed for the bathroom to wash his hands, the bedroom to take off his tie, the refrigerator for a bottle of beer, then to his chair to watch the news.

Mom put her hands on her hips. "If they're such idiots why can't you tear yourself away from that idiot box?"

I stood next to her. "And anyway, don't call them stupid, Dad. Why are you so prejudiced? They have good reasons for what they're doing. They're sick of living in poverty. They're mad about how they're treated. I don't think we can even understand how mad they are."

Mom gave me a warning look. I glared at them both. I was the only one in the family who had actually had conversations with Negroes about discrimination. Over the 1966-67 school year I'd attended monthly meetings of the Northdale Junior High Human Relations Club, which our social studies teacher Mrs. Glazer had organized in response to the previous summer's racial turmoil in Cleveland and Chicago. "How can we understand each other if we don't talk?" she had asked as she went around inviting eighth- and ninth-graders to come to the after-school "dialogues." Only a few did. There was a sharp divide between the Northdale kids, all white, and the Negroes who were bused in from Northdale Heights. Several thousand families lived in the unincorporated township, crammed in crumbling housing projects. The Heights kids had to get up earlier than us Northdalers, line up for the bus and ride twenty minutes to school, only to be funneled into remedial classes or vocational training. "Isn't it just another kind of segregation?" I'd asked at one of the first Human Relations Club meetings. "I mean, you're bused here for integration, but then we're not in any of the same classes." One of the handful of Negro kids said it was called tracking. And that anyway, the Heights kids weren't here for integration. It was because the tax base in the township was too low to support a school system.

That led to a discussion about why we lived in two different places. One girl insisted that Northdale and Northdale Heights were just as bad as Dearborn and Inkster. This shook me up. Everyone knew that Dearborn, the western suburb where the Ford Motor Company had its headquarters, was a terribly pre-judiced place. I'd seen their Mayor Hubbard on the TV news spouting off about how he would never allow Negroes to live in his city, or even to play ball in Dearborn parks or shop in Dear-born stores or anything. He looked like Herman Goehring—actually, with his sweaty Porky Pig face, he was a dead ringer for Bull Connor, the Alabama sheriff I'd had nightmares about for weeks in 1965 after watching him on the news, eyes bulging, veins distended, screaming about the sanctity of segregation and turning fire hoses on civil-rights marchers.

Inkster was right next to Dearborn. Mrs. Glazer told us that when Henry Ford had built his first factories he also built housing for assembly line workers—in two separate towns. Dearborn for the whites and Inkster for the Negroes. We, all of us in the Human Relations Club, agreed that was outrageous. So it threw me to hear Northdale compared to Dearborn. The people in Northdale weren't ignorant, hateful bigots. Most were liberals. Most were for civil rights. Like my mom, who spoke of Dr. Martin Luther King in reverential tones and taught me to always address Negro adults as "Mr." or "Mrs." and treat them with respect. Most of Northdale was Jewish. I figured that meant we were all in the same boat. Weren't the Holocaust and slavery the same thing?

No, I had learned, they were not. My ancestors were not bought and sold like cattle. But my people had been massacred, I objected. Six million of us. And before that, what about how we were kicked out of Spain in 1492? "Did you ever hear of the Middle Passage, Randy?" Mrs. Glazer asked. I hadn't. "Do you know how many people were wiped out in the slave trade?" I didn't. "50 million. You could call that a holocaust, couldn't you?" Northdale kids were placed in accelerated-studies classes. We had the debate team, the Chess Club. The Negroes? They got slotted into trade training. The basketball team. Detention. "And while you're at it, we're Black," said a soft-spoken girl I'd seen in the halls but never in any of my classes. "Don't call us Negroes. As if we're some whole other species or something."

Now, as Dad scowled at the TV and Mom scowled at me, I thought about calling that girl. Andrea. Tell her I thought the people on Twelfth Street had a right to set things on fire. When the Human Relations Club had fizzled out in April, I'd decided to go ahead and read some books Mrs. Glazer had recommended. *The Fire Next Time*, *The Wretched of the Earth*, *The Autobiography of Malcolm X*. Between the books and what I saw happening on the TV news every night, I felt like I'd learned a lot. By this summer of 1967 I was convinced that Black people had the right to rebel. I reached for the kitchen phone, but realized I didn't even know Andrea's last name, let alone her phone number. I stood there feeling like a hypocrite.

Mom's focus, meanwhile, wasn't social justice. "While we're at it," she said to Dad, "could you possibly swear a little more? I'm not sure your thirteen-year-old daughter has heard quite enough just yet."

"Fourteen, Mom." Well, I would be in two weeks.

"For Christ's sake!" Dad thundered. "Will you two shut up!"

"Don't you speak to me like that, Bill Stei—"

"Goddamn it!" He jumped out of his armchair and towered over Mom. "Would you please fermez your fat bouche for once in your life!" He reached to the television set and turned up the volume just as the announcer promised that "WXYZ-TV's coverage of the riots, with exclusive on-the-scene footage from the corner of Twelfth Street and Claremount," would return after these messages. Spittle flying from his lips, Dad bellowed, "The shvartzes are burning down Detroit. I don't give a good goddamn about that. Let them destroy their own homes. But for all we know they may be on their way to Northdale. They may try to burn down our house too. Can you possibly comprehend that this is more important than whether you will have to wait a few more minutes for your next feeding?"

A splash of flame lit up Mom's neck. Her hairline, the strawberry blonde of her college yearbook photo faded to mousy brown in middle age, flared into a scarlet halo framing the crimson burnish spilling across her face. She stood very still, skin glistening with sweat, hands fisted, long red fingernails digging into palms.

Please don't have a heart attack, I thought. My own pulse pounding in my ears nearly drowned out Bill Bonds as Channel 7 returned to the newscast. Fourteen years with these mental cases—these racist mental cases!—and I probably had high blood pressure myself.

Dad sat back down. He made a big show of watching the TV for several long minutes while Mom and I stood in silence watching his jaw grind. "Oh for god's sake," he said, turning away from the TV. "Look, Ruby, just forget it, I didn't mean—"

Taking small, careful steps as though she were crossing a shaky suspension bridge over rushing rapids, Mom walked down the short hallway to the back of the house. The bedroom door slammed.

Dad went back to watching TV. "Turn that thing down, Randy."

"What?"

"Turn down the volume on the television set, please."

"Are you kidding?"

"No, why would I be kidding? It's too damned loud so I am asking you to turn it down. Just do what I say, young lady, and stop being so fresh."

"You're the one watching it, you're the one who turned it up, you're the one screaming at everyone," although now I was the one, my voice high and shrill, which I hated but couldn't stop. "You're the one who insulted Mom, you're the one who's such a bigot you can't even—you think everyone's so stupid but you act like some Neanderthal from Alabama or something—you—you—"

He jumped up. Reached for the TV. Turned the volume down himself. Sat back down. Picked up his beer and drained it. Looked behind him, out the window. Yeah sure, I thought, you're wishing Elliot the brainiac was here for you to have a sensible conversation with instead of us hysterical females.

"Get me another beer, Rand." I stood there sputtering. "Or are you too prejudiced against your old man to do him a favor?" He thought he'd jolly me out of it? "Close your mouth, Randy." He smiled, teeth showing but tightly clamped together. "Especially since you don't know what you're talking about." He paused. "Look, it's hot, everyone's tense, it's been a long day. Just get me a beer and we'll forget about it."

Something red and fiery flared between my eyes. I won't forget about it, you asshole, I thought.

Wow. I called my dad an asshole. Even if he didn't know it. A fucking asshole! Shock, guilt, a little fear, as though god might strike me dead for thinking such a thought, except we didn't believe in god, and as I opened the refrigerator and took out a bottle, I was smiling. You don't scare me, you asshole, I thought. I am, in fact, laughing at you.

I closed the fridge. I leaned back against it. I held the bottle up to the place on my forehead where Dad had ignited the red spot. Cold now. Solid. My skull, sturdy, thick and hard, guarding my mind, which he couldn't touch. Impenetrable, like a castle keep.

I closed my eyes. I imagined that the weight of the beer bottle against my face was the noseguard on the helmet of a suit of armor. I was a knight of the round table. Sir Lancelot's haughty song from *Camelot* hummed out of me. My face went numb under the icy bottle. I opened my eyes and looked into the living room. You disgusting bigot, I thought as I brought Dad his beer, I am no longer in your sway.

I heard a car door close. I held the screen door open as Elliot carried in the pizza. I figured I should go get Mom.

With a sudden deep yearning I tried to remember the last time Mom and I had acted out a Broadway musical, lip-synching to the original cast album. Was it Camelot? Mom had played Guinevere, I remembered. I'd sung both Arthur's and Lancelot's songs. Now, as I moved into the hallway, I hummed. It must not be forgot ... tears gathered in the corners of my eyes.

The TV brought me back to today. Dave Diles was interviewing a police officer. But the camera zoomed behind them. Someone was screaming. Diles turned and we all watched three cops beat a Negro boy about my age. They kept hitting him with their nightsticks—the cracks and thumps came through loud and clear. Kicking him too. He was trying to cover his face with his hands but there was blood pouring down.

You could see buildings on fire down the block. People running. I heard screams, then the rumble of tanks rolling down the street.

"It's like Vietnam." Elliot threw Mom's car keys onto the lamp table and crossed in front of the TV to take the pizza to the kitchen. "Except that's jungle."

"So is this," Dad said. "Or might as well be. What do they know from civilization?"

You fucking asshole, I screamed as loud as I could without letting the words out of my mouth. I decided I should go eat in the bedroom with Mom. Let the two cavemen enjoy each other's company.

"Randy." Dad said. "Bring me the bottle opener. The beer was ever so kind of you but it ain't much good if I can't open it."

I ran to the kitchen and grabbed the bottle opener, crossed back to him in three big strides, dropped it on his lap. Then I was gone.

"Like the Arabs," I heard him tell Elliot as I headed down the hall. "Don't the shvartzes remind you of the Arabs? I mean if they had even an ounce of smarts—"

"Which, Arabs or Negroes?" from Elliot.

"Either. Both. I mean, Jesus H. Christ, not an ounce of smarts between them. Who fights a war they can't win? Against a superior enemy? Look at them, destroying their own neighborhoods. Like the Arabs. They goad Israel into attacking and naturally we trounce them in six days and now they've got what—one-fifth of the territory they had two months ago? It boggles the mind. They make their own situation worse. And they expect to be treated like equals?"

"Nobody says the Arabs should be treated like equals."

"No, of course not, I meant the shvartzes."

"Dad, you really should call them Negroes."

"Shvartze is not a racialist word."

"Oh come on, just say Negro. To keep Mom and Randy quiet if for no other reason."

"Right. The brains of the operation."

I knocked at my parents' bedroom. "Mom? Pizza's here."

"Not ..."

I could barely hear her. I pushed my ear up against the door. "What?"

"I said I'm not hungry. Eat without me. I'm going to bed."

That sucked my appetite right out. I ended up in my bedroom.

I laid on my bed for a while waiting for my stomach to settle. Sweat prickled my arms and legs as the sound of gunshots echoed from the TV in the living room. Was it the Detroit police shooting more Black people, or had Dad switched to some Western? Either way, I wanted to drown it out. I got off the bed, stepped to the dresser and opened the record player case. Turning it on, I stuck the forty-five adaptor into the center of the turntable. I slid the closet door open and pulled out my records.

Keeping the volume low so as not to disturb Mom on the other side of the wall, I sang along with my singles for the next hour or so. Crooning with the Supremes about not hurrying love, chanting with the Beatles about only needing love. It only made me feel more unsettled. How would love stop the police from beating people up? Or end discrimination? Why should anyone love Mayor Hubbard? I put on my newest single. Was respect more important than love? Why can't there be both, for everyone? Well, if I have to choose I'm with Aretha any day of the week. Choose what, anyway? How to fix the world? Music was wonderful, but people were getting killed, right here in Detroit, not to mention Vietnam, and even Israel, which was supposed to be the place that answered the Nazis and solved everything. Everything was all wrong everywhere, and music wasn't going to fix any of it, that much I knew.

I put on Marvin and Tammy. There's not a mountain so high, I pledged, that it would keep me from getting to wherever the action was. They'd had revolutions in Russia and Red China, and much closer, too, in Cuba. People did fight to make things better. As soon as I was old enough, I would set out, like a thane on a noble quest, to find the army of good and take my stand against evil and oppression.

I decided to make it official. Take a vow. Checking that my door was firmly closed, I staged a knighting ceremony to consecrate myself to the cause.

I took my shirt off to look strapping, muscular. I grabbed the ruler from my desk and touched it to my forehead and each shoulder. I pulled out one of the tacks holding my shiny new Sergeant Pepper poster to the wall and, biting my lip, pricked my index finger. I touched the tip of the ruler to the trickle of blood. Breathing deeply, closing my eyes, hefting the ruler as though it were as weighty as Excalibur, I said, "For justice and liberation. Ignoring all privation. This I swear." I touched the blood-tipped ruler to my forehead. "I dub thee Sir Randy." I bowed my head. "Fighter for freedom." I opened my eyes and raised my arm, stretching my sword toward the ceiling.

Just as I felt righteousness surge through me, Elliot banged on my door. "Dad says come out of there and eat some dinner." Putting my shirt and glasses back on, I piled my records in the corner. I pushed the door open, swept past Elliot and out of my room.

Twenty-four hours later everything was still off kilter. I sat at the picnic table on the screened-in back porch eating corned beef sandwiches and macaroni salad with Dad, Elliot and Tanteh Vera. Elliot and Tanteh Vera had picked up the food at Lieberman's Delicatessen on their way from Palmer Park. Mom hadn't emerged from the bedroom since last night except to go to the bathroom. She hadn't even eaten as far as I knew.

Had a new era begun here in our house as well as out there in the world? Was Mom on a hunger strike like Gandhi or something? Would she stay secluded the rest of the summer, not talking to anyone, not even me, or, worse, consigning me to the role of go-between, mediating between her and Dad? Would she starve? What would I do without her, quarantined with my fascist father and hypercerebral brother?

All day Dad had acted like nothing was wrong. He didn't go to the library but I didn't know if that was because Mom was barricaded in the bedroom—he'd slept on the couch—or because he was afraid of encountering Black rage as the uprising entered its second day. He mostly stayed at his desk down in the basement, working on his dissertation. I was glad. I couldn't stand the sight of him.

This wasn't the first time we'd clashed, especially as we watched the six o'clock news. Always before, though, the flare-up had passed. This was different. After what he'd said last night—about Black people, and Arabs, and to Mom—he disgusted me. I felt like a partisan trapped in enemy territory.

I wondered how Dad had pulled the wool over Mom's eyes back when they were dating. And if Mom had fallen for his nice-guy act, would I too end up with some arrogant, war-loving racist who'd order me around and call me fat? No, skin and bones as I was, flat as flapjacks up top, I was pretty sure I'd inherited Dad's and Tanteh Vera's thin genes. Anyway, I couldn't picture a husband at all.

Since the afternoon, when Dad had come upstairs and called Tanteh Vera, I had looked forward to her arrival, although I knew she was coming under protest. Dad had insisted over the phone that she couldn't stay in her apartment, but he also said it wasn't safe for her to drive herself to Northdale. Elliot would go get her. She must have said Dad was being ridiculous because he grabbed at his gut, which meant his ulcer was acting up, and asked her would she please cease demeaning his intelligence. She must have pointed out that Palmer Park was miles from the trouble spots. He said, "Who's being ridiculous now, Ma? Use a little sense, please. It's spreading. They could reach your neigh-borhood in no time." He listened for a minute then said, low, through tight lips, "Look, whatever I may have said about your … neighbors … you're still my mother and I can't leave you there to get shot or set on fire." His jaw muscle bulged. "No. No … friends. Just you. Ma—don't—Ma, listen to me. Bring a toothbrush in case you have to stay overnight. Get your purse. And watch out the window for Elliot. That's it. End of discus-sion. If you ever want to see your grandchildren again."

Now, as I chewed my sandwich, I watched Tanteh Vera watching Dad. He and Elliot were reading some old Edgar Rice

Burroughs science fiction paperbacks while they ate. She'd shaken her head and clucked her tongue when they'd opened their books as soon as we all sat down.

"Honestly," she said, "didn't anyone teach either one of you how rude that is? Don't you know that normal families chat while they eat dinner?"

"Long live abnormality. I'd think you'd agree, Ma," Dad said, then went back to his book.

I shrugged apologetically at Tanteh Vera, who forced a strained smile my way. Where did you go wrong with him, I wanted to ask her. Why did he turn out like this?

And how come Dad's brother was so different? I'd heard that Uncle Lenny was quite a favorite with his high school history students. Unlike Dad—whose nickname at Northdale High, Elliot had told me, was Der Fury, one more reason my high school years promised to be just peachy. Uncle Lenny didn't speak much, no doubt because of his stutter, but you could tell he had an open mind. He didn't flip out if anyone said anything against the war or the system or the powers that be. He wasn't even crazed about the need for a Jewish state and all that stuff. Neither was Tanteh Vera, come to think of it. Mom and Dad were another story altogether.

It had come out early last month. That solid week in June when the news was all about the war between Israel and the Arabs. One night midway through the six days, I'd made the mistake of wondering out loud what the Palestinians' point of view was. After all, their country had been taken away. They lived in miserable conditions crowded into refugee camps. Maybe their anger was justified.

"Miserable conditions is their way of life, you moron," Elliot had answered. "They don't have houses like regular people. Haven't you ever heard of Bedouins? Didn't you see Lawrence of Arabia?"

"And Israel is our country, Randy, not theirs," said Mom. "We simply took back what was rightfully ours."

Elliot was right, I was a moron, because instead of shutting up I pressed on with my point, insisting that there would never be peace unless we tried to understand how the Arabs saw things.

That—trying on the other fellow's vantage point—had been one of the main principles Mrs. Glazer had taught us in the Human Relations Club. Last fall one day after school she'd brought in a young married couple who'd recently moved to Detroit from the Middle East. She'd met them in the English-as-a-second-language night class she taught. "But they're the ones who've really taught me," she said, introducing Jaber and Amirah Alrami. She said they'd opened her eyes about what was really going on, "even though I resisted like the dickens, didn't I?" The two smiled but were silent. They seemed real shy, and they were obviously uncomfortable, and then a few of the Black kids went over and introduced themselves, and I watched them give each other the Black Power handshake. I tugged up Karen Kornblatt. She and I went over to them too. But when we said hi and told them our names and reached out our hands they just nodded and shook them stiffly. I had a Star of David hanging around my neck—Mom had given it to me when I was ten and told me to wear it always, to show that I was proud of my heritage—and I saw Amirah Alrami take it in as she shook my hand.

By the time of the Six-Day War I didn't wear that star anymore, and so far so good, Mom hadn't noticed. After several subsequent sessions of the Human Relations Club I knew that what I'd thought of as the Jewish star was in fact the symbol of the state of Israel. And I no longer wanted to be associated with that country in any way. The Alramis had spun my head around. Old kindly-eyed, white-maned David Ben-Gurion a conniving bigot? Pennies donated to plant trees used to push families out of their villages? Good jobs for Jews, ditch digging for Palestinians? I started by arguing every point, defending Israel no matter what Amirah and Jaber quietly said about their homes, their families, their rights, but after a while my words started sounding hollow even to me. By the end of the two hours, I'd gone speechless. What I had just heard wasn't the version I'd grown up on, Israel as the happy ending to the Holocaust. This was the truth, and it wasn't pretty. I concentrated on not crying.

With everything that had been going on lately in this country—the Vietnam protests, the Black uprisings—my world had been changing, and I hadn't found it hard to let go of the corny old patriotic baloney I'd been fed as a kid. Hadn't shed a single tear as my red, white and blue illusions fell away. In fact, it was a thrill to be swept into the camp of rebellion. No to the war. No to the pigs. Letting go of Israel was tougher. It was like, here I was, not quite fourteen years old, four years to go before I'd pack my bags for college, and I found myself leaving my parents' house. I'd still live there, of course. We'd still be a family. But in some irreversible way, I knew, I'd be on my own.

During the Six-Day War I had managed to summon enough common sense to not tell Mom and Dad about the Alramis and how they'd opened my eyes at the Human Relations Club meeting. But I had tried to apply Mrs. Glazer's put-yourself-in-the-other-guy's-shoes approach. Memo to Mrs. Glazer: Your methods don't apply in the Steiner household.

Dad blew his top. The Arabs have no point of view, he yelled, except that of terrorists and murderers. If a Jew doesn't know who the enemy is, after all that has happened to us, if the Jews don't concentrate on protecting themselves—"and that means Israel!"—we'll be wiped out once and for all. "They want to finish off what Hitler started," he roared. "Drive us into the sea! Mass murder! That's the goddamned Arabs' goddamned point of view! What in the goddamned-son-of-a-bitch world is the matter with you?"

"Randy Hitler," Elliot called me, adding, "Are you a Nazi or what?"

I'd ended up shaking. Mom had walked with me back to my bedroom, sat down on my bed with me, taken my hands in hers. Hers shook slightly too. I thought she was upset about Dad being so unreasonable, yelling like a maniac.

"Randy," she said softly, and I nodded, eager to hear her take. "Randy, what have we done wrong?" Her voice trembled. "We are Jews, Randy. Our people have barely survived. There is only one reason we exist at all today. Israel. The Jewish people have our own country." Which struck me as a stretch. I mean, we lived in Northdale, not Netanya. How was Israel our country? "We have our own army." Again with the our. "This is the only guarantee."

"Guarantee of what, Mom?"

"No more Hitlers. Because of Israel."

"How does Israel guarantee that? How can stealing someone else's country stop there from being another Hitler?"

Mom looked at me like she'd never seen me before. Like she'd just remembered I was adopted or something. She asked, "Is that a serious question?" I nodded. She closed her eyes. Her voice even lower, her lips quivering: "I—I don't know what your father and I have done wrong that you would even ask that question. That you would question your own people."

My guts were churning. "But Mom, how can what Israel does be right just because they're Jews?" She shook her head sadly, giving me that what-planet-are-you-from look again. "No, really, I mean, I bet those white people in the South say the same thing about what they do to Black people. I bet they tell their kids, 'we're right because we're white.' That's what it sounds like—"

"How dare you compare this—"

"I'm just saying that's what it sounds like, like just because Israel is Jewish they have the right to do all these awful things to the Palestinians. And how is that any diff—"

"It is fundamentally different, Randy Steiner, and if you can't see that, if you believe your own people are no better than some ignorant hillbillies in Mississippi, I shudder to think in what direction you're headed." She closed her eyes again, took a deep breath, squared her shoulders, opened her eyes and looked at me. Squeezed my hands. "Randy, I don't know who's been talking to you, but you shouldn't be so gullible. The Middle East is not the South. The Arabs are not like the Negroes." She squeezed again. "Randy. Randeleh. We're talking about Israel, honey. Our homeland. Our future."

I wanted us to be on the same side. But she'd just blown it. Homeland? Who did she think she was kidding? Our roots were in New Jersey, and before that Russia. She was going biblical on me? Making a divine claim for our blood lines going back to the so-called holy land? I felt like puking. And our future? Come on. Bill and Ruby were not about to relocate, I knew that much.

Mom was breathing quietly. I felt her waiting for me to return to the fold.

"What about Uncle Eeb?" I said. "How can you only care about the Jews when our own relative is a Palestinian? What about how his family had to leave? I know he never talks about it, but still. For all we know, some distant cousins of ours kicked his family out of their house in 1948." She shook her head sadly. "Okay, but Mom, really, I mean it. What ever happened to two sides to every story, like you always say?"

Not this story, she said. Not Israel. The Holocaust was the worst thing that had ever happened in history. Because of it we had the right to our own land, wherever it might be, and the right to do anything required to keep it strong.

"Otherwise," Mom said, dropping my hands, standing up from my bed and stepping toward the door, "the Nazis win." She pointed at me. "You're right, Randy. There are two sides. Ours and the Nazis.' Whose are you on?" She turned. She was out the door.

I opened my mouth to call her back. Then I bit my lower lip. Lost cause, I thought. Don't say another word about it.

I hadn't, for the last six weeks. Now, after last night and Dad's performance in front of the TV, I'd decided never to speak about Black Liberation to these people either. What was the point?

These people. I wondered how I could be related to them. I looked across the picnic table at Tanteh Vera. She chewed her sandwich methodically. She watched Dad read. Deep inside her eyes I saw something grim. She flicked her gaze toward me. I flushed, caught staring at her.

She smiled. She wiped her mouth with a paper napkin, put her silverware on her plate, and rose from the table. "Come on, Randeleh. Let's wash the dishes."

"Okay." I picked up my plate, and Dad's and Elliot's.

"Then we'll call Aunt Dorothy. See what she thinks about all this." Great idea. I did have some decent family. Too bad they didn't live in Detroit. "All right, Bill?"

Dad looked up from his book. "Hmm?"

"Is it all right with you and Ruby if I make a long-distance call? I'd like to check in with your aunt and uncle."

"Sure, fine, Ma." He turned back to his Burroughs.

The call to New York was a bust. Aunt Dorothy and Uncle Mickey weren't home. Dad and Elliot came inside. El announced that he was going to a friend's house and left. Dad turned on the TV and watched his pals the pigs terrorize Black people for a while. Then he climbed down to do his thing at his desk in the basement. The house went weirdly quiet. Mom remained entombed in the bedroom. Tanteh Vera took a shower and said goodnight. She was sleeping in my room. I'd volunteered to spend the night in the hammock on the back porch.

It was after ten o'clock. I stood out there, looking through the screen at the night. Sucking ice, sweat streaming down my back. Will I always be misunderstood, I wondered, always alone? One more year of junior high. Then three years in high school. It seemed like I'd have to wait forever until I could search out others of my kind.

I unlatched the porch door, stepped out of my flip-flops and into the backyard. Blades of grass melted into the soles of my feet. It felt like standing on a damp mop.

I looked up. Stars blazed. A mosquito buzzed by my face. I swatted it away. Holding my finger against the sky, I traced out a couple of constellations. The Big Dipper, Little Dipper. Cassiopeia. I looked for Leo, my favorite, my horoscope sign. The lion. Fearsome. Fearless. As I hoped someday to be.

VERA'S WILL.

V

The Talking Cure

I hung up the telephone. I stood staring at it.

"Well?"

"Well, that was my brother."

"I know that, turtledove." This was Babe's latest thing, calling me weird-ass names from bygone eras. She was lying on her bed in our dormitory room. She'd stopped studying and started eavesdropping on my phone conversation a few minutes earlier. The thin cotton curtains fluttered beside Babe's bed as late-afternoon April air, lightly laden with the scent of new greenery, blew through the open window. Conversation, laughter, birdsong, the sound of frisbees colliding with trees floated up from the courtyard three floors below where folks were hanging out before Friday dinner. "I heard your end of the conversation, sugar plum."

"Then you got the gist of it."

"I know Elliot is not going to be trying to fix up baby sister with his med school cronies anymore."

"Damn straight!" I snorted. Then I sighed. Babe's hands were on my shoulders. I hadn't heard her get off the bed and take the four steps across the room to where I stood facing the wall phone.

"So you finally came out to him."

"Mm hmm. Yeah, I guess I did." I leaned back, letting my head fall against Babe's chest.

"And?"

"Ouch! Hey, that hurt."

"Oh, sorry, milady, guess I found a sore spot." She paused. "So you were saying? Is everything copacetic with you and Elliot?" I shrugged. Babe tightened her grip on my shoulders and turned me around. When she saw my face she said, "Oh shit. What did he say to you, Randy?"

Without waiting for an answer, Babe gathered me in. I hugged her back, savoring the aroma of the coconut oil she used on her Afro. She swept the books and notebooks off her bed onto the floor. We laid on our backs side by side, Babe's feet extending a good three inches beyond mine.

Babe was taller than me. In fact, my friend was big all over, but so elegantly proportioned that her parts almost seemed to float, hips, breasts, elbows, graceful neck all perfectly fitted along her broad frame.

The first time we'd met, here in this same room, the sight of her had blown me away. It was the first week of our first year at the Big U. The University of Michigan, at last. I'd arrived the day before, having bugged Mom until she'd agreed to drive me and my clothes, records and books to Ann Arbor on the first permissible day so I could check in at the dorm at the earliest possible moment. Since Mom had left—all sad-eyed, doing her best to guilt-trip me, her baby leaving home and all that bullshit but I'd resisted, pushing her back into the car, dropping a desultory kiss on her cheek—since I'd sent her on her way I'd been wandering around the campus relishing the feeling. Free! On my own, finally!

Yet I was also uptight. So many unknowns—especially my roommate. The university had sent me her name earlier in the summer. Babette Poole. All summer, I'd idled away many hours wondering about her. The name sounded kind of snooty. I worried that she was from a rich family. She probably had blonde hair and went skiing in the Alps; old Mount Brighton wasn't good enough for her. Yuck. She was no doubt anti-Semitic to boot. On the other hand, maybe she wasn't privileged at all. From the Upper Peninsula, maybe, her father a laid-off iron miner. Her mother French Canadian—that would explain the first name.

Babette might be terribly naïve, having grown up in the U.P. boonies. To someone like her I'd be exotic, a real city slicker. What a trip it would be showing her the ropes, acclimating her to Ann Arbor, teaching her to toke—that would be awesome, to be the one to introduce her to the pleasures of reefer.

When I'd thought more about it, though, I'd realized that neither snooty-rich Babette nor U.P.-poor Babette was a likely profile of my roommate-to-be. She might very well be someone like me. From the Detroit area. Angry, radical, revved up by the last five years of what Dad punningly called "revolting behavior." That would be far fucking out, if she was totally pissed off about the war and racism, grossed out by Nixon and Hoover and the whole fascist-pig government.

That first day I'd spent an hour or so checking out the records at the student bookstore in the basement of the Michigan Union, then I'd gone upstairs and sat in the lobby for a while. Licking an ice cream cone and wondering whether Babette's wardrobe was heavy on Che T-shirts and tie-dye like mine. If she carried a copy of Chairman Mao's little red book in her knapsack like I did.

Had she read *The Autobiography of Malcolm X*? Would she like my Angela Davis and Allen Ginsberg and M.C. Escher posters? Did she wear a bra? Shave under her arms? Eat meat? I hoped she'd be into my black light for late-night sessions with Captain Beefheart blaring.

I took the long way back to East Quad. Please, please, please, I thought as I crossed the Diag, let her be a freak. Smart, for sure, but let her be at college for the same basic reason as me: not to train for some bourgie rip-off career as a capitalist robot but because coming to college was the easiest way to get away from home and besides, Ann Arbor in 1971 was a fantastic scene. Not as good as in '68 or '69, those were the best years, and many's the time I'd lamented not being born earlier, missing my chance at SDS, missing the BAM strike, the ROTC protests. But things were still happening here. If I learned something in the classroom too, cool—but it would have to be something real, not that plastic bullshit the powers that be manufactured to keep their nation of sheep asleep.

But this Babette, oy oy oy, who knows, I thought, grinding my teeth as I passed under the Engineering Arch and stepped onto East University. Please, please, please, let her share my basic human values. She must, I reassured myself. Why else would she live in East Quad? Unquestionably the coolest dormitory on campus, and home of the Residential College. RC billed itself as an intimate liberal-arts community within a great university or some such crap but everyone knew what it really was: U of M's hippie school. Pot smoke drifted down the halls, and so did the music of Jimi Hendrix, Dr. John and Laura Nyro, and so too long-haired boys and bell-bottomed girls, and all summer I'd been thinking that soon Babette and I would too, and that we would enrich the drift with Hound Dog Taylor and John Mayall, Barbara Lewis and Dinah Washington, all of whom I hoped Babette liked or we'd have a bad culture clash right away.

I'd worked myself into quite a tizzy over meeting my roommate. Then, when I did meet her, I nearly plotzed. But it wasn't over any of the stuff I'd been obsessing about. It was something shallow, something I liked to think I didn't care about at all. Her looks.

Jesus Christ. She was so fine.

She was something else too, something a little less obvious, not as easy to define. Which it took me a little longer to divine.

Babette—Babe, as she quickly informed me—and I had introduced ourselves and made awkward small talk for a while. Then we went down to the cafeteria to have dinner together. I was tongue-tied. My heart pounded like I was speeding but I couldn't figure out why. She actually asked me to stop staring at her. Weeks later she told me she had thought I must have never met a Black person before or was flipping out about rooming with one. I was mortified to hear that she had taken me for a bigot, but looking back on my behavior I understood why, and I apologized, tardily, even though by then we both knew exactly what had been going on.

I was smitten. Instantly. I knew from the moment I saw her that this was the woman I would walk through doors with. Doors I had not even known I'd been hiding behind.

Within a day, I knew something else: Striking as she was, and she had as curvaceous a bod as any va-va-voom pinup poster, Babette Poole was no girly-girl. I didn't know the lingo yet so the word "butch" didn't leap to mind, and even if I had it might not have because she was such a mix of different modes. Finger-nails painted deep blood red—toes, too, I saw when she took her socks off at bedtime—yet never a lick of makeup. No earrings, never a dress or skirt, but rings on her fingers, gold and silver bangles up and down her arms.

I liked the way Babe strutted. I also liked that she was soft. It was part of what made her irresistible, that essential sweetness hiding under a hard shell. It reminded me of those suckers with candy inside. I wanted to lick her.

I did, pretty damn soon. It's shocking how fast Babe and I became lovers. Even more so when you realize that neither one of us had ever done anything like this before.

Before the first month of our first year at college was over, Babe and I were an item.

I assumed she was an old hand at this. Her kisses—on our seventeenth night as roommates, and I counted, because believe me, those first sixteen nights yearning toward her across the miles-long chasm between our beds were torture—her kisses when at last she bestowed them were luxuriant, unhurried, expert and exploratory. So I thought she'd done this before.

She had not, she told me when we were able to form words again, any more than I had. She was scared, just as much as me. And—here's the holy shit part, the miracle, I mean the Jesus freaks could have easily recruited me over this had they cared to take credit for it—she was as bowled over by me as I was by her.

We were what each had been waiting for without either of us knowing it.

For three nights in a row—that would be nights seventeen through nineteen—we kissed. Just kissed. Goddamn, her tongue drove me crazy. Her teeth. The skin on her neck, the tender, hidden crease where it met her hairline.

After three nights of that, we were both nuts with lust. I don't know why we didn't go any further until the fourth night, but by then there was no question of holding back any more. Embracing on my bed against the wall, our lips swollen and sore, swollen below too, sore with desire, we pressed against each other. Grappling, sweating, bodies entangled, we rolled off the bed and onto the floor.

For a second everything stopped. Babe had landed on top of me. I looked up at her and she was grinning but her eyes were filling with tears. I put my hands to her cheeks, straining toward her, an entirely new feeling engulfing me.

"What?" I whispered.

"I can't wait anymore."

"I don't think we have to." Nudging her off me, I sat up, leaned over her and began to unbutton her shirt. Pulling her up slightly, easing her arms out of the sleeves, dropping the shirt on the floor, holding one arm under her, dropping my other arm until it touched her torso. I rested my elbow on her belly. I reached for her breast. She shuddered and I let myself breathe, I let myself go, I let myself make love with this wonderful woman.

We did not turn out to be each other's one true love, Babe and I. We did not last as girlfriends beyond that first spring, in fact just about one year before this day of Elliot's phone call. Maybe there was too much else going on, getting acclimated to college, studying, meeting a million new people. Realizing we were lesbians and then, slam, wham, getting hip real fast to the fact that we weren't the only ones. Discovering that there were some damn cute girls out there. Messy scenes. Jealousies. Maybe I was too needy, maybe she was too driven. Probably it was just too soon. It doesn't matter. It worked out. We worked it through. We had a hot few months as a couple—astonished to find love and wild to discover sex, getting it on at a fever pitch, in a fervor to make up for the lost high school years when we'd watched, lonely, locked out, as our straight peers mastered a dance whose steps we just couldn't get. We were so absorbed in each other that we both nearly flunked out that very first semester and barely got our acts in gear to do any better the second. And then we had a few months of hurting each other as we uncoupled on a grand scale. The old-time dykes in Ann Arbor still talk to this day about the human wreckage—women wooed and dumped—left in the wake of our brief stint as lovers.

Somehow we managed to hang on to our relationship, to what turned out to be the core of it, which was a thick-or-thin friendship made not of sex, as it turned out, but of a similar way of looking at the world and shared ideas about where we wanted to go from there. Where we wanted the world to go.

Once in a while someone, usually white, often straight, commented that it was funny we were so close when it seemed we were so different. Me a skinny motormouth Jew from the suburbs and her a shapely, serene Black woman from Detroit proper. Babe would look at them and say, "Did it ever occur to you that there's more going on here than meets the eye? That Randy is together with a capital T? And"—here she'd draw herself up to full height and raise her voice—"that I am not nearly as serene as you seem to think? Perhaps you are confusing Randy with some kind of concentration camp resident. And you may have mistaken me for your aunt—you know, the one you pour onto your pancakes."

That shut them up. We stuck it out. Stuck together, friends for life, because we thought alike.

Being teenagers in the sixties had opened our eyes big-time. We hated this fucking society, with all its ways of destroying people if they weren't rich or white or straight or male. We burned with ambition. But it wasn't the kind of ambition that drove the creepy short-haired denizens of the engineering school or the career-minded feminists who had started applying in droves to law school, convinced that there lay the route to women's liberation. We wanted to smash the system. And help create a new one. A world where everyone has what they need and exploitation is a bad old dream. Socialism.

We had more than our ideals in common. Our mothers, for example. Within weeks of becoming roommates we had discovered that both our mothers were fat. Both thought we needed more meat on our bones. Both seemed to be coping with missing us by expending considerable energy on trying to plump us up via frequent care packages. These parcels soon gained dorm-wide renown. Word would go out that one had arrived and people from the farthest reaches of East Quad would assemble outside our door, hoping to share in the largesse. From me, salami, brisket, cheeses, pumpernickel and challah breads, seven-layer cake, noodle kugel, cans of tuna, coupons for ice cream. Tupperware containers full of frozen homemade chicken soup. From Babe, Tupperware containers of homemade macaroni and cheese, greens, meat loaf, cornbread, cans of sardines, crackers, devils-food cake baked from scratch by her granny, plastic bags full of washed and cut-up celery and carrots "so you get a little actual nutrition and stay healthy" as her mother's note said.

Babe's father had died when she was twelve, keeling over with a heart attack right on the assembly-line floor of the Mack Stamping plant where he'd worked for twenty-three years. Her mother worked in an elementary school, like mine, only she was a custodian. Babe was at Michigan on a full scholarship from the UAW. Obviously, Babe's life had been harder than mine. Somewhere along the way it occurred to me that that's why she seemed like a grown woman when I first met her, whereas I was just starting to enter adulthood.

Soon after we arrived at school that first autumn, Babe had become involved in Abeng, the Black students' organization at East Quad. Through people she met there, she hooked up with some Black dykes. That was one of the things that contributed to us pulling apart as lovers that first spring. Some of her Black friends weren't thrilled with me tagging along when she hung out with them, and she had started feeling a sexual tug toward "my own people," as she put it to me.

The evening she'd told me this, I'd sat on my bed watching her as she picked out clothes for an Abeng meeting. I said something whiney about her being racist toward me. At that she twirled around, planted herself in front of me, and treated me to a twenty-minute treatise on what racism is. About this country's five-hundred-year history of genocide against African people. About slavery. About what her own grandmother had endured, "including, you might be interested to know, from all those nice Jewish ladies she cleaned house for. I enjoyed wearing their children's hand-me-downs, mm-hmm, yes ma'am, I surely did."

I winced, and looked down at the floor. She continued, quiet, enunciating each word, with "a little advice for you, Randy. You had better do some studying of your own to follow up on this little history lesson I just gave you. Learn the real meaning of racism. Which you will never experience." She took a deep breath. "You and I are not equal in this fucking society. We can't have a friendship based on some bullshit snow-fucking-white fairy tale." I sat stock still on my bed, staring at the floor tiles. "Look at me." I lifted my head. She had a thoughtful expression on her face, not the disgust I'd expected. In a voice even lower than before, she said, "Randy, from now on, don't you ever accuse a Black person of being racist toward you. There's no such thing. You have to be the group in power to oppress anyone, and we Afro-Americans most certainly are not in power. Get it?" I nodded again. "Well, I hope you do. And another thing. From here on out, don't you ever rely on me or any other Afro-American to help you work on your racism. Now now, wait a minute, close your mouth. I'm not saying you're a racist, exactly. But you were raised as a white person in this society and there are some things that you were fed along with your cream of wheat or your lox and cream cheese or what-not. Even if you don't know it, it's there inside you. You have to root it out. But don't expect me or any other Black person to hold your hand or help you assuage your white guilt. That is not our job. OK?" I nodded. She took my hand. "OK. Listen, Randy. We have a lot in common but we also have a lot not in common and the biggest thing is that I'm Black and you're white. Now I don't happen to think that particular divide is uncrossable, especially not when you love someone—"

"You still love me?"

She squeezed my hand. "Shit, Randy, we've got too much between us at this point for me to stop loving you just because your extremely white-ass self made a mistake. Don't get me wrong, you make many more of that kind of mistake and it's a different story. Like I was saying, we have some things in common and we have some things not in common. But when you love someone you can cross over. It's like there are bridges. The thing is, it's just not up to me to build them."

The vise that had clamped over my chest loosened. Air entered my lungs. "I get it, Babe. I'm sorry."

"That's what it's all about."

"Maybe I should transfer to the engineering school."

"Uh-huh. And this would be to?"

"This would be to become a master bridge builder."

"Oh lord. Save me from a Jew and her punch lines."

That was a year ago. Now it was spring semester of our second year. About three weeks of classes left, then finals, then we'd be out of East Quad forever. Babe and I had already secured a cheap summer sublet on the Old West Side. We'd both be working, she at the Institute for Social Research and me at the Big Ten Party Store out on Packard Road. Our plan was to work from mid-May to mid-August, saving as much money as we could, then book on over to San Francisco for the last two weeks of the summer. We'd been hearing so much about the gay scene out there. It sounded like a major trip. We'd both been getting all goofy, constantly singing that song about wearing blossoms in your hair if you're heading to San Francisco.

After my brother's phone call, we lay side by side on Babe's bed. The frisbee players had vacated the courtyard for dinner and it was quiet except for the singing of sparrows and starlings. Babe waited for me to answer her question. What had my brother said to me when I told him I was a lesbian?

When I didn't say anything, she asked, "How much of an asshole was he?"

I thought for a minute. "You mean, like on the one-to-ten scale of assholeism?"

Babe barked a laugh. "Uh-huh, right. Wherein one is the opposite of asshole. Which in this case would mean he sang hosannas thanking Jesus that his sister's a homosexual."

"And ten would be—?"

"And ten would be he called the president, not to mention mommy and daddy, all of whom are on their way over here right now and they're going to throw handcuffs on you, wrap you in a straitjacket, arrest you for sodomy and put you in jail and a mental hospital for the rest of your life."

"Oh, I don't know, maybe an eight. Or am I overdramatizing here? Seven?"

She turned onto her side and leaned on her elbow facing me. "You know what, honey bun? You're too shook up to be an objective judge of how big an asshole your brother is. Let me decide. Just tell me what he said. Come on, you'll feel better."

"Okay. He said he wants to see me."

"So?"

"So he's bringing books."

"What kind of books?"

"Medical books. Medical textbooks."

"Fuck a duck."

"He'd already figured it out. He was just calling to give me one last chance, as he put it, to tell him he was wrong." Babe took my hand. "But he'd already done his research."

"Medical research? So-called?"

"Yeah. It seems he went to the medical school library and looked up homosexuality."

"And surprise, surprise, the medical experts affirmed his view." Babe said the word "experts" with a sneer. "That homosexuality is—"

"And especially lesbianism, because women are always sicker, you know, women are really just sickly, lesser versions of men all in all—"

"Goddamn! He didn't say that!"

"No, he's never actually said it, but I know it's what he thinks. Or not even thinks, consciously. Knows, so-called, deep in his guts. That women aren't quite full human beings. Isn't that what it all boils down to?"

"How true." We were both quiet for a minute. "And how ironic. When the truth is that it's males whose humanity gets sucked out of them." Babe looked at me, then continued softly, "Like Elliot. Would a fully human being tell his sister she isn't one? And why? Because she loves?"

At the moment I loved Babe so much. Her tone. Her body, solid and soothing. When I'd hung up the phone I'd felt faint. Like a whirlwind was swirling me into the ether. Thank goodness Babe was here to grab me and let me hold on.

I squeezed her hand. "No, my brother is no mensch." A light bulb went off in my head. "Oh my god—even that word, mensch. You know what it means, right?"

"I do by now. A good person, right?"

"Yeah. Or just a person. As in 'a real human being.'" Babe nodded. I shook my head angrily. "Fuckwad. Even Yiddish."

"What?"

"Mensch means human being. But literally it means man. So a human being is a man."

"Why would you think Yiddish would be any better than English? It's all the patriarchy, missy." This time I nodded. Babe let go of my hand, sat up and looked out the window. "It's dinnertime. Tell me the rest of what Elliot said and then let's go down to the cafeteria."

"I'm not hungry. He said he's researched homosexuality and he understands what happened to me—"

"He said that? 'What happened to you'?"

"Yep."

"Asshole."

"We've established that. Anyway, he understands what caused it—"

"Caused your disease?" As Babe's voice got louder my mellow mood melted away.

"Yeah, my disease, although I guess he didn't use that exact word."

"What word did he use, Randy? I really want to know."

"Condition."

"He said you have a condition?" I looked at her. Suddenly I was helpless. Shaking. She trembled too. "And I suppose he said he has the cure?" I leaned against her, nodding. "It's in the medical books, is it?"

Yes, I whispered. My brother is going to bring medical textbooks here to our room on Sunday afternoon, I told her. He's going to explain what happened to make me ill. And he's going to tell me about the cure.

He threatened me too, I told Babe. He said if I didn't cooperate he'd tell my parents I'm a lesbian. And they won't be as understanding as I am, Elliot had said.

Babe squeezed my hand real tight. "That is bogue. Totally bogue."

Our monthly Marxist study group wasn't scheduled to meet for another two weeks. Our weekly women's consciousness-raising cell had suspended sessions after it came out that one of the supposedly straight members had been secretly exploring her sexuality with one of the dykes, whose lover couldn't get over her monogamy hang-up, which had made itself known in a messy scene at Pizza Bob's on State Street, where she'd found them sharing a Favorite submarine and licking the sauce off each others' chins. So I told Babe I didn't know what she meant by suggesting that we organize a collective response to Elliot's effort to cure me.

"Gawk," she said.

I craned my neck and looked around her, toward the door. It was Saturday night, eightish. The Flame Bar had barely begun to fill. Babe was treating me to a night out before my big session with Elliot. We'd walked to the bar from the Fleetwood Diner, where we'd pigged out on fat cheeseburgers and platters of fries. The Fleetwood was our favorite dining establishment—Babe's because of the food and mine because of the graffiti in the bathroom that read "Fleetwood flies are fried in butter." Now we were sipping beers, sitting in one of the Flame's back booths near the jukebox. Surveying the place, I took in Sam and Stu, the straight brothers who owned the place, standing behind the bar looking bored. I spied Sunflower, the acid-addled barmaid floating around cleaning ashtrays. I started to wave, but she didn't see me. I looked around once more, but couldn't find whoever the hot babe was Babe wanted me to get a gander at.

"Who?" There were a few familiar faces. One or two other baby dykes from East Quad, a couple of slightly older women from what we called the community to distinguish it from the campus, Aphrodite the beautiful drag queen who had mussed my hair maternally as we walked in, a handful of bearded guys I knew were in Gay Liberation Front. But I didn't see anyone worth gawking at. "Who am I supposed to be—what? What are you laughing at?"

"You! You crack me up." I drank some beer and waited. "Not gawk as in stare like some kind of rude moron, Randy." Oh. I chuckled. "You got it now?" I nodded. "G.A.W.K."

"Okay, fine, but that's not exactly a sentence, Babe. How was I supposed to know you were referring to the Gay Awareness Women's Kollective?"

"Because we're talking about what to do about Elliot, you dufus. Do you think I'm going to interrupt that to tell you to look at a pretty girl?"

"W-ell."

"Never mind. Whatever. Anyway, what about bringing GAWK in? Have some of the GAWK women in our room tomorrow when your brother gets there."

"So he'll be outnumbered?"

"Among other things."

"Outsmarted?"

"Quite possibly."

"You think so? He's pretty fucking intelligent, Babe."

"He's an idiot, sweet pea. When it comes to anything that matters, like love for instance."

She had me there. Elliot was my brother and I still loved him, I guessed, but if he loved me, signing on with the sex police was one fucked-up way to show it.

"Okay, fine, the more the merrier. Who should we ask?"

Babe slid out of the booth. She approached a couple standing in the aisle, hands around each other's waists, swaying and singing to a lezzy-friendly Dusty Springfield refrain. I watched her kiss them each hello, put her arms around them, start to talk. She pointed toward me. They all kissed again and she moved on. She joined some women in their booth. She motioned to me to come over but I shook my head and stayed where I was, drinking my beer. She shrugged, and I watched her buy everyone a round. I signaled Sunflower to bring me another.

Sunday afternoon. Elliot was due at two o'clock. By one-thirty the troops had arrived. Besides Babe and me there were four lesbians—a teaching assistant in the new women's studies program, two AATA bus drivers and a Human Rights Party activist—and one gay man we knew from the food co-op.

We discussed strategy. Should we stay here, everyone crammed into our little room? It would be physically uncomfortable. That's good, someone said, let the little prick squirm. But it would be just as unpleasant for us, eight people piled into a room barely big enough for two. No, not just as bad, came the answer, because we can all lean on each other. Which in itself shifts the dynamic even further in our favor, it was next pointed out.

On the other hand, we could move the whole thing down to one of the first-floor lounges. That way we would make public something my brother saw as a shameful private matter.

Elliot arrived early, interrupting our deliberations. I let him in. We didn't hug. I saw right away that he was pretty freaked out too. He kept adjusting his glasses, clearing his throat, chewing his lip. Shifting the fat, heavy book he was holding from hand to hand.

After I introduced him to everyone he said to me, "So do you want to go down to The Cellar or what?"

"I'm not hungry."

"No, I mean we can talk over coffee I guess."

"We can talk here."

He looked around. "Randy." He had on his Wilhelm voice, the one he used to try to pull rank on me or act paternal. That voice always pissed me off but for once I clamped my jaw shut and said nothing. "This is personal, Randy. Come on, let's go." He started toward the door.

Three dykes, including Babe, got there first. They blocked his way. "You may not have heard the news flash, Elliot," Babe said, "but the personal is political."

Several "right on's and "dig it's" to that. Elliot said, "Oh Christ," sighed, laid his book on the desk and leaned there, folding his arms across his chest. The matter, it seemed, had been settled. This would be a group discussion, and it had begun.

I hadn't pictured myself sitting silent while everyone else argued my case. But uptight as I'd been waiting for Elliot's arrival, I had not foreseen what a total bummer it would be when he actually started in on his spiel. As he did, jittery, talking fast, his voice's timbre rising, I wanted to be anywhere but there. I wished I were some sort of den-building, hibernating animal, a woodchuck or something. I wanted to burrow into a deep, hidden tunnel, seal the entrance and curl up.

As soon as Elliot said, "You know, I partly blame myself for your being mixed up," I started to shut down. When he went on, "I really regret telling you in high school that the reason you didn't have a boyfriend was because you're too much of a person," I leaned my head against the wall, rolled my eyes and closed them.

Thank goodness Babe had organized a backup team. I could not deal with this. My brother had diagnosed my lesbianism as a sort of phobic reaction to the opposite sex, caused by massive pre-Oedipal issues in early childhood that in turn had disrupted the natural evolutionary drive to reproduce. I was underdeveloped psychologically, it seemed, just as I had been a late bloomer in terms of my physical development, and because of my stunted psyche I mistook the normal impulses of female friendship for abnormal, morbid sexual attraction.

A chorus of "Morbid—what the hell!?" came from the crowd on the beds. Someone said, "Now she's a necrophiliac?"

Elliot ran a hand over his mustache. I knew the gesture. He was telling himself to be patient. He considered my friends idiots, but he couldn't just dismiss them if he wanted to convince me of his case. He kept his tone even. "Morbid doesn't only have to do with dead things. It is also a medical term. It simply means diseased."

Babe spoke evenly too. "Now we're getting to the point. So according to you, Randy's diseased."

"Not according to me. According to the medical experts." Elliot patted his book. He picked it up. "The psychiatric experts, in particular."

"Oh, I see." Babe took three steps, from the door to my brother at the desk. "Show me." He leafed through the psychiatry textbook, found what he was looking for, handed it to Babe. We were all quiet as she read. Then she lifted her head. "Mm hmm. Just what I expected." She turned toward us on the beds. "Freud."

"Of course" and "what else is new" from our friends.

"Oedipus, you know—"

"And don't forget penis envy—"

"Don't worry, I won't. It's all about your father, Randy," Babe said. Ugh. I hunkered against the wall, wishing again for the silent safety of an underground den. "You see, my dear," and here Babe slipped into a Viennese accent, "it seems you have failed to transfer your attachment to your father onto a proper male figure." Some tittering at that, and out of the corner of my eye I saw our bearded friend Jack make a rather crude hand gesture, which roused Elliot to resume his effort.

"Look, you can laugh all you want—"

"Thanks, love," from Jack, with a wink.

Elliot looked away. "You can laugh, but this is science. Medical science. You really can't argue with it." He turned toward me. "The sooner you get treatment, the sooner you'll get well."

"Why, you arrogant motherfucker." Whoops. He'd made Babe mad. She was in his face now, holding the psychiatry book in both her hands above his head. I wondered if she planned to smash it against his skull. If there'd be blood on the walls soon. "This isn't science, medical or otherwise. This is centuries of superstition, bias and religious dogma masquerading as science."

Elliot stood his ground. "Freud wasn't superstitious—"

"And you don't know a good goddamn about what Freud said. Oedipus, Electra, we're not talking about Greek drama here, we're talking about human emotions, and Freud knew, as you and your so-called experts do not, that human emotions don't follow some rigid script."

"Okay, sure." Elliot's voice was low, controlled. "Oedipal impulses can go awry—"

"Awry my ass. You chose your experts pretty carefully, didn't you?"

Elliot looked wary. "What do you mean?"

"I mean you haven't even read the Kinsey Report, have you? Let alone Juliet Mitchell?" Elliot shook his head. "I didn't think so. She's got something to say about Freud and Oedipus and all, only her take on it doesn't fit with your take on it so you aren't harking to this particular expert."

"It's not a matter of—"

"And she's female, which also disqualifies her, I'm sure."

"That's irrelevant. Why don't you stick to—"

Their exchange reminded me of a class rap. These were the little talks GAWK and GLF members gave at U of M classes when a teacher invited us to make a presentation on homosexuality and the gay liberation movement. I'd taken part a couple of times. Inevitably, after we'd explained that same-sex love was natural and healthy and argued that it should be illegal to discriminate against us, some jock or pre-med student would raise his hand and cite the "authorities," religious or moral, and the "evidence," scientific or psychological, to prove us wrong. We'd sharpened our debating skills cutting these turkeys down to size. Those times, I'd found it exhilarating. Not now. As Elliot and Babe argued, with occasional additions from our friends in the peanut gallery, I slumped lower against the wall, wishing it would end.

I appreciated them standing up for me. But I knew it would do no good.

My brother might give up. He might decide to wait me out, hoping the passage of time and accrual of maturity would bring me back around to heterosexual health. He might even change his mind. Someday. Maybe he'd realize he was wrong, that I was who I was and that by rejecting that he'd lost me.

But that would be too late. For he had. Lost me, I mean. And he was lost to me.

As Babe lectured and Elliot sputtered, the strangest thing happened. My brother started to disappear. It was as if I was peering through the wrong end of a telescope. He was a dim mass, receding. He tumbled backward, shrinking further and further into the mists of time and space. Until at last I couldn't see him at all.

I closed my eyes. His voice seemed to diminish, too, thinning first to a whisper, then a whistle, then vanishing altogether, swallowed by too great a distance. I heard nothing, not even an ancient vibration like that left by some stray cosmological event.

I leaned against the wall. I waited for it to end. Across campus they were building machines so sensitive they could detect echoes of things that happened eons ago in far-off galaxies. With these instruments scientists could listen, and see, and, almost impossibly, it was as if those events were occurring now. Maybe this will be like that, I thought. Elliot in East Quad on an April Sunday trying to talk my heart away. Maybe it goes on forever. I guess everything does, with family. The intensity fades a bit, eases into a lower frequency, but like a quasar sending signals across vast emptiness, the reach is toward infinity.

No—I gave myself a shake—I was out of range. It was sad that my brother was stuck in a flat world, but I had moved on. All that was left between us was a void. An expanse Elliot and I could never cross. Not if we traveled at the speed of sound. Or even the speed of light.

Don't Ask Don't Tell

"But how will he ever get back on track?"

"Oh, for crying out loud." Dorothy holds up a hand to shade her eyes and looks at Vera. "Don't be such a party pooper. We're all worried about how Willy'll do when he's discharged. But it's time to relax." She jiggles ice in a tall glass. Chugs some lemonade. "Hold on now, I see you going all stiff on me. Cut it out." She swats a hand at Vera, swiping her arm playfully, trickling icy drops. "Can't you ever just be, Vee? I mean, it's a holiday, woman. The birds are singing. Look on the sunny side."

"That's all well and good, but he's—"

"Vera. That's enough. I'm not kidding now." Dorothy is right, as usual. Birds are indeed singing, up in the two great oak trees that shade Peggy's yard. Bumblebees buzz among the flower beds. I should loosen up, enjoy the day, Vera thinks. Maybe, if things go well in the next few months—"Oh, now she's giving me the silent treatment. I swear, Vera Steiner, if you weren't my sister-in-law—"

"All right already! I give up!"

"It's about time. Now listen here—"

"No, you listen, Dee. I can't just will myself to stop worrying about Willy—wait a minute, don't roll your eyes—I can't seem to do it on my own, but if you and Mickey can take my mind off him, please be my guests."

"Huh." Dorothy pushes her sunglasses down her nose. She looks Vera up and down, then covers her eyes again, satisfied. "Well all right."

"So you'll take the assignment, Mrs. Resnick?"

"Mmm-hmm. With Mr. Resnick's help. And Peggy's."

Yes. Peggy. If anyone can make Vera forget—why did it take Willy so long to get out of the wheelchair and onto crutches, when will he graduate to a cane, when will the doctors finally wean him off the medication for pain, how much longer will he be restricted to day passes, why hasn't discharge day come yet, and when it does where will he go—if anyone can obviate the anxiety, it's Peggy Lean.

"Speak of the devil!" Dorothy's off the swing, up and opening the screened door as Peggy struggles onto the back porch with a platter of raw hamburgers. "Hand those over, woman. Are they seasoned the way I told you?"

"I believe so, sir!" Peggy passes the plate to Dorothy and gives her a sharp salute. "Hamburgers present and accounted for! Sir!" Then she crumbles into laughter and joins Vera on the porch swing.

Dorothy snorts. "Well, you may think I'm bossy, but wait till you taste these burgers I'm going to make." She steps off the porch and onto the lawn, calling out to Mickey at the grill. "Those coals ready, hon?" He nods, and mimics Peggy's salute. "You too, huh? Well, I don't give a damn. Be that way, every one of you. You'll be singing another tune soon. And Vera," she calls over her shoulder as she hurries toward her husband with the meat.

"Yes, sweetie?"

"Don't forget—I want that potato salad good and chilled, woman."

"Yes, s—"

"Don't you dare!"

All three laugh, Dorothy as she delivers the ground beef, Vera and Peggy swaying, legs inclined against each other, listing back and forth on the porch swing in the summer breeze.

"Too bad Lenny couldn't come. And if only Momma and Daddy were here." Ruby resplendent, bust tucked tightly into a hot-pink halter-top dress, its loose skirt draped against the grass. Cheeks almost as bright, she sits cross-legged on the ground, plate piled with potato salad on her lap, hamburger in hand. "They love picnics."

"Well, they were certainly invited."

"Oh, no, of course, Peggy, I didn't mean that—"

"And don't forget the twins, this would be nice for them too," Vera says.

"That I'm not so sure of," Ruby replies.

"Yeah, Ma," Willy puts in. "From what Ruby tells me those two hellcats are a little fast for this gathering."

"Hellcats?" Vera wants to defend Bud, at least. "Why— maybe Rosie's a little—"

"A little? Ha!" Ruby throws her head back, snorts. "I don't think you've heard the unexpurgated version of her escapade at Kensington Lake last month with Harold Gluck—"

"Gussie told me—"

"Ha again! Momma doesn't know what really happened. Rosie was afraid Daddy'd lock her away for life, and she badgered me into covering up for her."

"I'll be damned. Nevertheless, what I was going to say is that Buddy's not like that. Not so wild. Sweet girl. I wish she were here."

"But Ma," Willy says, "they're twins. Identical twins, which means they share the same set of chromosomes.

"Yes?"

"Sixteen-year-old twins, Ma." His professorial tone.

Vera tenses. She feels a nudge in her side—Peggy's elbow— and finds the long neck of a bottle of beer, frigid, slick, sliding between her fingers. She looks at Peggy, who winks. Vera takes a swig. "Yes, I see your point, Willy. I guess they'd be a handful."

"That's putting it mildly. They'd be a recipe for disaster. A day like this? Sun, end of summer, harvest time—"

"What do they know from⸻⸻vest time?" Mickey says. "They're not country girls."

"Thank you, Uncle Mickey."

Vera's brother, lying on the gra⸻ with his arm around Dorothy, gives one of his goofy grins. "You're welcome. What for?"

"For permitting me to clarify my point." Willy clears his throat. "I've been doing some reading in current chemical research. Surveying the literature, well, as much as it's possible in the hospital library, though they have given me access to the medical texts, and the journals that come in for the staff, which is unusual, very nice of them to make an exception for me. So I keep up to a certain extent. Don't let me mislead you, I'm no expert yet, not at all, and I don't even know if my area of specialty will end up being biology and genetics. As you may know, I've been taking the time to sample many fields before I decide. At first I was perhaps a bit obsessed with structural dynamics—you know, orthopedics, the chemistry of muscular change, atrophy and regeneration, and so on, and I guess it doesn't take a psychological genius to see why. But I got off that kick." He swats away a mosquito. "Moved on to the endocrine system, cardiopulmonology, and of course neurology, which is in many ways the most fascinating of all. I guess you could accuse me of being a bit of a gourmand—"

"You do seem to have fine taste—" says Dorothy, grinning at Ruby, who, eyes glued to her beau, is oblivious to everyone else.

"Actually, I meant more in the sense of indiscriminate gobbling, Aunt Dorothy. That is, if you look at the etymology, the precise meaning of gourmand, as opposed to gourmet, which is probably the word you meant to use."

"Uh huh." Dorothy shrugs at Vera, who tries to apologize on behalf of her son with her return look.

Willy hasn't stopped talking. "—which demonstrates that the role of hormones in the female physique, as well as the female psyche, is only now beginning to be clearly understood. Of course, we've known about estrone for at least fifteen years now, but there's a fellow at Stanford who's working on breaking it down, isolating its components and identifying—"

"Willy."

"Yes, Uncle Mickey?"

"So nu, what does all this have to do with the sun, the harvest, the Rose Bud twins?"

"Oh. Right. Sorry, I tend to get too technical for a layman's audience." Vera exchanges another amused, embarrassed glance with Dee. The way her son is monopolizing the conversation, it is as though he's showing off, but—oh, of course. Look at Ruby, drinking him in. "To bring it down to laymen's terms, the point simply is that at their age—"

"Sweet sixteen, and have they ever been kissed!" Ruby's face is the color of the ketchup with which she's saturated her hamburger. Willy ought to be using her as a visual aid, Vera thinks, for her hormones certainly seem to be on the loose.

Willy pats Ruby's shoulder from his perch on a lawn chair above her. "At their age—"

"Rosie, anyway. I don't think Buddy's been out on a single date—"

"Yes. As I was saying, Ruby, the role of chemistry in human physiology has been barely understood until now. But isn't the body subject to the laws of natural science as much as any fruit-bearing plant? Doesn't it only stand to reason that the female organism, subject as it is to such extreme fluctuations, so many complex chemical reactions that are as closely linked to chronological cycles as is the annual agricultural pattern, fallow and fertile, would respond in intricate ways to, say, a day like today?" Ruby is beet red. "Now, don't make the mistake of interpreting this teleologically. That of course is an absurd fallacy. There is no grand design. But even though it's a result of random selection, there is a symbiosis at play. Systems interacting. The plants, the animals, insects—"

Peggy, out of the side of her mouth, to Vera, "I do believe he's expounding on the birds and the bees."

"Trying hard to conceal it," Vera whispers back.

"Not succeeding. Get a load of Ruby."

The girl fans herself. Then she leans back, elbows on the grass.

"And the sun, which of course is basically electricity." He stops, looks at Ruby on the ground below him. She turns her head, meets his eyes. He runs his hands through his hair, rushes to conclude. "The point is simply this: there are forces at play both inside the bodies of the twins and in this yard, the air, the sky. And at this point in their development, Ruby, your sisters are more or less at the mercy of these forces. So, although I'm sure they're great girls, we should all be glad they're not here. They'd be exhausting. Do you see, Ma?" Vera smiles. "Ruby, do you see?"

She nods. Lifting her left forearm in a languid sweep, she says softly, "It's like what you told me about electrons colliding." Her hand brushes his leg.

He colors. "That's correct." He turns the other way. "Everything is energy, Uncle Mickey. You may think you're sitting still but in reality, on a microscopic level, there's constant motion. Everything interacting with everything else to create something new. Take for instance nuclear fission—"

"Fusion," almost inaudible, from Ruby.

"Maybe, in the future." He turns, looks down at her. Vera can't read his expression. He leans back, lets his head fall against the lawn chair. Is he in pain? Probably just tired. This is a big outing for him, the first full day off hospital grounds. Ruby sits up, squats next to him, and slowly, delicately, begins to massage his legs. A visible quiver pulses across his thighs. He bites his lip. Closes his eyes. He's clenching his teeth, Vera can see. It doesn't take an Einstein to understand what's happening here. Peggy clasps Vera's hand. She's looking at her sympathetically. Doesn't she think I'd be pleased? Things couldn't be working out more perfectly. Soon we'll be a family, she thinks. At last. "All matter is energy," Willy mutters. "Bodies in motion. Friction. Heat."

Vera itches for a cigarette. It's stuffy here in Peggy's little vestibule. Ben waits at the wheel of his car. In a minute they'll hit the road. First this goodbye.

"We'll visit," Vera says.

Hands, her friend's and hers, hold tight. A tear reaches Peggy's lip. Vera puts a forefinger to it. She touches her thumb to the other corner of Peggy's mouth. Gripping either side, she tries to lift it into a smile. No use. Teardrops stipple her friend's face.

Vera steps in a little closer. Her palms cradle Peggy's wet cheeks.

"Peggy," Vera says, then has to wait a minute. Finally, only: "Thank you."

"Oh, please." Peggy's voice, husky, trying for hearty. "You have nothing to thank me for. It's been ... we ... you're ... oh you know ..." She swallows. "Gosh, look at us, two sad old sacks. It's a happy occasion! Willy's heading home! And getting married! A happy ending." She makes a gallant attempt at a smile.

Vera can't even try to return it. "Peter and Ruby picked him up an hour ago."

"So!"

Vera commands herself to finish. "So that's it, I guess." Peggy's eyelids flutter desperately to dam fresh tears. "Look, Peggy. We'll visit. Detroit's not so far."

"Right. Sure."

"And you'll come to the wedding." Where we won't dance, Vera thinks. As we never have.

Peggy's head drops. She folds into Vera. They hold each other. Peggy's face pressing into Vera's neck. Peggy's mouth against her, shaping words Vera doesn't want to hear. She might say something herself. Something reckless.

She's come so close. She must not risk it. Soon she'll be settled, both her sons alive and well, a daughter-in-law, and a home, for Vera is to live with Ruby and Willy in the house Peter has loaned them the money to buy. Soon, too, grandchildren, she hopes. At last, she will not be alone. At last, again, a normal family of her own. That is the life she wants. Not this. Not even if her heart begs …

If only she could have both … No. You're a realist, Vera Steiner, she reminds herself. Save the silly fancies for the safety of sleep. In the silent overnight hours, everything's allowed. People can't control what they dream. This, though, is clear cold day. It's time to go. She squeezes Peggy one final time, pulls away.

Will I ever see her again, she wonders. A year from now, will it be as if she doesn't exist?

We never even kissed, she thinks. She flees.

OCTOBER 1950

"Listen to me, bubbeleh. It's all a question of—you're listening?—so look, it's all a question of attitude. Here's what my Louie used to say: Life is work, life is survival, life is lending a hand to your fellow man. Ten percent inspiration, ninety percent perspiration. A worker's fulfillment comes from contributing to the class struggle. Happy shmappy, that's what Louie said, he should rest in peace, and you could do a lot worse than to take his advice."

"Happy shmappy. Very helpful. I'll make a note of that." Vera takes off her reading glasses, stubs out her cigarette, and folds the museum guide she'd been reviewing. In her peripheral vision, Dorothy with an arch expression. "But tell me something, Cel. Since when have you got religion?"

"Religion? Feh! What are you talking about?"

"He should rest in peace?"

"Listen Vera, don't start up with me, just because we're a couple of alteh kockers doesn't mean I won't let you have it. I'm still your older sister—"

"Hey, I only—"

"Louie was a doll. A prince among men, a—"

"Of course he was. I'm only asking, you said rest in peace, which implies—"

"It implies no such thing. Always so literal you have to take everything, Vera. It's an expression, that's all. So I'm full of bubbe meisehs, it doesn't mean I'm not also a modern person. And you can be damn sure it doesn't mean I all of a sudden believe in that god mish-mosh. Understood?"

"Understood. So—"

"So let me get back to the point."

"Good," says Dorothy. "You were about to explicate the Rivera mural when your sister so rudely interrupted you."

Isn't Dorothy pleased with herself, Vera thinks. As well she should be. For Dee convinced Celia the time was finally right to visit Vera, arranged the trip to coincide with a gig, and she and Mickey even paid Celia's train fare.

Vera watches Celia scrutinize the mural that covers the walls of the Detroit Institute of Art's vast entry hall. She hadn't been prepared for the joy of seeing her again. She'd grown used to the distance between them, which after all had been there since even before she left New York. Since Peter ousted her, which soured Celia, unlike Mama and Mickey, on her tainted sister.

Vera pictures Celia the ten-year-old tease. By fifteen she'd been in the sweatshops, like Vera. Only unlike Vera she never really got out. Celia had known the switch from stitching for the boss to organizing for the union wouldn't make her rich. A lifetime of ease was never her goal. She's had what she needed— fulfillment, family. And now that she's getting old—can you believe it, sixty soon—even with Louie dead and her boy Bernie, too, killed fighting the fascists in Spain, she isn't alone. Still lives with Bernie's widow Adele and her brood. And she has her daughter Estelle and her kids. All in Bayonne. A step up from Passaic, at least. At the same time, though, defeat: she wasn't purged, exactly, the treatment was a bit gentler than that, but this past spring the garment union to which she'd given thirty years had pushed her out. Retirement, they called it.

"Joe McCarthy's henchmen," Dorothy had spit when she told Vera on the phone. "They don't deserve to be called trade unionists." A little pension they gave her. A gold pen. Vera knows Celia will not speak of it. It's a principle, Dorothy has explained: as a socialist Celia will not criticize the union, not even when the union ousts her for being a socialist. "I'll tell you one thing, woman," her sister-in-law had said, the phone line practically melting from her heat. "They're shooting themselves in the foot. The union—hell, not just this one, all of them, the whole damn labor movement, giving in to the red scare, getting rid of their best people—the unions in this country will never be the same. They're cutting off their own arms and legs. Without the Celia Kupfers of this country we wouldn't have a Wagner Act. Unemployment, Social Security. What in the world are they thinking? Louie must be turning over in his grave."

As expected, Vera doesn't hear it from Celia. Nor does her sister speak of Hersh. But when she'd gotten off the train yesterday, after they'd clasped then stepped back, she'd pressed something hard and sharp-cornered into Vera's pocket. "You'll look at it later," she said. "When I'm at Gussie's."

Hersh's medal. On loan from his daughters in the Soviet Union to his family in the States. The chance to show off the Order of Lenin is what lured Celia to leave Jersey for the first time in forty-five years. Every summer a week at the shore, a room with Louie and the kids. Occasionally in autumn, a drive in the country for a treat. Maybe she'd been waiting. Could it be, Vera pondered as she sat at her vanity last night engrossed by the mirror's light glinting off the gold star, that Celia stayed put all those years awaiting word from Hersh? Concerned that he know where to find her? Convinced that he would?

He didn't. But his girls did. It was Gussie's doing. After the war she and Ben had spent one full year searching for his sisters and brother, from whom he'd had no word since 1940. Inquiries at upstate New York displaced person camps. Letters to refugee organizations. They even considered a trip to Europe but they couldn't swing it financially so more letters and telegrams had to do. Without telling Celia, Gussie included Hersh in her inquiries. Nothing paid off for Ben. Chana, Gitl, Alter, gone. Hersh, however, was found. Or at least what happened to him.

A package had arrived in Jersey last fall. Cyrillic script—that alone had sent Celia fluttering to pop a nitroglycerin pill under her tongue. Inside, the medal. And a letter she'd rushed to the Russian Orthodox church for translating.

He was a hero after all, as the sister who idolized him had always believed. Party member for forty years. Taught Marxist theory at a Moscow institute. With the war, old as he was, he put on a uniform. Fought the Nazis. Was captured. Organized discussion groups among the POWs. Tried to lead an escape. Was shot down.

Last night Vera had run the medal's sharp corners along her arm. She looped the shiny red ribbon around a finger. We knew nothing of his life, she thought. As he knew nothing of mine. Bemused, bushed from the emotion of seeing her sister again, she'd lain in her bed and wondered at the turns things take. She tried to remember Freyde, so long ago. Why, the siblings are dying in order—that makes Sol next. Terrible thought! She ought to slap herself in the face! It holds a perverse interest, though, wondering how Celia would react. Her sister has never made up with their prosperous brother. Funny—finally, somehow, she's made her peace with Vera. In the scheme of things, then, Sol's crime is worse. Weirdly comforting.

Today Celia seems her old self as she explicates the mural. "Look how the assembly line devours the workers," she says. "Look how Rivera shows industry—what it is, and what it could be. Imagine what it could be without the bosses, Veraleh." Her old self. Yet not. Celia's eyes sag, dragged down by bags that descend into concave wrinkled cheeks. Her nose seems bigger than before—can that be? Does something like that change? Her chin blends into jowls. She looks like Winston Churchill mated with a basset hound. Her hair is completely gray, and thin, high on the forehead. Only five years older than Vera and Celia is an old lady.

She reminds Vera of Papa. First sight of her yesterday at the train station had given Vera a start. Something in the tilt of Celia's head. Her stance. More than anything, once they began to chat, walking to Ben and Gussie waiting in the car, it was her sister's hands. Like Papa's, always in motion. Cutting into the air to emphasize her points. Gesticulating fiercely when, as now, she articulates a political stand.

"So okay. The artistry is impeccable, this I assume you know. Nu, you're still the artsy-shmartsy one, aren't you, Veraleh?"

"No, Cel, I've passed those duties on to Ruby."

"Fine, so Ruby, do you agree that this mural reveals an artist at the height of his powers?"

"I do, Tanteh Celia." Ruby smiles at her husband's aunt. "And the scope is terribly impressive too."

Celia beams. "This one I like, Vera. Good taste she's got. So tell me something else, Ruby. What do you think of Rivera's symbolism?"

"For me, it works, Tanteh Celia."

"Good. Me too."

"But I can't help wondering if Bill would feel the same way."

"Bill? Who's he, the art teacher where you work?"

"No, Bill! My husband."

Celia gives a questioning look all around. Vera taps her foot, waiting for someone else to explain. When no one does she says, "Willy." A twist of annoyance travels up her spine. She digs into her purse, finds her pack of cigarettes, pulls one out. "He wants to be called Bill now."

"Bill! You're kidding me." Celia looks at her quizzically but why should I have to explain, Vera thinks, and says nothing, taking a cooling suck on her cigarette. Celia turns to Dorothy, then back to Ruby. "Our adorable Willy. I'm supposed to call him Bill now, you're telling me?"

Ruby smiles. "That's right, Tanteh Celia. Bill. He feels it's more—"

"It sounds like a cowboy or something," Celia says. "Like he should be out on the range herding cattle." Ha! My sister agrees with me, Vera does not say aloud. Ridiculous. A grown man— why, he's in his thirties now—changing what he's called. Celia's chuckling. She lays a hand on her brow to settle herself down. "Sorry, dolly," she says, shifting the hand on to Ruby's arm. "I don't mean to belittle your husband, or you. It's his name, he's got every right."

Ruby shoots a triumphant smile at Vera. "Exactly."

"However, I have to say, and I'm sure you don't mind, his old aunt, I know him from the minute he was born, remember, Vera?" Yes. Celia was there. "So he's not a cowpoke, this we know. But Bill? It has an, I don't know, I guess a goyishe ring to it. Wouldn't you say, Dorothy?"

"Leave the shiksa out of it, you tricky old girl."

Dee's smart, Vera tells herself, and discreet, although it wouldn't kill her to take my side. The last couple of visits Vera has had to hold back asking Dee to put in a good word for her with her son and daughter-in-law. She's probably being ridiculous, but lately she feels out of place in the home they share. It's nothing specific. Looks, whispers, the set of her son's shoulders, his wife often too busy to chat. It may be time to get my own place, she thinks, leaning against a pillar, cigarette pressed between her lips. I don't want to be a mother-in-law out of a Catskills comic's routine. That isn't me. Not twenty minutes ago as they entered the museum Celia had complimented Vera's dress, purse, make-up, shoes. "So smart, so chic," she said, "it's one thing I'll say for you, Veraleh, always the latest look. An old girl like you, still sharp as all get-out."

She doesn't want to move. So there are tensions. There are in any home. She'll try harder. Go to bed earlier, so they can have the house to themselves. Stay in when they go to the movies.

Cook, clean. I'll offer to do the marketing too—no, then Ruby will feel she's trying to take over.

Smoking, running her eyes over Ruby, round in the middle, burnished hair gleaming, thick, Vera decides to talk with Dorothy later. She always has a helpful thought or two.

"Goyishe?" Ruby's revving up. "Tanteh Celia, aren't you being silly?"

"I am?" Vera recognizes Celia's amused expression, goading the girl, the way she used to Hersh long ago.

"Sure you are. There are plenty of Jewish Bills."

"Name one."

"And that's beside the point anyway."

"So what's the point?"

"Willy is a child's name. It isn't dignified. A nickname, really, not a proper name at all." Ruby had said the same thing when she announced the change last spring, so it shouldn't have this impact again, but it does, like a blow to Vera's midsection. Willy, the one she searched for all those years. "He's a scientist, Tanteh Celia. Soon he'll have his doctorate. He needs a serious, adult name." Ruby whips her head around, looking past the art lovers lingering in the lobby, and locates her mother-in-law by the smoke furling from the pillar. Eyes drilling into Vera's, Ruby enunciates: "He's not your Willy anymore."

Is it a competition, then? Vera modulates her voice so it's as mild as can be. "It's his business, Cel." Takes a casual puff. "Anyway, it's old news. So tell us, Ruby dear, what would Bill think of the mural?" She smiles at Ruby.

And just like that Ruby softens. Returns Vera's smile, a hint of apology as if rescinding her claws. "Oh, I don't know, Vera. But you know he hasn't inherited the Resnick family leanings."

"I have to agree, a Steiner all the way."

"Which means what?" from Celia.

"Steady yourself, Cel. Bill's a free-enterprise man."

Her sister staggers, hand to her heart, the old Harold Lloyd stupefaction routine. "No! Don't tell me!"

Vera nods. Dorothy takes Celia's hand, mock-solemn. "He's young still. One day he'll see the error of his ways."

Ruby's giggling. "You gals are too much. Tanteh Celia, you're kidding, right?"

"No, dolly, I'm not. I think if Willy—excuse me, Bill—is a proponent of capitalism, it's a shanda of the first degree. Vera, think how Mama and Papa must be turning over in their graves." And Hersh, Vera thinks, and watches Celia think the same. Her sister gives her head a little shake, goiter flapping, gray wisps of hair fluffing back from her face, and aims a sham-stern look at Ruby's distended womb. "Well, we can always hope." She points at Ruby's bulk. "The next generation at least, maybe they'll see the light."

"And on that note ..." Ruby is clearly eager to move on. Vera knows her proletarian dramatic masterpiece sits in an attic drawer, the half-finished revision of her nearly-award-winning play piled under old copies of The Masses. Willy—Bill, damn it, Bill—frowns on all that. One more thing I wasn't there for. Not that I'd have made him a flaming red, he'd have needed Celia for a mother for that, and even she would have had a hard time countering Peter. But I might have widened his perspective, helped him see beyond his well-provided-for little self, held his heart open. As it was, no one did. There's something missing in him. As if he's organized himself around a hollow core. Only Ruby draws more from him, and who knows how much, or for how much longer.

"All right already, on that note, let us return to Rivera. Which is a very fine place to be indeed, and I want to thank you all for bringing me here this morning." Celia blows kisses to the three. "Now, I'm sure you'll agree that this is socialist realism at its finest, but more than realism, it's heroism on a grand scale. Because first of all don't forget that Diego Rivera is a hero. Ask Dorothy, she was there when they tried to save his mural in New York from those Rockefeller thugs." Vera has heard this tale from Mickey, so proud. "Same story, different town. Big deal, the Motor City. Ha! The motor that drives industry is the working man. That's what Rivera shows, and that's why Rockefeller tore it down. Don't think Edsel Ford didn't dearly want to do the same thing here. What an artist, this Rivera, how he thumbed his nose at them. Look at it, Veraleh! The sweep, the majesty of the working man! Is there anything so grand?"

"Excuse me a minute, Celia." Dorothy touches Vera's arm. "Vee, where's Ruby?"

"Isn't she—she was right there—my goodness, you're right. Where'd she go?"

"She's probably looking at the mummies. You know she's got her drama students doing *Antony and Cleopatra.*"

"Cleopatra was a slave owner," Celia says, tearing her attention from the mural.

"Cleopatra was a great African queen," her sister-in-law replies without skipping a beat. "Chew on that, comrade. I'm going to poke into some of these exhibit rooms and find her."

Vera has her reading glasses on again, comparing the curators' take on the Rivera mural with her sister's. She tears them off at the sound of yelling. It's coming from around the corner in the next room, breaking the museum's decorum.

"Vera! Help us—hurry!" She rushes toward the sound of Dorothy's voice. "Over here!"

What in the—oh. This is it. Calm, she tells herself. This happens every day. Dorothy is on the floor, arm around Ruby, who's grimacing, gripping her gut.

Vera strides toward a guard who just passed the door. "Dee, Ruby, stay still," she says. "I'll bring back some help. And Celia can call Willy from the phone booth in the entryway. Then we'll get you into a cab."

The waiting room empties out. The celebrating has begun.

Willy running to the elevator. Gussie and Ben just behind. Lenny, Peter and Mabel next, Rose and Bud bringing up the rear.

"Go on, Vera." Dorothy gives her a push. "Get up there and see your grandson."

"In a minute." She hadn't expected to feel so overwhelmed. Images of the last baby boy she held flood her mind. How fleeting that was, then how endless the emptiness.

Dorothy's hand stays on Vera's back. "What are you waiting for, woman?" She kneads a thumb between the spinal knobs.

Vera grabs Dorothy's other hand. "Come with me."

Silence. A few more days, then it will never be quiet again in this house. Vera's surprised at how weepy she is.

So tiny. Her grandson, can you imagine? Purple-faced, bawling like a—like a baby, she thinks, and she chokes a little, tearing up again as she chuckles. He's Ruby's, of course, and Bill's. But some grandmother he'll have, she thinks. He can come to me for anything. Famous failed mother. Finally another chance.

Midnight. Willy's not back yet. This is good. Staying by his wife's side. Vera hopes he can figure out how to be a father. He should let Ruby, full of love, be his guide.

Vera can't sleep. She'll call Peggy! She skips down the steps to the kitchen. They've spoken what—two, three times in two-and-a-half years? Each time excruciating. Over the phone, Vera had metamorphosed from a poised, articulate person into a mumbler, gauche, bungling the expensive minutes until they were both happy to hang up.

This won't be like that. Peggy's the perfect person to share her joy. She was there, she knows what her boy went through. She'll be thrilled, Vera thinks. For Bill, for Ruby, and me.

Vera picks up the handpiece. Pauses, finger poised over dial. It's late. How rude. We haven't talked since New Year's. I'll wake her.

Oh, Peggy won't mind. She dials the operator. Pictures the squat phone next to Peggy's bed ringing, Peggy jolting awake, hugging the blanket as she sits up to answer. Vera tenses, excited as a kid, as she hears the receiver picked up.

"Hello?" Sleepy woman's voice. Not Peg's. "Hello? Who is it?"

Vera plunks the black plastic handset into its cradle. She thuds upstairs. Slips under the covers. Closes her eyes. As if she'll sleep.

My Dirty Laundry

In June of 1974, after our junior year at the University of Michigan, Babe headed south to spend the summer on her uncle's farm and I got a job at U of M's laundry facility, a huge industrial plant out on the sparsely inhabited North Campus that did all the wash for the dormitories and the medical center. Bedding, towels, surgical scrubs, tablecloths, uniforms. They had a regular work force but took on a few students in the hot weather when there was more to wash.

Those first few weeks I felt like I was doing doctoral-level linguistics research just trying to understand my fellow workers. Appalachian accents so thick and lush you could practically smell coal dust, taste moonshine. Then there was the heat. That laundry plant was the hottest place I have ever been. Those first two months, a typically steamy Michigan summer, I learned more about the human body's reaction to high temperatures than I would have in four years of medical school.

I often found myself musing about Dante's Divine Comedy and which level of the inferno the laundry most resembled. I leaned toward Canto 14. The rain of fire would be the constant drizzle of colorless hot cotton dust that misted the air throughout the cavernous facility, imbuing it with a strange starchy odor, tickling nostrils and the backs of throats. Then there were the big gray-white sheets that the workers fed through the massive steel mangle one at a time, two people holding the ends taut and slowly stepping forward as their partners stationed next to the machine guided the material onto the rollers, on the other side two more women catching each sheet as it rolled out, scorching their hands on the material and scalding their lungs breathing chemical gusts released along with the bedding. Obviously, this would be Dante's "sheet of flame."

But maybe I was being too literal. Perhaps the plant was merely purgatory, and its heat like the cleansing fire that sears away sin. Although how this place of hellish toil could possibly parallel heaven's anteroom I could not see.

At first I didn't think I could stand it. I didn't feel nearly as sturdy as the regular workers seemed to be. Some of those women had been working there fifteen, twenty or more years. Then there were the younger ones like Lydia Tammy Talmadge. All of nineteen years old, Lydia Tammy was a short, scrawny, awkward little thing. When she moved her thin bones jangled up against each other like an assemblage of twigs making each others' acquaintance in a windstorm. She had that pale, parched look, those brittle features and narrow mouth I saw on so many of the Appalachian women. She didn't talk much. But one lunch hour during my second week when we sat at the same picnic table out back and I asked her how her morning had been, she launched into a lament in her reedy, already nicotine-pickled voice, about how she was "going to get the hell out of this place, but soon, you better believe it, honey. You are sorrowful mistaken if you think I'm a-gonna spend my best years in this particular pitiful location."

Lydia Tammy and most of the other workers smoked. With that, the long hours indoors under bright fluorescent lighting and the cotton dust they breathed day after day, most of them had dull, mottled skin and phlegmy breath. Their backs were stooped to varying degrees. The veins on the older women's legs bulged, purple, twisted and crawling like blood-gorged worms. Yet they came to work every day. They went home and cooked and cleaned and put the kids to bed. And they got up the next morning and did it again.

They had no choice. There was a recession going on. What better jobs were there for them? Black women, white women, most of them had migrated from the South with their families, the fathers, brothers and husbands hiring on at the Ford factory in Ypsilanti, the women settling for much lower laundry wages. The best-educated among my co-workers were high school graduates. Many had less schooling than that. They considered themselves lucky. They had a union. Medical benefits, vacation, sick days. They didn't complain. They just kept coming to work. And so, beginning that June of 1974, did I.

I was assigned to the main mangle. Like some monstrous omnivorous plant with roots descending to unknown depths, it hulked smack in the middle of the floor, which was roughly the size of Crisler Stadium, home of The Mighty Wolverines, Go Blue! as the decal slapped on one side of the behemoth proclaimed. Like a defensive guard challenging all comers, the great grease-streaked steel bulk loomed, rollers revolving, steam bellowing, pistons firing.

The big mangle was unbelievably loud. But that was only part of the racket. There was the clatter of rickety bins being loaded, unloaded and wheeled around, soiled laundry heading to washing stations 1, 2, 3, and 4, newly clean material rolling toward the driers, dry pieces parceled out among the big mangle, small mangles, and various hot presses. I thought pushing those bins around must be the worst job at the place, but some of the women considered it a choice assignment. They said they liked to move around.

All the other machines were arrayed around the main mangle. What a cacophony. Engines, rotors, motors whirring and sputtering. Metal parts slapping against each other. Chains clanging. And always, everywhere, under and over and beyond every other sound, the rhythmic, locomotive hiss emitted by the steam presses opening and closing. Despite the volume there was something soothing about the vaporous sibilance as it pulsed through the place, whispering a sultry "husssh-husssh-husssh" that slipped under my skin.

I was relieved at how easily I fell into camaraderie with the team I joined on mangle duty. I'd been really nervous that I wouldn't fit in, that these tough women who talked in tobacco-roughened rumbles would take one look at me with my wire-rimmed glasses, uncallused hands, hear one word out of my mouth, roll their eyes and write me off. They didn't. They welcomed me.

Two middle-aged mangle hands took me under their wing. Wanda Harrington was white, with such a heavy hill-country lilt that I had to concentrate really hard to make out her words. Caroline Hotchkiss was Black, born in Kentucky, moved to Detroit when she was twelve, now living in Ypsilanti and proud to be putting two kids through Eastern Michigan University. They showed me the ropes, including shortcuts with the work and ways to cheat the timeclock. When I confided my nervousness about the big machines, they both went all maternal on me, taking extra time to make sure I got the hang of the job. Slapping my back and yelling to be heard just before the end-of-shift bell sounded on my first Friday there, Wanda said, "You might be a soft little college girl, Randy, but as far as I am concerned you are a full-fledged mangle gal now." As the foreman walked by, Caroline added, "Anybody messes with you will have to reckon with us."

Work was hard and god it was hot, but I soon got the hang of it and settled into a routine. That summer I got the best sleep of my life. I'd take the bus home, get off on State Street in front of the U of M administration building, walk past the big black spinning cube and continue through to East Jefferson and my little studio apartment two blocks down. I'd crank up the air conditioning, strip and shower, throw together some dinner, grilled cheese sandwiches, that sort of thing, read or watch TV for not very long at all, then fall into bed and lie there, dead, undreaming, until the alarm woke me for work. Sometimes on weekends I'd stop in at the Flame and have a couple of drinks, shoot the shit with Sunflower, play the jukebox, dance a little if a friend or two showed up.

VERA'S WILL

I couldn't think on the job because of the noise and I didn't think at home because I was too tired. Maybe that had something to do with why, when fall came around, I decided to stay on instead of returning to school for my senior year.

I ended up working at the laundry for two years. I never did graduate from college.

Mom was not pleased. There's your classic understatement. Her daughter the laundress? This she could not stomach. Her daughter the dropout, bad enough, but she was prepared to be patient on that front.

"Look, that's what kids are like these days," she told Auntie Rose on a Saturday that September. I had driven home, popped a load of clothes into the washing machine. Over coffee and bagels with Mom, Auntie Rose and Uncle Eeb, I had just dropped the dropping-out news.

"They all want to experiment a little before buckling down," Rosie agreed. "It's what they do these days. And what's the harm? A little breather before she gets her degree. Right, dollface?" She chucked my cheek, grinning at Eeb.

Mom nodded. "Sure. When she goes back she can really get serious, and don't forget, she's still got years of graduate school ahead of her." Uncle Eeb was silent as usual, but I felt his eyes on me. Was he as surprised as I at Mom's plan for me to stay in school forever? "Thank god she doesn't take drugs at least." I saw no need to correct her on this, since daily pot smoking and a few LSD trips did make me a virtual teetotaler compared to most of my friends. "The rest she'll sort out. I consider this an elongated study break. She's earned it."

I cleared my throat. Better get the rest over with. "Glad you're cool with this, Mom. So I figured since I'm not in school I should work."

"You are so smart" from Auntie Rose. "Make enough, you can save some, and then you can backpack around Europe, like, Ruby, did I tell you, my friend Mitzy's girl is doing?"

"She's not going to any Europe," Mom replied. "No decent doctors if she gets sick, unscrupulous characters take advantage of a young innocent girl, no thank you. She wants to work, good, we'll find her something right here—"

"I live in Ann Arbor, Mom—"

"Fine, in Ann Arbor if for some reason you feel compelled to stay there and pay rent when you could live here at home for free. You can tutor schoolkids, something like that. I'll call the teachers' union, find out how to set it up. It probably doesn't pay much but it'll be good experience."

It was now or never. "Thanks, Mom, but you don't need to. I've already got a job. Matter of fact, I'm staying on at the laundry."

I don't remember details of the ensuing conversation—or lack thereof. What precisely Mom said—or didn't. When exactly Auntie Rose and Uncle Eeb made their getaway. Where Mom went. I only recall a sudden freeze. Me suddenly alone, sitting there shivering on a formerly sunny Sunday.

Mom didn't ice me out forever. That only lasted for a few days. She simply posted a fence around a region of my life—work, the way I spent most of my waking hours—and set about skirting it until it became routine. She never spoke of my job, ever. And neither did I.

I lived to regret this. For we had now cemented a pattern, already well in place, of sidestepping difficult issues. We both meant well. All those silences born of love. The two of us desperately erecting walls—to protect us, we thought, to safeguard what we had left. Which was precious little by the end. Instead of constructing a bulwark, we cranked open a fissure that eventually grew too wide to traverse.

I'd long since given up on Dad. But how I wish Mom and I had been able to hold fast.

Instead, our conversations—and we still talked often, big phone bills on both ends—devolved into one-way information-delivery systems. Mom loading trivia about Northdale or Hollywood or the uninteresting lives of her teacher colleagues onto a rushing conveyor belt, me idly eying the detritus tumbling down.

That's how it went, from September 1974 when I started full-time work at the laundry and for the next ten years until Mom died. She'd ask about my health. My weight, which she worried was way too low. My studies, as she quaintly referred to any fiction I was reading, were also an acceptable topic. And she'd fill me in about the family. She seemed particularly devoted to charting engagements and marriages, even if the bride was a fifth cousin once removed I'd never met. She made sure I got invited to every wedding and baby shower, buying opulent gifts in my name.

Occasionally she sallied forth with a vague inquiry like, "So how's life?" I answered, "Fine." And there we were.

It was as if, cast out from a faintly remembered homeland, we were forever trying to make our way back to that place of perfect safety. Like sailboats becalmed on a motionless sea, we never made it to shore.

I found it ironic that Mom was ashamed of my laundry job. She was a worker too, but like most teachers she considered herself a "professional," occupying a loftier position than everyone else who labored for a wage, like Uncle Eeb manufacturing Mustangs at the River Rouge plant. This daughter of thick-accented up-from-the-slums immigrants was a snob. Worse, she'd started criticizing the civil-rights movement for "extremism." Echoing Dad's cracks about the anti-war protests. Referring to feminists as "ugly man-hating sickos." Refusing, of course, to even listen to anything about Palestine.

On that September Saturday in 1974, I resolved to stop letting it shock me and to accept that I had no way to please her. I did one more load of clothes, loaded the car and left.

Back in Ann Arbor, I met with my academic advisor the next day. She'd agreed to see me even though it was a Sunday. I told her I wouldn't be coming back to school. When she asked why, I was at a loss.

"Why don't you think about it and try to explain," she insisted.

We sat in agonizing silence on the loveseat in her East Quad office. I gripped my hands together and looked down at the floor. Finally I looked up at her, tried to smile, and said, "I'm a lesbian." I felt dishonest, though. This wasn't news. It had already been three years since Babe and I first got it on. What did it have to do with work and school? Then I startled myself by saying, "I mean, I came out of the closet." My voice quavered. My hands shook.

She said, "You need time to get through this, don't you?"

I felt a rush of gratitude. I wished she'd hug me. Then she did, she hugged me, and I wasn't crying but I was kind of crumbling against her.

I was a little in shock because until that moment I had actually thought that coming out had been pretty much of a breeze. I'd filled in all my old Northdale friends the summer after my first year in Ann Arbor. Elliot of course had known since a year ago last spring, and though that hadn't been pretty I was well over it. Mom I'd told about six months ago. Compared to some of the horror stories I'd heard about parents' reactions to their children's coming out, hers hadn't been so bad. She didn't disown me, or put me in a mental institution. She didn't assault me physically. She wasn't even loud, and Mom was a shryer. She didn't shrivel me with one of her famous angry glares. In fact, she didn't look at me at all. The conversation was brief. It ended with her announcing that we would never speak of this again. She still hugged me at the door when I came home for the weekend. We still stayed up late together watching old movies. But I obeyed her. I never spoke of my life. Now we'd added my job to the list of forbidden topics.

As my advisor and I separated from our hug I whispered, "I guess I just need to gather my wits."

And I guessed that's what I would continue doing at the laundry. Keep your hands busy. Distract your mind. I've never been able to turn off my brain, but there at the laundry I did. I could not hear myself think in the midst of all that noise.

In August of 1976 I was twenty-three. I'd been at the laundry a little over two years. One sweltering Thursday afternoon we'd spent our lunch break sitting outside at the picnic tables cooling off in the muggy ninety-five degrees. Now, only twenty minutes later, little pools of sweat puddled on the gray concrete floor at our feet. As I stood holding the end of a sheet, shuffling forward while Caroline fed the ends into the mangle, I glanced at her face. Droplets hung under her eyes and around her nose and at the corners of her mouth and trickled into the creases of her neck, which shone slick with wet. It occurred to me that this would be how she'd look if she were crying. We moved sluggishly, as if drugged. The washers, mangles, driers and presses gave off blasts of heat that could rock you off your feet, especially if you hadn't been drinking enough water and were a little dizzied by dehydration, something Wanda was always warning me against.

There was a surreal shimmer to the place. Things seemed to be happening in slow motion, an effect that only intensified when someone screamed. I felt it before I heard it. The scream traveled up my spine loud and strong, high and fast as a blast-off, and I felt my feet leave the ground. I looked around. We were all aloft. Jolted upward by the power of that scream, the whole place had jumped. Then we touched down and everyone stood still.

Her screaming didn't stop. She seemed not to take a breath. She became that scream, and the rest of us, in thrall to her endless pain, became dreamers, immobile, stuck in that dreadful state where you can't move and you can't wake up. Hours seemed to pass like that. Probably it was a few seconds. Then Caroline shouted, "Who is it? What's happened?" She twisted, trying to find the source of the screams, and locked onto Lydia Tammy Talmadge, writhing at the big press at the other end of the plant.

Caroline grabbed Wanda's arm and those two middle-aged mangle gals did the fifty-yard dash in nothing flat.

Now everyone got moving. Some ran toward Lydia Tammy. Others headed the other way, toward the office. Shouts of "call an ambulance" and "get her some ice." I followed Wanda and Caroline.

Lydia Tammy's mouth was agape as she howled. Skin stretched taut against her cheekbones. Knees buckling, she still stood, held in place by the grip of the press locked on her arm. Blood seeped down from the press, dripping onto the floor, diluting a sweat pool and dying it pinkish yellow. I felt like I might throw up. I turned away. The loading-dock guys, Luther and Jake, were trotting toward Lydia Tammy. They got to her just after Wanda and Caroline lifted the top of the press.

As its weight came off her arm, the limb slid down. All of Lydia Tammy followed, folding onto the floor. A pale green surgical scrub top billowed behind her like the freshly laundered wing of a leafy, verdant angel. Flesh and fabric were soldered together.

Relieved of its captive, the press released a stench. I stepped back as the smell of cooked meat reached me. Luther lifted Lydia Tammy. With Jake clearing the way in front of him, he ran, carrying her limp form toward the rear door where I heard the ambulance siren approaching.

The van hauled Lydia Tammy to University Hospital, its eerie strains fading as it pealed away along the same route clean laundry traveled at the end of every work day.

In the plant, things were at a standstill. Everyone had shut down their machines. Some of the washers and driers were still running through their automated cycles but that was it. Their muted hum was a shadow of the usual workaday clamor.

The women stood clustered in little circles. Nervous bursts of conversation alternated with long silences. A puff of cigarette smoke shot down my throat. I coughed. Just then Jim Stickney, the foreman, came striding through.

"All right, everybody," he said. His voice was loud, his tone jocular. He was smiling his fake good-buddy smile, eyes dead as always, combing his thin yellow hair in a transparent effort to appear relaxed. The women's faces tightened as he walked around them. "Look, I'm not going to write anyone up for having a smoke, I understand, everybody's got to unwind after something like this. But you've had your break now. Put out your cigarettes and let's get these machines going. It's time to get back to work." No one moved. Wanda placed her cigarette between her lips and took a slow, deliberate draw, squinting as she let the smoke seep out her nostrils. Caroline, one of the few who didn't smoke, put both her hands on her hips and cocked her head at the foreman. He stiffened, and his combing faltered, but he maintained his sham grin. "What? You got something to say, Caroline?"

"I ain't said nothing."

"Well, you were looking just then like you wanted to."

"When I want to speak I will speak. Don't you worry."

"Well, okay then. Now you gals get moving. You-all are still on the clock." Turning away, he started to reach for the power switch on a mini-mangle.

"Look here, hold up." Caroline. Stickney dropped his arm and turned back to her, lifting his eyebrows as if to say, all right, what now? She took a kerchief out of her jeans pocket and mopped her face. Her other hand stayed planted on her hip. "Here's the thing, Jim. We all are upset. We just watched that little girl get nearly kilt in that goddamn press—"

"Now, now, no need for profanity." He spoke as though to a child.

"I said we just watched that goddamn press burn Lydia Tammy's arm off, and all you goddamn sons-of-a-bitches management going to do is tell us stop smoking and get back to work?" Caroline was shouting now. "Is she not a human being? Does it not matter what just happened here? And you know this ain't the first time, you goddamn bastard. What about Raylene Craymore? That goddamn mangle crippled her for life, and you and Mr. Johnson and this stingy university have spent the last two years doing your god-damnedest to cheat her out of her workman's compensation. What the hell is wrong with you people?"

"That's right! We are human beings!" It was Wanda, still holding her cigarette, thrusting it forward for emphasis. Her voice was shakier than Caroline's, higher pitched, but she stood stalwart next to her, green eyes flashing, pale face going red.

A flicker of fear brought the foreman's eyes to brief life. Then they went dead again as he tried on a sad, humane expression. He took off his glasses and stood there, his brows furrowed deep enough to plant cotton in. He stepped toward Caroline and Wanda, shaking his head and looking at them with a compassion so counterfeit it wouldn't have bought two pops out of the lunchroom vending machine. All the women looked at him looking like that. They looked at each other. No one made a move to start back to work but no one refused either.

Then out of the blue: a high, thin laugh. It had come from me. I clapped my hands onto my mouth but it was too late. Wanda whipped her head around to locate the laugher. Next to her, Caroline swiveled. "What the hell is so goddamn—" she started, but then she sighted my face and suddenly hers changed. She starting chuckling low in her throat.

Swiftly it spread. Just like that, the scene shifted. Sixty-some women stood in the middle of that shop floor and laughed, falling into each other. Holding each other up. Slapping each other's hands. The foreman made his getaway. Soon it became obvious he had been busy, moving from machine to machine, flipping switches. The guffaws grew faint. Caroline stood up straight and listened. Then Wanda, and one by one the others. Steam was pulsing again. Chains were clanging. The machines were calling us back to work.

No one wanted to be first. Especially when we could see Stickney, back inside his glassed-in little office where he spent most of every day drinking coffee, smoking cigarettes, combing hair, overseeing. Nobody wanted to give him the satisfaction.

Caroline stepped up to Wanda. She put her arm around her shoulder. She whispered something into her ear. Then Wanda put her arm around Caroline's shoulder too. Arms draped around each other, the partners sidestepped to me. They sandwiched me between them. My arms went around each waist.

Caroline and Wanda and I stood there like that, watching the other workers, who soon started moving. In twos and threes, the members of each machine's team found each other and joined up. I got a sudden image of how it must look from above, like a number from one of those old Busby Berkley musicals, women moving gracefully about, forming into pairs, trios, groups of four and five coming together in patterns. Geometric shapes. Stars. Flowers.

When each team was together, only Vernell Vance, Lydia Tammy's press partner, stood alone. She took a long, ragged breath and then I felt her, small and sweaty and still shaking, crammed up against me. Caroline and Wanda had taken her in for a mangle gal.

We'd go back to work. But Vernell was on mangle duty now. Nobody was touching that press.

Next morning it was hard to get up. I hadn't slept. Lydia Tammy's scream was lodged in my spine. Every time I'd started to drop off, the whip crack of her scream yanked me back awake. When the alarm clock rang at six-thirty my eyes were already open. I'd been lying there trying to pump myself up to face the place again.

I thought of the others. Caroline and Wanda and the rest. This wasn't the first time they'd been through something like this. Were they lying in bed sighing about how they couldn't go to work this morning? Hell no. By now every one of them is up, I thought, waking kids, making breakfast, packing lunches.

I took the bus to North Campus. I got off, crossed the street and stepped onto the long paved approach to the laundry plant. Rising up to greet me from the expanse of green lawn on either side of the sidewalk, the clicking of cicadas calmed my nerves.

As I got closer I saw some men standing in front of the laundry. They weren't walking but they were holding picket signs. What the hell? Was this about Lydia Tammy?

I drew near. About a dozen guys. Black and white, some in faded gray coveralls, some wearing T-shirts and jeans. Their signs said "Unfair to Labor" and "No Contract No Work." I was flabbergasted. A strike, at the laundry! But who were these guys? They didn't work here. I'd never seen any of them before. I approached the picketers and asked what was going on.

Several of them talking at once, they told me they belonged to the International Brotherhood of Electrical Workers. Their union was on strike against the university. When had the strike started, I asked. Two days ago, on Wednesday. Why hadn't I heard about it? Why hadn't there been anything in the Ann Arbor News? The strikers shrugged. "We're not worried about that," a rangy guy in an Eastern Michigan cap said. "We don't need to be on the news. We'll get our contract." Until they did, they'd be reporting for picket duty every morning. They had to in order to collect strike benefits.

"So everybody turned around and went home?" I asked.

A short, squat guy with salt-and-pepper hair pulled back into a ponytail—a Hell's Angel-looking guy, the kind I would veer away from on the street—looked at me. "Who do you mean?"

"The women, all the others, the ones I work here with. Are they gone already?"

"Gone? They're inside. Why would they be gone?"

I paused. Something was strange here. "Well, you're on strike and you're picketing. I assume our union is honoring your picket lines."

"No, that's not necessary. Let me get Leon." He walked over to a younger fellow and brought him back.

"Hi, I'm Leon. I'm the picket captain." We shook hands. I asked why my co-workers had crossed his picket line. He smiled. "Oh, don't call it like that. It's not like the ladies are scabs or anything. We're not asking anybody to stay out. We're just here to make a point, but you don't need to get yourselves in trouble. All the other unions, we know they support us, but they can all keep working."

"You're saying it's okay to go in to work even though you're out here picketing?" He nodded, and smiled. "Well, okay, if you're really sure."

He patted me on the back. "That's what I'm saying, hon. You'd better go on in to work or they'll dock you, won't they?"

I went inside. After I clocked in and put my lunch bag in my locker, I went to the mangle. Caroline and Wanda were already working. Wanda said, "Morning," and handed me an end of sheet. Caroline nodded a quick hello from her station feeding the other end onto the rollers. Neither seemed very sociable. Both looked down at their hands as they silently handled the sheets.

It was the same at every station. Usually each work team functioned as a unit, like a marching band stepping in cadence to the pace set by the machines. This morning each worker seemed a person apart, moving to her own unhappy rhythm.

We're all blue, I thought. It's what happened to Lydia Tammy. The thought actually cheered me. I wasn't so weak. The accident had hurt us all.

Boy, did I read them wrong.

When I went outside for the mid-morning break, I found everyone standing instead of sitting around smoking as they usually did. They formed a semi-circle around one of the picnic tables. Caroline stood on the bench.

"It just ain't right," she said. For someone who hadn't spoken three words all morning her voice rang out sure and strong. "It goes against everything I feel deep in my bones."

"Me too," someone yelled out. "That's right" from someone else.

"You just do not cross a picket line. You just don't do it," Caroline said. "Am I right or am I wrong?"

"You are right, honey!" This came from Wanda, as she jumped up onto the bench next to Caroline. I turned toward Vernell, who was standing next to me at the back of the crowd. She beamed. "When I come in here this morning," Wanda continued, "when I walked on in past them guys out there on strike, I just felt sick inside." Lots of "me too"s and "uh-huh"s from the workers. "All morning I have stood inside there and felt ashamed of myself. I mean, what the hell, you know?" More affirmation from the women. "I don't care what those guys say, it just ain't right, you know?"

"So what do we do now?" The voice came from somewhere in front. Everyone started talking. Caroline and Wanda whispered to each other for a minute. Then Caroline lifted both her hands and asked everyone to pay attention.

"Look here," she said. "This break is over in five minutes. The question on the table is, are we going to just go back in to work like usual or what?" Almost everybody shook their heads no. "Well then, are you ready to do the right thing? Are you strong enough to do right by them guys on strike out there—"

"Even if they are too dumb to know theyselves what the right thing is!" Wanda sang out. She cracked everybody up. A few people clapped as they laughed.

"Well, she's right, you know," Caroline said. "If we do this we are on our own."

"Y'all know good and well it's always the women got to make things right! We got to strike!" Holy shit—I hadn't noticed Vernell move away from my side, but there she was, standing in front of the bench below Caroline and Wanda, throwing her fist into the air and yelling at the top of her lungs. She was a different woman than the shaking, quaking casualty of yesterday. Maybe this was about Lydia Tammy after all.

Caroline took Wanda's hand. They raised their clasped hands in the air, making fists of their free ones and raising them too. "Okay, then," Caroline shouted. "Let's take a vote. Listen up. The question we are voting on is this: are we going to honor the strike of our brothers in the electricians' union and not cross their picket line like goddamn scabs? All in favor say aye." Every voice rang out. "Opposed say nay." Not a sound but the cicadas. "Well, let's go tell old Jim Stickney and then let's get the hell out of here!"

We followed Caroline, Wanda and Vernell into the laundry, all of us clapping and chanting, "Strike! Strike! Strike!"

There was a pause during which I assumed Caroline and Wanda were informing Stickney that we were going to honor the IBEW strike. They must not have waited for his reply; the chanting and clapping started up again real fast. We moved like a drill team toward the locker room. We grabbed our stuff. As smoothly as if we'd rehearsed for weeks, we reassembled and marched out the front door.

We swept the strikers into a real picket line. I noticed that someone had pulled Luther and Jake off the loading dock. Back and forth we all walked in front of the University of Michigan industrial laundry. Chanting, "No contract! No work!" so loud that we drowned out the cicadas' drone.

We picketed for about two hours. Marched through what would have been our lunch hour. The strikers shared thermoses of lemonade with us laundry workers. It tasted great, puckery and sweet, just right for picketing under the hot sun.

Then, at one o'clock, Leon started collecting the picket signs. The strikers gathered their trash and pulled out car keys. Their picket shift was over, Leon explained. He also said that the laundry wasn't one of the sites on their picket rotation for next week, so we could plan to go back to work Monday.

"That all works out real fine," said Caroline. There were smiles all around, back slapping, hugs. I was thrilled at the thought of heading home to a nice long nap and uneventful weekend.

Wanda clapped her hands for attention. "Wait up, y'all," she said. People had begun to drift away toward the parking lot, but they paused. "We done real good here today." Wanda smiled widely and I noticed for the first time that she was missing a tooth on top. "I am just not ready to say goodbye. So how about everybody come on over to my house and we'll have us a barbecue? What do y'all say? Caroline and me, we'll stop and get some hot dogs and hamburgers, and somebody else can get some beer and pop and chips, you know what I'm talking bout, we'll have us a nice, relaxing summer afternoon. How bout it?"

There were hoots of agreement, more clapping, and people started organizing themselves to share rides and pick up supplies. Wanda went around giving directions to her place in Ypsi. When she came up to me she said, "You ride with me and Caroline, honey, I know you don't have a car."

"Um, listen, Wanda, thanks a lot," I said, "but I can't come. I'm not feeling too good."

"Oh, no. What's the matter?"

"I think I'm coming down with a stomach flu. I was feeling bad all morning, I was thinking I was going to have to go home sick." I did feel queasy in my stomach, lying to her.

Wanda touched my cheek. "Why, you are hot, Randy. OK, we'll drop you home before we go to the store." Why did she have to be so nice? I shook my head and mumbled something about it being too far out of her way. She looked at me for a long minute. "Well all right," she finally said. "Go on and take the bus. But you call me tonight and tell me how you're feeling."

I nodded. I went over to Caroline and said goodbye. Then I headed down the long walkway. The cicadas were going strong again, thundering their angry August song as I waited for the bus.

I never went back to work at the laundry. I never saw any of those women again.

I never called Wanda. Never spoke to Caroline. Never heard whether Lydia Tammy recovered. Never explained, or apologized.

I spent the weekend hiding. From everyone and everything, but mostly from myself. Pitiful little closet case.

For that had been all I could think of when Wanda started organizing the barbecue. How I was a big lezzie who would never fit in at the backyard bash. How everyone would drink a few beers and loosen up, start talking about their husbands and their boyfriends, how sooner or later someone would ask me about my boyfriend. And what would I do? I could lie, making up a boyfriend, giving him a name and various characteristics, or simply say I wasn't seeing any steady guy right now, but either way, commission or omission, it would be a lie lie lie. Or I could tell the truth, come out to all my half-crocked co-workers right there in Wanda's backyard. Oh, that would be special. That would be a real treat. Telling a bunch of back-country church-going straight women that I was a lesbian. Watch their faces twist. Hear their voices fill with disgust. Feel them pull away.

Those had seemed to me to be my choices as I'd quickly gauged the situation while Wanda and the women settled on who would buy what for the barbecue. Lie, and hate myself for it. Or come out of the closet, and invite them to hate me.

My calculations had taken only a minute. By the time Wanda approached me, I really had made myself sick. So I took the coward's way out. And took to my bed. Where I stayed pretty much all weekend.

The phone rang and rang but I didn't pick up. On Monday I called the university personnel office and quit, arranging for them to mail me my final check. The phone finally stopped ringing on Wednesday.

I never forgave myself for fleeing the laundry and betraying my friends. It took Mom dying for me to figure out why I'd fled.

It was almost eight years later, spring of 1984. I was in her room at Sinai Hospital on Outer Drive on a stormy Sunday afternoon. Dad had spent a few minutes that morning then left for the library. My flight home to Brooklyn was set for that night.

I'd been sharing small talk with a nurse as she changed Mom's IV drip and checked her chart. Mom was unconscious. I was in shock: I had just found out she'd led the nurse to believe I was a professor. She'd probably said something like, "My daughter is in English literature at the university." So she hadn't lied outright, which would have been important to Mom even if it was a fine distinction, some might say a false one ethically speaking.

The nurse's name was Lourdes Narciso. I remember it because she treated Mom with such tender care even though she had a ridiculous number of other patients and even though Mom was pretty clearly a lost cause, and at the same time she dealt with me as gently as if I were a wounded animal she'd spotted lying on the side of the road. Whenever she came in to work on Mom she talked softly and steadily to me. She had just been telling me about her son, a medical student at Wayne State. She was very proud. Then she said, "Like your mother. She is so proud of you, Randy." My smile was, I'm sure, tinged with skepticism. Nurse Narcisco said, "Oh, she is. She told me so when she could still speak. And why wouldn't she be? An English professor at a great university in New York—that is a very wonderful thing. A daughter like that would make any mother proud."

I was flummoxed. If I kept silent—back to ethics here—I'd be colluding in Mom's pathetic lie. If I told the truth, that I was "in" English literature only in the sense that I was the department secretary, I would be confessing something sad and awful about my mother and me.

I never cry in front of strangers, but tears pretty well solved my dilemma. I didn't tell Nurse Narciso the truth. I didn't join Mom's lie. I skirted the whole issue by falling apart.

In a secret corner of my heart I'd always hoped that one day, somehow, Mom and I would recover each other. I would burst from a phone booth all shiny and sparkly, and dazzle her with my super self. She'd shriek Eureka and love me for, not despite, who I'd turned out to be. Now that chance was lost.

I stopped blubbering. Cleaned up my face. Gathered my things. I thanked Nurse Narciso, hugged her, and asked her to give us a minute alone. She patted my back, said, "See you next month, dear," and was gone. I stood over Mom. Listened to her chuffing breaths. Held her hand. I kissed her forehead. I left.

On the plane all I could think about was a conversation we'd had six months earlier, my last visit home before she was first hospitalized for liver failure. She'd been in the basement washing clothes. I'd followed her downstairs. Ronny, the other English Department secretary, had been urging me to confront Mom about how she dealt with my lesbianism. His idea was that I should reach out, express how much I needed her to acknowledge me. I tried, but it came out bitter, an attack.

"Stop shoving me back in the closet when you talk to the

relatives," I said. "I know you lie. I know you say I'm dating men. Why can't you tell the truth? When are you going to accept that who I am is fine?"

She got all tight-faced. "Let me see if I have this right. Do you want me to make a sign? I should carry it around, saying my daughter is a lesbian?"

"Yeah, Mom, that would be a good first step."

Weary distaste turned her mouth downward. She busied herself shifting clothes from the washer to the drier. She said, "You know, Randy, I'm not like you. Maybe I don't want everyone to know everything. Maybe I don't care to hang my dirty laundry out for the world to see."

Now, in the plane, as I watched the Manhattan skyline approach and tried to blot out the memory of that awful scene, Wanda and Caroline's kind faces came to mind. And it came to me why I had run away from them.

That August afternoon eight years before, as I'd struggled over whether to go to Wanda's for barbecue, I'd let a stupid stereotype of backward hillbillies overwhelm what I knew to be true. They were good people. They understood solidarity—hadn't they shown it just that afternoon? Now, in hindsight, I was sure they would not have done me wrong. If I had gone to the barbecue, if I had come out to them, all of them together over hot dogs or privately in ones and twos over the weeks and months, it would have been all right. Maybe not perfect, or even great, with everyone, at first. But if I had trusted those workers enough to stick together we would have come through.

Took me long enough to wise up. Well. They say you don't really grow up until your mother dies.

I got the call at work a week later. After Elliot told me, I hung up the phone and looked down at my desk. I laid my palms onto it and felt its substance. I laid my head on my hands and smelled a hint of varnish. I thought: this desk exists. My mother does not.

I touched my lips to my wrist. I kissed myself and tasted salt. I thought: this is me, alone.

Truth and Consequences

Perhaps purgatory is something like this. Searing in the midday summer sun, surrounded by sweaty, yelling men. Watching a boring game that never ends, stranded up here in the nosebleed seats so you can't even see.

And then doing it again next week. Bounce downtown in Ben's Packard. Hank Greenberg's history, still you'll come, he insists. He has tickets. Compulsory attendance.

What piffle enters your head, Vera Steiner. For these are halcyon days. Several levels up from limbo. Remember hell? There may have been no deadly dull baseball then, but that's because there were no wide-eyed little boys to dirty your dress with their ice-cream-sticky hands, gobble hot dogs dribbling ketchup down the chin, jump up, yelp, clap, and wave a Tigers pennant on a pointy stick, missing your eye by barely an inch. This is paradise, or as close as life gets. Messy, populated, plumb full of pleasures as palpable as the Good 'N Plenty your grandson politely requests during the seventh-inning stretch. Heaven is the hard wood of Briggs Stadium bleachers polishing your bum to a benumbed, glossy sheen.

Has there ever been a child like this? "Elliot," Vera sings. Attention glued to the game—can he possibly understand it at his age?—Elliot lifts a hand as if to swat his name away. She can't stop bothering him. "Belly boy." His lips purse—and oh! he puts his hands to his hips. Big-league consternation. Could you plotz from the pleasure of it? Certain he's made his point, the toddler concentrates on the diamond again. Bending behind Elliot's back, Vera whispers to Ben, "Couldn't you just eat him up?"

"Watch this," is Ben's reply. He extends his fingers toward Elliot's waist.

The two of them pestering the poor kid. She stays Ben. "Wait a minute. Watch." Elliot's tongue tips out of the corner of his mouth.

"Oy" from Ben.

Vera grabs his hand. "Sha. Hold on." The grandparents grip each other, gasping down the impulse to giggle as Elliot, perfectly focused, follows the game.

He's smart as can be, but still, he's only three. Surely Elliot can't grasp the intricacies—"Infiewd fwy wule," he shrieks, jumping up. Flailing pennant nearly skewers Ben. Who ducks, ends up lying half on Vera's lap. Laughing, the two of them, as the tot scowls and Al Kaline fouls out.

December 1953

Squirming in her arms, a baby girl! Is there no magic Ruby cannot perform?

Last winter, when she'd said she was p.g. again, Vera had been concerned. Ruby hadn't worked since Elliot was born. She had talked of returning to the classroom soon, putting El in nursery school or dropping him at the deli every day with Gussie and Ben. That would have removed the burden on Bill. When Elliot came he'd taken a teaching job himself, science at a suburban high school, and he'd been doing double duty ever since. Adult Ed at night, to bring in extra cash. Naturally he had no kechas left to exert himself on his dissertation. He's wanted that Ph.D. so badly. They should wait for another baby, Vera had thought. First things first.

She must have been nuts. Bill will be Dr. Steiner soon enough. But Daddy again—and to a girl! A gurgling, wriggling, curly-headed sprite, with dewy brown eyes fringed by long lashes that tickle your neck when you press her against you to burp. A wiggly chubby little body exuding heat beneath the fuzzy flannel your fingers gently rub.

She smiled at me! I don't care what Gussie says, that's not gas!

Elliot's getting sleepy. He'll never admit it. She remembers his father was like this too, stubbornly resisting bedtime, and wonders at what age he outgrew it.

Sitting on the piano bench, Elliot nudges ever closer to her. His head has fallen against her breast. Still he makes an effort to play. Nonsense notes, dissonance from a three-year-old, but when she peeks at his face the expression is intense. Lips puckered, sucking at his cheeks. And then, oy, with the tongue—out it comes, slipping from the corner of his mouth—and sure enough, his brow contracts. Maestro, if you please! She has no doubt this boy will do grand things. She'd clap but has no free hands. Right arm around El, Mary cradled in her left.

"Tanteh Vera?"

"Hmm?" She shouldn't have let Bill talk her into being called that. She's their grandmother, not their aunt. Back when Elliot was born Bill had given her a whole song and dance. "Grandma" is too corny, he said, "bubbie" too old-world. You're so refined, he said, not like Gussie. Vera had insisted on the Yiddish word, tanteh, but conceded the larger point. Which she regrets. It's almost as though Bill and Ruby want to distance her from their kids. Which makes no sense. She lives here. Heats a bottle and feeds the baby when Ruby's too bushed. Plays piano with El, reads to him. She frequently babysits, like tonight. Ruby and Bill are at a ZOA shindig, some bigwig from Israel pitching for alms. Aunt my foot. Why did I ever let them ... oh, forget it, she tells herself. Tanteh Vera? Fine. Let it be. "Yes, Elliot? But whisper now, because it's time to go to sleep."

"Okay," he whispers. "I just want to say that I love my Superman PJ's."

Oy. She kisses his cheek. They'll sit another minute. She just gave them both their baths. Soft skin. Sweet scents. It took a lifetime, but luck has finally come her way again. Two little ones to love. And years ahead for the loving.

The first twinge comes when she hears Ruby and Bill get home. A queer tension sweeps in with them. Strong enough to enter every room, climb stairs, penetrate doors and walls: it reaches Vera as she reads, radio tuned to jazz at low volume next to her bed. Passes through her like an augury.

The two of them in the kitchen. A hissing exchange of whispers with an angry edge. Ruby spewing outrage. What about? Vera shivers, reaches for a smoke, freezes. She's sure she hears Ruby spit her name. Then Bill, sputtering, hushing his wife—and, audible in his nearly inaudible voice, shame. Anger. Irritation. "Don't aggravate me," Vera hears him say. Something about "the end of the line" from Ruby.

Ruby's stomp up the stairs, then his. A door closes, hard.

Vera lies stiff as a mannequin between icy sheets. A perfunctory knock, then her door opens. Bill sticks his head in. "Ma, would you turn the radio off? That junk you're playing is bothering Ruby."

"Of course, dear." She flicks the dial.

The click echoes in half-dreams throughout the night's restless sleep. A guillotine drops. A trigger cocked. Piano wires snap. Shattering glass. Vera trapped in a windowless room.

She comes fully awake long before dawn. She lies listening to winter-bare branches thrashing in the wind.

January 1954

She's been making too many mistakes. Sam even had to speak to her. She'd better watch it. Soon this job, this goddamned job, twenty-four years counting that philistine's riches, may be all she has left.

Every day as quitting time nears, she could scream.

It's tempting. Throw her hands up, let the chips fall where they may. What difference would it make? There's nothing she

374

can ever do to make things fit. She knew it once. Forgot for a bit, or let herself be convinced. Now it is manifest again.

A countdown is under way. She can almost hear the metronome tick-tick-ticking. As she gathers her things, five o'clock every day. Huddles into coat and hat. Climbs onto the bus and drops in her coins. Trudges through two blocks of snowy slush to the house. Drags her feet inside.

Ruby's getting ready to lower the boom. Only a fool could miss the clues. Since the night of that Zionist dinner last month, nothing is the same. Vera has an idea what happened, but she doesn't investigate. Vile things under that rock. She won't be the one to turn it.

Doesn't matter. When the sun goes down you know. Ruby has turned off her glow.

Sam Pleck was at that ZOA bash. He came in to the office the next morning gushing about sitting with Ruby and Bill— and Ernest Steiner, Peter's brother. "Fascinating fellow," he said. "Quite a business sense." Sam said he had left early, for Ada was home with a head cold. Which left Peter's brother with Ruby and Bill. A fancy dinner, wine flowing, catching up on family news. Did Ernest let something spill?

Now Vera watches Woodward pass. Should I do it myself, she wonders. Bow out gracefully? Find a place, say it's time to go, a young family doesn't need grandma in the way?

No! She presses her forehead against the bus window. It isn't fair, she thinks. I haven't done anything wrong. Not in what seems a million years. Will malicious gossip from a meddling former brother-in-law do her in?

She seizes up. This is a Friday. It will be tonight, she thinks. I just know. They're going to confront me. And Bill will drive me to Gussie's. Park me back in the attic. Over the weekend he'll bring my things.

They can't! I'm fifty-six. God, I can't control my thoughts, I'm not a machine, I have feelings, they'll never go away, but I haven't done—for pity's sake, I haven't done any awful thing in thirty years. Three decades sequestered. Is there a more eloquent plea?

No. I won't beg. Despite everything, I have my dignity.

Are you nuts? Do you hear yourself, Vera Steiner? At this late date, dignity? Don't be a fool. Do whatever it takes. Go to your boy. Make your case. Stop him from doing what his father did. Breaking up the family, again.

Willy—Bill! I gave up every chance at love. Because I loved you more. Don't make it not matter. Don't discard me. I'm your mother. You can't shake me off like so much dirty, shoddy debris—can you? Deny Elliot and Mary their very own grandmother?

Her shoulders are shaking. Compose yourself, Vera, she thinks. People will see. Still facing the window, she pushes into her purse, pops the compact. Dabs with a tissue at her eyes. Applies lipstick. Lightly powders her cheeks. Permits herself a long, raggedy sigh. There. All right. Face the music.

She needs to gather her wits. She glances at the street again. Oh dear—she's missed her stop. By a lot. The bus is nearing Fenkell. She flips her wrist. Five forty-five. If she has an appointment with doom, is she obliged to be prompt?

She rides to McNichols, gets out near Palmer Park. Walks east. Sugar's. This will do.

"No," Vera says. "I don't dance."

"Aw, sure you do, darlin', sharp lookin' lady like you. I bet you could even teach me a step or two."

Vera smiles and shakes her head. Isn't this just perfect, she thinks. I'm being pursued.

She sips her gin, watches the girl's back as she heads toward the other end of the bar. Notices anew a woman sitting a few stools down, short dark hair, fingers wrapped around a highball glass she's been nursing since before Vera came in. The woman looks her way. Vera quickly turns. Better not to meet anyone's eye. On the other side, right next to her, another gal. Drinking beer. Strong hands. But soft, I bet, Vera thinks. Hands that know how to ... where to ... I'd better get out of here. You see how they do it? Entice you with … nothing tangible … a taste beneath the booze, beyond the smoky haze a fragrance … whatever it is, it's sweet, it surrounds you, invites you in. A warm, woozily welcoming fog into which you might easily wander and find yourself forever lost. You sit, you order a drink, you look around, and, god, it's like quicksand, you're powerless against this wave of wanting to sink into a woman's arms.

No—not true! She's been strong for so long. Day in, day out, she resists.

Vera has never found anyplace she belonged. But she's held strong. She hasn't done wrong, or not for a very long time.

Today of all days, she won't be lured. She can hold out. She came here to ensure that. And she's passed the test. Her heart may be flawed, but her will is insurmountable.

She drains the gin from her first and only drink, finds some change in her coin purse for the tip, stands, heaves on her coat, pulls out gloves, knots scarf, glances about. She meets the high-ball sipper's eyes. They exchange a smile. Why not? She's ready for the cold. She leaves.

"Veraleh, dolly, it's been a pleasure you dropping in for dinner. And staying after for tea—such a treat! You can stay as long as you like as far as I'm concerned, we haven't talked like this in a million years—"

"I hear a but coming, Gussie."

"No but, Veraleh, only I'm afraid Ruby and Bill, they're worrying where you are, you don't think you should give them a call already?"

Her tone is mild, but Gussie's look is shrewd. Vera is reminded again that this one is nobody's fool. She clearly knows something is up. She may even know what it is. They have never spoken of Vera's … problem … yet Vera suspects that Gussie has long known the ugly truth. Does she also know of the tension in her daughter's marital home? Has Ruby said something? Asked Gussie's advice?

Vera peers at Gussie, who has converted her expression to guileless concern, and shrugs. "Guess you're right." She rises. "So I'll call."

"Sure. Call, sit back down, have some more kugel, we'll talk—"

"No, Gussie. I should go." Gussie starts to say something, then stops. "What, Gussie? What is it?"

"Nothing, Veraleh. Only—" Gussie gets up, stands beside Vera, puts her hands on her shoulders, rubs. She kisses the top of Vera's head. She lifts the telephone handset off the wall cradle, gives it to Vera. "So call. Whenever you want. Ben will drive you home."

Bill answers on the first ring. "Ma! Where've you been?"

"Did I worry you? Oh, I'm sorry, Bill. I had dinner with Gussie and Ben."

"You could have called. We were waiting to—"

"I'm calling now, dear. We're just having some tea, and then Ben will drive me home."

"No. I'll pick you up."

"Oh, don't bother, you must be tired—"

"I'm coming, Ma. Ruby wants me to ... there's something."

I know, Vera wants to say. Poor boy, human relations have never been his forte. "I'll be waiting. Be careful driving in this snow. Bye."

She gathers her things. Waits by the door. Gussie's hands on her shoulders again. A peculiar feeling. Almost peace. This must be what comes over the condemned as they mount the gallows to face their fate.

Ruby's standing at the kitchen door, dish towel in hand, as Vera and Bill rush in, stamping wet white from their feet. Vera feels herself being inspected as she doffs her wintry things. Ruby shifts her eyes to Bill—undoing his boots, wiping them fastidiously, lining them up in the closet beside his wife's, not meeting her gaze—then back to his mother.

Vera hands Bill her coat. She looks directly at Ruby. He couldn't do it, she wants to say. I knew it would be you.

Vera and Ruby at the kitchen table. Outside, howling wind. The snow has thickened. A real winter storm, then. Here, inside, a pause in the silly little conversation. Upstairs, the children sleep. Bill in the master bedroom working on his thesis. Oh hell, Vera thinks. Get it over with.

"I'm surprised, Ruby," she says.

"At what?"

"Beating around the bush like this. Fifteen minutes of small talk? That's not like you."

"Fine." Ruby's eyes flash. Cheeks flush. "I was trying to be nice, but you know what? You're right. Let's get down to brass tacks." Still, she dawdles, looking down, fiddling with her wedding ring. "You know," she looks at Vera across the table again, "this really should have been Bill."

"Oh?"

"He should have been the one to tell you. We've talked about it enough. And he promised. But there's something weak in him." Vera opens her mouth. "No, don't say anything. There is. All that pain, the hospital years, of course in some ways he's really tough, he has to be to have gotten through that … but he's also weak. Inside."

"He—"

"I said don't speak. You made him like this, Vera. You damaged him. Took something from him when you left, or, well, I don't know, it would take psychoanalysis and that's one thing Bill will never do … look, I'm getting off the topic. Which is you, not him. I only wanted to explain why I'm going to say this when by rights it should come from your son."

"All right. That's clear. So say it."

"I think you know." Still being pokey. Vera reaches for her purse, then remembers Ruby has asked her not to smoke except in her bedroom. She claims to be allergic. "You want a cigarette. Well, there, you see. one of many things you won't have to put up with anymore." Vera stares at her. "Okay. I'm not being fair. Here it is. Bill and I would like you to find your own place." The wind seems to shift direction. A blowing branch knocks up against the window. Vera wraps her arms around each other. Her eyes stay on Ruby, who turns to the window, clears her throat, looks at Vera again. "Do you understand?" Does she suppose that's enough, Vera wonders. Just like that, she says it, I'll agree, that's it? "Vera? We're asking you to leave."

I don't want to make this harder. For them or for me. I'd probably do the same thing in their place. Only—no, no, no! She spurts: "Why?"

"Pardon me?"

"Why are you asking me to leave?"

"Vera." For the first time, when Ruby meets her eye, it's in the old way. My friend. Vera thinks. Cruel of me to put her in this position. I know perfectly well why she wants me out. Should I force her to speak the words? Once the truth is said out loud, how will I survive? I'll never find my way back a second time.

A familiar feeling of defeat settles over her. In a strange way it's better than the confusion of impulses that has wracked her all day: fight, give up, fight, give up. She starts to stand.

"Vera, wait." Ruby's lips are quivering. Tentatively, Ruby reaches for Vera's hand. Vera shrinks back. Ruby's voice goes small. "I promised myself I'd be mean. Don't think of her as your friend, I told myself. As a wonderful human being you should be embracing, not banishing. Because I'm not a callous person. Vera, I'm not." Her face is wet. Her expression says "forgive me." Vera wonders if she ever will. "Forget she's a person at all, let alone family, that's what Bill and I told ourselves. Do what must be done. Consider her a disease. Because, we've got to protect the kids, don't you see? Mary especially. If there were a vaccine, like that new polio shot, it'd be different, but it's not that sort of … don't you see, Vera, we can't take the risk."

VERA'S WILL

Vera's jaws clamp tight. Anger, fast and clean as a bullet, pierces her, clearing away the stupor of fear and confusion. "No. Frankly, Ruby, I do not see."

"But—"

"I may be many things, Ruby. I make no claim to sainthood. But I am not a disease." She pauses. She must find a way to change Ruby's mind. If she can win Ruby back to her side, she's sure Bill will go along with his wife. She asks, in her sincerest voice, "Ernest told you about me?" Ruby nods. Vera takes a deep breath. "And Bill ... how long has he known?"

If she can understand exactly what she's up against. If she can find ammunition with which to fight.

She has to try. Something pulls at her. Pride? My god, yes, despite everything, Vera still has her pride. Like a general rallying the troops, some long-submerged piece of her psyche urges her on. Uncharted region deep inside, a voice piping up. Saying: last time you didn't fight. You must tonight.

Ruby fingers her ring, casts her eyes down, answers Vera's question. "How long has Bill known? He won't say. I think since at least his teens. Before he ran away in college." Vera struggles against nausea. Oh god. How he hates me. This—his children—his ultimate revenge. Always the walls, so tall. Do I imagine I have the strength to vault them? "Quite a while he's known," Ruby repeats. Then, very low, her voice quavering, she adds, "I didn't. All these years, I thought I knew you, Vera. I ... I loved you. You lied to me."

The words linger, reverberating like a violently plucked violin string. Vera's determination dissolves, replaced by a feeling curiously like relief, as if absolved from an impossible responsibility. Ruby doesn't like it that I lied, she repeats to herself. And if I'd come clean? Shown her the hidden truth of me? She almost laughs. All this would be happening exactly the same.

Vera rises, pushing against the table, her joints creaking. She's getting old. Her bones have begun to decay. She turns toward the stairs.

"Vera, wait," Ruby whispers.

No, Vera thinks, setting her lips tight against each other and shaking her head. You can't have it both ways, Ruby. You can banish me. But you can't get me to agree that I deserve this pain. She heads to her bedroom to pack.

MARCH 1954

It still surprises Vera what she'll tell Dorothy, in letters, anyway. Since she moved into this snug little Palmer Park apartment, she's been writing once, sometimes twice a week, and Dee, darling gal that she will always be, writes right back, and so they have quite a dialogue going. The topic: Vera's problem.

This thing she's spent most of her life avoiding and that everyone nevertheless seems to believe defines her. No matter how she tries to hide it, lock it away, there it sits, smack in the center of her existence, like an ugly old heirloom she hates but can't discard, maybe because she's had it forever, maybe because, despite everything, she loves it a little too.

Her first night here, exhausted after the move, sitting alone sipping sherry wishing for the weight of her grandchildren on her lap, Vera had asked herself, and Dorothy in a letter, what more she could have done to keep the family together—six weeks ago, or thirty years. After all, she had not, since that single afternoon with Florence, acted on her desires. Her behavior was always impeccable. She lived modestly, respectably, giving nothing away of the shameful yearning that never eased. Yet somehow it had shown.

Bill knows. Ruby knows. Why can no one, least of all herself, let it go? *The only thing I can think*, she'd written, *is that I still want what I can never have. I wish I could accept that I just don't fit, stop wishing for, well, you know, Dee.*

The reason you can't is simple, Dorothy promptly wrote back. *You're human. You want love. If that went away, if you gave up, you'd hardly be alive at all.*

No, was Vera's reply. *Maybe for most people that's true. But it isn't—it can't be—for me. What I want isn't what you call love, Dee. It's something base. An affliction. Without these feelings I'd have had a normal life. I've suppressed them—but I've never known how to make them go away.*

Dorothy's next letter was a jolt. Now Vera rereads it as she smokes tonight's final cigarette and listens to March winds lashing leafless trees. *Affliction? Base? That's a bunch of hooey, Vee—which furthermore Mickey says he told you thirty years ago. He can't understand why you still can't see. And I have to agree. I know it's hard. But I also know other gals, I've told you this before, Vee, and some fellows too, and they all walk on the same side of the street as you, and you know what, woman? They have what you call a normal life, or I don't know, maybe they don't, I'm the last one to know what normal means, this crazy existence, your brother and me, but do you see what I mean? They live, Vera, they live, and the world is hard on them, I know this, honey; don't get me wrong, because please do not forget that I know all about this hard world, but they figure that's the world's problem, not theirs. Why can't you do that too? Why can't you accept that you're okay?*

Why? Vera sucks in a deep draft of tobacco smoke, closes her eyes, pictures Mary, Flo, an anonymous gal or two with whom she's shared never more than a drink or a dance the once or twice when she couldn't stand the solitude and stopped in at Sugar's place. Aside from the fact that the entire world, every social structure, every authority, disagrees—what if Mickey and Dee are right? It would mean she's lost most of her life for nothing. Held herself in, lived without love, let her family fall apart, wandered in a wilderness of loneliness, all for no good reason.

No. That can't be. She has done the right thing. Forsaken her own heart for the sake of her family, kept to herself because it was the only way to keep clean. It has not been a wasted effort. It cannot have been.

Not Alone

Fuckers. Assholes. Fucking assholes.

Redundant, I admit. Unoriginal. Well, give a girl a break. I was too irate to come up with more eloquent exclamations. Anyway, the words dwelt only in my head. I couldn't very well start shouting "fucking assholes" in a subway car crammed with workers sweltering their way from Brooklyn toward another day of wage slavery in Manhattan.

It was eight a.m. on the last Tuesday in June 1986. I had just squeezed onto the D train for the ride in from Flatbush. Gripping a pole slick with sweat, I held the New York Times in my other hand and caught sight of the lead story.

The Supreme Court had upheld "sodomy" laws. They had issued the decision yesterday—the day after the Lesbian and Gay Pride march.

Two days ago I had marched, as I did every year on the last Sunday in June. I had felt lucky to be there, as always. In fact, I'd been choked up most of the day. That's the kind of sap I am. I mean, there I was, striding down Fifth Avenue with half a million of my kind. For once, we were the majority. Not outsiders, for once. We weren't safe, exactly, because gay bashers prowled the edges so when you left you had to be careful not to end up isolated the way so many of us were so much of the time. But there, on the avenue, we were none of us alone. We showed ourselves. We were seen. We dazzled under the summer sun's hot spotlights.

One day a year, we were home.

How wondrous that was. The sense of belonging in the world that straight white men must awaken to, unaware, every morning. Exquisite, and strange. It's why the parade brought such a mix of joy and pain. Because you couldn't not notice the change. The difference between this feeling of freedom and the way we lived every other day of the year. You couldn't not think about it, and so in the midst of this splendid display, this thrust for justice, this gaudy giving of notice that we weren't going away, right at the moment you fell in love with every drag queen's glamour, every swaggering bulldagger, and vowed to fight on with them until all our rights were won, right in the middle of all this, how good it felt reminded you of how hard it usually was. And the contrast took your breath away. And you dreaded the next day. And the broad avenue tapered to a slender strip. The street, the parade, the whole day a tightrope. You an aerialist performing a high-wire act, teetering atop a dream of liberation, real life waiting below. Balancing between elation and the inevitability of descent.

As I marched I had grown teary-eyed thinking of that old slogan, "We are everywhere and we shall be free." I looked around at my people. My gorgeous, glorious family. Dykes on Bikes and Salsa Soul Sisters, Black and White Men Together, Lesbian and Gay Labor Network, Street Transvestite Action Revolutionaries. The Stonewall veterans up near the front, rotund, bearded Ed Murphy strutting like a war hero, bejeweled Marsha P. Johnson sashaying like a beauty queen. A white-haired woman carried a sign reading "I love my gay son." Waves of cheers for her group, Parents of Lesbians and Gays. Tears, too.

In previous parades I'd looked at the parents of gays and lapsed into a daydream. Maybe one year, I used to think, Mom will surprise me—fly in to the city, ride in the PLG van. I'll leap onto the running board, reach in through a window, and my mom and I will ride down the avenue clasping hands.

That fantasy had died with her. Now I held on to another vision. That one of these years I wouldn't march alone. Of course, I was with my friends, fellow activists I planned to work with until the earth rose on new foundations. Nonetheless, it struck me as ironic. Here I was, demanding my right to kiss women without losing my lease, when I hadn't kissed a woman in a very long time. Decrying the fact that I couldn't hold hands with a woman on city streets without fear of violent attack. When I had no woman's hand to hold.

Both last year and the year before, when we had reached the end of the march route, folded up the banners, the straights saying their goodbyes, the rest of us moving on to the festival to eat, drink, watch performers, dance, I had yielded to a blend of exhilaration and loneliness that did me in. I wasn't unacquainted with it. Yet I couldn't rise above it. Like an inebriate overcome by her accustomed brew, I succumbed. I'm going home, I told everyone. Nah, I said when someone urged me to stay for the dance, I don't feel like dancing. Too tired, tomorrow's a work day. But that hadn't been the real reason. Not last year nor the year before. I'd wanted to stay, I'd wanted to dance, but I'd been pretty sure that staying would only make me feel more alone. Unloved.

This year I was determined not to surrender to that morass. I'd go to the dance on the Christopher Street pier. My best friend Babe was going, and others from our group including Linda Rojas who'd moved here last fall from Texas and with whom I'd struck up a funny little flirtation lately. I'd dance, I'd buy a drink or two. I'd have some fun, goddamn it. Mom ain't here to disapprove any more, I told myself. Maybe she was what was holding you back and maybe she wasn't, but either way, Randy old pal, this sad single gal shit is getting tired.

I grabbed one end of the big lavender banner at the front of our contingent of street-fighting socialists, returning the grin Linda Rojas shot me from the other, and moved forward matching her pace. I let the day take me over. Its gleam, its grandeur. Marching for liberation. What else matters?

This year, as always, our group impressed the crowd with our brightly colored banners, our verve, the volume of our voices.

"Fight back," we cried, and the crowd echoed, "Fight back." I swallowed as the lump in my throat swelled. Thousands cheering and applauding. People we'd never seen rushed in to grab placards and head downtown with us. Others, on the sides, raised fists, voices ringing out together, joining our chants against President Reagan and Mayor Koch and Archbigot O'Connor.

On Fifth Avenue a couple blocks below Fourteenth Street we paused and dipped our banners to salute two beloved community elders who I'd heard used to have some kind of little store around here. Sitting on folding chairs, shaded by parasols held over them by a gaggle of younger men, George and Walid waved, smiled and blew kisses. They both looked very frail. I knew that one of these years we'd pass this corner and they wouldn't be here. But for now they were, old as the hills and gayer than the morning sun, and seeing them gave me a jolt of joy as it did every year, a feeling of kinship and continuity and somehow, I don't know, something like roots. As we lifted our banners and moved on I raised my fist, and out of the corner of my eye I thought I saw Walid raise his in a shaky return salute.

That was two days ago. Yesterday the country's highest court had affirmed the laws against our lives. We could parade all we liked. We were criminals still.

The sexual acts we committed (not lately, in my case, but I had every intent of committing them again, soon, and isn't intent nine-tenths of the law?) were banned in half the states. Now the Supreme Court had declared that these laws criminalizing our sexuality were constitutional.

We were, they declared, guilty. Every pussy-eating girl of us, every cocksucking boy.

Now I stared at the Times. I fumed as the train rattled along. A blinding pain behind my eye told me I was grinding my teeth; I stuck my tongue between my molars to force myself to stop. In the packed subway car I couldn't maneuver to open the newspaper so all I knew was what the front page told me. Bowers vs. Hardwick. Bowers was the attorney general of Georgia. I had never heard of Michael Hardwick until this morning. Now the whole country was reading about his crime.

One night, this Michael Hardwick had been in bed with his boyfriend. Or maybe it was a one-night stand. Whoever it was, it was a man, and he was in Michael's bed, in Michael's bedroom, in Michael's home. In Atlanta, Georgia. Where a pair of police officers had proceeded to enter Michael Hardwick's apartment, and then enter Michael Hardwick's bedroom, and then arrest Michael Hardwick for the crime of entering his man or letting his man enter him, or maybe not, maybe it was a manual affair, oral, anal, we don't know the details, but the police put a stop to it. For that night, anyhow. Once Michael Hardwick got himself bailed out of jail who knows how long it had taken him to head right back to criminal conduct? Not long, I was sure. Funny thing about sex. Love. You can't legislate it away. Even if the Supreme Court says you can.

The train emerged from under the ground and swung out over the East River. Flexing my knees to keep my balance as we lurched across the Manhattan Bridge, I glared out the window. Usually I loved this part of the ride with its magnificent view. My beautiful Brooklyn Bridge off to our left. Beyond it the harbor, Statue of Liberty to one side, to the other the waters of the Verrazzano Narrows heading out for their rendezvous with the open ocean. Usually I gloried in it. This morning I couldn't stand the sight.

The summer heat was already thickening the air into a gloppy soup. The Statue of Liberty shimmered in the steamy haze, grim green giant glimmering like a monstrous mocking mirage. My grandparents must have passed that statue when they arrived in this country. I pictured them on the boat. Children. Pale, rail-thin after a crossing spent puking into buckets, miserable, scared, the voyage in the packed, unventilated poverty-class quarters seeming never to end. Then, at last, the statue! Come, you must not miss this sight! They rush onto the deck. They stand there staring, subdued, awestruck as much at how the prattle of Yiddish, Italian, Romanian, Greek subsides to silence as at the icon itself. The sight swiftly recedes. In moments the ship starts to dock at Ellis Island. Everyone dashes belowdecks to gather their belongings and prepare to disembark. A rush of movement, bewildering to the children.

I found it impossible to picture Grandma Gussie, Grandpa Ben or Tanteh Vera at that age—what age? I realized I didn't know any of the details, when they came, how they were treated. Had they remembered it all, to their dying days? Or was it a jumble of confused images, a blurred set piece culled from books and film, the emotional memory inauthentic, the authorized feelings of awe, hope, love for the new land of freedom superimposed on the actual experience? Oh well. They were all dead now. I'd never know.

I do know one thing, I thought as the train started moving again. That statue is a goddamn lie. Ask the descendants of slaves. Ask Native people, or the Japanese-Americans forced into internment camps. Or Puerto Ricans whose country has been occupied for almost a hundred years.

Ask Michael Hardwick.

I didn't get much work done that day. The phone on my desk rang and rang. Good thing my boss, head of the university's English Department, wasn't in. She had left last week for her summer research trip to London. First she'd plied me with a ton of tasks. Type the new departmental personnel list. Confirm next spring's course listings. Copy and distribute the CVs of freshly minted Ph.D.s applying for the two tenure-track positions and the twelve slots allotted low-paid, no-benefit adjunct scum. Plus I'd been covering Ronny's work for all these months while he'd been on sick leave. Well, fuck it. I couldn't concentrate on any of that. Not with everyone calling, asking me if I'd seen the news.

Everyone was in shock. Everyone was afraid. Above all, everyone was angry. Two days after the great gathering, we knew we had to get back into the streets. And this time, we were in no mood for a parade.

At noon Linda Rojas rang. She said a new group, Lesbians and Gays Against Discrimination, or LGAD, had joined with the more established Gay Rights Council to call for a six o'clock protest at Sheridan Square. At five-thirty we were there, distributing hastily scrawled signs declaring, "We Won't Go Back!"

By six the postage-stamp park, and the sidewalk in front of it, was packed. The crowd spilled into the street. We numbered about a thousand when the cops showed up. They started directing traffic around the congested intersection of West Fourth Street, Christopher Street, and Seventh Avenue. They didn't make a move to force the swarm to back off.

They were smart. People were pissed. One touch from a nightstick, one shout of "remember Stonewall" and it would have been 1969 all over again.

While the sound system was being set up, I walked onto Christopher Street. I looked at the bagel place. Where it all began. Of course, it hadn't been a bagel place back then. It was a bar. The Stonewall Inn. And of course, I knew the rebellion that took place those June nights seventeen years ago wasn't the literal beginning; that was in the 50s, with the Mattachines and Bilitis, and, going further back, in Germany with the sexual emancipation movement before the Nazis. But we commemorated Stonewall every year on the last Sunday in June because that was the night the drag queens and bull dykes, sissy boys and bar butches took it to the next level: they fought back. Cops had raided the club. A standard event, it would never be routine again. By the end of the week, rocks hurled, police cars crushed, parking meters uprooted and thrown through windows, the boys in blue were bruised and scared, and our side attired in newfound pride. A new battle cry had been voiced: "Gay power!" Soon a group would spring up, named after Vietnam's freedom fighters: Gay Liberation Front. Soon a movement.

Seventeen years ago. Now here we were again. Time to fight again. And it wasn't just the court. Reagan and Congress were trying to set back what gains we'd won. There was the religious right.

And a virus was mowing my brothers down. We had to win funds for AIDS research and care. We had to stop the church's campaign against condoms. I ground my teeth. Once again, I felt, we needed a new movement to propel the struggle to the next stage.

"Testing one two three." The sound check broke through my musings. There'll be plenty of chances, I told myself. Today's today. Michael Hardwick, here I come. I pushed my way back through the crowd.

A big, middle-aged, crew-cut woman was bellowing into a bullhorn. "My name is Every Dyke and I represent the lesbian nation!" A great roar rose. "I only have one thing to say to the judges. You may think we're a bunch of perverts that you can roll right over, but we are more than that. We are an army of lovers, and an army of lovers cannot fail!"

A softspoken young guy from Black Men United stepped up next. "Sisters and brothers," he began. He looked at the people, and at the traffic backing up on Seventh Avenue. "Sisters and brothers," he tried again, louder, competing unsuccessfully with the taxicabs' honking horns. He turned to his side and crooked his finger, summoning two tall, lean men in leather vests. They bent, interlocking their fingers to create a sturdy platform, and boosted him up so he towered above everyone. "Sisters and brothers," he said again, and now, as if his voice were a roar, the crowd grew silent, heads upturned, struck by the heroic figure he cut up there. A stillness came over us, as though we were waiting for the words of an oracle. "The supremes want to push us back into the closet? Jerry Falwell? Reagan? Pope John Paul George Ringo? Well, we have got news for all of them, the whole tired right-wing, bigoted, backward crowd. We have got news, don't we?"

"Yes!" shouted a thousand voices.

"And here's our news: They say get back—"

"We say fight back!" The answering call swelled up from what suddenly seemed like thousands of throats, tens of thousands, millions of suffering people exploding into action, silent no more.

The "fight back" chant continued for several minutes. Finally it started to fade. Babe was next in line to speak. As she was handed the bullhorn, she pulled me to her side. "Will you hold it for me, Randy?"

"Sure." I held the horn before her, putting my other arm around her waist to bolster her. I couldn't tell if her trembling was nervousness or anger. As soon as she opened her mouth, I knew.

"I'm Babette Poole and I'm from the gay caucus of People Against Intervention in El Salvador—and you are beautiful!" Her voice boomed out, confident, powerful. "Do you know how beautiful you are?" Clapping, shouting, hooting. One voice called out, "How beautiful, honey?" Babe smiled, looked in that voice's direction, and said, "You are exquisite, my sisters and brothers. You are gorgeous, you are stunning." More applause and shouts of affirmation. "But I'm not talking about how good looking you are. I'm talking about your spirit. Our spirit! They can't beat us down, and that's a beautiful thing." Babe raised her hand to quell the noise. When she spoke again, it was in a different tone. "You know, they will always try. The harder we fight the harder they'll try to push us back. That's what's behind the Hardwick decision. The Supreme Court is their ace in the hole. That's where they go when they're scared of the people's struggle. Remember the Dred Scott decision? That was because slaves were rebelling. Refusing to be enslaved. But you know what?" Her voice was slowly rising in volume. "The Supreme Court—the racist, slavery-upholding highest court in the land—couldn't save slavery. Do you remember how we ended slavery?"

People were listening, nodding, looking serious. God, she was something. God, I loved her. A little shiver danced down my spine as Babe orated. God, I was lucky. We'd been thrown together as college roommates—pure chance, yet here we were, fifteen years later, still tight as the fist Babe raised, working the crowd. As I held the mike and listened to her angry eloquence, it seemed to me that she had barely aged. She'd changed her style a bit—cornrows had replaced the Afro of 1971 and she moved a little stiffly since banging up her knee in a motorcycle accident a few years back—but her substance? Not at all. Babe was the same firebrand she'd been at eighteen.

"It took a war, sisters and brothers!" she shouted. "It took a bloody civil war to free my people!" That's right, people yelled. War! "Well, we've still got that racist, bigoted, slavery-loving Supreme Court down there in Washington, thinking they can rule over us, thinking they can hold us down, only this time they think they can drive us back into the goddamned closet! Can they?"

"No! No! No!" It was as if a thousand people were one.

"So what are we going to do?"

"Fight back!"

"Yes, we are going to fight back. We are going to fight so hard that if they don't give us our civil rights we are going to give them another goddamned civil war! Am I right? Are you ready?" Babe looked at me, mouthed, "Help me," and pulled my head so we were cheek to cheek at the bullhorn, and we both started chanting, "Civil rights or civil war!"

The crowd picked it up instantly. "Civil rights or civil war! Civil rights or civil war! Civil rights or civil war!"

The chanting grew louder. As it continued, a young guy I'd never seen before came up to Babe and said, "I'm Dean Larkin, from LGAD." They shook hands. "You were great."

"Thanks."

"We should probably wrap up now."

"I don't think so."

"Well—"

"There's too much energy still. We have to announce what's next."

The "civil war" chant was dying down. People were watching Babe confer with Dean. Someone shouted, "Let's march." Others picked that up. Someone else yelled, "Boycott the Fourth!"

Babe's head shot up. "That's it," she said. "Dean, that's it—the Fourth." She leaned over the mike again. "Boycott the Fourth! Boycott the Fourth!"

394

A new wave of enthusiasm rolled over everyone. I was jazzed. This thing wasn't over yet, not by a longshot.

In three days, New York was slated to host what was being touted as the biggest Fourth of July celebration ever. It was the 100th anniversary of the Statue of Liberty, and the city was pulling out all the stops. Diplomatic ceremonies with dignitaries from France. A show of military might, warships steaming into New York harbor, fighter jets zooming overhead. President Reagan was going to make a grand entrance on the battleship USS Iowa.

The hooplah for the Statue of Liberty Centennial Fourth of July would fall on a Saturday. Newspapers were predicting that a million people would go down to Battery Park for the festivities.

Babe and Dean came out of their huddle. As she lifted the mike again, my old friend winked at me.

We were going to crash the party.

Saturday, July 4, 1986. Noon. Sheridan Square, again. Five thousand this time. Every one of them bursting with so much angry energy it felt as though we were collectively plugged into an invisible power source overloaded with electricity. About to explode.

I helped Nathan Lowenstein set up the speakers, turn on the portable generator, hook up the microphones. Nathan was straight. He'd been an activist since the Columbia University sit-in of '68. Watching him load batteries, twist wires, plug in mikes, fiddle with the volume settings, I thought he could never have known back then that he'd be here today, amplifying the complaints of a bunch of hopping-mad lesbians and gays. Nathan wasn't my only straight friend who'd come. He'd brought at least a dozen others. They checked in with Linda Rojas, then fanned out to volunteer for security, hold signs, quietly do whatever was asked.

I was glad they were here. If anyone ever again tried to claim the left wing was anti-gay, I'd point to this day as proof to the contrary. My friends are with us, I'd say. We're not alone.

I turned toward the folks packed in front of the park. A sea of handmade signs filled West Fourth Street. The best, clearly the work of an artist, featured a caricature of the statue, lips curled in an ugly snarl, and the words "Miss Liberty? You Bet I Do."

The rally began. It was clear from the start that the crowd was edgy, more interested in action than words. Willing to sizzle under the blazing July sun, but not to stand still. By the time the fourth or fifth speaker started, people were calling out that it was time to march. Everyone was itching to get down to Battery Park.

We moved onto Seventh Avenue, taking over the street in a single mass wave. Cops in riot gear surrounded us. Helmets on their heads, nightsticks at the ready. Would they try to block us? Attempt to force us uptown, away from Battery Park? I exchanged a tense glance with Babe and Linda. No one had applied for a sound permit. No one had told the police which way we planned to go.

I watched a group of "community affairs" police officers in light blue jackets arguing heatedly with the uniformed lieutenants. Then one of the blue jackets shook a lieutenant's hand. Word went down the ranks. Dozens of cops on motorcycles revved up in front of us. The rest lined up along our sides. They were letting us start. We headed downtown.

"The Fourth of July is a lie! The Fourth of July is a lie!"

Our ranks swelled as we snaked our way south, people joining in from the busy sidewalks of Bleecker, Sixth Avenue, Canal Street. Marching down the canyon of lower Broadway, our chants echoed off the old buildings looming on either side.

"Hi there, girlie-q." Someone tugged at my hand.

I looked down. A wheelchair had pulled up alongside me. "Hey—Ronny. I didn't see you before."

"I was running late, missed you at Sheridan Square."

"How you feeling?"

He smiled and shrugged. "Better now that I'm here." A feather of guilt tickled my scalp as I realized I hadn't seen Ronny for several months. He'd been off work on medical leave for over a year. The last time I'd seen him he was in the hospital with pneumocystic pneumonia. Today he seemed better than he was then—he had some color in his cheeks and wasn't coughing— but he was drawn and awfully thin. And the wheelchair was new. Couldn't he walk anymore?

"Wondering about my wheels?" Ronny asked.

"You're a mind reader now?"

"You haven't exactly got a poker face, Randy." Thought I did. Thought I played my feelings close to the chest. "Don't worry, I'm not as weak as all that. I just figured this might be a long day and we might walk a long time, and—"

"And I wouldn't let him come unless it was in this chair." A tall drag queen decked out in a slinky, shiny red number and pushing Ronny's wheelchair turned toward me, holding out a bejeweled hand. "Since Miss Thing here is too rude to introduce us—"

"Sorry, hon," Ronny said.

"Whatever. I take it you're Randy?" I nodded, and we shook hands. "Bess Truwoman. Pleased to—"

"Bess who?" Ronnie yelped. "Yesterday you were Sally Forth."

"Yesterday our esteemed president wasn't in town. Today I'm in a rather firstladylike frame of mind, if you please. Now, Randy, as I was saying before this boor interrupted, I'm very pleased to meet you."

"Me too. You—what?" Babe was grabbing me, pulling me forward. "I—nice to meet you, Bess, sorry, guess I'm needed up front."

White marble pillars loomed ahead. A line of police barricades, blue wooden sawhorses locked each to the next, blocked the steps in front of the federal courthouse. As the front marchers reached them, Dean from LGAD stopped. He looked around uncertainly. Nathan nudged Babe to join him. "Tell him we can take these steps," he said.

Oh shit, I thought. Here we go. Dean's going to think Babe's an irresponsible radical. But when she walked over, they talked, nodding, arms around each other's shoulders.

Meanwhile, behind us, the thousands were inching forward. Soon there was physical as well as political pressure to climb the steps and claim the courthouse. People were jostling, pressing up against our backs. There was no choice but to go forward.

And then, in a flash, it was done. "The Fourth of July is a lie! The Fourth of July is a lie!" In what seemed like magic, almost as if the chant itself had accomplished the deed, barricades were toppled, flung to the sides, and everyone surged up the steps. I felt a sting in my palm and found a blue wooden splinter. There was no time to pull it out.

"Give me a hand," Nathan barked. He hefted the generator and PA system while I grabbed the big speaker. Grimacing as metal brushed against the splinter and pushed it deeper into my skin, I hustled to help Nathan get the sound up to the front before the crowd overwhelmed us.

I glanced at the cops. Gripping their nightsticks tight but standing still. Holding back, as they had the other night. Recognizing that they couldn't win this fight.

We rallied at the courthouse for fifteen minutes or so. There was no way anyone would listen to more speeches than that. "March! March! March!" The crowd was psyched. Hot and antsy. "Let's go!" people yelled. "Take it to the statue!"

We hurried once again to get the sound system in place. We waited while Dean and Babe—eager new militant and veteran rebel, the day's ad-hoc leadership team—moved to the front. Then we went on.

"Gay, straight, Black, white, together we struggle, together we fight!" That one picked up steam as we rolled down Broadway. I'd never been on a march that moved so fast. The pace was bruising. At times I was trotting. Christ, I've got to start working out, I thought, huffing and puffing and hoping to heaven that we wouldn't break into a run the way anti-apartheid marchers in South Africa did. I'd thrilled to pictures of their demonstrations but I was in no shape to emulate them.

"What the fuck—" Someone slammed into my back. I'd stopped short along with the others in the front line but the force of inertia drove everyone else forward, a ripple effect that lasted several minutes, people stumbling, grabbing onto each other until finally the whole march halted.

Babe took the mike. "Sisters and brothers, we are at the corner of Broadway and Wall Street. Wall Street—that's who the Supreme Court serves. Why do you think they want to keep us down? Why do they uphold anti-gay laws? To keep the people divided, that's why. Keep the workers from uniting to fight back—against Wall Street!" People cheered like crazy. "So sisters and brothers, we shouldn't be surprised to find that there is a wall of police officers greeting us here at Wall Street. They say we can't go any further."

"No! No!" lots of voices yelled. "March! March!"

"That's right!" Babe shouted. "We have the right to march. But the cops say otherwise. Apparently this bash they're giving in Battery Park isn't open to the likes of us. Liberty! It's a sham!"

"Liberty's a sham! Liberty's a sham!" This new chant rolled like thunder from the lead of the march to the back. As they chanted, people pushed forward. Jesus. Behind me, someone's hot breath on my neck. Not ten feet in front of me, cops arrayed in riot formation.

Hundreds of them. Reinforcements had just arrived, speeding up from lower Broadway in vans and jumping out to block our path. They lowered the visors on their helmets, spread their feet in the ready stance, thrust nightsticks up. I heard a whinny, smelled something pungent, turned to see mounted police lining up. On the other side motors revved: a line of motorcycle cops.

Horses. Harleys. Guns. Nightsticks. I ground my heels against the pavement to hold steady as thousands pushed behind me.

The standoff went on. I was soaked with sweat. Each time the person behind me chanted his hot breath raised the hairs on the back of my neck.

"This is Captain Amione. You are ordered to disperse." The jerk held his bullhorn right in the faces of Dean, Babe and Nathan, who'd been talking to him, trying to negotiate an acceptable route. They backed off a bit as his voice blasted into them. "I repeat. This is an illegal assembly. You must disperse, by order of the New York Police Department."

Someone yelled, "What ever happened to the First Amendment? Oh, I forgot—no faggots need apply."

Amione again: "You must disperse. This march is over. If you remain in the street you will be arrested. This is your second warning."

Dean and Babe put their heads together for an instant. Then Dean walked into the crowd and started talking to people in twos and threes. Babe grabbed Nathan, Linda and me.

"Listen, here's the deal," she said. "The relationship of forces is too uneven." We nodded. There were thousands of us, but there were hundreds of police, and they were armed and dangerous. "We just can't get through them."

"So?" Nathan asked.

"So we go around them."

At this moment, Babe explained, Dean and others from LGAD were spreading the word. We would all disperse—or appear to. In reality, everyone would keep moving, find their clandestine way to Battery Park, where we'd reassemble and rally. Take side streets, stay together but in small groups. We'll see you in a half hour, they were telling everyone. Meet at the northeast entrance to the park.

"Perfect," Nathan said. I was impressed. He had nearly twenty years of experience with street tactics, and Babe had won his seal of approval. "Let's get the sound to the park."

Babe, Linda, Nathan and I started walking north. I looked behind. The street was emptying fast. The cops were taking off their helmets, wiping sweat from their faces, shaking hands.

We crossed Pine Street, kept walking up Broadway. I turned back one more time. The cops were heading downtown. Not a single one was looking up our way. "Let's do it," I said.

We slipped left, onto Cedar Street. The next left was onto Trinity Place, and then we were heading south again. Down to Battery Park.

Thick crowds filled the Statue of Liberty centennial celebration —but not so thick that they didn't part when several thousand people stormed in chanting, "We're gonna beat back the Reagan attack!" My heart was pumping. We did it! We were here, protesting right in the heart of the hypocritical celebration of "liberty."

We had reassembled smoothly. The police never saw us coming. Thousands of them were deployed for the festivities, but most were concentrated at the southwest end for the official ceremonies. So we had no trouble gathering, forming ourselves into a tight, cohesive bloc, and stepping lively into the park in cadence to "Beat back the Reagan attack!"

We swept through the park, voices raised, signs and banners held high. The column of protesters crackled with renewed energy. We were making ourselves heard, and as hopped-up and loud as if we'd begun minutes before, not several hours ago.

Once or twice as we topped a rise in the grass we'd get a glimpse of the harbor. The Statue of Liberty, surrounded by warships.

"The Fourth of July is a lie! The Fourth of July is a lie!"

Startled looks from some of the tourists, scared, shrinking away as we plowed through. Others, New Yorkers, I suspected, nodded and applauded as we passed. A few folks stepped in to join us. I had no idea if they were straight or gay, but I was gripped again by the certainty that we were not alone.

New York. A rush of love for my adopted hometown gushed up my gullet. Some people came here from other countries hoping to escape poverty; some from small U.S. towns fleeing homegrown bigotry. One way or another, struggling our way forward. No thanks to that nasty green statue.

We marched all around the park. Not a soul could miss us. I wondered what the tourists would tell the folks back home about the hot, sunny July 4 when what must have seemed like a million enraged homosexuals rained on Miss Liberty's parade.

Eventually someone ran up to say she'd seen the cops regrouping, donning riot helmets again. We stopped to consider what to do. I leaned against a monument of some sort, a tall stone pedestal topped by a great bronze eagle with a fifteen-foot wingspread. I glanced up at it. One more stupid symbol, I thought. What this country needs is more justice and fewer statues.

"Randy, give me a hand." Babe interrupted my reverie. "Help me get Dean up there." At my puzzled expression, she said. "We can rally one more time, use this bird as the stage. It'll draw a lot of attention. Plus, we'll be able to see if the cops start to move in. It'd be nice not to end the day in jail."

Babe and I scooped our hands to give Dean a boost while Nathan grabbed him under the arms and pushed him up. He got his knee onto the pedestal, then pulled himself up to stand. then climbed another 10 feet up onto the sculpture itself.

Babe grabbed my arm. "Now you, Randy." What? Me? "Get up there, and I'll throw you the mike."

"No, you go, Babe."

"I can't, hon—my knees won't make it. Just go ahead. You'll know what to say."

"No I won't—hey, Linda! You go!"

"She's right," Babe said, turning to Linda. "We need to hear from a Latina."

We gave Linda a boost, Nathan pushed, and Dean reached down from his roost atop the eagle, holding on to a wing with his other hand. Once she was up, I threw the microphone to her. She started rapping, and soon had the crowd eating out of the palm of her hand. She had a way of linking everything together— Central America, racism, police brutality, the Hardwick decision. She talked about her own family, and how her grandparents had been pushed off their farm during the Depression, and how outrageous that was since Texas was really Mexico's land. And—I'm not sure what else she said because, well, maybe it was the heat or my creeping fatigue, but the truth is I started zoning out a little, no longer catching her specific words, starting to just groove on her. Linda Rojas was beautiful. Not movie-star pretty; her face had too much character for that. Dark eyes seethed. Short black hair shone, glinting beneath each fiery sunbeam. She was beautiful because she was where she belonged, up there on the eagle. A leader. A fighter. Something swelled in my chest. She threw her fist into the air and I clapped, even though I hadn't heard her precise words.

"Now you." Babe tapped my ass. She and Nathan lifted my left foot.

"What?"

Linda was leading a new chant—"Money for AIDS, not for war! U.S. out of El Salvador!"—and it was hard to hear over it.

Babe leaned in to my ear. "You get up there now, Randy. Dean's doing fine, but I want you up there with Linda too."

"Shit. OK." I reached for the top of the pedestal. Standing on the platform of Babe's and Nathan's hands, I pulled myself up. I reminded myself again to get to a gym. My biceps strained. The muscles in my thighs quivered. Ninety-nine-pound weakling. I wasn't going to make it. Then Linda was bending over, hooking her elbows under my shoulders and pulling me the rest of the way. I leaned against her, wobbly but safe, high above the pavement. Dean was on her other side, holding onto the eagle's right wing and speaking to the crowd. I grabbed the burnished hot metal of the left wing with one hand and with the other steadied myself on the cooler stone of the narrow perch I shared with Linda. She held the wing too, her fingers wedged against mine. She put her other hand on my shoulder to steady me.

"Scared of heights?"

"Kind of."

"Worth it, though. Right?" She squeezed my shoulder.

I nodded. Definitely.

After Dean spoke a line of police moved ominously close. I'd been petrified that Babe expected me to speak. I had no talent for it. Luckily, all I had to do was shout, "Let's go!" I threw the mike down to Nathan, who hastened to set up the sound, and we headed back to the streets.

Not all the thousands stayed all the way. Enough did, though. It was amazing. We marched along South Street past the Fulton Fish Market. We even stopped for another rally. On the waterfront across from Brooklyn, we paused at the offices of the New York Post and let the editors have it for every anti-gay, every racist, right-wing lie their rag printed every day. Then we headed back uptown.

People were pretty tired by now. As we trudged along, there were stretches when we didn't chant. At one point Bess Truwoman walked through offering drinks from a gallon water jug.

I took a slug and handed the water to Babe. "Where's Ronny?" I asked.

"He's wiped out," Bess said. "I wasn't ready to leave, so I got somebody to take him home."

"How's he been doing?"

"It's up and down. He's got a while left, I think."

We walked in silence side by side for a bit, then Bess pecked me on the cheek and moved on.

Linda nudged me. "Look at those heels," she said. "The whole way. That's got to hurt."

Bess's head tossed back toward us. "Piece of cake."

We made it back to Sheridan Square at about six o'clock. After a few wrap-up words from Dean and Babe, people patted each other's backs, kissed, hugged, and drifted away.

As he disassembled the sound system, I stepped over to Nathan. "Thanks," I said, and reached out to shake his hand. The straight boy surprised me—stepped forward and engulfed me in a big hug. His beard scratched against my cheek. As he pulled away I saw tears in his eyes. "It was a very good day," he said quietly. He embraced Babe and Linda, then he waved and walked away, pushing the sound cart up Seventh Avenue.

Linda, Babe and I wearily crossed the street to Tiffany's diner for dinner. We chewed, too pooped to talk much. Linda drank glass after glass of iced tea. "That was my mother's drink," I told her. She smiled.

Full, thirst quenched, eager to doff clothes stiff with sweat, the three of us descended into the West Fourth Street subway station. Linda and I kissed Babe goodbye and she boarded the F train to Park Slope. We took the D line. We sat in silent exhaustion as the train whisked us to Brooklyn. I knew Linda lived a couple stops past me in Flatbush. As the train approached my stop, I rose. I reached to shake her hand goodbye.

"Hey, hold on," Linda said, grasping my hand and pulling me back down. I winced as I plopped onto the bench beside her. "Why the face?"

"Splinter in my hand."

"Sorry." She loosened her grip. "So how come I don't rate?"

"Huh?"

"Babe gets a goodbye kiss and it's just a handshake for me? What's the matter, Randy, don't you like Mexicans?" Oh my god, what an ass I was, making her think that, and all because I was too nervous to … when actually I … I opened my mouth to apologize, but she stopped me, splaying her fingers across my lips and chuckling low in her throat. "Chingao, you're easy to tease."

She looked at me, dark eyes lit from deep within. She slid her fingers off my mouth, laying them lightly on my cheek.

I smiled, shook my head. "I'm a shmuck, what can I say?" I opened my arms, leaned in, and clasped her, hard. Her hair smelled like almonds. Her fingertips felt pristine, cool against my face, like the first dew after a long, dry night.

The train slowed, and stopped. I unwrapped her and jumped up. "This is me," I said. "See you."

"Soon, I hope," Linda replied.

*

I bounded up the stairs, let myself in to the apartment and glanced at the clock above the stove. Only eight o'clock. The night is young, I thought, then let out a silly little whoop. Strange to be in such a giddy mood. Only an hour ago I'd been wiped out. Half-dozing on the train beside Linda, I'd expected to plod the three blocks home, wash up, collapse onto the bed and stare at the TV until sleep fastened my eyelids together. Instead, I was wide awake. I stripped, stuffed my clothes in the laundry bag, hopped into the shower.

"I would have danced …" Someone was singing. Good golly, c'est moi, I said out loud. Confident the people in the next apartment couldn't hear my voice over the pounding water, I continued belting some of my favorite corny show tunes, spreading my wings, warning ducks and chicks to scurry, celebrating June all over hills and meadows. At this rate I'd work my way through the entire musical-theater canon. Once, a few years ago, at a potluck I'd hosted for members of the university union's bargaining team, Ronny had knelt to inspect my record collection and announced that I must have been a gay man in a previous incarnation. "It's the only explanation," he said. "Who else would listen exclusively to musicals, disco and R&B?" Your theory's flawed, someone objected. No opera. "Give her time," Ronny had replied. "She's young yet. Hasn't developed a feel for tragedy."

He was young then too. I didn't know how long I'd been standing, singing, the shower's icy waterfall refreshing my sun-seared scalp and skin, but now I shuddered, chilled to the core. I turned the faucet. I stepped onto the bathroom rug. I was shaking. Why had I made the water so cold? Why did I always go too far?

Why was I like this—happy one minute, the next plunged into a glacial gloom? I stepped into the main room. I'd opened the windows when I arrived, but my tiny studio had been shut tight all day, so although the early evening air had begun to circulate it was still plenty hot. Good. I stood, huddled inside a thick, plush bath towel. I waited to warm up.

VERA'S WILL

Ronny's okay for now, I told myself, Jesus Christ, it's been a great day, think about that. I stopped shivering. Threw off the towel and threw on underpants and a tank top.

I slumped into the chair at the foot of my bed, picked up the remote control. But I didn't click the TV on. I sunk deeper, running my hands along the frayed fabric on the arms. This chair was the one piece of decent furniture I owned. Everything else was made of thin boards of pressed chips, assemble-it-yourself jobs that, since I was the self who'd assembled them, stood all rickety and lopsided, the bookcase, for example, perpetually threatening to slide its tenants off warped, overloaded shelves. This chair was the genuine article. It had been Tanteh Vera's. I'd taken it back to Ann Arbor when Mom and I cleaned out her apartment the day after her funeral, and I'd lugged it on every move since, even paying to ship it to Brooklyn when I moved east in 1980, otherwise encumbered only with clothes, records and books. The velveteen upholstery, thinned by the years but not worn through, was a dusky pink, shot with swirling black abstract lines that echoed the understated art deco design. The scalloped back was at once graceful and sturdy, firm and plush, supporting your spine yet also inviting you to your ease.

I sat fingering the cushy fabric and yelped as the sliver snagged a thread. I closed my eyes and all at once I was in my dead grandmother's apartment, a dozen years before, sitting in the same chair. I'd been taking a break, I remembered, as I helped Mom dispose of Tanteh Vera's stuff.

I had never seen my grandmother much—Thanksgiving, some Saturdays—so her things had been only vaguely familiar to me. I was bummed, but not horribly so. The saddest part was how little special there seemed to be. Her clothes, her furnishings, everything struck me as having a generic quality. Tasteful, self-contained, giving nothing away about the inner life of the fashionable divorcee. I'd spent an hour climbing to retrieve things from closet heights, boxing dresses, gloves and hats to be donated to Goodwill, then I'd sat down to rest. I picked up her silver cigarette lighter from the lamp table next to me. She hadn't smoked for a decade, yet there it lay. "To remind myself," I imagined she'd say. "This lighter symbolized my self-control."

I swallowed, shot through with sudden sadness, replaying the conversation I'd had with Sugar the day before at Tanteh Vera's funeral. The lighter seemed to burn in my hand. I dropped it back onto the table. It glinted in the Saturday afternoon sunlight pouring through the picture window.

"Getting sentimental in your old age?" Mom was staring down at me. What was with her? All day she'd been snapping at anything I did or said. At one point she got a paper cut and I heard her curse Tanteh Vera under her breath. I was taken aback. I'd thought she'd be feeling carefree—the old bitch is finally out of my life kind of thing, for I knew there'd always been tension between them although I'd never understood why. But she was on some whole other trip. A couple of times I'd caught her picking up a book or a blouse and looking at me as she held it. I thought I saw tears. Or maybe the dust was stirring up her allergies. "Are you going to sit there all day or help me?"

"Okay, okay." I got up, grabbing the lighter and jamming it in my jeans pocket as Mom turned away. We worked quickly and quietly after that. Threw out a lot of stuff. Put some aside to take home or distribute among the other grandchildren. Jewelry, chochkes.

Then I found a shoebox filled with old photographs. Sepia-toned, from the 1920s and 30s, I guessed. I shuffled through them.

There were two or three of my grandmother and her sons when they were very young. Dad at about five or six. Uncle Lenny maybe three or four. Tanteh Vera must have been in her mid-twenties. She was striking. Sharp cut of her features, firm line of her mouth. Stunningly turned out, in each shot wearing finely tailored outfits. More than that, she had a presence. You could sense it, you could feel her intensity even in fifty-year-old photographs.

Most of all it was her eyes. They seemed to bore into me.

VERA'S WILL

I stared at the ancient photographs, trying to identify what it was about my grandmother's deep brown eyes. In one snapshot, probably from the 1930s, Tanteh Vera walked briskly down a street with another woman. In another, hair graying, after the war, she posed with her grown sons in their military uniforms. In both, something indefinable about her drew me in and warned me off, as it had in life.

I glanced back and forth between the shots of her as a young mother in the 1920s and those from the 30s and 40s—and I realized that there was not a single photograph in which she was smiling. Now I knew what I saw in her eyes. Sorrow. It had been there all along. Right through to her last days in the nursing home. Until she called me Mary and we sang that song and I glimpsed a capacity for happiness long untapped.

Now, thanks to Sugar, I knew what I had never known. Tanteh Vera's secret source of sorrow. She'd been so alone. A wave of grief and guilt washed over me.

I opened my eyes and found myself back in Brooklyn, Fourth of July, 1986, but I felt the same sick feeling I had in my grandmother's apartment in 1974.

Jeez, get over it, I told myself. It was a secret. How could you have guessed? Still. Shit. Here I'd been, Big Miss Dykeola, and there was my own grandmother, hiding, closeted, forever on her own. Okay, there was nothing I could have done to give her back those years, no way to undo what the world had done to her. But I could have recognized her. I could have come out to her. Claimed her as my own.

I grabbed some tissues, blew my nose, wiped my tears. What the hell, Randy, I thought. She's dead twelve years. You're doing the right thing, you're trying to change the world so it'll be better for everyone.

Only not for her. My slim, sophisticated, soul-shriveled grandmother. The one who was like me.

I jumped up, the remote control clattering onto the floorboards. I had to see those pictures again. Burrowing into desk drawers, pulling cartons out from under the bed, pressing my lips together against the sting of the sliver, climbing into the back of the closet, at last I found the old gray shoebox.

I sat back down on Tanteh Vera's chair. I opened the box, flinging the top aside. Piles of photos. I made a neat stack on the table next to me. There were other odds and ends, too, things I must have hurriedly stuffed in as Mom rushed me to finish up that day after the funeral. A pair of glasses. I sniffed, but none of my grandmother's Chanel Number Five scent was left. Two monogrammed handkerchiefs, neatly folded, VS in a tight stitch.

Next I pulled out a letter opener, long and sleek with a dangerously sharp point. I set it aside. Finally, a ring. It was very simple, a thin tarnished silver band. It couldn't have been worth much, but it stopped my heart. This ring was mine.

I'd forgotten all about it, but now it came back. Tanteh Vera had promised it to me when I was four or five. It must have been someone's birthday, one of the rare times she was at our house. I sat on her lap, dreaming the smoke rings she blew into fairy castles, dreaming myself inside them rescuing damsels in distress. She held her cigarette in one hand; with the other she played with my curls. "Ow!" I yelped as something snagged in my hair. She disentangled herself, took off the offending ring, and held it out to me, apologizing. It was kind of pretty but kind of plain. I turned it over. On the underside was engraved a single letter. "What's that say?" I asked Tanteh Vera. Speaking so quietly I doubt anyone else could hear, she told me, "That's an M." An M! "For Mary?" Yes, she murmured, and asked me if I liked it. Nodding enthusiastically, I tried to put it on, but the ring fell off every finger I tried. Tanteh Vera held out her hand. I slipped it onto her fourth finger.

She'd leaned down, her smoky breath hot against my ear as she whispered, "The ring is yours, Mary. I'll keep it for you until you're big enough."

I'm thirty-three now, I thought. That ought to be big enough. I put the ring on. It fit. I felt a calm descend and decided I'd look at the photographs some other night.

VERA'S WILL

As I picked up the empty shoebox it made a slight rustling sound. I stuck a couple fingers in, ran them along the sides until they came up against something crackly and dry. I held the box up under the table lamp and saw an envelope wedged flat against one side. Careful not to tear, I pulled it out. Inside were two sheets of paper. I unfolded them and spread them across my knees. Tattered, crinkled, ink smudged, but legible, both.

One was typed; it looked like a chart. The other was a letter, neatly handwritten on ivory note-sized stationery.

I looked at the typed sheet first. Some sort of grid. Horizontal and vertical lines drawn in, probably using a ruler. Four rows of three columns each. A calendar, obviously, for the lines divided the sheet into twelve boxes, one for each month. The first two boxes on the top row were empty. Inside the boxes for each of the other months a date was typed, starting with Saturday, March 20, 1954, and followed by the next nine, through December 18, 1954. A schedule—but of what? I turned it over, and found most of the back filled with writing in two different hands. I recognized some of it—tiny, crabbed, all uppercase, printed—as Dad's. At the top he'd written, *Here's the schedule Ruby and I would prefer. The kids and I will come to Palmer Park. I trust these dates are convenient. I will draw up next year's in December.* Below that, in a neat, elegant cursive, was this: *It will be lovely to see the children on the Saturdays you've noted. I also plan to be with them on birthdays, holidays, other Saturdays, as well as occasional Sundays, summer afternoons, after school— sometimes even at their own house, so kindly do what you must to prepare Ruby and yourself for such an ordeal. Do I need to remind you that I am Elliot and Mary's grandmother? I have a right to love them (as their other grandmother agrees, which you're welcome to confirm with Gussie), and they have a right to grow up knowing me. We are, however distasteful you find the fact, a family. I will not allow you to deny it.*

Were we? A family? I'd never known that it was set down on paper, but the truth was that Elliot and I had seen Tanteh Vera pretty much once a month, on a Saturday, and almost always at her apartment, just as Mom and Dad had apparently dictated back when I was a baby. It gave me a weird feeling, a squeamish mix of shame and pride, to witness what felt like Tanteh Vera's last stand, here, on paper, in her own lovely script. She'd tried to assert herself, refuse to be shunted to the side. Yet it hadn't worked: this much I knew from my own memory.

I saw why when I read the next lines, again in Dad's hand, even tinier, more tightly spaced. *There is a chromosomal link. To this extent you are correct when you speak of "family." This genetic circumstance, however, confers on you no "right" with regard to the children. I reiterate that the schedule is as I have typed it on the reverse side, and if you persist in trying to expand it Ruby and I will deny you any contact at all with Elliot and Mary.* Dad had deviated from block-printed letters to sign his full name, *Wilhelm Steiner*, but then, below his signature, he printed two more sentences. *Frankly, Mother, you surprise me. You never fought like this for Lenny and me.*

Oh. I wasn't used to feeling sympathy for my father. I stood, shakily, the two sheets of paper falling from my lap. I went to the bathroom, ran cold water, splashing my face, drinking. Okay. Okay. I went back to my chair, sat down, laid the page I'd just read into the shoe box, picked up the other, smaller, one, ivory notepaper covered with Tanteh Vera's writing. I flipped it over—no more surprises, please—but the back was blank, so I turned again to the front.

Dear Bill—and immediately I stopped short, for it occurred to me that this was a letter my grandmother had never sent. I was about to read what Dad never had. I took a deep breath and read on. *It's been five months now. I've stuck to your rules. Although I'm holding out hope that one day we can throw that damned schedule away, I want you to know that until then I will continue to abide by your wishes. And I want you to know why.*

I suppose it's actually rather simple. You have never asked for—you never expected—anything from me. Not for the last thirty years. Not since you were my little Willy. Now, at last, there is something. Even though you pose it as an ultimatum rather than a request, and even though I have no real choice in the matter, I have come to understand. You have a family now. You are trying to do right by them. For that, I gladly do what you ask. For you, Bill, for Ruby too, and Elliot. And for Mary, who won't remember all the nights I rocked her as a baby. I'll remember, and I'll love her just as I've always loved you. The difference will be that somehow, I swear, she'll know it, as you never have. This is all I have to give. Only all my love,

Your mother

I started to cry. Oh god, isn't this just typical, I thought. A great day—a step forward in the struggle for liberation—and you end it blubbering alone in your pitiful little room. But Tanteh Vera, so alone. And Dad, reduced to wreckage, I now knew, since long before I was born.

And me? What was wrong with me, to always be alone? I rose and put on a record. Aretha Franklin, exquisite and soul-piercing as always, sang about needing to find an angel in her life. I laid my head against the chair. I thought of how Mom had never wanted to hear about my life, never asked if I had a girlfriend, yet seemed to always know I didn't. She used to warn me that I was just like Vera. "If you don't watch it, Randy," she'd say, "you'll end up like your grandmother. Old, bitter, and alone." No I won't, I'd protest. I'm happy, I've got lots of friends, a full life, I'm not bitter. "Maybe not yet," Mom would counter. "But just look at your lips. They're getting thinner and thinner. Tighter and tighter. Just like hers."

I'd hated Mom's assumption that every lesbian was doomed to an empty life. Now I wondered if she'd seen something else about me, some inner essence of unlovability.

Aw, snap out of it, my Jiminy Cricket side chirped. Aretha's album had moved on to the next song. Catchy little number about a woman from Texas. The beat started getting under my skin, and, come on, Randy old gal old pal, Jiminy said, the only thing unlovable about you is that you've convinced yourself you're doomed. Nobody likes a crybaby. Tell you what: Let's put some clothes on. Get out of this dump.

Yeah, I thought, it's not even nine o'clock. Saturday night in New York City, for heaven's sake. I should call someone. Do something.

Novel idea. What the hell. I switched from the tank top into a muscle shirt. I pulled on some baggy shorts. I found ten dollars and a couple subway tokens.

OK, I thought, now what? Shlep in to Manhattan, I guess. See who's at the Duchess tonight. Have a drink, get up my nerve, find someone fetching, ask her to dance.

Come to think of it, I was dancing a little already, singing along about that Texas sister, my voice swooping up and down with Aretha's.

Wait a minute. Wait just a goddamn minute. Manhattan my ass. I fumbled in my knapsack, felt for my phone book, found the number. Dialed.

Linda answered after two rings.

"I'm not waking you or anything, am I?"

"Randy?"

"Oh, sorry. Yeah."

"No, you're not waking me at nine o'clock on a Saturday night."

"Right. Actually, that's just what I was noticing."

"Hmm?"

"That it's nine o'clock on a Saturday night."

"Uh-huh."

She wasn't making this easy for me. But I thought I heard a smile in her eyes. "So, anyway, look, I was wondering if you felt like some company." I wondered, if she let me come over, how far into them she'd let me see.

"Took you long enough."

"What?"

"To call me."

"You mean—"

"—Oh, I'd better stop teasing you. Come on over. You know how to get here?"

"Yeah, I'll just hop the Flatbush Avenue bus."

"Right. And pick up a bottle of wine."

"OK." I blushed, glad she couldn't see.

"That way you can loosen up and give me one of your world-famous backrubs."

"My what?"

"See you in a few." She hung up. Boy, these summer nights. They sure could steam up fast.

Linda was waiting outside her building as I walked up. She kissed my cheek and squeezed my hand. I winced. She looked at me quizzically.

"Splinter," I said.

"I'll take it out. Come on."

We climbed the steps of her building. She opened the door and held it for me. I imagined thousands of voices cheering. I felt an impulse to turn and wave. Maybe next year, I thought, maybe next Pride parade, I won't be alone. We stepped into the elevator. We ascended. We kissed, this time on the lips.

Maybe I never was.

SUGAR'S

Is it weakness or strength, this dalliance, at this late date? Peter would call it weakness, or worse. Dee would say strength. Gussie'd smile, shrug, perhaps offer a hug. Ruby and Bill, well they'd just avert their eyes and walk away, a sequence they've perfected over the years. Not that any of them will see. Not that there's anything, really, to see. Just Vera, here, balanced atop a bar stool, head up, spine straight, ladylike legs crossed, toes touching the stool's bottom rung. Facing forward. Handbag on the bar next to her drink. Fingers thrumming to the rhythm of each successive jukebox tune.

In the mirror behind the bar bottles multiply. Vera amuses herself by trying to read their backward-print reflected labels, occasionally catching her own eye if she can find it above and between. Still here. Sometimes the sight stirs the faintest frisson of something like satisfaction. Like peace. A sliver of defiance, if that could possibly be. Not active transgression, it's not as if she does anything she should not, ever. She forbids herself, forever. A hint, however, a subterranean hum, imperceptible, yet it persists. It exists—she exists. Vera Steiner. If she's stuck to the rules, Peter's rules, Bill's, the world's, if she's forsaken every chance for one kind of touch in favor of another, passed every night uncaressed to purchase the occasional grandmotherly afternoon, it does not mean there is no need. By now an ancient ache, as accustomed as the swollen joint on her big toe to which she has learned to accommodate by stepping a certain way, just so, in order not to aggravate it, not to call up a sudden splash of pain.

What is the accommodation in this case, the way she lives with her inner affliction for which no pill will ever provide relief? A dalliance. But only with a place.

This place. Bar, stool, bottles, mirror. She comes now and then, as today, a late afternoon springtime walk across the park. A sandwich, sometimes, usually a drink, rarely two. Fingers itching to hold a cigarette after five smokeless years, drumming twitchily instead. A chat, now and then, with Sugar behind the bar if she's not too busy, or someone else, someone perched here like her seeking an hour's cheer among others like herself.

Not that anyone here is anything like her. Vera is ancient, seventy-one, decades older than these girls, why she could be their grandmother some are so young. Age isn't the point. They are her kind. Co-ed, clerk, whatever they do, whoever they appear to be in the outside world, here, inside, they are themselves. They are seen.

An hour's reprieve. This is all she seeks. At this late date. To see herself, and to be seen. Balm.

She can never entirely relax. There are dangers here. Twice this year Sugar's has been raided by the police. Late night both times, lucky for Vera, safely home asleep. And shocks, of a sort she'd never have foreseen. She remembers the first time she saw Bud at the bar. Fifteen years ago: what a start they'd both had. A pause, a shaky breath, and then they'd struck a silent pact, nodded, smiled, turned back, each to her conversation, Bud with a group of pals in a booth, Vera with her neighbor at the bar. Sleepless that night and several after, Vera worried whether Buddy's childhood crush on her had twisted into this, whether she'd unwittingly warped Ruby's sister, if only by proximity. Though the kid did seem happy, at ease, chattering away, dancing, throwing back a frosty mug of Stroh's, and when she saw her at Gussie and Ben's, Bud's grin was as shy and sweet and unselfconscious as always.

Then came that day, eleven years ago now. Summer afternoon, stationed here at Sugar's on her usual stool, and in the mirror she saw Bud enter—only this time who did she steer through the door but Vera's own granddaughter, Mary, barely five years old, and what in the world was her foolish young friend thinking, bringing a little girl to such an unsavory place? They caught each other's eye, as always, in the mirror behind the bar, Vera's blazing, saying, Buddy, are you nuts, what's got into you, and widening at what she read as Bud's reply: there's nothing wrong with this place. With us. Why, she even winked! Then Sugar hustled Buddy and Mary to the furthest booth, and Vera made sure to keep her back turned to them as she lit a cigarette, finished her drink, gathered her purse, paid and left Sugar a generous tip, rose to leave.

As she'd stood she heard the jukebox shuffle records and a new song had started up, a favorite of hers, lovely tune, sugary sentiment about how to love, how to give it your all, pure malarky, hard to see how it applies to anyone here, but she'd wanted it to, wanted to imagine that Bud and her pals would find a way Vera never had. It's the drink, she knew, that looses such crazy ideas in her, she was loopy to fancy an easier time in store for the younger gals, a day they might be allowed their love complete, she knew she was nuts to let a romantic tune swell her chest with such nonsensical dreams. Nuts or not, she found herself laying her purse back onto the bar and joining the handful of snuggling couples shuffling around to Sinatra's croons. Placing herself facing the wall, carefully keeping her back to the booths, she stood and swayed and smoked. Alone, eyes closed. Then she felt her right hand clasped and raised to rest on someone's shoulder, felt someone's hand firm against her back, felt herself led. She opened her eyes, saw a soft smile spread across an open unlined face. She closed her eyes again, and danced. She didn't let her head drop forward to rest on the girl's chest. She kept her left hand low, at her side, squeezing her cigarette lest she let it go and let her hand be held. Just so, she had danced.

Now, more than ten years on, everyone who's ever truly known Vera, known her truest self yet somehow loved her all the same, is gone or out of reach. Those days and nights with Mary in Passaic so long ago they're a fading dream. Flo, who knows, the thought of her a gut punch Vera's learned to avoid. Mama she misses every day, every moment some days; she supposes this would surprise these young bar habitués, that missing your mother persists till your old-lady days, but yes dear, she'd say if she were asked, yes it does. Darling Buddy gone some years now, that awful car crash, poor Gussie, how she'd grieved, god what a rotten deal that was, and Vera misses Bud a great deal too, the one with whom she'd shared a silent bond, a secret Bud had kept yet seemed unburdened, unashamed.

Mickey and Dee more or less retired, they never make it to Detroit anymore. The grand best-friend correspondence has slackened—arthritic joints rule out long letter-writing sessions on both sides—so Dee is only ever a voice on the phone. Cherished voice.

Meanwhile Mary is Randy, almost grown up, nearly a stranger from their infrequent visits, shy and awkward with Vera, but obviously normal, a regular teen, and she certainly doesn't remember that single Saturday her Auntie Bud lost her mind and brought her to this wrong impossible spot. So that worked out all right.

Vera sighs. Her body's too stiff to try even the simplest dance step. Not that anyone would join her, not anymore, and anyway the stuff they dance to these days, loud rocking noise, it's not for her, hell they don't even touch, just gyrate around—except if a slow song comes on, a Motown number by the Temptations, that one she loves for how it reaches inside, taps her dessicated soul, squeezes, makes her forget to breathe. She doesn't get up, though. She's content to watch.

It's come down to this. A short walk through Palmer Park. A bar stool. A drink. A chat. Sugar's. Where she dallies on an infrequent afternoon. Watches herself in the mirror. Watches them dance. Sees herself, and is seen.

CPSIA information can be obtained at www.ICGtesting.com
Printed in the USA
LVOW11s1310050315

429363LV00003B/121/P